WILLING

LESLIE NOYES

blender
PUBLISHING

blended genres with a twist

This is a work of fiction. Names, characters, businesses, places, events, locales, and incidents are either the products of the author's imagination or used in a fictitious manner. Any resemblance to actual persons, living or dead, or actual events is purely coincidental, except for the dog who is as close to the real "Obie" as the author could make him.

Published in the United States by Blender Publishing
An imprint of Leslie Noyes Creative Consulting
Bennington, Vermont, USA

ISBN: 978-1-7357448-0-3
Designed by Leslie Noyes

First Edition, 2021

To the Green Mountain Goddesses—
Thank you for your wise counsel and for reading
the manuscript at least 52 times with seeming enthusiasm.

And to R.G.—
Thank you for allowing me to borrow your voice for
Kit and for your expertise in all things Southern.

WILLING

BEFORE

IT'S NOT THAT I don't love the men I sleep with. I just don't love them after we get out of bed, or off the couch, the rug, or wherever we've satisfied ourselves. I like men. I appreciate them. But I don't need to love one on a permanent basis. This doesn't mean I'm promiscuous or dishonest in my relationships. I'm always clear at the start of an affair about what the future holds and so far I haven't had any complaints.

If you've had your heart broken as badly as I have—the kind of broken that takes years to heal but never quite does; the kind that forever after leaves an abrasion to ooze fresh blood if you're stupid enough to even glance at it—well then, you understand where I'm coming from, and why I'm content to leave love out of the relationship equation. After my last disastrous love affair five years ago, I slammed the door with the valentine pinned on it and nailed it closed for good. I haven't regretted it, not even once.

I'm content. Or rather, I *was* content until C. made his entrance.

The all too delectable C. notwithstanding, I need to state that I don't see the fountain of youth in every young person who walks by, which isn't true of a number of middle-aged men of my acquaintance who have divorced their first wives for women young enough to be their daughters. As a woman of a certain age—meaning that I'm over forty—I'm contemptuous of the belief that rejuvenation can be found between the legs of someone who barely sidles past the jailbait threshold.

If this opinion seems harsh, my friends will tell you I can be swift to judge. And, this time, that old reprobate, Zeus, lover of irony, mortal women, and practical jokes, couldn't resist the challenge my opinion contained.

Of course I don't believe that any deity, from among the pantheon I might choose—including Yahweh, God of my people—is meddling in my life; but it's a more comforting conceit than to accept full culpability for my own mistakes.

Whatever you choose to believe about meddlesome gods or fate, my ironic little lesson arrived on an otherwise unremarkable February afternoon, cloaked in the form of a lanky twenty-three-year-old man-child.

Two men later, I'm still reeling.

PART ONE
~ C. ~

CHAPTER 1

C. is standing in front of the liquor cabinet in his family's great-room kitchen, his back to me. The last time I saw him, about three years ago, a bronze-colored braid hung past his shoulder blades. There was something delightfully anachronistic about that long braid. I'm caught by its absence, as well as by how curly his hair is cut to collar length. Braid or no, C. is a sight to see, broad shouldered and slim in a way that rarely lasts past a man's early thirties.

This last observation is academic, since I'm more than twenty years C.'s senior. The eldest of my friends' three sons, C. spent the last few years ski bumming out West, as well as in Europe and Australia. He did not go off to college at the usual age because he had no idea what he wanted to study, having too many interests rather than too few.

Earlier this evening, when I bumped into his mom, Mel, at the grocery store, she told me he's finally decided what to pursue and has been home since fall, applying to colleges. For now, he is working at Stratton Mountain, less than an hour from home. C. became a certified ski instructor at the amazingly young age of sixteen. Mel says the ski school there was happy to have him back.

C. turns and exclaims, "Hi, Mom. Hey, Liz!"

Crossing the room, he relieves us of the grocery bags we're holding. He deposits them on the kitchen island and helps me out of my coat. C. and his brothers have always been well mannered in a way that most of the young men my daughter brings home are not. I find the Larkin boys all slightly unnatural though thoroughly charming.

Transferring my coat and his mother's to the pegs beside the door, C. says, "Nice surprise. It's been too long." His blue eyes twinkle.

I smile. "Agreed! So, when your mom invited me for dinner, I couldn't refuse. It's great to see you."

"Back at you." He rubs his hands together. "Can I get you something?" He tilts his head toward his glass on the counter. "The Aberlour is good."

I wrinkle my nose. "Scotch is your drink, not mine."

In the past, the glass of Scotch he often poured for himself before dinner jangled me. His parents share a European view of youth and alcoholic beverages, so 4:30 p.m. on a Friday afternoon was, and continues to be, happy hour for everyone in this household. Since none of the boys has ever showed signs of abusing the custom, I try not to judge it. But, that old-knee jerk reaction I used to experience when C. was younger twitches through me. I need to adjust that; he is a young man now, no longer a boy.

Returning to the liquor cabinet, C. contemplates the contents. "There's a nice selection of reds." He pulls a bottle from the wine rack and pivots to display it. "How about this?"

"Tell me why it's the one for me." I expect a short dissertation in the language of a wine aficionado will commence.

He doesn't disappoint. "The 2005 Yering Station has a floral fragrance and deep fruity notes. Plum and cherry mostly," he adds, his hand fisted around the bottle. "Kind of spicy, with a vanilla and oak finish."

I shake my head. I'm amused by his polished recitation, another trait that sets him apart from my daughter's friends. Diana turned nineteen in October.

"Sold," I say. His mom has begun organizing appetizers on the kitchen island. She orders a glass as well.

"Where are your brothers?" I ask as C. lifts down wineglasses.

"Harry is at a friend's house. Drew is upstairs in front of his computer. You know how he is. He'll show for dinner."

The Larkins are casual friends although I've known them for years. C. is three years older than Drew, and five years older than Harry, the baby of the family. Mel and I met at our library's book sale, bonding over the fiction table. Finding ourselves next to each other in the check-out line, we decided to continue our conversation over lunch. These days we get together only a few times a year—life seems too busy for more—but we always pick up where we left off.

"So what have you been up to?" C. asks as he uncorks the bottle.

I think about how to answer, then decide to do a top-level skim. "I'm shooting a wedding at the Manchester Village Inn in a couple of weeks. They've remodeled since the last event I shot there, so this after-noon, I took a look at the public spaces for possible lighting issues." I'm unable to keep a new weariness out of my tone.

"That bad? You sound like I do when it's my turn to mow the grass around here," C. says.

I laugh. "I think I'm suffering from a bit of wedding fatigue."

"Too much giddiness makes me uneasy, too."

I grin but answer seriously, "I would rather take pictures of the great outdoors, but it doesn't pay the piper."

"I'm surprised you don't like portraiture, since you're so good at it."

"You've seen my work?" I ask, pleased he enjoys what I do.

"Like, on your website?" C. says, as if I'm a little slow.

"Of course. Well, thank you. I enjoy shooting people if not quite as much as landscapes. Like your mom, I'm always curious about what motivates us humans. Curiosity makes her a good doctor and me a good people photographer. It's just . . ."

I pause, not understanding what has me so dissatisfied with my work these days. Specializing in weddings and portraiture has paid well enough for me to own my own home and support my daughter. These substantial benefits, however, don't change the fact my work has become less satisfying.

Perhaps, having forsworn love for myself, all those starry-eyed cou-ples and oaths of eternal love and obedience are wearing on me. I just don't know, and until I can articulate the problem for myself, I'm not going public with it.

"How about what you've been up to?" I ask. "I want to hear about your skiing adventures. And what's happening with your applications. Any early acceptances?"

"I haven't decided where I want to go, so I didn't apply for early acceptance."

TheLarkin boys have been home schooled because Mel and Ham believe they provide a better education than the local schools offer. Both parents took a step back in their careers to make that commitment. Mel works at a clinic, and while Ham is tenured, his track to get there was a little longer than it should have been for a man of his accomplishments.

C.'s parents were fine with his decision not to apply to college immediately after finishing his high school requirements. He hung around at home for a year taking a couple of online courses. Then, he decided to do some ski instructing and parlayed it into a travel adventure. His parents supported that choice, too.

I'm not sure I could have been so relaxed had it been Diana. Particularly if it ended up, as it did with C., that her year all over the map would become two years and then three.

No matter Mel and Ham's display of solidarity with C., they must be relieved he is home and headed for college this fall.

I wonder how it will be for him to be so much older and possibly more mature than his classmates. Age differences are more pronounced when one is young. C. has always been shy, although he is outgoing at home. His introvert tendencies seem at odds with his looks. In public, he manages to appear sophisticated and polished, but his sangfroid is manufactured. I've always thought his real-time knowledge of human experience is thin. At least it was thin before he began his travels. His interactions with his ski students and off hours at the resorts where he worked—Steamboat Springs, Colorado; Courchevel, France; and Perisher, in Australia—have probably increased his comfort among strangers. I hope so, because if not, college is going to be a hard and lonely landing.

"No favorite school?" I say. "I'm surprised. Remind me where you applied."

"Columbia, Princeton, Dartmouth, and Brown."

"Quite the pantheon. Is Dartmouth your safe school?" I ask facetiously, because none of the schools he's mentioned are easy entry.

"Ashburton is his safe school," his mother interjects. "Because Ham is tenured, tuition is free and we have no reason to believe he wouldn't be accepted."

"Nice perk," I say as C. hands me my Shiraz.

He brings his mother her glass as well, circles the counter, and, his ultra-cool yet self-conscious manner still evident, slides onto the stool next to me. He takes a sip of his Scotch.

"I hear behavioral science is taking you off the slopes," I say.

He nods. "Doesn't the idea that what we do is as much about brain chemicals as conditioning intrigue you? I love the Dr. Jekyll and Mr. Hyde overtones."

"The subject is indeed fascinating. Too bad the knowledge of how to alter those chemicals is as yet largely a mystery. There are a lot of medications but they don't work for everyone. I'd love to fix a bad mood with the right mix of chemicals—chemicals more natural than pills, like a shot of spinach with a side dose of extra trace minerals." I don't add that I suspect the solution to whatever ails me is more complicated than the Popeye fix.

As I take a sip of the wine, which proves as good as advertised, C. tilts his head, observing quizzically, "Your eyes are very green tonight."

My glance flashes to his. Is he flirting with me? I shift my glance to his mother. She raises her eyebrows, her expression amused, seemingly comfortable with her twenty-three-year-old son flirting with her forty-five-year-old friend.

But is he flirting? If he is, his three years on the road didn't move him past novice abilities, or he is going about the process so carefully that it is hard to assess. Yet, there is something unmistakably appraising in his gaze, something more man than boy. I decide our age disparity makes it okay to notice what he may be up to, but less okay to feel the flutter of arousal accompanying that notice.

No matter what my insides are doing, I'm a safe target for his practice, since nothing can come of it. I decide to be flattered and leave it at that.

Affecting aplomb, I reply, "Hazel eyes tend toward green or brown depending on the colors around them." I've always appreciated my light eyes and complexion, which friends say are striking with my dark hair. The rest of my family has brown eyes. I theorize that a marauding Cossack inserted the green eye color into the Silver family's Jewish gene pool a couple of centuries ago in the old country. "The green of my scarf is making my eyes look greener tonight."

He nods, apparently satisfied with this answer.

Mel looks up from arranging cheese on a board. "I meant to compliment you on that scarf."

"Thanks. My mother sent it for Hanukkah. She has a good eye."

I like to think I inherited her artistic eye, although I'm relieved that some of her less stellar traits have passed me by.

"Are my eyes bluer when I wear blue?" C. asks.

A zing of sexual awareness travels through me as his eyes meet mine. This is a new game for him, one I would expect more from Harry, a born lady's man if there ever was one. Coming from C. it's a surprise. Boys his age can be painfully self-conscious or obnoxiously vain. Either way, they spend plenty of time in front of the mirror. C. should know how his clothing enhances his beauty, so I don't think I'm imagining that he is flirting.

Amused, I say, "I suspect so, but I don't think I've ever seen you in blue, so I can't offer a definitive answer." I glance at his mother, who smiles. "Mel, care to weigh in?"

"All my sons should wear more blue and less black."

"Ha!" C. exclaims, smoothing a hand down his flat stomach and the black T-shirt he is wearing. The shirt says, "There are two kinds of people in the world: those who can extrapolate from incomplete data."

I laugh, but worry that for all his sophistication, accomplishments, and amusing T-shirts, C. remains ignorant of the life experiences I would expect him to have acquired at the cusp of adulthood. Has he lived

head, which I refer to as the Victorian, gives an emphatic thumbs-down to the rest of what I'm contemplating. The Victorian is my internalized mother. She shares with the corporeal version a rigidly nineteenth-century code of honor. It overrides her Jewish-mother tendencies—not that she has all that many.

Shooing my inner mother away, I do a quick calculation involving probable outcomes if I were to take C. to bed. In our twenties, we think we know what we want. In reality we don't have the life experience to accurately anticipate where our actions might lead. We are often shocked by the result of those actions. As the true adult in this kitchen, the one capable of weighing the odds of this ending in disaster, it's up to me to decide what happens next.

By the time I put my glass down, the pause between C.'s revelation and my response has become a little too long. I close the distance between us. "C.," I say, "do you have a girlfriend?"

I'm actually asking whether he's a virgin. It's a delicate subject I'm unwilling to probe directly. I expect most young men his age have rid themselves of their virginity, but C.'s path to adulthood hasn't been typical.

His eyes meet mine. I think he is too intelligent to miss what I'm really asking. But, he is also young enough not to perceive the nuance in the question. I brush a knuckle over his cheek. He sighs, breaking eye contact. His hand rises to trace the same path mine took. He mumbles, "Not at the moment."

"So you've had—" I'm about to say, *So you've had sex.* I don't finish, deciding it's better not to be so explicit.

"Yeah," he says. "Of course."

"Ah." I nod as if in understanding. In truth, I don't know whether he's telling me he's had sex or only that he's had a girlfriend. I recall seeing a couple of young women his age hovering at his last piano recital. Maybe one of them is his not-at-the-moment girlfriend.

He must have had opportunities to fool around during his travels. Youth is full of opportunities if you can get out of your own way to notice them, and après-ski bars are reliable pickup spots.

Since he isn't elaborating on that less than enlightening "Of course," I'm no more in the know about his sexual experience than I was before. Worse, I've no doubt embarrassed him as I have myself. Yet, I can't help stirring the pot . . .

Leaning slowly toward him, I set my hand lightly on his shoulder and gently trail it higher until I'm cupping the back of his neck. I let my palm rest there, giving him the chance to pull away.

This is where before and after divide. I've calculated the odds and I've decided they favor me. Our glances hold. C. doesn't look away, step back, or suggest the Red Sox look promising this year. I kiss him softly, a mere brush of my lips against his. He stands very still, a tall blue-eyed statue in my kitchen.

I let my hand slide down his chest as I step away. "You know this can't be real," I say. "I mean, it's a fantasy with no future."

He says nothing, then murmurs, "But it might have a *right now.*" Color blooms in his cheeks at his own brazenness.

I raise my brows. "Okay."

His eyes widen for a second and then he raises his glass, intent on draining it.

"I think you're smart enough to understand the rules here, but I'll give them to you anyway," I say, watching his glass empty. "You will not tell anyone. Most definitely, you will not utter a word to your brothers. *Ever.* Our secret. Got it? The same for me."

My only confidante, my best friend, Arielle, wouldn't approve, so I won't be recounting this little adventure to her. I've reached the age where I accept that total honesty isn't always the best policy. Nor do I feel the compulsive urge of my younger self to confess every little transgression on my conscience. If I'm going to do something this iffy, I must be willing to pay the price, and that includes keeping my own counsel.

I wait for confirmation from C. He puts his glass on the counter and nods.

"Another understanding we need to share—this will happen only once."

C. nods again. "Secrets are interesting." His mouth twists, part smirk, part smile.

An *interesting* remark, though one I don't choose to examine at the moment. Instead I warn, "If you tell anyone and it gets back to me, I'll say it is a lie even if you flatter me by telling it."

"I'm not a child," he says, as if this isn't evident.

"I know who you are. Definitely not a child." I squeeze his arm, sorry to have insulted him, yet reassured he understands the perils of what we're about to do.

As much as he hoped for a yes, getting one seems to have surprised him. As for me, it's probably a stupendous conceit to believe I have something to teach him. Although there must have been any number of ski bunnies and the Internet is a richly pornographic world for anyone of legal age, I nevertheless tell myself I'm doing him a favor—the next girl he takes to bed will have a more enjoyable experience than if I'd dismissed his idea and kept making the salad. "Come on, then." Taking his hand, I lead him through the house to the stairs.

While we climb, I question my sanity. I have watched C. grow from a child into a lovely young man. *What am I doing?* I'm not corrupting a minor—as if this detail makes taking him to bed more acceptable.

Busy worrying about the right and wrong of what is about to happen, I don't realize C. has made a thorough study of my backside until I hit the upstairs hall and twist to check on him. Two steps below me, his focus takes a second to rise to my face. I raise my eyebrows. He raises his. We laugh as I lead him cross the hall to the bedroom.

I have coveted C. for a long time. He is beautiful—a chrysalis in mid-metamorphosis from tender youth to the man he will become. I realize it is a cliché to compare him to a butterfly, but it is the best I can do; recently emerged from the cocoon of childhood, he remains vulnerable to what the world has in store for him. I can't entirely comprehend the protectiveness I feel for him, or the lust.

This thought should be a flashing red light. Unfortunately, my brain has already thrown the switch and my body is blind to anything but what I want, and I want C.

He comes to stand next to me in the shadowy bedroom, the streetlight outside the window providing the only lighting. In front of us, my high-backed antique bed seems to take up far more space than it did when I made it this morning.

I contemplate what should happen next while I wait to see if he will change his mind. To occupy myself, I pull a matchbox from the nineteenth-century commode I repurposed as a bedside table. We need enough light to see each other, but not enough to make what we're up to blindingly clear. I light a few candles and set two on the commode, a third on the painted dresser near the door.

Since C. shows no signs of bolting, I sit on the bed and motion for him to join me.

He sits down, cozying his thigh next to mine. Throwing me a quick glance, he settles one hand a little behind me, but he doesn't move closer.

I kiss his cheek. He turns to face me, his eyes not meeting mine. After his show of bravado in the kitchen, this suddenly shy C. is the one I remember. I kiss his lips. They part enough to let me in. Happily, he is not sloppy with inexperience. Surprisingly subtle, it takes only a few seconds for him to join in with a lovely display of finesse.

I give him points for overcoming his reserve when his hands rise to the buttons of my shirt. His fingers tremble the tiniest bit as he fumbles with the button between my breasts, though by the time he reaches button number three, he's doing fine.

I shrug to slide the shirt off my shoulders and peel one bra strap down. "Touch me," I suggest, guiding his hand to my breast. His fingers are hot against my skin as his thumb rolls across the nipple. It puckers instantly.

Emboldened, he pushes the bra cup down and studies what he sees. I wish I could be younger and prettier for him. But I don't say this, because I have other gifts to offer; the compensation of his youth to my experience will be fair.

I lean against the pillows feeling almost as ill at ease as he appears. I remind myself that this is what he wanted. It is what I want too, although the last time my curriculum vitae included seducing young men, I was his age and so were the boys I took to bed. I roll the tip of a finger over my breast. "I would like you to kiss me here."

My directive hasn't drawn him closer. *Uh-oh.*

Perhaps this is a situation where his too-facile intellect is useless to him, a second benefit to the lesson, separate from the more obvious ones. Whatever is going on in his head, after his initial hesitation, C. leans in and flicks his tongue over one areola.

"Nice," I murmur, tugging at the hem of his blue T-shirt. He raises his arms. The shirt lifts up and off. I toss it at the end of the bed.

"You look good in blue. It makes your eyes very blue." Although I noticed the color of his shirt before our outing, and thought it flattered him, I didn't say anything about it. Based on the last few minutes, I consider whether the choice to wear it is significant. His eyes meet mine. He grins. I have my answer, one that leads to another—he may more culpable for us ending up here than I have been giving him credit for.

"I'm betting you look better in nothing at all." I touch his chest, running my palm down to his belly. His grin widens.

C.'s chosen sports are skiing and fencing. His hours at swordplay and on the slopes have done nice things for his body.

"You," I tell him, "are beautiful." I bend to flick his nipple, a sweet pleasure. Hardening the tip of my tongue, I flick again. He groans. I suck. Touching him is a delight. His skin is silky—pale from the lack of summer sun, and so taut it could be glued on.

As my hands skim his chest, emotions roil inside me. I remember being this young. How I felt cripplingly insecure inside my own skin, yet thought I knew everything and resented the adult world for not allowing me the chance to prove it.

Is that how C. feels right now? He presses against me, hard inside his jeans. I lift far enough away to puff warm breath over the little disk I've been worrying. He arches, wanting more.

"Your turn," I say, pulling away.

This time he shows no hesitation. His tongue circles. He pulls my nipple between his teeth and adds a teasing tug. Lovely. When he nips me, I remember he has a creative streak. The animalistic bite and his ready erection are reassuring; no matter my physical imperfections, I have stirred his inner beast. I reach down to trace his denim-covered length. Still sitting at the side of the bed, C. thrusts into my hand.

I pull him down, twisting so I'm on top.

His skin is hot to the touch. I trace a finger over his hairless chest. There will be hair in a few years as he matures. For now there is only a golden line starting a few inches above his belly button. I kiss my way from collarbone to stomach until the waistband of C.' jeans hinders further exploration. Straddling his legs, I unzip him. He lies very still, watching my hands.

"I think," he says, "I won't last long." He doesn't look at me.

"Don't worry, I don't expect you to."

He groans when I liberate him from his jeans. Blue shirt; no underwear. *Interesting.* And so is his cock. The head is a graceful bell, the shaft long and thick. He smells clean and slightly sweet, the musk of sex not yet present. I take him in my mouth. He rears, sucking in a harsh breath. As I go down, he goes off. He pushes himself into my throat as he spends. He tastes as sweet as he smells.

"Oh God," he groans, bending an arm over his eyes. There is a moment of silence. "Sorry," he mumbles.

Sipping from a glass of water I keep on the bedside table, I consider what I can do to make him feel better about his instant orgasm. I set the glass aside and lie next to him. His cheeks are flushed, his head turned away under one forearm. Thick blond lashes lay tight against his cheeks. I draw a fingertip up his chin.

"That was flattering. It means you found me exciting," I say, meaning it.

"Come on." His arm drops away. But his eyes focus on the ceiling, not on me. "As if that was fun for you."

"It was. You were delicious." I tug at his arm so I can look into his eyes. "I loved bringing you off." I kiss his forehead. My feelings are tender. Bending, I lick a nipple. "You made me feel irresistible, like a great seductress," I murmur as I nip him.

He finally shifts his focus to me. I give him credit for the contact, although I'm discomfited by the uncertainty in his gaze.

Determined to return him to more cheerful emotional terrain, I say, "Lucky me, my gorgeous young thing, I predict that in about ten minutes, you'll be ready again, as well as a little less sensitive. I plan to take full advantage of that fact—and of you." I walk my fingers up his chest to his chin and rub my thumb across his lips.

I've said the right words because he pushes my hand away and takes the lead. We settle into some serious kissing. If his kisses are a predictor of bedroom skills to come, we are about to have a really good time.

"Can you taste yourself?" I murmur against his lips as we break apart. "It turns me on to kiss you after you've spent in my mouth."

He doesn't answer. Instead, he goes exploring with his tongue. When he finds my ear, I shiver. I divest myself of the rest of my clothing. No matter C.'s willingness, I feel self-conscious; I am not young. I have had a child. There are stretch marks, and gravity is working its wicked way with me.

C. breaks off to watch me reveal myself. Thankfully, he doesn't run screaming from what he sees. He strokes his hands down my shoulders, shaping his palms around my breasts and into the concavity of my waist.

"Your skin is so soft," he says, his hands on my hips.

I hum in appreciation. "The female of the species is supposed to be soft. Remember that. Women are not supposed to look or feel like men with breasts."

He makes his own humming sound. I don't think he's the least bit interested in sexual politics at the moment. Deciding to do some exploring myself, I run my hand over his flat stomach.

He slants his mouth over mine. His kiss is ardent. When we come up for air, I taste my way around the firm curve of his jaw. He turns his head to capture my mouth.

I guide his hand into the warmth between my legs. He breaks the kiss to watch his fingers as I rub them up and down my slit, then over the sensitive nub beginning to swell under our ministrations. I'm drenched where he touches me.

When I release his hand, he continues to stroke. I open wider to encourage him. He pushes a finger gently inside me. "You are so wet," he says. "And hot." The look in his eyes drives my temperature up another notch.

"A clue to how much I like you," I say. Breaking eye contact, I glance admiringly at his cock, which, right on schedule, has resurrected itself. Then all I say is, "Mmmm . . ." as he finds a particularly sensitive plea-sure point.

We both watch his finger move in and out, glistening with my juices. "Very nice," I moan. My eyes close. "Make it nicer; add another finger."

He complies.

"Harder, please," I say. "A little rough is good. Think about how you touch yourself. I doubt your stroke is gentle for long."

"Wow," he exhales, looking shocked. I laugh, amused at his reac-tion to my seeming knowledge of his private habits, enjoying his fingers pumping in and out of me. At least his surprise doesn't affect his ability to multitask. Shocked or not, he finds a rhythm I like—a divinely stim-ulating rhythm. I groan softly. "Stroke me with your thumb, please."

When he complies, a low purr of contentment vibrates from my throat. "Don't stop. I'm really close."

He adds a little twist to each thrust, stroking my clit with the thumb of his other hand. I'm making little moaning noises on each exhale.

"C., sweetie" I breathe. "You don't have to, but I'd love you to put your mouth there." I push myself into his fingers, making sure he knows where "there" is.

As if reading my mind, he answers as he thrusts again. "*Fanny Hill.*"
His long blond eyelashes throw shadows on his cheeks. He is exquisite,
this man-child I've taken to bed. He rotates his hips, swiveling from
side to side. I moan. He bites his lower lip and shudders with pleasure.
Because I have almost swooned with my own, he swivels again.

Although there have been many men in my life, there's been quite
the gap since the last boy I took to bed—a two-decade lapse. The previous boy became my husband. Come to think of it, he was fair and blue-
eyed, like C., but less muscular. I hope C. is heading for full maturity
with the wisdom age entails. In my opinion, Dan never got around to
crossing the line into adulthood. He did, however, cross another line
and kept right on going—out of my life and into someone else's.

For a moment I feel profoundly melancholy. Life is such a heavy
accumulation of gains and losses. I wonder what the loss will be from
this, since the gain is obvious. But how foolish it is to waste my attention on philosophy when I have a gift from the gods in my bed.

Having noticed my psychic abandonment of him, C.'s brow furrows. "What?"

"Nothing. Nothing at all." I push the lock of hair that stubbornly
insists on falling into his eyes behind his ear and wiggle a little where he
has me impaled, giving him a silly, come-hither look.

Reassured, his hands slide from my knees to my hips, his fingertips
slightly rough from outdoor chores. C. is a Vermont mountain boy and
more—he can chop wood and grow a garden, devour eight-hundred-
page histories of ancient wars, and, when seated at the family piano,
play Chopin with passionate abandon. I note that we are currently polishing another skill he can add to his list.

He pushes my knees off his shoulders. They fall open with the
pleasure-pain of muscles drawn taut from knee to groin. Touching the
moisture where we're joined, C. lifts his finger to his mouth and tastes,
watching to see what effect the gesture has on me.

My internal temperature climbs several notches as the tip of his
tongue laps his glistening finger. "Don't tell me you learned that from

a movie," I say, "because if you did, I'm pretty sure it wasn't rated R."
I constrict my inner muscles around his cock.

He throws his head back and thrusts. "It's my own innovation. Like it?"

His eyes tell me he already knows the answer. Behind the defense of his carefully maintained self-possession, I can see the man he has the potential to become: formidable in bed; sure of his sexual power. But then he blinks and grins and returns to what he is at present—a happy, well-pleasured twenty-three-year-old, his attention focused on his cock. Arching, he puts space between us so he can observe his slick wet slide. I observe it too. His penis is a lovely, dusky red.

"Fuck me." I roll my pelvis up to suck him in.

He plunges deep. His eyelids flutter closed. "Yesss . . ." he moans, thrusting faster.

In a sinuous slide of skin against skin, he comes down on top of me. Our mouths meet. He finds a rhythm that suits us both. I rest my hands on his chest, rubbing my thumbs across his nipples. C.'s devouring kiss indicates he likes the stimulation. The power of his thrusts and driving intensity make me think I am about to see his sangfroid finally crumble. I tilt up to meet him, wrapping my legs around his waist. He thrusts faster, grinding into me, pushing me up the bed. I begin to sizzle.

I cannot always achieve a second orgasm, but it is happening now. Restless, I trace his rib cage from front to back. His spine is a chain of small knobby hills covered with silken flesh. It rises from the center of a shallow valley where the long, powerful muscles of his back meet. My palms slide lower to cup the firm globes of his ass, shaping the lovely concavities where thigh and gluteus muscle meet.

We are slick with sweat, two bodies in frenzied motion. There is no sound outside the collision of our flesh, of breath shortening as we climb toward climax. The room is musky with the scent of sex.

"Oh. God," C. gasps. "Liz—"

I can't believe he's still capable of speech, even if his vocabulary is reduced to single syllables, delivered one panting breath at a time. I can't believe I'm coherent enough to notice. Even as my brain starts to sputter, as every pleasure receptor fires, I reach between his legs and massage the smooth skin behind his balls. His breath catches. He groans. I think, *I've done it*; C. is finally inside that gorgeous body without his brain running interference.

There are no more words and no more thinking for either of us. He is pumping, twisting, losing himself. Arching up on locked elbows, he throws his head back in an agony of pleasure.

I contract around him as he comes. My shoulders rise off the bed as my own orgasm begins, the pleasure so intense it swallows all sound, all thought, exploding outward from where we are joined, burning me to ash.

CHAPTER 2

FOR A WHILE neither of us moves. I wonder what C. is thinking but don't ask. Side by side, we rest in a haze of flickering candlelight. Lacing my fingers with his, I squeeze. He squeezes back. "I'm going downstairs," I say a moment later, sitting up with a sigh. I slide my feet to the floor. "You might want to take a shower."

He sniffs his underarm, then lifts his chin to sniff the air. "Right." He nods, understanding the particular after-sex cologne he is wearing will make what we've been doing all too obvious to anyone who might get close—like his mother.

I leave to find him a towel. I consider returning with a washcloth as well. It can be sweet to clean a lover post coitus, but in this case it would be a little too much like swabbing the baby. I decide against it.

C. is sitting on the edge of the bed grinning when I return. I throw him the towel. Wrapping my robe around me, I head downstairs. It's late, so I decide I'd better make something quick. Maybe an omelet.

I'm beating eggs a few minutes later when C. fills the doorframe, showered and blown dry. He looks as he did when we walked into the house two hours ago, except for the wash of color across his cheeks.

"Thank you," he says solemnly. I can tell from the way he is standing that he has worked his way out of his body and back into his head.

"Thank *you*," I reply. I leave off beating eggs to hug him. Going up on tiptoes, I press my cheek to his. There is tension in him that was not in evidence when I'd left the bed. I wonder how to traverse this awkwardness. Now that our axis is once again vertical, I'm guessing he doesn't have a clue about how to move forward. I'm not sure I do, either. Releasing him, I glance at the food on the counter.

"I think I'd better go," he says.

With a nod, I step aside, leaving a clear path to the door.

He takes it quickly, as if the door may lock itself and trap him here. Pulling his jacket from the hook over the radiator, he zips it hastily, searching for his scarf. Finding it under my coat, he winds it around his neck and grabs the doorknob. A blast of cold air sweeps into the kitchen. I wait for his exit, feeling tense—almost panicky—hoping this hasn't been a terrible mistake.

The door closes, but C. remains on this side of it. He strides back to me. I'm pulled into his chest for a passionate open-mouthed kiss. When it ends, he's grinning again. "I hope you know I love your food, but it's late. I've got to go."

"A care package for the ride home?" I suggest.

"No thanks. I'm not hungry for anything but you." With this delightful parting sally, he whirls himself out the door.

I stand in the middle of my kitchen grinning, trying to figure out where he borrowed the line.

Ten minutes later, I'm forking up eggs when my endorphin high flatlines, leaving me slightly sick to my stomach. I put the fork down and push the plate away. *What have I done?*

The Victorian sputters, unable to find words. "Go away," I tell her. "I've read C. correctly." At least, I think I have. Banishing my internal mom for the second time today, I reassure myself that everything will be fine. Better than fine. C. had his lesson in how to please a woman, a skill he's well on his way to mastering. It is as simple as that.

But what if Mel and Ham find out—or even suspect? C. doesn't have to tell them. There are countless ways he could give himself away. The recognition that this is possible, even probable, slams into me. My stomach flips. I find this possibility all too easy to envision, as well as altogether horrifying. My hand rises to my mouth.

Everything hinges on C. playing it cool, understanding we aren't at the beginning of some passionate doomed love affair. I'm hoping what I said to him before we went upstairs has stuck; our evening together was a one-time event meant to move him more securely into adulthood.

But God, how do I look Mel or Ham in the eye, whether they suspect or not? I carry the plate of congealed eggs into the kitchen and scrape them into Obie's bowl. Tail wagging, he happily scarfs my uneaten dinner.

My untouched glass of wine remains on the counter. I take it with me, plopping into one of the wing chairs in the dining room window alcove. Staring into the darkness outside, I continue to fret. Obie places his head on my knee. He rolls his eyes to mine. I give him a reassuring pat.

Playing it cool is C.'s favorite game. I decide he won't spill the beans deliberately, though he might tell one of his brothers. He's close to Drew. Finding the story titillating, Drew might tell someone else, perhaps one of his World of Warcraft friends. Who knows where it would go from there.

Shit. I have rules about whom I sleep with. Boys hardly over the drinking age have never been on my approved substance list. I down a generous swallow of wine, underscoring how far I've traveled past C.'s recent alcohol eligibility. I hope taking him to bed is not another mistake to add to my legion of mistakes with men. My ex-husband wasn't the first or the last. I give the man who came after him that honor. That mistake was almost fatal and caused lasting damage. If C. turns out to be a mistake—and I don't know that he is—he's definitely a new twist.

Blowing out a breath, I tilt my head into the chair, remembering. C. really was lovely—beautiful, sweet, and deliciously lovely.

Unfortunately, lovely mistakes are the worst because they are so damn complicated in the aftermath. You can't just shudder, wonder what you were thinking, file your lapse under experiences to be avoided, and move on. Lovely mistakes are the men you cannot be sorry about; the ones who make you sorry: sorry they're gone, sorry you aren't over them, and, worst of all, sorry you won't ever be over them.

My heart barely healed each time a man broke it. Shattering into smaller and smaller pieces with every loss; I swear, the last time there was nothing left but tiny shards.

That's why I instituted The Rules, which are nothing like that controversial little book published in the 1990s about how to catch a man. Mine are about how to enjoy the maximum pleasure from one before sending him on his way.

A headache twists into my temples. Until C., the age of my lovers has never been important. Now that I've slept with a young man, or a man-boy, or whatever C. is at the blooming age of twenty-three, I decide, somewhat arbitrarily, to set the do-not-cross line at thirty. I don't cringe when I think about sleeping with a man who is thirty. Twenty-eight causes a slight shiver. Twenty-three? How could I have done that?

Why didn't I think a little harder about the fact that I'm friends with C.'s parents, who are my contemporaries. Another dreadful thought, one I've been pushing away since I propositioned C. in my kitchen, forces itself to the surface; C. is a mere four years older than my daughter. What if Diana were to find out? I put my hand over my mouth, closing my eyes against the vision of how she would react. Our relationship might never recover.

I must have lost my mind to believe the risks of taking C. to bed were worth the rewards.

Raising my wineglass for another swallow, I think about how often I don't see my mistakes coming. Then, I tell myself to stop panicking. I don't know for certain whether C. was a mistake.

He appears in my mind's eye, naked, the way he looked when I pulled off his jeans, his eyes almost feverish, his body flushed with arousal.

I've disdained older men for sleeping with—and marrying— women as young as C. Do those men obsess about their young lovers? Do they sigh over the incredible, pore-free skin layered like silk over muscle and bone? Or are they more interested in the prowess the possession of such a young woman bequeaths to them?

I don't feel powerful. I feel ridiculous.

Maybe C.'s a mistake I didn't see coming *and* I'm a hypocrite for having acted on my desire for him. Yet this thought doesn't stop me from remembering C.'s body, so firm I could practically bruise myself

34   LESLIE NOYES

rubbing against him. A tide of lust folds me over my glass, heat pooling between my legs where I'm still tender.

At the bottom of the goblet, a few drops of blood-red liquid remain. Unfortunately, I can no more read wine stains than tea leaves.

Since my intentions were for the best, and since I can't predict the future, I decide a prayer might be fitting, although I won't direct it at Zeus. That old goat is probably laughing his head off about the mischief he's instigated.

"You made your point," I tell him. "*And*, I still don't approve of old men sleeping with young women any more than I approve of what I just did." Rolling my shoulders, I stand to take the glass to the kitchen.

The God of my people prefers standing prayer to abject cringing, so as long as I'm up, I tell him—and any other deity who may be eavesdropping—that I meant what I did as a catalyst for good, to help C. become more confident about women and, in the process, more confident overall.

Since it pays to be honest with higher powers, I also admit I meant to enjoy myself. There's no prohibition about enjoying sex in my religion, as long as you enjoy it responsibly—which is where I may have crossed into the no-fly zone.

"Oy! Come on, Obie. I can justify taking C. to bed six ways to Sunday but it won't change a thing." Setting my glass in the sink, I knock my knuckles against the butcher-block counter. A few salt crystals stick to my skin, escapees from seasoning the eggs. I press them onto a fingertip and flick the granules over my shoulder. I have no more faith in superstitious ritual than in prayer, but at this point I'm willing to consider all options.

CHAPTER 3

A WEEK LATER, I'm at the Manchester Village Inn. My videographer and I are standing at the groom's door. I knock. After a couple of seconds, the patrician best man I enjoyed focusing my camera on during last night's rehearsal dinner pulls the door open.

"Graham, nice to see you." I always try to memorize the wedding party's names.

Patrician specimens like Graham are off-limits according to my mother. She preferred that I date and marry within the tribe, which means I've been fascinated with fair-haired WASPs since puberty. Not that Jewish boys aren't almost as fascinating, since our small Massachusetts town contained so few. I don't discriminate. Except that from now on I'm only sleeping with men over the age of thirty. I judge Graham to be in his early fifties, so he qualifies.

"Lizbeth," he says. Smiling, he steps aside so I can walk into the suite.

I like that he remembered my name as well as how he pronounces it, emphasis on the *beth*; his diction pure New England boarding school.

I changed my name from Elizabeth to the shortened version when I was in college. My friends never used the extra two syllables, plus the legal name change irritated my mother, an important factor in the choice to do it. I was in major rebellion at the time, which has moderated over the years into an edgy truce. I continue to use Lizbeth officially, although most people call me Liz—efficient and to the point, just like me. My nearest and dearest are allowed to call me Lizzie, a diminutive I find a little too cute, but like well enough when it's imbued with affection.

Graham acknowledges Tim, the videographer I partner with at

most weddings; working with a videographer allows me to concentrate on the still images.

I scan the room, reading the light and compositional possibilities. The decor has a Scottish theme including black-and-tan tartan chair upholstery and curtains. A faux fire flickers from the fieldstone fireplace. There is a large Audubon duck print hanging above the mantel.

The groom, Jerry Goodman, is in his mid-fifties and about to tie the knot on his third marriage. He is leaning against a desk talking with his brother. Their dad sits in a nearby club chair, a cane by his side. All of the men are in shirtsleeves and hold champagne flutes.

"Ready to do some posing for posterity?" I ask.

Robust and squarely built, the groom jokes, "Isn't that what we're here for?"

His bride, whom I've already photographed prepping for the walk down the aisle (first time for her), is a pretty young woman named Heather.

Just because I'm not interested in love for myself doesn't mean I don't wish Jerry and his bride every happiness.

Since the incident with C., however, I'm more sensitive than ever to disparities in age and the off-kilter power dynamics that can result from May-December pairings.

Heather is a supple thirty-something Pilates instructor. Jerry is an investment banker with far more life experience and years. I suppose it's possible that Heather has a few tricks up her sleeve to equalize the power balance. Or, the groom could be so crazy in love or lust that the rich to not-so-rich, young versus not-so-young relationship politics will not arise between them.

Graham meets my eyes. I think he's been watching me. He shrugs. I smile. Are we on the same wavelength about this couple? Not that it matters. My job is to document their wedding; my opinions are not significant to that purpose.

"Looks like we interrupted a toast," I say to the room at large. An empty bottle of Veuve Clicquot rests on the desk. A second unopened bottle tilts at a rakish angle in the ice bucket next to it.

The bride and her party are not as relaxed as the groom and his friends—no surprise. Jerry and his best men do not have to dress themselves in petticoats, squeeze into SPANX or boned dresses, or stand in shoes of ankle-breaking heights until it is time for the ceremony because sitting could wrinkle their gowns. For the groom and his merry men, the only difference between today's attire and what they wear to work is the style of suit and added boutonniere.

While Heather and her mother remain keyed up about the details— the flowers, the cake, the food, the music—Jerry is cheerfully taking a ribbing from his brother, who is telling him he isn't allowed to have any more weddings.

"How about another round?" I ask. "I'd love some pictures of you all raising a glass to the groom."

"We aren't going to argue with more champagne." Jerry chuckles. He reaches for the unopened bottle and begins untwisting the muselet.

Good pictures capture the moment when action and emotion peak. To get it right, a photographer must constantly multitask, seeing not only the key elements of the image—in this case, the groom and what he is feeling—but all the other details as well. Before I learned this lesson, I shot a delightful picture of a bride with a light fixture positioned as if it were growing out of her head.

I click a few shots and preview them. The empty champagne bottle is in the frame, looking like an out-of-focus blob sliding toward Jerry's stomach. I push it out of the way. He looks at me as I bring the camera up and winks, popping the cork. I discovered last night that Jerry is relaxed in front of a camera. While I shoot, I continue to monitor details, watching for stray hairs, weird shadows, and that Jerry doesn't bend an arm or leg in a way the camera will interpret as a virtual amputation.

"Here goes," the man of the hour announces, tilting the bottle to top off his brother's glass. When he gets to his father, he takes the glass, refills it, and carefully hands it back. His dad is in his eighties, information he proudly shared with me last night. He's a little wobbly, though mentally sharp as a tack.

I ask Jerry to do the handoff again. "This time, can you take a half-step to the left before you hand over the glass?" I don't like giving a lot of direction when I'm doing reportage but sometimes it's unavoidable. Jerry backs up as directed, which prevents the shadow he was casting onto his father's face. Grinning, he hands his dad the glass a second time.

"It's a sweet image." Turning the camera, I offer the preview window for their inspection.

Graham moves in to look. "Nice."

I reset the camera to capture mode. "Ready for a toast?" At Jerry's nod I ask, "How about gathering in front of the French doors?"

I'm going to need the auxiliary flash to overpower the remaining afternoon light slanting through the windows. To prevent harsh shadows, I bounce the flash off the ceiling.

Jerry hands his father his cane. "Where's Rols?" he asks, helping his dad into his jacket, then watching the older man grip his cane to cross the room.

"Last time I saw him he was heading next door for his tie," Graham says.

Jerry picks up his phone and texts. Graham leans in to see what he's doing. He reads aloud, "Hop to, Rols, the photographer's here."

While we wait for his friend, Jerry, Jason, and Graham put on their jackets and boutonnieres, which Tim and I record. Still waiting, we confer about the list of pictures we want to take of the groom, including individual shots with the groomsmen. We also want to reshoot Jerry's dad to reenact pinning the boutonniere on his son's lapel; the video and stills we have so far aren't good enough.

"Rols, glad you could join us," Jerry says with good-humored sarcasm.

I look up, catching the eye of the up-to-now missing groomsman. I'd planned to ask everyone to raise their champagne flutes. Instead, I feel as if I've been punched. Hard. I would breathe if I remembered how. Like a rabbit under the shadow of a hawk, I go still, as if only stillness can save me.

Rols, whom I only ever knew as Roland, continues to lock eyes with me. He hasn't aged in the years since we parted—or, to be accurate, since he parted from me and took my heart with him. Roland is how The Rules began.

I manage to look away. My body unfreezes. I take a step back, hitting the wall behind me—a good thing, because it holds me steady while I reel. I've been afraid of this moment for years. Now it has arrived, as awful as I imagined. I gulp for air and choke on it, coughing into my hand.

My former fiancé and biggest mistake is neither short nor tall, with even facial features and straight brown hair. It's his eyes that are arresting: They are an amazing violet-blue. His voice is also lovely—as sweet and smooth as bourbon.

Whether this unintended meeting is a happy surprise for him is hard to know; his expression gives nothing away. I know exactly what kind of a surprise he is for me. I feel as if my skin has shrunk. A few sizes too small, it can hardly contain the emotion welling behind it.

"Hello, Liz," Roland's sweet voice says.

I push away from the wall and force my gaze to meet his. Roland's lips pull into a smile.

Jerry states the obvious. "You two are acquainted."

Neither of us offers to explain our acquaintance. I don't, because we aren't acquainted anymore. Roland's reasons are his own. I can't believe he's here. Why wasn't he at the rehearsal dinner last night? How does he know these men? I don't remember him ever talking about a Jerry or a Graham. Did he meet Jerry at his synagogue? Is he an old college friend? Roland doesn't live in Vermont, he lives in New Jersey. But then, these men are all metropolitan New Yorkers and the world is smaller than most of us realize.

Lifting the camera to my face, I hide behind the viewfinder, trying to distance myself from the bizarre reality in front of me, where the man who shattered my heart is examining me with careful concentration.

If there is any good news, it's that the moment I've been dreading for years has not turned me to stone. It is still possible, however, that I'll coalesce into a pillar of salt and then crumble. Not that I'll be doing any crumbling in front of Roland. I have too much pride for that.

I clear my throat. "Could everyone move a little closer together?"

I wonder if Roland can hear the raw note in my voice—apparently this is what I sound like when the past shows up to strangle me.

Roland and I were together for just over a year when he announced he couldn't do "this" anymore and, without another word, walked away.

His children, Sadie and Rob, in their midteens, were opposed to him remarrying. They'd lost their mom barely a year and a half before in a terrible car accident that killed her instantly. When Roland left he said he couldn't make their loss worse by continuing to see me.

Diana had her own issues about me pairing up with anyone other than her father. I wanted to give all the kids more time to get used to our combining families, but Roland had made up his mind and wasn't changing it.

I understood. And I didn't. A few weeks before he walked out, Roland called me his *beshert*—a Yiddish term meaning he saw me as his destiny and soul mate. He asked me to marry him, although he wanted to keep our engagement secret until the two-year anniversary of Laura's death had passed. I understood and agreed.

To give him credit, after he left he called occasionally to make sure I was okay. Hearing his voice was torture. It didn't matter. I always picked up the phone. In the end, I didn't think I'd survive if I didn't wipe him entirely out of my life, so I blocked his number and unfriended him on Facebook. I haven't communicated with him since.

"Toast or roast, let's do this," Graham says. In the viewfinder, my attention snaps from my former fiancé to the best man. He has definitely been watching me. I don't know how long, although it's been barely a minute since Roland walked into the room. Graham tilts his head. It's a question, a different one from Jerry's. I don't respond.

"Let's raise a glass," he says, laying a hand on his friend's shoulder. "To the groom, chief financial officer of Highland Equities, and soon to be chief diaper-changer at home."

I click the shutter, attempting to focus on my work. The camera is hard to hold steady in my shaky hands.

After the laughter dies down, Roland says, "May you be granted the warmth of love for all your days." He lifts his glass high. I am reminded, as if I need reminding, of his sweetness and why I love him. *Loved him.*

Jerry's dad leads the men's shout of "*L'chayim!*" They drain their glasses.

I snap the shot and a couple more, then roll my shoulders to release some tension. It doesn't help. My head begins to pound. If I'm a trifle impatient as I document the good-humored enjoyment of the occasion among the men, including the reenactment of the boutonniere pinning, I'm too professional to show it. But I desperately need to get away from Roland.

Finally finished, Graham sees Tim and me out. He asks if there is anything he can do for me, resting his hand on my arm for the barest second.

I reply to the question, not the question's subtext. "Could you help gather the wedding party for the formal pictures? I'll seek you out when it's time."

"Happy to oblige." He touches my arm again.

I don't think I've become completely stupid, even after the shock of seeing Roland, so I trust my observation that Graham is able to say as much between the lines as within them.

"Pre-wedding reception next?" Tim asks as the door to the suite closes behind us.

"In the Safford Room," I confirm. Approaching the elevator, I tell him, "I'll meet you in the rotunda in a few minutes."

"Sure. No problem." I'm given a searching look as he hits the Down button. Tim knows me well enough to sense something isn't right, but he doesn't ask what is going on, for which I'm grateful.

Detouring to the bathroom, I dig some Advil out of the camera bag to take with water I cup in my hands. Back in the upstairs vestibule, I walk to a sitting area where a couple of sofas are arranged between the staircase and long windows facing the street. After setting the camera bag on a side table, I rest my palms against the freezing windowpanes. It's 4:30 on a Sunday afternoon and almost dark. The shops lining the green are mostly in shadow except where old-fashioned iron streetlamps illuminate the marble walks and dirty snow along the curb.

Why can't I get over him? Five years should be long enough to forget or at least not to feel this aching sadness. I rub my temples. It is too soon for the Advil to have touched the headache.

My ex-husband Dan was not Jewish. His uptight Puritan ancestors helped found the Massachusetts Bay Colony. A favorite theory for how Dan got to be Dan is that his overstarched relatives couldn't do conflict, or dialogue conducted above a murmur, and bequeathed their lack to him.

Dan rarely fought back when challenged. He just backed up until he eventually backed out the door, never to return. Before he left for good, I managed to provoke him into expressing his opinion that I was an "overbearing bitch"—his exact words. I called him fickle and a whore because long before we were through, he'd begun horizontal auditions for my replacement, a fact I suspected for some time but didn't have confirmed until the last days of the marriage.

Dan may not have said so until the end, but years before we split our interactions made me feel I was a shrew. In contrast, Roland said I was a pushover and meant it.

In my world and Roland's, feisty woman are the norm. A woman has to be manically controlling for anyone to notice she's bossy. In the mirror of Roland's love, I was my best self: loving, funny, generous, capable. I found the experience intoxicating. Yet, he threw away the love I found so miraculous. Though I understood his reasons with my head, my heart remains bewildered to this day.

"Lizzie—"

My hands cover my mouth. I pivot to see Roland striding toward me. I wish I could pretend he isn't here. Unfortunately, we've already locked eyes.

"How are you?" He stops a few feet in front of me, his honeyed voice sparking memories both lovely and terrible because we won't be making more. As if we are dear friends who've been unexpectedly parted and just as unexpectedly reunited, he extends his hand.

I go hot then cold then hot again in a single second. It's bad enough to be standing so close to him; I can't imagine what his touch would do to me. When I don't lift my hand, his glance follows mine to the gold band on his finger.

I knew he'd remarried six months after he left me. I saw the announcement in *The New York Times*. He pushes his hands into his pant pockets. I take a step away.

"You look well, Liz. I've always hoped we would bump into each other. Vermont is a small state, right?"

The sound of his voice—so smooth, so sweet, so full of caring— slices into what's left of my heart.

I cross my arms over my chest. "You know where I live. If it was so important to *bump* into me, you could have done it long before now."

He blinks. "Diana is well?" he asks, disregarding the accusation. "You know I will always want the best for you and Diana."

I can smell his cologne. It isn't the scent he used when we were together. It's a relief to find it different, yet also makes me sad.

My life divided when Roland left. There was love and then there was a wasteland of grief. I take another step away from him. I'm angry at his presumption. He has no right to want anything for me. Yet, as always, he has stated his want so tenderly. Roland is a genuinely kind man, another reason why I've found it so difficult to let him go.

"I know you didn't want to have anything to do with me after I—" He doesn't finish this thought, skipping over the part where he abandoned me. "I respect that, Lizzie. But I want you to know I've come to recognize how out of my mind I was after Laura's death."

As if I hadn't figured that out a long time ago. But hearing his admission brings all the old feelings to the fore, particularly the anger at myself for not having the wisdom to understand that anyone who loses a spouse, and so shockingly, is going to be fatally flawed emotionally, and for a long time after the fact. Roland was primed for dalliance, not long-term commitment.

This hard-earned knowledge led me to Rule Number Two: beware of men in the first year of widowhood. They are lovely, appreciative bed partners; they are not relationship material.

Echoing this thought, Roland adds, "It was a mistake to date so soon after Laura died. I wasn't ready for a relationship. I was too desperate to recover what I'd lost. Lizzie, you paid for my ignorance and I'm more sorry than you can imagine."

I hate that he keeps calling me Lizzie. He lost that right a long time ago. I also hate the concept that he was out of his mind to love me. Oh, I know it isn't what he meant, but that's *how it feels*.

"Got it," I say. "I understood your reasons at the time. I still do. What I don't understand is how two years after Laura died was too soon for you to be with me, but a few more months made it possible for you to marry someone else." I meet his extraordinary eyes. If bumping into me is what he wanted, let's see how he feels about high-velocity impact. "You didn't even know her when you left me, did you?"

I'm sure he heard the hurt, incredulity, and accusation in my tone. I give him credit for continuing to hold my gaze. He reaches out to take my hand. I pull away. "Please," he says, and reaches out again.

At his touch, I don't melt. Nor do I turn to stone. I don't feel anything. My surprise at this turn of events keeps my hand in his.

"I did love you, Lizzie. But Rob and Sadie—they were so lost. I wasn't capable of navigating my own grief, never mind what my children were feeling. So, when you were so distressing to them and their reaction kept getting worse, I couldn't handle it, no matter how I felt about you."

"I told you I understand. But you haven't answered the question: What made it okay to meet and marry another woman within six months of walking out on me?" I pull away. He doesn't offer resistance.

Rubbing fingers over his mouth, he sighs. "I don't know why, Liz. Maybe because the kids didn't object to Becca. I guess I wasn't as demonstrably enamored." His eyes widen at what he's admitted, but he doesn't try to correct himself. He looks away, which is just as telling.

Neither of us says anything for a second.

I'm trying to decide whether he didn't love Becca as much as he loved me, or just didn't show his children how much he loved her. Since that first attempt didn't go well, I can see where he'd want to try a different methodology when dating new wife candidate number two, to make her less objectionable. From the way he isn't meeting my eyes, I'm guessing I can take what he said at face value. Does he *demonstrably* love Becca now?

I can't believe Roland could marry a woman he didn't feel passionately about. That the man before me isn't—and maybe never was—who I judged him to be, makes my knees wobble.

"I need you to know I accept responsibility for what I did." He returns his gaze to mine. "I'll understand if you can't do it, but Lizzie, I'm asking for your forgiveness."

"Why now? This isn't Yom Kippur. The season of forgiveness is months away." My tone holds more sarcasm than I'd like.

"I'm taking the opportunity God has handed me." He smiles ruefully.

Roland is more religious than I am. It isn't a surprise he wants to stand before God on the holiest day of the year, when we ask God to forgive our failings of the year before—to clear our sin list. The goal is to start the new year with a clean slate, wiping out not only our sins against others, but our sins against ourselves. But first we need to take our best shot at amends to those we've hurt. If Roland's a little late on this one, over the millennia God has proved lenient about balancing his accounts. Otherwise, we'd all be pillars of salt like Lot's wife.

"Ah. So this was just necessity and opportunity colliding," I say. I wish I were as lenient as God. Staring into those beautiful violet-blue eyes, I remember what I used to see there. Tonight, I see affection— maybe even love. A minute ago, before he offered his theory about why he could marry Becca and not me, my heart would have broken all over again. That isn't my reaction now.

"I was devastated when you left. Your apology doesn't change how much I loved you, Roland. Or that for a while you loved me. But time doesn't stand still, does it? What happened changed me. Like you, I've changed and moved on."

"What hasn't changed is that I owe you a real apology."

I might have valued an apology from the Roland I loved. But I'm not sure I know this man—a man who would marry a woman he doesn't consider *beshert*.

Unable to look at him, I glance out the windows. Night has fallen. I need to fall apart, but in the privacy of my own home. Right now, I have a wedding to shoot. No falling apart allowed.

It occurs to me that I'm furious. The possibility that Roland isn't who I thought he was, isn't the man I've been pining for these last five years, leads me to some disturbing conclusions that I don't want to contemplate. I fantasize about shooting him, and not with my camera.

I turn into his gaze and offer my own truth. "Look, the responsibility for what happened isn't all yours. Obviously, I made a mistake, too. I should have been wiser. We both should have been wiser."

"It was a bad time. I knew I had to break our relationship off but I didn't want to hurt you. I said I was sorry then, but my apology was perfunctory. I was so conflicted. could tell you didn't believe I was sincere, which is why I'm saying I'm sorry again today. I'm sorry I hurt you, Lizbeth." He brings his hands together in front of his chest.

I take a single step toward him. "I want to be gracious, Roland. But you need to accept that no amount of sorry, not then and not now, will change how I felt when you left me." I refrain from admitting that I never loved anyone the way I loved him. I've only ever shared *that* sad fact with Arielle. Right now I feel—I feel confused and a little numb, the way you do in the immediate aftermath of an accident, in those swift seconds when you can't quite understand what has transpired, right before the pain roars in.

"Lizzie." His tone is so sweetly sympathetic it sounds like pity. My fantasy changes. I'm not going to shoot him, I'm going to deck him with my camera bag. But I only walk to the table to hoist the bag onto my shoulder. Time to be on my way. Looking Roland in the eye for what is likely the last time, I say, "I accept that you're sorry. *I'm sorry, too.* Consider yourself forgiven. I hope you found love, really I do."

Roland holds out his hand again. I don't take it. Instead, I do what he did when he walked out five years ago; I leave without looking back.

Walking away this way felt great when I imagined it more times than I can count. I'm balancing a giant cosmic scale. But I don't feel as if I've weighed in on the side of righteousness. I feel hollowed out, as if this confrontation with Roland has ripped something essential out of me—the last little bit of love for him I've been hoarding these last five years.

A tear dribbles down my cheek. I swipe at it. Rather than wait for the elevator, I take the stairs. It's hard not to topple under the weight of the bag as all of the adrenaline pumped into my system in the last few minutes begins to ebb.

Life is full of tough lessons. The one I learned from Roland is to let the resilient others of the world battle their way to love. I've taken myself out of the game. Love is fickle and cruel and I can't survive its vicissitudes another time. Hence, The Rules. And nothing in the last few minutes has changed my feelings about the direction I'm heading, not one single iota.

※

The process of shooting a wedding is so ingrained that I hardly have to think about what I'm doing—an excellent happenstance since my brain is mostly AWOL. Training my camera on everyone except Roland, I document the ceremony, arrange the de rigueur formal group portraits with Graham's help, shoot the new husband and wife's first dance, and click through the toasts, cake cutting, and happy guests boogieing the night away.

Four hours after Jerry and Heather joined themselves together, the party is winding down. At some point while I was ignoring his presence, Roland slipped out. It was a relief to realize he was gone.

The musicians begin a set of standards, accurately judging the mellowing mood of the crowd. Tim and I are killing time, waiting for the bouquet toss and the couple's leave-taking. Graham leads a handsome woman onto to the dance floor. I've noticed he hasn't been partial to a particular partner.

I miss dancing. Roland was a good dancer, unlike Dan. Graham smiles at me as he fox-trots past.

I snap a couple of pictures of the dancers, including Graham, who obligingly turns the woman in his arms into my lens, right as the camera's memory card fills up. I squat on my heels to reach into the bag where I store the extras.

The tune ends. Graham disengages from his partner. I see him heading in my direction as my fingers find a fresh card. The drape of my velvet tunic's neckline falls away from my body as I bend forward, deepening the vee of my neckline, should he be paying attention. I like wearing loose knits when I'm shooting because they make bending and climbing easier. Being curvy, I also find that suggesting my curves is more flattering than hugging them.

When I was younger, I tried all the diets—Atkins, Weight Watchers, South Beach—without discernible effect. Eventually I accepted I'd never be tall and willowy like Arielle. Turns out, there are plenty of attractive men who appreciate my ultra-female shape. I've an inkling Graham might be one of them. I could use a new lover, and the best man has potential.

Unlike a *beshert*, a lover is a delicious meal you want to eat over and over again until you eat it one time too many and lose your taste for it. And, although a lover may not nourish you the way a soul mate can, he'll never break your heart. I may feel hollowed out by the encounter with Roland, but with The Rules in place, there is no reason to go on a man hiatus just because the guy who broke my heart and drove me to create those Rules just bruised that tender organ again. In fact, all the more reason to begin a new affair that steers far from love.

I'm not being deliberately obtuse; I'm aware of the feelings Roland has churned up—the ones I can't even define because they're such a tangled mess at the moment—won't disappear in a puff of valentine-shaped smoke if Graham shows an interest. But he could be a nice spritz of Solarcaine for the burn.

"Lizbeth." He joins me as I rise to my feet, leaning his shoulder into the wall beside us. "I wanted to make sure you didn't leave before I had a chance to say how much I've enjoyed watching you work." He meets my eyes for a second and then glances at my neckline. His mouth lifts ever so slightly at the corners.

I smile as his glance returns to mine. "How nice of you to say so. I enjoy what I do." He can take that any way he likes. I'm *mostly* referring my photo work, even if it's less true than it used to be.

"Although you don't enjoy Rols," he says, slipping his hands into his pockets. He relaxes into the wall, waiting for my reaction. When he doesn't get one right away, he adds, "Pardon me if the observation sounds impertinent."

This isn't an apology, it's more of an encouraging prod. I give him points for his vocabulary. The word "impertinent" is so Miss Manners. Should I satisfy his curiosity? Since he may have the answers to a few questions I'd like to ask, I say, "I noticed Roland's wife isn't here." Roland isn't really any of Graham's business, but as much as I don't want to ever set eyes on my former fiancé again, the fact that his wife of four and a half years isn't in attendance has piqued my interest.

My question, posed as a statement, probably sounds a little desperate. It probably is.

"Their three-year-old, Lauren, is running a fever so Becca stayed upstairs with her. They almost decided to stay home, because Lauren was clearly coming down with something. That's why they weren't at the rehearsal dinner last night," Graham says. "And tonight, Roland wanted to be here for Jerry, but didn't think it was fair to leave Becca and the baby alone for too long."

Roland has a baby? A baby named for his dead wife? I drop the camera's memory card. My haze of numbness dissolves, hurt roaring in to replace it. While I work on breathing, Graham bends to pick up the card. He places it in my palm.

I curl my fingers around it, deciding I can't cope with this information right now, even if I asked for it. I hesitate for a second then say, "How are Sadie and Rob?" I never blamed them for what happened, just as I didn't blame Diana.

"Rob is in his last year of college—computer science like Rols. Sadie is a freshman at Vassar, so not too far from home. They're good kids. Losing their mother like that was a terrible tragedy."

"It was. I'm glad they're doing well." I don't ask Graham to convey this sentiment to Roland. I don't ask how Sadie and Rob adjusted to Becca. I don't think I want to know.

The same way it isn't good to talk about your divorce on a first date, you shouldn't talk about an old lover with a man who interests you. I suppose that's another Rule. I ask, "Do you have children, Graham?"

"A son, Whit. He and his wife Emma are expecting my first grandchild in May."

"Congratulations. You and your wife must be thrilled." I'm certain he isn't married but confirmation is always good.

He laughs and touches my arm. "My ex-wife and I are indeed delighted. Do you have children, Lizbeth?"

"Call me Liz." I tell him about Diana. Our conversation sounds like small talk but we're doing a little dance around each other, trying to decide whether we might like to dance closer. In the years since Roland, I've learned that love isn't everything. Getting physical without emotional attachment can be exhilarating as well as relaxing, as long as the man in my bed is skilled and aims to please.

Tipping the camera, I slide the memory card in. Confirming all systems are go, I say, "I appreciated you stepping into that little vortex in Jerry's room."

Graham smiles. "But you aren't going to tell me about it, are you?"

"No, but I thank you all the same."

"You are welcome." He studies me for a second, then asks, "Do you live in the area?"

"In Ashburton." After his little fishing expedition, I give him additional credit for not pressing me for the revelations he didn't receive.

"Cute town. I'm in Manhattan during the week. I try to make it up to the house in Dorset a couple times a month."

Dorset is a little piece of the Connecticut Gold Coast snuggled into the hills of Vermont. Jerry has a house there, too.

"May I call you the next time I'm heading north? I'd like to take you to dinner."

"That would be delightful."

He touches the backs of two fingers to one side of my neckline and lets them drop a couple of inches before withdrawing. Awareness shivers through me.

He smiles and ambles away. I lift the Nikon and scan the room for picture-taking opportunities, marveling at how quickly the winds of change blow in.

The last wind blew C. into my bed. It's hard to know whether that was for good or ill just yet. At the thought of C., lust plows through me. I press my hand to a chair back. I can't think of him without this accompanying zing of desire. "Don't mess with me again, you big jerk," I tell Zeus, since I suspect he is the mischievous wind that blew C. into my bed and sent Roland crashing into me tonight.

A woman walking past swings her glance in my direction, her brow wrinkling.

Did I say that out loud?

CHAPTER 4

ARIELLE STUDIES THE STILL LIFE on my dining room table. Her newest bowl, decorated with a band of shiny white glaze brushed with blue, and colorful paste flowers, is sitting on a white linen cloth, the dove-gray wall acting as our backdrop.

I toggle between the last two shots I've taken, displayed on the PowerBook screen in front of us. "This or the last one?" I ask.

In the later image, I used a white fill card to reflect light into the bottom of the bowl and onto the petals of the blue delphinium resting on the table. I wait for her decision.

It takes a full minute. I know because I noticed the time on the monitor as the first shot loaded.

"The one with the fill," she finally decides. "It's a cheerful bowl. It wants happy light."

My friend has a tendency to refer to objects as if they have feelings. It's her way of asking for what she wants while giving the responsibility for her decision to objects, animals, and even weather patterns. Why she needs to cede control of her world this way is a mystery I've never solved.

"I agree. Let me do the bracket." I vary the f-stop, two behind the setting I used for the test shot, two after. The images we are shooting are for wholesale use in marketing her wares. "What's next?"

She reviews her checklist and glances into the kitchen where the counters are piled with her plates, bowls, dishes, platters, and vases. "Only the dessert bowls and vases."

Arielle has a ceramics studio behind her house. She sells to craft stores around the country. Her style is distinctive, influenced by antique Asian and English porcelain. The way she combines pebbly salt and high-gloss glazes with paste and brushwork is unique, and her work is in demand.

I possess what I consider the typical photographer's sense of order, not that I haven't met messy photographers, but they seem more the exception than the rule. In contrast to my house, Arielle's overflows with pottery and books. Then there's Miu-Miu. When we tried to photograph there, the cat launched himself into the middle of the set with predictable and disastrous results. So, we shoot here. The bungalow architecture, along with my spare decorating style, complements her pottery, and Obie, unlike Miu-Miu, is content to snooze in the next room.

"I really appreciate you pushing me to begin earlier this year. I can't believe I'm going to have images so far ahead." Removing the bowl from the table, Arielle walks into the kitchen. "I keep thinking I should declutter so we can try shooting at my house, Miu-Miu notwithstanding. If only I can figure out where to start the cleanup."

"Admit you're content with your clutter—unless you aren't telling me something? Are you unhappy with these shots?"

She rolls her eyes. "Are you crazy?"

"Then why change the status quo?"

Arielle starts doodling on her checklist. "Actually, I've been feeling a little hemmed in lately—there's my stuff, my sister's stuff, my parents' stuff. I could probably manage to go through Dad's things, but it would be weird to get rid of Mom's since she's still among us, and I bring her home from the nursing home for visits. Having family pieces around is comforting, but for whatever reason, I'm feeling more confined than comforted by so much history enveloping me. It never bothered me before. So why is it bothering me now?"

✳

Arielle's parents were a lot older than mine when they started their family, so she's dealing with issues I haven't had to face. "Since that's the case, can you ask your sister if she wants any of your parents' memorabilia or furniture?" Arielle's older sister, Anna, lives halfway across the country in Kansas City.

"I suppose I could," she says, not looking at all sure as she returns to the dining room with eight dessert bowls in her arms. Her face twists into a grimace. "I just don't understand why I'm suddenly bothered by what has never bothered me before."

"Because you're human like the rest of us?"

"Not you!" she says with mock horror.

"I'm antsy, too. And I'm not sure why, either." I shrug. "Until we have a clue, let's solve an easier problem, like where to shoot the dessert bowls. Figuring that out has got to be less fatiguing than exploring our existential angst."

She laughs and looks around the room.

"How about the sideboard for the white-on-white bowls?" I suggest. The 1930s-era sideboard has laurel motif detailing and is painted an electric blue that should complement the bowls.

Head cocked, she contemplates the suggestion.

Arielle and I have been friends since college. I met Dan through Arielle when we settled in Boston together after we graduated. Even though my friend and I fall on opposite ends of the personality spectrum, and most other spectrums as well, our inclinations manage to complement each other.

I may come to conclusions faster than she does, but I never discount the quality of her thinking or begrudge how long it takes; when Arielle finally decides what she wants, she's thoroughly considered her position. My own positions are more subject to change and mishap—C. being a perfect example, although the jury continues to deliberate about him.

In the past, C. and I were not in touch unless there was a foreign movie one of us wanted to see, so not hearing from him isn't unusual. His mother and I don't stay in touch all that much, either, relying on grocery store sightings to catch up and make plans. Neither situation has occurred in the six weeks since that movie date with benefits. I hope this means the status quo is holding steady.

Arielle sets the bowls on the table and strokes her long white-blond ponytail, staring at the sideboard. I study the images on the computer, starring the shots I like from the last few brackets. As I finish, she says, "Let's use the sideboard. And go with grapes. The bowls want the added color."

"Let's do the blueberries, too. A unified color palette is pleasing."

"Okay. Nice idea."

I'm surprised by how quickly she accepted my suggestion. Not that Arielle isn't decisive in her own way. She camps alone in isolated places, for God's sake. As for me, I don't sleep anywhere I need to cross a field in the dead of night to use the facilities. Or where a comfy mattress isn't available with help close by if I fall off it. Since her forays into the deep woods have yielded hair-raising stories of encounters with moose and bear, encounters that demanded quick, life-preserving decision-making, I reason that Arielle can make instant choices, but they tend to happen when I'm not around.

No matter our differences, we have a twenty-seven-year history of college escapades, shared agony over boys, and, as adults, the trials and satisfactions of running our own businesses, along with a similar eye for beauty. We also share a skewed sense of humor in response to life's many paradoxes and the mayhem that keeps our wheels spinning.

"Guess who contacted me yesterday?" I ask, as Arielle collects the fruit from the refrigerator while I rearrange the lights around the sideboard. My friend is almost as Victorian as my mother in her views about what goes on between the sheets. Arielle would not approve of what happened with C.—not that I totally approve, myself.

Arielle tilts her head in question.

"Here's a clue: Think open zippers."

Returning with the fruit, her eyes narrow. "What does he want?" She reviles Jay and for good reason.

"What he always wants." Although his e-mail said only that he was attending a green building show in Albany to exhibit his company's countertops made from architectural salvage. He included an encapsulated image of his hand gripping his erection along with the comment,

"See what happens when I think of you."

I used to enjoy his overt come-ons. These days I prefer to be seduced with flowers rather than overexposed selfies.

I hope Graham is a flower man and that he will be in touch. At the end of the wedding, he mentioned he wouldn't be in Dorset again until closer to April, so I don't expect to hear from him until then, although he sent me a quick e-mail saying he'd seen the wedding shots and thought they were great.

I position the tripod and focus the camera. Finding a good angle, I snap a shot to check the lighting while Arielle arranges fruit in a bowl. "I've been done with Jay since the incident with no plans for a reunion," I reminder her.

She turns to scowl at me.

When I first got involved with him, some months after Roland left, I was hardly functioning; however, I'd been hired to do some reportage work for a company in Waitsfield and it was winter, when business is always slow to nonexistent, so I dragged myself three hours north, up Route 100, the two-lane "highway" that twists through the Green Mountains. Jay was my liaison. He'd taken me out to lunch a couple of times when I was shooting for his company. He did so that day.

His timing and approach were impeccable. "You seem a little down," he observed at lunch. "What's going on? I hate to see good people feeling bad."

Jay was tall with an attractive smile. I was too depressed to deny how I was feeling. Layering on the sympathy, he had no trouble pulling the story out of me. Afterward, he said what I desperately needed to hear, even though I didn't know it until he told me I was too sexy to be alone for long and Roland wasn't the only man who had noticed me.

"Let me help you through this," he suggested, laying a hand on mine for the merest instant.

Jay let me coax his own story out of him, a tale about the frigid wife he adored. He told me she wouldn't go to counseling with him. He loved his kids and being a family, so he slept around to satisfy his sexual needs until his wife discovered what he had been doing and left him. This confession was clearly meant to garner my sympathy. I didn't have much, since my husband probably told that same tale about me to his lady friends. Not that my lack of sympathy was an impediment to sleeping with Jay.

He became my first lover after Roland, and the beta-test for The Rules. He was impossible to trust and therefore impossible to consider for a relationship. Jay inspired the first rule, the one about sleeping only with fatally flawed men. And, boy, was he fun.

Arielle didn't approve. She told me that the last time I'd done something as dumb as sleeping with Jay was when I dyed my hair purple in college. My hair had to be bleached first and instead of having a professional do it, I did it myself, burning the hell out of it. I ended up with a pixie cut. It didn't suit me. Nor did the purple.

I've always felt she let me off easy about Jay, especially after what happened.

Jay and I saw each other when an opportunity presented itself, since he lived at one end of the state and I lived at the other. I knew he had other lovers. I knew because he loved to talk about them, details included. He encouraged me to do the same. Sharing such details never turned me on—the opposite, in fact.

But even with Jay's flaws—and condoms—the sex was hot, dirty, and oh-so-satisfying. Best of all, my heart never fluttered, not once. How could I not be profoundly grateful to him for showing me I could enjoy sex without Cupid putting in an appearance?

Then, he wrecked it. The first and last time he stayed over at my house—Diana was with her dad—I'd forgotten Arielle planned to drop by with website text she wanted me to review. Jay and I were in bed when she knocked. I came downstairs to unlock the door. Jay followed me down to the kitchen in nothing but partially zipped jeans.

Arielle handed over her folder. I had a flash drive of images for her. While I went to grab it off my desk, Jay, in a move that shouldn't have surprised me—knowing who he was—asked her if she'd like to join us.

Obviously she declined. She was also gone by the time I returned with the drive.

The next day, after Jay left, she told me what he'd said.

I stopped being available to him. There was no point discussing why. But enough time has passed, apparently, for him to try running his flag back up the pole. Must be that available women are thinner on the ground of late, or he was fonder of me than I thought. I'm betting on door number one.

"I can't do anything about past mistakes. I can only *not* repeat them," I tell Arielle. I'm not just referencing Jay, but she doesn't know that. Nothing bad has happened to C. or because of C., as far as I know, but that doesn't stop me from waiting for a shoe to drop. "I'm deferring judgment as well as punishment to higher powers," I add. "If you could defer your own judgment until we reach the pearly gates?"

"You're Jewish. You don't believe in the pearly gates," Arielle retorts. She adjusts the position of the bowls, tilting the top one in the stack forward, placing the bowl filled with fruit more to the front. "And it's Saint Peter at the gate, not God."

I snap a shot of the arrangement she's made. "Details, Details. But, while we're on the subject, please don't point out what an idiot I was to start with Jay. He had his uses." I'm defending him because he saved me when I needed saving.

I study the image I just snapped and walk past her to move the bowl stack a tiny bit to the right.

"Liz, you might have only—" She flutters her fingers, unwilling to say the words, then continues. "But as far as we know, Dan—"

She doesn't complete that thought, either, because she doesn't need to. Dan, like Jay, was not faithful. She joins me at the monitor. I leave to adjust a light, asking her to hit the shutter, then return to wait for the image to process.

"How could you be attracted to that guy? I don't get it."

Arielle can be as intent as a dog with a bone, even if she is a cat lover.

"Was. I was attracted. Not anymore, okay?"

She looks at me and rolls her eyes.

"What do you think about the bowls?" I don't understand why she isn't relieved to hear I'm finished with Jay.

Pushing the fruit containers out of camera range, I motion for her to peer through the viewfinder as I arrange a couple of grapes to cover a hole in the arrangement. "Good?" I ask.

She nods.

I pick up the fill card. Holding it vertically, I slowly angle it forward and back, looking for the sweet spot where the light reflecting off the card throws the best highlights onto the tableaux we've arranged. When I find it, I say, "Hit the shutter, please?"

As we again wait for the image, Arielle pats my back. "I shouldn't be giving you such a hard time." She glances from the monitor to me. "At least Jay popping up is a distraction. You haven't been yourself since you saw Roland. I've been worried about you."

I shake my head. "I wish I didn't feel like I'm still shoving my feelings about him into a box already bursting at the seams."

With a shudder, I remember the weeks after he left when I couldn't sleep, when my body ached, bruised by loss, my emotions so close to the surface the most ridiculous things could make me cry. A few days after Roland left, I remember sobbing inconsolably when an egg rolled off the kitchen counter and smashed to the floor.

The worst part was pretending. I didn't want Diana burdened by my sadness, so I pretended to laugh at her jokes. I pretended excitement when a new client contacted me about work. I pretended I was going to survive when I thought I would die of grief.

"I guess I'm kind of a mess. He uttered those five words—'I wasn't as demonstrably enamored'—and it was like he broke an evil spell he cast when he left me. Except, I don't feel liberated. I feel like I've had something big ripped out of me, and it hurts like hell."

"I'm sorry it hurts, but don't hit me if I tell you I'm glad it happened, even if you feel like you have a doughnut hole through your middle."

I can't help laughing at this image. "Is that why I've been craving sweets? Though seriously, I can't get over what he said." I shake my head and let out a whoosh of breath. "I wonder if Roland feels better for having made the confession that Becca wasn't his *beshert, at least not when he married her—if I didn't imagine the implication of his words.*"

"I don't care how he feels. I'm just glad he showed his true colors."

Picking up the spray bottle filled with glycerin water, I spritz the fruit to make it shine. "If my theory is correct, he wants to stand before God on the holiest day of the year having done his best to make amends." I set the bottle down and look at Arielle. "Do you think he's made amends to God for marrying a woman he didn't consider his soul mate when he proposed to her? Not that God hasn't already forgiven him even if Diana hasn't."

My daughter hated Roland because she feared he would usurp her place in my heart. After he left, she hated him for making me unhappy.

"Whatever his reasons, accosting you at the wedding was selfish. And, if he actually married that woman in a this one will do moment? That's just . . . just—"

"I don't know." I interrupt, running my hand along the top edge of the monitor. "People are complicated. Now there is a baby. I'm sure he loves the baby. And isn't for me to judge what kind of love and how much is right for anyone other than myself."

"This is good, yes?" I point at the screen. Talking about Roland makes my throat constrict. A less fraught topic would be welcome right about now.

"Since you told him he was forgiven, he probably thinks he can forget about it."

This is my friend at her most loyal. I start the bracket. "Forgiving and forgetting aren't the same. I don't think he'll forget, any more than I can." I shake my head. "I need to hope my doughnut hole doesn't take five more years to mend. I'm all in for a miraculous healing."

"You're already on your way," Arielle says.

"You think?" I ask hopefully. "I'm ready to live in the moment—but this is the dessert bowls moment. Want to add a napkin to soften the hard line of the sideboard in background?"

"The bowls like it clean. No napkin." Arielle pats my back and heads into the kitchen to fetch the second set of bowls.

An hour later the shoot is over and we are repacking pottery into the big milk crates she uses for transport.

"You need to pick a couple of pieces before we've put everything away," she says.

"I don't want to take something you need for the show."

"Lizzie, it doesn't matter. You spent two days shooting for me, something you've done twice a year, every year, since I came home to take care of my parents, and you've never let me pay. Let us also not forget I introduced you to Dan. If every cupboard in your kitchen were stuffed with my pottery it wouldn't entirely cover what I owe you for that misdeed."

"Friendship? Priceless." I quip, but then say, "You need to stop with the business about Dan. It isn't your fault I fell for him." Then, to make Arielle happy, I choose a big salt-glazed bowl with a shiny Wedgwood-blue and white border.

CHAPTER 5

HEAVING THE FORTY-POUND dog food bag into the trunk, I hear my mobile buzz. Reading the display, I smile and say, "Graham, how are you?"

"Hey Liz. Glad to catch you. I'm fine, but far too busy."

"That doesn't sound like good news." Graham and I have plans for lunch tomorrow, and to spend the rest of the day and night together. As promised, he called in April and we've gotten together a few of times.

The mystery of how Roland knew Jerry has been explained. Graham told me they were friends as economics majors at Rutgers. They'd lost touch after graduation. A couple of years ago, they reconnected on LinkedIn. I'm still sorting out how I feel about Roland. I definitely don't long for him anymore. More like, I long for what I thought we had. Maybe that's okay. Maybe I need a new goal—*to find the lasting version of the relationship I had with him*. Right now, though, I'm still healing, so it's business as usual, which means living by The Rules.

Graham is great appreciator of life and good at acknowledging what he enjoys, a trait I admire. He's also easy company, which leaves me perplexed about why I'm not that into him. I suspect it is because I associate him with Roland. Maybe if I found him more interesting in bed, I would forget how we met. Graham is a pleasant lover, but the heat we generate is stuck on medium.

"This merger is a Rasputin project," Graham is saying into my ear. He is working on a huge and complicated bid for some company that is taking up all his time.

"We keep trying to finish the damn thing off but it keeps springing back to life with new complications."

I've had a wedding to shoot every weekend Graham has managed to make it up to his Dorset house. We've found it almost impossible to coordinate our schedules past a late-night sleep over.

"I'm afraid I don't have good news again, Liz. I'm not able to drive up tomorrow. We'll be working yet another weekend. I'm hoping this is finally the end of it."

"Darn. I was looking forward to seeing you." This is true even if the sex isn't stellar.

"And I was looking forward to seeing you. Let's find our next window of opportunity."

Consulting our calendars, we go back and forth, searching for a weekend in June when he can leave the city and I'm not shooting. We make a tentative date for three weeks from tomorrow. I visited him in New York at the end of April, but saw him only long enough to sleep with him because he was too busy for more. Obie was with me. Leaving the apartment made me nervous for fear my dog might try to claw the door down when I left. The woodwork of Graham's gorgeous prewar apartment would have suffered, so while Graham worked from morning to late in the evening, I sat around and read, unable to venture forth to enjoy the city, except for walks with my dog.

After we hang up, I drive home, drag the bag of dog food out of the car, and dump it inside the door.

"Obie, my beautiful beast, where are you?" I call. The guy who never disappoints me prances into the room with a toy in his mouth. He leaps away when I grab for it. I manage to snatch the stuffed duck on the third try, thinking I should be more disappointed about not seeing Graham tomorrow.

If I can't get past how we met, I should let him go. I suppose it's likely we'll drift apart anyway. I think we're already doing it. Geography can be destiny.

✳

The happenstance of busy lives has also kept the Larkins and me from getting together. A three- or four-month gap is the norm. Yet I continue to imagine the worst, ascribing our lack of connection to parental knowledge and condemnation. I've considered contacting C. I need to know he's all right. Then I think I'm being ridiculous. He is a lusty twenty-three-year-old man. He's fine. I decide to let the dust settle—if there is any dust that needs to settle.

Mel and I eventually meet in the produce section of the local Price Chopper in June. She tells cheerful stories about C. and his brothers, reciting their recent accomplishments. I assume from her demeanor that C. has kept mum. Mel invites me to dinner. I suggest it's my turn. When Mel and Ham are not at work, they don't like to leave their aerie in the woods so, after some back and forth, I agree to dinner at their place next Thursday as long as I can bring something. We settle on dessert. Perhaps I'm tempting fate by accepting the invitation, but I need to see C. and observe for myself how he is faring.

As for Graham, we were together as planned last weekend. It was pleasant, yet I was very aware of how much his presence churns up memories of Roland. Comparing schedules when we parted, we discovered our next opportunity to see each other would be in late August. I'm not betting it will happen.

✳

It's a warm evening, the mountains rolling green and hazy into the distance, the air alive with birdsong and the chirping of insects as I travel the long drive to the Larkins' rambling white colonial.

Mel is off the porch and in front of me before I can extract myself from the car.

"It's been way too long!" she exclaims, reaching for the basket I packed with raspberry tarts for dessert. At the same time, she pulls me into a hug.

I stiffen for a fraction of a second before squeezing her back, hoping she doesn't sense the hesitation; hoping she can't intuit I'm practically squirming with discomfort. I tell myself good news is wrapped in her easy greeting. Clearly, C. hasn't done anything to tip off his parents.

"We've all been busy," I say. "For me, it's high wedding season. At least Diana is working in Burlington this summer and isn't home. If she were, I'd feel worse about having so little time to spend with her. I miss her terribly, but I'm busy earning her keep. Among other expenses, her car needed brakes and I'm having to assume some tuition Dan can't manage, so I can't not work. The good news is that I'll be able to cover all of her needs with a little left over. I'll get a small Diana fix when she visits in August before school starts."

Mel nods. "We've recently fallen into tuition tyranny ourselves, so I totally understand the overwork thing. Let's see . . ." She looks skyward. "What's better, a lack of leisure or a lagging bank balance?" She shakes her head. "No surprise the money wins every time."

We climb the porch steps. I say, "I can't believe I haven't told you how thrilled I am to hear C. was accepted everywhere he applied."

Mel holds the screen door open. She sets my basket on the kitchen island. "We're happy with his choice of Columbia."

"It's nice that he won't be too far from home," Ham adds. I wave hello to him. He is at the sink washing chicken pieces, and placing them on a platter.

"New York is going to be quite a change from Ashburton," I say. "Not in miles, but in other ways."

"Very true," Ham concurs. "He's in for a wonderful adventure. New York is great fun when you are young."

None of the boys are in evidence. For the first time in recent memory, Mel pours the drinks, white wine for both of us. I hear a Chopin etude from the living room, so C. is home, but busy at the moment.

Mel hands over my chardonnay as the last notes of the etude fade. Seconds later, C. wanders into the kitchen to pour himself a Scotch. He toasts me with a grin and comes to stand near, crowding me just enough to be noticeable. He says, "I've missed our movie nights, Liz. That last one was so provocative." He holds my gaze.

My mouth drops open. He sips from his glass, pulls a piece of ice into his mouth, and rolls it with his tongue. I remember how he used that tongue on me. Good thing I don't normally blush or I'd go lobster red.

Thankfully, Mel doesn't register my amazement at her son's daring because she's tossing a salad with her back to us.

Ignoring C.'s remark seems prudent. I say, "Hey—I hear congrats are in order—you're off to the Big Apple this fall."

C. grins but before he can respond, his mother interrupts to ask for his help, keeping him on the other side of the island to skewer vegetables for the grill. He manages to behave himself—although who knows how long that will last. I appreciate the respite, much too aware of the masculine shape of him in his loose cotton shirt and those form-fitting jeans that are in fashion these days. I wonder if he is wearing underwear today.

Oh God. "Nice wine," I say to distract myself. "What is it?"

As hoped, C. offers his usual connoisseur's description. The conversation continues on safe ground, especially after we agree there are no art films on the schedule before he leaves for school in mid-August.

✳

Dinner is delicious. Even Drew, who did his usual greet and disappear trick, reappears for dinner and joins the conversation. He compliments the raspberry tarts I made with the frozen remains of last year's crop from my backyard bushes—an unexpectedly smooth social interaction for him. Harry tells a story about a berry patch and some ground bees, an adventure that didn't end well.

As the evening progresses, I decide C. and I have sneaked under the family radar. Just as reassuring, I see no evidence he has suffered from our encounter.

Over dessert, the brothers discuss fencing. They will be helping their instructor with a demonstration in Saratoga next weekend. C. says, "I'm working on my straight thrust." He throws a glance in my direction and jumps up to demonstrate. He sends a pantomime sword through my heart. When he's finished, he holds his pretend rapier in front of his face and bows low, an eighteenth-century courtier in skinny jeans. He invites me to critique his technique.

"Masterful," I say without thinking. Full of merriment, his eyes meet mine. Only then do I connect what I've just said to his remark in bed last winter. I manage to keep my glance from swinging toward his parents. "But I'm no expert," I hedge, trying to cover my guilty embarrassment, which must be visible to all, no matter that they are clueless about what is actually going on. "Drew, what's your verdict?" I ask, to deflect attention.

Undeterred, C. looks me in the eye and says, "You underestimate yourself," as his brother drawls, "He's improving—slowly," thereby drowning out C.'s comment. This bit of brotherly snark thankfully shifts C.'s attention from me. I take a relieved breath as he thrusts a second imaginary blade through his brother.

If his parents or siblings notice the between-the-lines game C. is playing, if they register his surge of energy, perhaps they attribute it to his excitement about heading off to college.

I find no evidence that I've wounded him or our easy rapport, but whenever I see Mel, which I do again a few weeks later, I brace for bad news, wondering if I'll ever be rid of the flutter of anxiety whenever we meet. As usual, her news is good. Harry is away taking college-level math classes in Boston. Drew is doing research for his father, and C. is a counselor at the Ashburton summer arts and sciences program for high school juniors and seniors. Mel's friendly demeanor and cheerful delivery begin to close the book on C., no matter that my companion Guilt continues to shadow me.

CHAPTER 6

ASHBURTON'S MAIN STREET invites strolling with its arty stores and good restaurants. Colorful baskets of petunias, geraniums, and trailing *Vinca* hang from Victorian-style lampposts. More-colorful flora burst from oversized terracotta planters placed at intervals along the curb. The entryways to many stores and restaurants sport tasteful green or black awnings, shading interiors from the bright sunlight. Our downtown is New England picture-perfect on this late-July afternoon, the sidewalks crowded with locals and tourists.

Appreciating that our merchants and restaurateurs are in the money today, I'm not as pleased to discover the only available parking spot is a long block from my bank. A photo-editing deadline is looming, I'm irritated by the heat, and plowing my way through eighty percent humidity while dodging pedestrians has me cursing the need to deposit a couple of checks that arrived today so I don't have to raid my savings to help with Diana's final fall tuition payment. Focused on the lovely air-conditioned interior of the bank I've almost reached, I'm mopping the sweat beading my forehead when I hear my name shouted. Recognizing the voice, I pivot.

C. strides toward me. He is as beautiful as ever. Although it is almost two months since the dinner at his parents' house where he played at skewering my heart, all the feelings I thought I'd boxed up for good—lust, guilt, and longing—bloom as verdantly as if I'd been tenderly nurturing them since he left my bed.

As far as I can tell, C. has no such problem. He drops a casual kiss on my cheek and steps away. "Liz, great to see you," he exclaims, with that funny little gesture of his—rubbing his palms together in front of his chest. "I hoped to catch you before I left for school, and here you are!"

This is news. Or the kind of smooth repartee called for in situations like this.

A petite, hip-looking girl ambles to C.'s side. I figure her for an Ashburton student owing to her casually mussed hair, red lipstick, and artfully deconstructed clothing. C. pulls her into his body. "Liz, this is Isabelle, friend and fellow counselor."

From the possessive way he is holding her, I can guess what sort of friend Isabelle is to him. I'm pleased C. has a girlfriend. "Nice to meet you, Isabelle."

With a mischievous sparkle in his eyes, C. says, "Liz is one of my favorite teachers."

This would be cutely clever if the girl didn't ask, "I thought you were home schooled?"

I wait to see how C. will wiggle out of the little hole he's dug himself.

He doesn't disappoint. With his usual ease, he replies, "Oh, I was." With the same flip of his hand that started the whole thing that memorable February evening, he explains, "I had tutors for a couple of subjects my parents didn't teach." He casts me a knowing glance and says, "Like fencing."

She nods, satisfied with his answer. I am relieved when he leaves it at that. We chat about his plans as well as hers.

As they turn away to continue their errands, I can't help admiring C.'s broad shoulders, his narrow hips, that high firm ass. I remember the pleasure we gave each other and smile at his jaunty walk. Perhaps he senses me watching because he looks over his shoulder and grins.

The girl says something. He bends to listen, taking her hand.

They disappear into a coffee shop up the street.

My mood shifts. As much as I'd hoped C. would connect with a girl his own age, seeing him at it is another matter entirely.

It isn't that I have designs on him. That would be absurd, although it's impossible not to desire his sweetly mischievous presence, precocious intellect, and potent young body. But wanting and doing are not the same. I suspect this change in mood has more to do with his youthful optimism and witnessing his first foray into the intoxication of first love or infatuation—whatever is between him and Isabelle. At the very beginning of his adult life, the open road of possibility stretches out before him. I'm in the middle of my life with too much history stacked around me to face the future with the confidence he possesses.

If I'm jealous, it's of all of that potential.

C.'s obviously more confident than before we slept together; confident in real, rather than assumed, ways, which had been his style in the past.

It should be a relief to bid adieu to any worries about damaging him. I tell myself all is well, to buck up, to move on past him, and likely past Graham as well. Graham and I can't even pull off casual pillow friends. Our schedules won't mesh.

The lobby of the bank is blessedly cool. I pull out my deposit slip and endorsed checks. Waiting for a teller, I think, if we mirror what we experience at home, as the experts suggest, then C. is headed for relationship success since his parents are models of supportive and loving coupledom.

My parents divorced when I was in college. They were unhappy for as long as I can remember. This may explain what happened between Dan and me. Based on what went on at home, I didn't have a clue about how to make a marriage work. The best that can be said of my marriage is that Dan and I were loving parents and remain so, although we love Diana from separate sides of town.

Still, I worry that the strife Diana witnessed between us will affect her relationships. She professes not to be interested in dating. Without a good role model, I don't think she trusts herself to make good choices. I understand, yet I hope she will stay open to possibility.

A teller motions me to her window. While she processes the deposit, I wish I had presented my daughter with a better example of marriage than I gave her.

Back on the street, I notice the florist's window is filled with orchids. Some are white. Others have dusky pink petals with darker veining at the center. Shade plants with dark waxy leaves set off the flowers' sensual beauty.

I stop to give these floozies of the plant world closer study. Their shape—that female cleft and protruding stamen—are too openly erotic. I find them slightly disturbing, which only draws me closer to the window.

✳

"So, everything's good? Classes are interesting?" I ask Diana two weeks later. She texts often enough, but I'm old school and like to hear her voice. I plug my ear bud in so I can continue to touch up the bride and groom I shot the weekend before.

"Mom, I know the code. Say what you mean. That would be, 'Have you met any nice guys yet?'"

"No, sweet girl, it means, are you doing anything other than studying?" Good thing Diana can't see me roll my eyes because it would irritate her and she's irritated enough. "Not that studying isn't desirable," I add.

My daughter is more than willing to let me know how irritating, idiotic, or just plain out of touch I am when I display any or all such characteristics. When she's feeling charitable, which isn't often, she tells me I'm a good mom. Because such compliments are rare, her praise is deeply gratifying. My parents didn't provide a road map for good parenting skills any more than they provided one for relationships, although I have to give Mom—the Victorian—credit for instilling the right lessons no matter that her delivery method was less than ideal.

"I'm going to the opera Friday night with a group of girls from my history class," Diana says, throwing me a bone. "They're music majors and get free tickets from the department."

"Nice." I leave it at that.

"So, I'll see you in two weeks?"

"Yup. I've really been missing you and I'm excited that we can spend a little time together." I add, "It will be fun to see Karen, too. I'm staying with her. We haven't worked together since the beginning of the season. I'll be shooting through Sunday morning, though. How about we meet at the Farm at 1:00 and take a walk?"

The Farm is Shelburne Farms, fourteen hundred acres of fields and woodland with an immense horse barn that has been converted to an events space. The property was originally owned by members of the Vanderbilt family.

"Actually," says Diana, "I need new jeans."

"Okay, the mall it is." We'll probably walk the same distance there as we would at the Farm, only the view will be of store mannequins. "Shall we have dinner in Burlington on Church Street somewhere?"

"Sounds like a plan."

After we say good-bye, I notice the jade plant perched on the sill in front of my desk needs water. In contrast to my Jewish-mother tendencies with Diana, I'm a neglectful mother to my houseplants. Green things tend to die slow deaths in my care. I splash some water into the soil from the glass on my desk before turning my attention to the plant's new companion, purchased the afternoon I bumped into C.

Thus far the orchid has thrived in my neglectful care. I pour the last of the water over its gnarly roots. I see no sign of appreciation. Self-contained and sure of its beauty, the orchid is like many house cats of my acquaintance, who, I suspect, would happily swallow me if I were to suddenly shrink to a chewable size. I touch an elongated stamen, both transfixed and repelled by the flower's crass sexuality.

The DNA of the common housefly and humans is not so dissimilar—or so I've read. This could explain why a plant designed to lure insects has attracted a warm-blooded biped like me. It doesn't account, however, for the orchid's acquisition, since ninety-nine percent of my previous impulse buys took place in shoe stores.

I yawn. Compulsive about finishing tasks, I've put off lunch to finish correcting a file of images, knocking down shadows to pick up detail, as well as dodging in highlights where they are startlingly bright.

Although I don't find my work all that exciting anymore, producing good-quality pictures remains important to me. As I make the little corrections that separate my photographs from those of lesser professionals, whitening teeth and removing the stray frizz of hair, taking the shine off eyeglasses and bald pates, I've been contemplating my current lack of enthusiasm.

Does it have any bearing on why I slept with C.? Did I take him to bed hoping he would be the antidote to my creeping dissatisfaction with the way life is trending? If that were the case—and I don't know my own mind well enough to confirm or deny it—I'm as dumb as the men I've disdained for *shtupping* young women as if they are a magical age-defying elixir.

C. has had the opposite effect on me. I am more restless than before. Seeing C. with Isabelle seems to have made the malaise worse. Their youthful vitality reminded me that the wonder of new love isn't likely to ever be mine again.

I study the picture I've finished correcting, the last of the group. The bride is bent over the groom's arm in a swooning kiss we faked for the camera, although the sentiment was real enough. The image makes me feel a little queasy.

Or I could be queasy because I delayed lunch too long.

Lately, as I edit pictures of happy brides and grooms celebrating with their happy families and happy friends—everyone so happy, happy, happy—I'm sucked into the fairy tale and find myself yearning for a similar happiness of my own.

Thirty percent of all marriages end in divorce. The statistic doesn't alter my feelings. No matter how many times I shove those feelings into the "don't think about it" box, they slither out again.

It's unnerving, not to mention depressing. I need to understand, and understand fast, whether sleeping with someone young enough to be my son was my subconscious cure for what's ailing me. If so, it was a dismal failure. Seeing Roland hasn't helped, either. I definitely don't need another impetuous and possibly more consequential experiment like the one with C. I mean, what's next? Bungee cord jumping? Russian roulette?

A new and appropriately aged bed partner would be a better option. My bed was empty for a few months before C. filled it, and has been again, since Graham and I saw each other in June and didn't manage to connect in August.

I ponder a candidate to break the dry spell. The last time I stopped at my lawyer's office to review changes to my standard client contract, Elliot Carson, Esq., suggested we get together for drinks sometime. Newly divorced, he could be in fun mode rather than relationship-acquisition mode.

There is safety in the newly divorced, which happens to be Rule Number Four. Many divorced men are profoundly relieved to regain their freedom, with no desire to retie the knot anytime soon. Such men are perfect for my purposes.

Resolved to ensure Elliot and I have a drink is in the near future, I push away from the desk. Obie rests his head on my thigh with a big doggy sigh. His tail rises in an *I'm-hoping-for-attention* swish. My standard poodle has perfected the art of Jewish guilt, canine style.

"Okay, okay," I say. "I'm a bad mother to houseplants *and dogs*." I give his head a stroke. He dips into a downward-facing dog posture. His homage makes me ashamed; the poor guy should have been walked an hour ago.

Obie was the consolation gift I gave myself when Roland left me. He is grateful for as much or as little attention as I can spare him. Unlike many human males I've known, he has never held my failings against me. And, he's so much nicer to cuddle than my latest houseplant, even if a middle-aged woman whose dog is her most intimate relationship is a cliché I never thought I'd become.

Tilting his head, Obie looks quizzical as I reverse at the kitchen door and return to my desk. Although the orchid's blatantly sexual message is not the cause of my restlessness, it isn't helping. I carry it to the kitchen window where it will have less opportunity to seduce me. "Seduce the fruit flies instead," I tell it before Obie and I head outside.

CHAPTER 7

SAL'S PLACE is a narrow restaurant sandwiched between the bookstore and a real estate agent. The name is written in swooping gilt lettering on the window facing the street. Elliot and I are meeting here, ostensibly so I can hand over the contract he revised. I have a few last notes. I walk past linen-covered tables, checking out the wall art.

Sally Bartoli, the owner, is an enthusiastic supporter of the local art community. She uses the long brick walls of her eatery as a revolving gallery. This month, a watercolorist is showing his impressionistic paintings of the area.

I have shown here. And sold a few prints. I'd like to again, but I have nothing new to offer. The realization tenses my shoulders.

"Hi, Liz. What can I get you?" Ted, the bartender, asks as I slide onto a bar stool.

"Hey, Teddy. How are you?"

Teddy and I met when he was in high school. Years ago, I spoke to his photography class about life as a professional photographer. I've mentored him on and off since. "When am I going to see some of your work on these walls?" I ask. Promoting someone else's creativity is the next best thing to promoting your own. I smile encouragingly and order a gin and tonic, light on the gin, heavy on the lime.

It is early yet so there are only a couple other occupied stools. Ted picks a tall glass out of the collection under the counter and stays to chat while he mixes my drink.

"I've been too busy." He drops ice into the glass. "You know I've been stringing some for the *Ashburton Gazette,* right? Pays hardly anything but I like covering local sports."

"I've noticed your credit. I'll see a shot in the paper and think, '*That is way better than average.'* More often than not, the shot is yours."

"Thanks for noticing, but I confess, photography isn't my main interest right now. I formed a band with a few friends from college. We just signed with a manager and we're doing a college circuit this fall." He grins.

"That's great! I'm so pleased for you."

"But hey, how come I've never seen your work on these walls?" He sets my drink on a cocktail napkin and slides it across the counter.

I salute him with it before taking a sip. "I've shown some of my landscape work here. It was before your time. Like you, I've been too busy. Nothing else pays the bills like weddings." I shrug, as if my lack of opportunity for personal work is no big deal.

"Well, I think you should find the time. You shouldn't let go of what you love."

"You're a wise man." I take another sip of my drink. He's made it refreshingly sour with lime. Teddy is right; but as disinterested in the wedding biz as I am these days, I also haven't felt the least creative spark for anything else. Perhaps the tariff on earning a decent living in my field of interest has become a little boredom. At least I enjoy the tabletop stuff I shoot for Arielle. Maybe I should put her images on my website to see if I can pick up more of that kind of business.

Ted pulls out a card and hands it to me. On the front, a snarling cat in red is cropped to mostly eye and teeth. Across this graphic is a single word: "Tomcat." The flipside is fluorescent orange with a web address written in more red. "Our dates are listed on the website," Ted says.

"I'd love to catch one of your shows."

He smiles. "That would be great. Bring your camera!" he suggests, before moving down the bar to serve a new customer.

Waiting for Elliot, I tap the contract on the counter. Weddings keep me busy from early spring until late fall. I earn between $1,500 and $6,000 an event. It's hard to give up that kind of money to squeeze in other work. I lay the envelope down, knowing I'm making excuses; the problem is more systemic. My brow knits. Maybe I'm suffering from a

PART ONE
~ DARIUS ~

CHAPTER 8

"I'M SO GLAD you could make it." Jill Burton motions for me to precede her up the hall. The Burtons' house is open to the rafters, exposing the original beams of the converted barn. Large divided-pane windows offer a spectacular panorama of the Vermont landscape.

"This is my first free Saturday night since mid-June. I'm delighted I could be here!" I offer a grin.

"The usual?" Jill's husband Alex asks when I walk over to say hello. He mixes my favorite fall drink, a Kir.

The view out the windows has me wishing I hadn't left my camera at home. I've gotten out of my old habit of carrying it wherever I go.

The exact cast of the light and shading of the sun-tinted autumnal mountains is beautiful tonight. I could return to capture the view at the same time tomorrow but it won't be the same. The humidity will be different, which will change the light. There could be clouds or rain. Nothing about a landscape is exactly the same twice. Yet this thought isn't entirely an unhappy one, because this is the first time I've wished I could photograph anything in a very long time.

"It seems as if summer lasted about a week and fall is already well on its way." I turn to Alex. "My schedule makes our best seasons speed by."

"You should help on the farm. You know we always need volunteers." Alex chuckles. "Summer is a lot longer when you weed your way through it." He hands me the Kir. "You and I will catch up later, I hope, but for now I'm doubling as bartender and sous chef and I'm needed in the kitchen."

I wave him off, noticing an old friend in front of the appetizer-laden sideboard. Sheri is applying herbed goat cheese to a cracker as I join her. Once I've chosen a few nibbles, we seat ourselves on one of a pair of living room sofas. A fire in the fieldstone hearth adds welcome warmth to the evening.

"I can't believe I haven't seen you since you moved into your new house," I say. "Of course, I don't see anyone until the wedding season is over, unless they are attending a wedding I'm shooting." I've been so immersed in work, I haven't seen Arielle in weeks.

"Modern life . . . it gets away from you," Sheri says. "I'm glad I teach. It means the kids and I are on the same schedule, with summers off."

"So everything is good?" Like Elliot's, her divorce was final six months ago.

"Better. I mean, better not to be in the middle of the deep-freeze zone where Bill and I ended up." She grimaces. "I'm okay except for these weird moments of crazy irritation that crop up every so often. Like yesterday, when I couldn't find the peas I was sure were in the freezer. I flung everything out of it. I'm not kidding—frozen pizzas and packages of hamburger and baggies of stuff I could no longer identify went flying. Thank God the kids weren't home to see me acting like an enraged five-year-old. Did you ever do things like that?"

"After Dan and I split? Yup. Although once I had everything out of my freezer I think I stomped on it, too, before bursting into tears."

Sheri laughs. "Oh God, that isn't funny, but it's good to know I'm not the only one."

"Did you find the peas?"

"I did. And a couple of old Mars bars I'd forgotten were in there. Those calmed me right down. Plus, the freezer got cleaned out."

Laughing, I say, "At times like that it's good to focus on the positive." Our conversation moves on to the losers she's met on the dating site she joined. "Dating isn't a priority right now," Sheri concludes. "What matters is the kids are doing well—a miracle considering what they've been through."

"I'm glad." I've never tried the online dating scene, no matter the length of my dry spells.

We talk companionably until Sheri wants to refresh her drink. "Listen, you need to see the new house. I'll call to make a date," she says as she gets to her feet.

"I'd love that. I have a couple more weddings to shoot and then the season is over. Give me until the end of the month and I'll be there."

Sheri heads for the drinks table. Choosing to remain by the hearth rather than replenish my drink, I watch the flames as the sky darkens beyond the windows. I'm enjoying the warmth of the fire and the slight buzz from the Kir. The hum of conversation behind me is pleasant background music. I feel more relaxed than I have in months.

A spark leaps out of the marble hearth with a loud pop. I startle. At the same time, a hand brushes across my shoulder, sending goose bumps up my spine. I twist and meet merry gray eyes.

"Darius! How nice. I didn't know you were friends with Alex and Jill!"

"Lovely to see you, Leezbeth. An unexpected delight. And yes, we became acquainted when they purchased a few pieces from the shop."

"Let me guess. The Moorish fantasy over the dining table? It looks like a fugitive from the lobby of an old movie theater."

"You have good intuition. It is exactly that."

Having grown up in Lebanon, Darius speaks Lebanese Arabic and French—Lebanon having been a French colony. Although he has lived in America for something like forty years, his speech retains the pleasing inflections of his childhood languages, rather purposely, I suspect.

Setting a fresh Kir on the coffee table for me, Darius takes a seat on the couch. He must have asked Alex what I'm drinking. I appreciate his thoughtfulness. Holding his Scotch with two fingers curled under the tumbler's base, Darius settles himself. He takes a sip. On his pinkie, a chunky gold ring with a large stone reflects luminescent moss green in the firelight.

I admire the ring. "Seventeenth-century Italian," he says, putting his drink down to tug the bauble off.

"Did you buy it to match your jacket?" My mouth quirks; I'm not serious, although the stone is indeed a match for the forest green of his velveteen blazer. A foulard-patterned silk square peeks from his chest pocket. Darius's fashion sense is very old-world continental.

He puts the ring in my palm and shrugs. "It has been with me for too long to remember how I acquired it."

Solid gold, the ring is as heavy as it looks. I hold it to the light, admiring the pair of half-woman, half-serpent figures twining around what appears to be a large cabochon emerald. My credulity is strained by the idea Darius doesn't remember how something this singular came into his possession. My bet is he knows exactly where it came from but enjoys withholding the information. Being mysterious is his raison d'être. Not for the first time I wonder whether he is enigmatic by nature or because it burnishes his image of himself.

I hold the ring out to him. His manicured fingers, totally in keeping with his continental style, brush mine as he takes it back. A small frisson of awareness shimmers through me. I have known Mr. Mystery— as I sometimes refer to Darius in my mind—in a casual way and for a long time, without any evidence he'd want to take our acquaintance to a different level. Even so, awareness is blooming tonight.

"So, how's the antique business these days?" I ask, since I'm not about to call him out on his mystery shtick.

"I have new pieces. Stop by. But soon, *oui*? Buyers are coming from the city next weekend who will want the furniture you must see."

"Why *must* I see?"

"Because you will appreciate the Art Nouveau chiffonier I picked up at auction along with a Biedermeier bedroom set. Very beautiful. You will particularly like the Biedermeier pieces."

"If only my pocketbook were deep enough to buy a single Biedermeier anything, never mind an entire suite." I sigh.

Darius knows from previous visits how much I love the style. The sleekly streamlined European furniture reminds me of Art Deco, except that it came into vogue a century earlier. And, unlike a lot of Deco, it remains modern-looking to this day.

"Not so sad," Darius counters.

I tilt my head to the side, gesturing for further explanation.

"You are indiscriminate in your tastes, ma *cherie*." He tempers his criticism with a smile.

"I think I've been insulted!" I exclaim.

His eyes dance with mischief. "Leezbeth"—his tone is consoling, his accent veering toward the French—"if you had money, you would buy everything you like."

"And why not?"

He waves his glass, warming to the subject. "It would require twenty rooms to house your purchases and"—he grimaces, probably imagining the decor—"you would end up with a mishmash of neoclassical, Biedermeier, country Victorian, midcentury, and . . . " He strokes his beard for a second as he reviews the horrors of such an interior in his mind's eye and finally concludes, "And I don't know what else. Better to be limited by what you can afford—it gives you focus."

"Just because I mix periods doesn't make me indiscriminate," I say. "Although, I admit it would be wonderful to be a dealer like you so I could collect all the mismatched furniture I want and when I get tired of it, sell it off at a profit and start all over again." I raise one brow.

"Touché! Like to like, *oui*? You have exposed my secret." He laughs, clinking his glass with mine. I can't decide if he is flirting or treating me like a favorite pupil, one who is cleverer than he supposed. "So," he says after another sip of his drink, "what have you been up to since I last saw you—could it be last winter? So long ago?"

"What I'm always up to," I say. Two can play the mystery game.

Darius and I know each other through the small purchases I've made at his shop and my larger appreciation of his eye for exquisite antiques. We are fond acquaintances rather than friends. When my brain wearies of scrutinizing happy wedding photographs and I need a dose of something solid and long lasting, I've been known to pay a visit to his shop. I'm drawn by the size and age of the pieces he stocks, furniture that has made it through centuries of ownership in pristine condition, unlike so many marriages. An hour spent around

Darius's antiques soothes the cynic in me.

"Must I presume you have been collecting men again?" Darius asks, deliberately misinterpreting my comment, which referred to how much I work.

I have always *presumed* we know more about each other than we have confided. Our town has a population of about fourteen thousand, but the community of artists and professionals is small. This means most of us know each other if not personally then peripherally. For instance, I know that until recently, Darius was seeing a divorcée living in Old Ashburton Village, the high-toned town on the hill. But what does he know about me? Apparently more than I thought.

Sipping his drink, Darius watches me over the rim of his glass, the twinkle in his eyes daring me to be equally outrageous. On-your-toes banter is his stock in trade. He is being particularly provocative tonight. I admit to enjoying it. "Are you not the pot calling the kettle black?" I suggest. "Although men wouldn't be your interest."

His eyes glitter with amusement and a smile lifts one side of his mouth, the warm firelight highlighting the angular bones of his face.

Darius is not handsome, yet there is something undeniably sexy about him. He has high cheekbones, a wide jaw, and a prominent, slightly hooked nose that balances the strength of the rest of his features. He wears a neatly trimmed mustache and goatee, adding to his distinguished, European aura. His wide-set gray eyes, almond shaped and uptilted, are his best feature. Expressive and knowing, he uses them to hold your gaze in a way that makes him seem entirely present. I have never found older men of much interest, but Darius could be the exception. I don't know exactly how old he is but I guess he has fifteen or more years on me.

His ability to concentrate so intensely on another person, the way he is concentrating on me, must contribute to his success as a dealer. I don't need to bet that it contributes to his success with women.

When he looks at me, I feel like the most interesting woman in the room. It's a definite turn-on. And, whether feigned or not, his air of

night"—and suddenly everyone else is calling it a night, too. A sociologist could probably explain this phenomenon, but since we don't have one in attendance this evening, I'm left to theorize on my own, betting the lemming-like chain reaction has its foundations in pack mentality buried deep within the primitive cortex of our brains.

Tonight, Alex's emergency room doctor friend Bob rises to start the stampede. "I'm on at 6:00 a.m. I'd better get some sleep while I can," he says, and in minutes everyone else is collecting wraps and bags except me and, surprisingly, Darius.

Jill and I clear. Alex handles leftovers. Darius, elbows on the counter dividing the kitchen from the dining area, doesn't offer to tidy. Instead, he entertains us with stories about his interesting and sometimes exasperating customers. Once the dishwasher is full, Jill begins washing the crystal by hand. Darius surprises me by picking up a towel. I dry as well.

Forty-five minutes after the rest of the guests have left, the mess has been tamed. I pick up the a foil-wrapped treat Jill has set aside for Obs, and head for the guest bedroom doubling as coat repository. Darius follows. He retrieves his scarf and the Greek fisherman's cap he wears to keep the small bald spot at his crown warm on chilly nights like this. His leather jacket looks Italian. When I brush against it, I find it as gorgeously supple as the body part described by my one word of Farsi. I keep the opinion to myself, but feel it in a lovely tightening between my legs.

Ever the gallant, Darius holds my coat for me. I manage to push one arm into the corresponding sleeve, but my body doesn't remember the rest of the choreography. I get tangled in the other sleeve and wiggle, feeling awkward and a little embarrassed by my lack of grace.

My clumsiness amuses Darius. Once I have myself organized, he stands my collar up and taps my nose playfully with the tip of a finger. Looking into his twinkling gray eyes I can't help but wonder again about what he is hiding behind all that glitter.

As we leave the room, his palm settles between my shoulder blades and stays there. It seems obvious which way the wind is blowing, yet he hasn't made an overt move since that outrageous remark about the Kir, unless pressing me to show up at the shop sooner rather than later is his opening gambit. I decide to take him up on his offer and see where it leads. As he hands me into the car, I say, "Thank you for that lesson in Farsi. In the future I'll enjoy my favorite drink with new appreciation." I pet his coat and smile.

CHAPTER 9

MY AT-HOME WORK OUTFIT of T-shirt and yoga pants is fine for errands, though not for errands culminating in a visit to Darius's shop. I change into a periwinkle-colored jersey top with a deep neckline. The top tends to shift, exposing the lacy black straps of my bra. Paired with hip-hugging black pants, the outfit is flattering and flirty. I decide on high-heeled ankle boots and accessorize with a few silver bangles that jingle as I move.

Telling Obie to watch the house, I step into the overcast September afternoon. First stop is the post office, where I mail an additional album for one of the August weddings. At Stratton's Stationary & Gifts I pick up file folders, and, because I'm near, I stop at the florist to find out more about the care of orchids. Mine continues to flourish but I don't know if I need to move it away from the window in winter. I trust the information from the florist more than what I might find on the Internet.

Errands complete, I drive east on Main Street, which is also the main east–west artery bisecting southern Vermont. It is a two-lane with precious few passing zones for most of its hill-climbing distance into Brattleboro on the opposite side of the state. Darius's shop is located where the commercial part of the street begins to thin into a mixture of residential and commercial buildings.

I turn into the parking area. The house where Darius lives and does business is a grand Italianate Victorian. I assume it was built by the owner of the defunct shoe factory across the street. The factory sprawls over several lots. A century ago it was one of the largest employers in town.

I walk under an elaborate multi-pillared porte cochere. Steps lead to a wide wraparound porch. Recently painted in colors appropriate to the period, the house's clapboards are a deep red. Ornamental details are coral, with architectural flourishes in the same chocolate brown of the shutters. The house dwarfs the more humble dwellings around it.

A bell jingles deep inside when I push one of the eight-foot-tall exterior doors open to the narrow vestibule. Another set of doors with etched-glass panels open to the grand center hall with a massive mahogany staircase. Large archways lead to equally large rooms where Darius displays his wares. Over the windows, the house's original interior shutters softly filter late-afternoon light.

Assuming Darius heard the bell and will eventually show himself, I move toward the right front parlor. My heels click across the polished parquet until I reach a thick Persian rug blanketing the parlor floor.

It amazes me how quickly Darius's inventory turns over. Only a few pieces are familiar from my visit last winter. The front parlor is used to display sofas and fainting couches, clusters of ornamental tables and wood-framed fauteuil chairs with silky brocade backs, seats, and arm pads. Oil paintings crowd the walls.

A second parlor behind this one displays tables set with china as if visitors were about to arrive for a six-course meal. Dining chairs in styles ranging from French Provincial to Arts and Crafts tuck around the tables. Overhead, so many chandeliers glitter I can hardly see the ceiling.

I wander for a good five minutes without Darius making his appearance. The double doors to his living quarters at the top of the stairs are closed. I decide to complete my tour before going in search of him.

The Biedermeier suite I've been summoned to see is hard to miss in the front room on the opposite side of the hall. Pausing to admire the outsized furniture's amber-hued perfection, I hear Darius descending the stairs.

When I turn toward him, he smiles, though he doesn't advance into the room. Choosing to lean into in archway, he takes a typical Darius pose. One arm crossed over his chest, the other resting on it, he strokes his goatee awaiting my reaction to the bedroom set.

"Wow," is all I manage as I admire the massive bed and armoire, as well as the other components.

"I thought you would like them." His voice holds a note of pride. The furniture is polished to a high gloss, without a single scratch visible to the eye. Unable to resist, I stroke my fingertips over the gorgeous satin finish of an armoire door. Constructed of subtle grained birch, the door has been pieced to resemble moiré silk. I like the vanity best. Smaller in scale than the rest, it has three shallow drawers with ebony-and-brass pulls and a square mirror that pivots between birch pillars.

"The set is Swedish, as is the chiffonier in the back room," Darius volunteers. "Dating from 1840 or so."

"The set is very beautiful." I trail my hand along the vanity top, its surface mirror bright, so shiny it could be glass. When I look up, Darius is watching my hand. He raises his eyes to mine, the corners creasing attractively as he smiles, yet his usual twinkle is not evident.

I haven't yet figured out what causes his twinkle to come and go. I once knew another man who twinkled except when he lied. I don't think that is Darius's M.O.

"The chiffonier is in the next room. Not a tallboy, you understand, but a French sideboard. Sometimes Americans confuse the two. We will admire it and then I will make you coffee." He turns without waiting to see if I fall in step with his plans.

Amused by his assuming behavior, I trail after him. The chiffonier is indeed marvelous. It has an undulating shape with applied carved vines and leaves snaking over the surface.

We climb the stairs. This will be my first visit to Darius's home above the shop. He unlocks the double doors, gesturing me inside. I surmise the space was once several smaller rooms now combined into one. The overcast late-afternoon light slanting through tall windows makes me think of nineteenth-century Parisian artists' salons I've seen in vintage photographs.

On the same wall as the doors, floor-to-ceiling bookcases take up the entire wall. Opposite is a kitchen with artistically distressed ocher-stained cabinets fronted by a substantial butcher-block island. An old library table is surrounded by armless fauteuil chairs upholstered in colorful Kilim rug remnants. The other half of the room is arranged as a living room, a large abstract canvas above a graceful white marble mantel acting as the focal point.

The space is interesting and comfortable but reveals little about Darius I don't already know. There is a stone head on a pedestal near one window. Chinese ginger jars converted into lamps perch on side tables, along with many other small objets d'art, but no photographs of family or trinkets of the type most of us keep for sentimental value rather than beauty.

Only the painting over the mantel is different—notably less than fifty years old and shockingly modern by the standards of the rest. I walk over to admire it. Taking note of the signature, I turn my head in question.

"I used to paint," Darius says, joining me.

The landscape of hills and fields has a palette of soft purple and the acid greens of early spring. The brush strokes are exuberant.

I pivot to face him. "This is wonderful! Is it recent?"

"From long ago." His eyes move past me to glance at the canvas.

I notice a date brushed into the corner next to his name: 1984.

"Do you still paint?"

"*Non.*" He turns and walks to the kitchen.

I study the painting a moment longer. Finding myself sucked into Darius's Mr. Mystery routine, I join him at the island counter. "It seems a shame," I say.

"There is a long story, too long to tell in the time we have. I would like to hear more about your work. Do you do other kinds of photography or only the weddings? I think I should know this, but I do not."

Pleased by his interest, though noting his unwillingness to share his own story, I respond, "I enjoy shooting landscapes when I see one that interests me, and occasionally I enjoy portraiture and reportage, which is why I enjoy weddings, but I haven't exhibited in a long time." I don't say that I haven't found anything interesting enough to capture my interest since I-don't-know-when. I look over my shoulder at his painting. "Your painting really is marvelous. You know, if you would like to tell me about it, I have time to listen." I smile as prettily as I'm able.

He studies me for a long moment without any sparkle. He says, "I think it is too late for coffee. Do you like brandy, cognac? Perhaps wine?"

"Surprise me?"

He gestures to the high-backed sofa near the fireplace. The velvet upholstery is a deep blue. Pulling two snifters out of a cupboard, he uncaps a bottle of brandy with a pear imprisoned inside and crosses the room, bottle and glasses in hand.

"How is Diana?" he asks, as I settle myself on the sofa. He sets his supplies on the long Shaker bench he has repurposed as a coffee table.

"In her second year of college. She loves UVM and Burlington. She's a good student and a hard worker." It seems his painting days are to be approached obliquely.

"*Bon*. It is good to know. She was such a charming little girl. Most children climb the furniture. Diana did not. She asked good questions and listened to the answers. She is very intelligent, *oui*?"

I love hearing my daughter praised. I grin. "I've always thought there aren't many people her age who appreciate old things the way Diana does. I hold you responsible, Darius. She considered our visits here a great treat."

I arrange a few of the sofa's jewel-toned silk toss pillows around me. Darius pours. He hands me a snifter, setting the bottle next to a pile of magazines on the bench. Seating himself in a wing chair opposite the sofa, he swirls the contents of his glass before drinking.

I sip, tasting alcohol more than anything else. Darius props a loafer-shod foot on the bench. I recognize it will not work to steer the conversation to his story and try the brandy again. This time I taste a hint of pear and like it better.

"Your work winds down in late fall, I imagine?" Darius says.

"I have a few events to shoot in October and one in December. I never have more than a few bookings in the winter months."

He contemplates me as he sips his brandy. "A little breather is good for creativity."

"True." I assume that he, as a former painter, understands the relationship between creativity and fallow thinking time. "Will you go to Europe as usual this winter?"

"*Oui.* But not until mid-December."

I nod. Excellent. An affair with Darius will have a natural shelf life. He is seeming more and more Rule perfect.

As he takes another sip of his brandy, I say, "So, tell me about the painting." I am unable to resist shifting the conversation toward this latest mystery.

"You will be disappointed by how ordinary a tale you will hear."

"*If* I nod off I won't blame your story; I'll blame the brandy." I smile and take a small sip from my snifter.

Mr. Mystery—I am definitely dealing with him tonight—lifts a brow and takes a much larger swallow than mine. Otherwise he doesn't respond. I'm beginning to find his non-responses more normal than not. By the time he sets his glass down, I'm a little light-headed from my few sips. I realize I once again forgot to eat lunch.

"When I was young I intended a career in music," Darius begins. "I studied at the Conservatoire. In Paris." He pronounces the city "Paree."

"You are a musician as well as a painter? Quite the Renaissance man," I say admiringly. "What did you play?"

"Viola. I played the viola and conducted."

"I had no idea! Did you begin studying when you were small? You grew up in Beirut, right?"

"Until the mid-'60s, when I was in my early teens." Darius takes the last swallow of his brandy, then asks, "How much do you know about the region?"

"Not much. Wasn't Lebanon occupied by France before the Second World War?"

Darius nods. "Because it was on the Mediterranean and relatively stable, Lebanon was a tourist mecca. My father repaired watches and sold jewelry and small antiques to tourists. But after the Six-Day War, he didn't believe peace would hold. Friends in France sponsored us, so we emigrated. Papa opened a little shop and did well enough."

Looking around the room, I question my earlier analysis. Are the smaller art objects like the ormolu clock on the mantel and the little cloisonné bird sitting on the table beside Darius's chair mementos of his boyhood?

"But you didn't stay in France," I comment, wondering what brought him from France to the States.

"*Non.* I left the Conservatoire to graduate from Julliard." He puts down his glass. "It was not a popular choice with my family. As the only and anointed son I was expected to do my share of the work and to take over the shop one day. My father fought my leaving. When I did it anyway—following Julianne to the States—he refused to speak to me for many years. It wasn't until I became a success and he could read about me in the international press as well as brag to his friends about my accomplishments that I was forgiven."

I don't hear bitterness in his tone. And, I'm amazed he's sharing this much.

Turning to survey the bookcases, he walks over to extract a large scrapbook from a haphazard pile of art books and journals. He hands it to me before retaking his seat.

Resting the leather-covered folio on my lap, I open the cover to a clipping from the Sunday Arts section of *The Boston Globe*—a front-page story. Skimming, I read about Darius and his chamber orchestra premiering an Aaron Copland piece at Tanglewood.

"Did you attend the summer program there?" I ask.

"It is where I met Aaron." He pronounces "it" as "eet." Sliding a magazine out from the stack on the bench, he leafs through it in a way that suggests tension rather than interest. He says nothing more as I peruse the reviews.

So, not only did he have a successful career in music, he was on a first-name basis with one of America's greatest composers. Fascinating. The scrapbook's pages are stuffed with reviews of L'Ensemble, the music group Darius formed and conducted. The reviews are glowing. They document performances at Alice Tully Hall in New York, the Royal Albert Hall in London, and French, Italian, and German venues. I can't read the non-English clippings; except for some spotty French, I have no foreign languages. I scan for the name Julianne in the English-language clippings and discover that somewhere along the way she became Darius's wife. She was also the ensemble's flutist. Leafing through the pages, I note ten years of reviews from pretty much every major American and European city.

"I'm impressed. These reviews are amazing. But when did you find time to paint?"

"We didn't tour in December and January." He sets the magazine on the bench. "Painting was a way to wind down after touring. I hadn't any formal training but I enjoyed being creative in a medium other than music."

"I can understand how touring could become more of a job than a calling by the time you've been on the road for a few months." I flip to the last page and skim a glowing report about a concert in Chicago. The footer on the tear sheet is dated April 1984.

"Our last performance," Darius remarks.

I glance at him. He leans forward to take the book from me, carrying it back to the shelf. When he returns, he asks abruptly, "Would you like to stay for dinner?"

We regard each other. My pulse quickens. I nod, yes.

Why isn't he making music rather than selling antiques in a small Vermont town? Not that he doesn't do well and enjoy his work. Yet, every musician I know is passionate about the calling. How could Darius stop making music? What happened to L'Ensemble? Why have thirty years passed since he's picked up a brush? And how does his ex-wife fit into all of this?

As I shared with C., people's stories fascinate me. I love hearing where someone started out in life and how their path led to the present. Maybe that's what has kept me interested in weddings this long. I never tire of couples' stories of how they met and courted. I believe this genuine interest leads to the many referrals I receive—along with very good photography skills. Whatever is making me so listless about my profession isn't about my clients. Maybe it's the routine of the weddings themselves wearing me down.

Watching Darius open a cupboard and contemplate its contents, I wonder if he will answer any of the questions I have for him.

He turns, a box of Arborio rice in his hand. "Do you like risotto?"

"Very much."

"*Bon.*" The box moves to the counter. He pulls a bag of shrimp from the freezer, then bends to take an onion from a drawer in the island.

I walk to the island to watch him cook. "So you changed careers from music to antiques because . . . ?"

"It is what I knew from childhood. All the traveling was too much. And I wanted to be free in the summer for Christian's visits."

"Christian?"

"My son."

My eyes widen. "I didn't know you had a son. You are full of interesting surprises today." I suppose the many questions I'm asking could be considered nosy. I want to know him better, and tonight I'm willing to push a little way into his mystery shtick if that is what it takes. He's a big boy. If he doesn't like it, he'll let me know.

Darius shrugs, a quintessentially French gesture. "He lives in France with his family. I have two grandchildren, Thierry and Melisande." He flashes me a delighted smile. "I spend February with them."

The quality of this smile is different from the others he has bestowed on me. This one doesn't sit in the shallow twinkle of his eyes, but emanates from a deeper place.

As I register this difference, I also add up what he's told me—somewhere between Paris and Ashburton, a wife came into his story and exited it. "So, when Christian was a child, you and your wife had already split up and you had him with you for the summer?" I probe.

"*Oui.* From when he was five."

Surprised by this ready answer, I ask, "Did he live close by during the school year?"

"Unfortunately, *non.*"

I take a sip of brandy and set the snifter on the counter. "I can't imagine not being with Diana every day when she was little. It's lovely you've maintained close ties with your son, no matter how far apart you were living when he was a child."

He nods, acknowledging my compliment.

"But disbanding your orchestra . . . you never play the viola anymore? It seems such a pity when you were so successful with your music—and a talented artist."

"A ridiculous choice, from your practical Yankee viewpoint? To divorce, and at the same time give up so much success must seem very wrong to you."

So, the divorce and the end of the orchestra are related. I register this, as well as the rebuff. I'm not surprised. I've been waiting for it. But, he doesn't seem offended, so I don't back off.

"Many people might think so, although I try not to judge," I say. "I prefer to understand." I wonder why he didn't hire a nanny so he could take his son along on his tours. Many performers do.

Darius turns to the sink, measuring water and broth into a pot.

His divorce was a long time ago. His son was five when it happened and old enough now to have children of his own. Darius's silence makes me think that whatever took place in the early '80s still haunts him. When the silence becomes awkward, I say, "Divorce may be common, but it is not ordinary to anyone who has experienced it. The results can have an unexpectedly radioactive half-life."

He returns to the island with the pot, giving me a coolly assessing look. "It is true."

I decide on a last attempt to build a shared connection via

common experience. "There were days after my husband and I split when I wanted to give up. But Diana had lost Dan, too, and through no fault of her own. When we separated, she was around the same age as your son. She needed my emotional support. Plus, for me, it was work or starve because I had no savings. I'm sure you made the choices your situation forced on you, just as I did."

He looks at the onion and the knife he has pulled from his block. "Divorce is a difficult passage," he says. "When Julianne and I split up, I was tired of touring." His glance meets mine. "Don't imagine it was more than that."

Why does he expect me to challenge his version of events? It's hard not to feel judged, but I hardly know him, really, and decide this isn't about me as much as it is about how he feels about his own past.

"I was lucky to have some money put away so I decided to do something else, which is different from what you experienced. I'm sorry you had a hard time," he says.

"And I, you." I suppose it is possible he quit a successful career because he was tired of touring, though I feel sure there was more to it. "I hope you were able to be with Christian at other times."

"I saw him only in summer." He frowns. "It was not enough." Putting the palm of his left hand over the knife blade he pushes down, splitting the onion with a crisp snap. I wait as he dices half. The sweet yet stinging aroma makes my eyes water. He hesitates for a moment, as if he has something to say but thinks better of it. He chops the remainder of the onion, his strikes efficient and sure.

I admire how competent he is with his knife. Darius is competent at everything he does. Although, he might not be competent at relationships. I used to worry that I wasn't, before I decided my relationship skills aren't the problem; the problem is the men I pick—another reason I don't do relationships anymore. I have bad taste in men if consistency is the measure. No point wasting love on someone who won't stick around to enjoy it. The Rules protect me from my own weaknesses.

"Staying in one place appealed to me by then, not just because of Christian," Darius remarks. I shift my attention from his knife to his face. He looks impassively back at me. "I began dealing in antique jewelry and watches because it was something I knew how to do." He wipes his hands on a linen kitchen towel and leans against the counter, crossing his arms. "Ironic, is it not—to have left Paris and my father's shop only to re-create it here?" He offers another of his philosophical shrugs and reaches for a second pot from the overhead rack. He pours olive oil into it. "Life has been perfectly placid ever since," he concludes.

Sure it has. I know I'm getting the expurgated version of this tale. But Darius has trusted me a little, so I respect the reconfigured boundary he's drawn. As carefully edited as his story seems, he's moved his line in the sand a few inches closer to me. I suspect that Julianne left him, and when she did, she broke his heart. I base this conclusion not only on the little he's told me, but on how much I think he's left out.

There can be a lot of ego tied to rejection. I've seen men become serial daters after a divorce—the twenty-first-century version of a rake, seducing women only to spurn them once the seduction is complete, as if taking revenge on an ex-wife by proxy, over and over again.

I'm betting that whatever went down between Darius and his ex-wife wounded him to his soul, the reason why he hasn't married again. I don't think he's the revenge type, for all of the small judgments he's made about my reaction to his story. More likely, he's devised a system like my own, choosing to keep any sort of deeply felt connection, never mind love, far from his dealings with the opposite sex.

Darius meets every criterion on my list. From what I know about him, he isn't looking for more than I can deliver: fun in bed and out; interesting conversation; and possibly, a little deeply shared emotion, but only as a way of looking into the past to reinforce the desire never to return there. Darius and I have the potential to be the perfect pairing until he leaves for Europe, which will put a tidy end to the affair.

He moves his pots to the stove. Sipping my drink, I ask, "You haven't said why you stopped painting."

"I had some success," he admits. "I was represented at Pace in New York, and at a gallery in the Place de Vosges in Paris." He offers another shrug, this one accompanied by a little curl of his lip. "But I became bored."

"I'm sad you don't paint anymore."

He finishes adjusting the flame under the broth pot. "Painting took too much energy." His eyes regard me flatly.

Subject closed. I don't believe he was bored. Exercising your creativity is stimulating, often thrilling, because it draws emotion from deep inside you, emotion you often don't know you possess until it ends up on canvas—or captured by a camera lens and deposited on a computer chip, as is the case with me. On a good day, creativity is a glorious experience. On a bad day, when what is pulled out of you is painful—loneliness or failure or jealousy—it can be torture. Perhaps for Darius, painting required more emotion than he could expose to his own scrutiny. And perhaps, because I have no creativity to express lately, that he chose to toss his away is particularly distressing to me.

But. While I find him and his history fascinating, it isn't material to what I believe our mutual goals are for each other. It is best to remember that. "Can I do something to help?" I ask.

"You can be ornamental."

"Not one of my better skills," I joke.

He looks up from tending his pots, his eyes slowly sweeping from my face down my body. He says, "Have you considered your perspective may be skewed?"

I laugh. "Do you realize every time we get together, you tell me I'm wrong about something?" Because, really, he does. If I am being honest with myself, a small part of me is offended, but I'm more interested in what he'll say in response than in pursuing those feelings.

Darius narrows his eyes. "Is that what I do?" His voice is low and he gives me the deep attention I find so attractive.

"You do." My tone is light but I'm regretting what I've admitted, feeling exposed by his scrutiny.

"I hear you denigrate yourself and then I tell you the truth as I see it," he says.

"I suppose that is also what you were doing when you told me my taste is indiscriminate?" I guess his corrections bother me more than I realized, but he's taking my comment way too seriously, not that he doesn't have a valid point.

Turning the gas off under the oil, Darius rounds the counter.

He hugs me. I lean into him, enjoying his touch, yet my feelings remain unsettled.

"Why do you assume I don't like your taste, *ma petit colombe*? I thought we agreed that I have far-ranging tastes as well?" He pulls away a little. His eyes sparkle with amusement.

He just called me his little dove. I assume he is being ironic, since I am sparring with him, if good-naturedly. "You might want to consider," I say, giving it back to him, "that if my tastes weren't so indiscriminate, I wouldn't be here."

"To see . . . me?" He cocks a brow.

"Exactly. I like the ground solid underfoot," I joke. At least I think I'm joking. With Darius, it is hard to predict how a conversation will end. He is challenging, which excites me even though it makes me uneasy—or maybe especially because it makes me uneasy.

"You feel the ground is not solid when you are around me?" he asks with another shrug. "Leezbeth, the ground is never solid. You must be nimble; you must learn how to balance when what is underfoot shifts and sways—and accept this is how life is, a constant shifting."

I frown at this idea, because I've spent the last five years making sure the ground isn't merely solid underfoot but hard as concrete. I will need to watch what I say around this man because he imbues my every statement with gravitas. Breezy is not his style, at least not tonight.

He squeezes my shoulders. "I have offended you in some way."

"Of course not!"

"I am just an old man, you know. One who holds the conceit that he has picked up a soupçon of wisdom during his lifetime, wisdom he would like to share with others he believes might benefit."

Was I not in a similar position with C., the older woman offering life lessons? Apparently I like to dish it out but I'm less comfortable on the receiving end.

"Ah. How sweet. I love presents," I say, attempting a quick attitude adjustment. I pat his chest, which is firmer than I would have thought.

Darius laughs and strokes the nape of my neck, sending a little tremor of something—excitement? anticipation?—down my spine. "We understand each other then, ma *chérie*?" He squeezes me into his body. "I am forgiven?" His breath smells sweetly of brandy.

"I was not offended." His hand strokes down my back. A new frisson of awareness sparks.

I meet his eyes. He kisses my temple. I lean into him, deciding we definitely want the same thing. His arm tightens around me. I can't decide whether Darius is dangerous or dangerously exciting. When his hand lifts to my shoulder and slowly drifts down my arm, my heart speeds. Unfurling my closed fist, he lifts it between us and kisses my palm. The gesture is courtly. And very, *very* sexy.

I don't know what to do or if I'm supposed to do anything. This in itself is unsettling; I almost always know how to respond to men. While I'm trying to figure out my next move, Darius releases me. He returns to his place behind the counter and kindles the flame under the saucepan. Dropping a pat of butter into the olive oil, he begins browning the onions.

I decide to be ornamental because I can't come up with anything else to be at the moment.

✻

The risotto was delicious, as was the wine Darius served with it. After our rocky middle passage, we have moved on to easier topics. He wants to know about where I have traveled. As we sip tea and nibble on slices of pear and the soft cheeses he's set out for dessert, we compare notes about Paris, London, and Montreal, because I have not been lucky enough to journey farther afield.

He asks whether I like to read and what is on my night table. He is reading a book about New York under Dutch rule. I am reading *Hamilton*, which gives us intersecting themes to discuss about the American ideal. I learn he began his business in New York City, his interests moving to large European furnishings when stock market millionaires wanted grand furniture suited to their monster-sized apartments and the houses they were building. I also learn he moved to Vermont ten years ago when he tired of the city, and that he misses the land of his childhood for its sea and food and architecture.

"So," he says after we talk about the itinerary for his upcoming travels, "what do you do during the winter months when you have less work and more time on your hands?"

"I catch up on marketing and do the home projects I have no time for during the wedding season when I'm not sulking about gray skies, bitter cold, and snow and ice. Having turned forty-six last month, I have experienced way too many northeast winters. I wish I could go somewhere warm, just for January, February, and maybe March, because I love the rest of our seasons, but it is hard to travel with a big dog. I probably can't afford it anyway."

Darius rests his chin in his hand and taps his lip. "I might have an idea for you, but I must speak with a friend before saying more."

"I'll look forward to your idea, since I don't have any of my own." I drain the last of my tea as all of the clocks in the shop strike 8:00 in a great, slightly off-tempo cacophony. "I'd better go." I yawn behind my hand.

I manage the man-holds-the-jacket faux pas de deux—as I have dubbed our coat dance—far more gracefully than I did at the Burtons'.

When we reach the vestibule, I ask, "Will you let me reciprocate and make dinner for you?"

"*Avec plaisir.*"

"Next week? I'll call."

"I look forward to hearing from you."

We reach for the door handle simultaneously. I wrap my fingers around it. He wraps his around mine. Neither of us lets go. With my body on heightened alert, I draw in a deep breath. My stomach flutters, as if full of butterflies rather than risotto.

We pull the door open hand in hand. The crisp night air makes me shiver . . . or maybe it's his touch. A live current hums through me. Darius pulls away. I turn to say good night and, oddly dizzy, steady myself with a hand on his shoulder. He looks into my eyes.

The silence stretches. I think maybe Darius will kiss me, but he only smiles and murmurs, "*Bonne nuit, ma chérie.*" Then, breaking the mood, which may or may not be significant, he asks, "You are safe to drive?"

"I'm going five blocks, the weather is placid, and the last wine met my lips an hour ago."

He shakes his head. "I have offended you once more."

"You have not."

"*Je suis profondément désolé,*" he says, ignoring my denial.

"No, really. I'm just not used to anyone watching out for me." What is also true is that instead of hearing Darius ask that question, I heard my mother.

"*Oui,* I do care for your welfare." He rubs my back.

"*Bon,*" I say, using one of the handful of French words I committed to memory during high school language classes. The others are: *très, déjeuner, nuit, et, vous, tu, moi, chat, chen, and colombe.* A very limited vocabulary.

His eyes twinkle.

I decide, to hell with it, and go up on tiptoes to buss his cheek. He puts his arm around my waist and squeezes, but doesn't kiss me back. Offering him a jaunty wave, I walk to the car as he watches over me from the porch. The wave makes me think of C. The entire C. situation suddenly seems like a lark compared to simply trying to navigate a conversation with Darius. I get into the car thinking I keep getting tangled up in—*in what?* I have no idea. *No idea* seems to be my new mode of operation. I don't know why I slept with C.; I don't know why my work is no longer satisfying; I don't know what it is about Darius that unsettles me.

So much for concrete underfoot.

CHAPTER 10

MY PHOTO SHOOT UNIFORM doesn't include dressy skirts made for twirling. Or sexy tops, so when I told Diana that Darius has invited me to Waltz Night, she insisted on coming home for the weekend to shop for an appropriate outfit in the nearest metropolis. I'm excited about the invitation. I love to dance.

Two months into spending time together, Darius has yet to make his move. I could make the move instead; however, intuition continues to suggest he not only enjoys control, he requires it, so I'm waiting him out. Besides, waiting is a certain kind of turn-on, and the invitation to Waltz Night gives me hope that the wait is almost over.

"What do you think of this one?" I ask Diana. She and I study my reflection in the full-length mirror of the dressing room. The dark-red bodice is tightly fitted, with a deep square neckline and tight three-quarter-length sleeves. I don't usually like clothing that fits this close to the body, but in this case I find the top flattering.

"The color is great. And I like the rose." She touches the petals of an oversized black satin flower pinned to the obi-like sash. "It adds drama and works with the skirt."

I twist to check the rear view. The blouse plunges past my bra, with a strategically placed thickness of fabric to hold it together at the mid-back. A wide sash circles the waist.

I smooth my hands down the skirt. The hem rests eight inches above my ankles. Made of black chiffon, it hugs my hips before opening into sixteen gores that ripple softly at my slightest move. "The blouse is a little expensive for my budget. Let me try the beaded top again."

"Too much black," Diana says, removing the top from my reach. "You always say men like color. I'm with them. Red makes your skin glow. It's more dramatic and feminine than that boring jacket. You have a pretty back, Mom. I say flaunt it."

"I'm not the femme-fatale, red-blouse type."

"Where do you get these strange ideas?"

For a woman who chooses affairs of the body over those of the heart, I suppose I should have embraced a more outré version of the femme fatale in my clothing choices long before now, but overt sexiness isn't something I enjoy. This preference is likely owed to being reared by my Victorian mother. I like clothing that suggests rather than shouts. My compromise is sexy lingerie—Victoria's Secret sexy, not Fredrick's of Hollywood sexy—resulting in a nice package to unwrap. For instance, I always wear stockings with skirts, rather than pantyhose. The men I sleep with seem delighted with my philosophy.

I wrinkle my brow at the blouse, debating.

My daughter chides, "It isn't like I'm suggesting you wear pink ruffles. There is feminine and there is *feminine*."

She has a point. And, the red is flattering. "The blouse is outside my comfort zone—my pocketbook's comfort zone," I think aloud, looking at the price tag. I take it off.

"Guess it's time to expand the old comfort zone, huh?" Without waiting for me to finish putting on my clothes, Diana grabs the blouse and heads for the cash register.

I had a good year. I suppose I might as well celebrate with an expensive red blouse cut down to there. It will enhance my ornamental powers. I'm looking forward to what those powers might accomplish on Waltz Night.

✳

On the hour-long drive home from Macy's, it's my daughter's turn to tell stories. I've regaled her with tales of the past season's out-of-control brides, their stressed-out mothers, and the antics of assorted drunken groomsmen and guests during the trip to the mall.

I ask if her classes are still interesting at the halfway point.

"All except for 104B," she says.

"Translate, please." Diana has adopted the irritating habit of referring to her classes by their course catalog numbers.

"Advanced trig. I don't understand why an international studies major needs advanced trigonometry."

"How about you should be well rounded? When I went to art school I studied photography. Period. I graduated with a fair amount of knowledge on the subject, but ignorant about almost everything else."

"Whether that was worse is debatable, Mom. These days it takes a master's degree to know as much as you probably did about your major when you received your BA. All these Gen Eds are killing me."

"But you will know how to balance a budget and a lot of other things I learned the hard way. I had to educate myself in everything about the photography business except how to develop film, which, it should be noted, became an obsolete skill once digital cameras were invented. I'm not sure your comparison holds."

"I want to study Chinese, not transcendental numbers. I'll have to cram all of the courses I'll need into my last two years, if I want to go into international affairs. And get this—the first time I can take an actual elective is my senior year. You have to admit that's ridiculous."

"I suppose."

We drive in silence for a few minutes until I ask, "So, how about guys? Met any cute ones lately?" I know I shouldn't ask but I'm her mother and can't help myself.

I'd hoped Diana would meet a nice boy in college, but so far it hasn't happened. There have been boys, but not nice ones. The warning signs were practically written across those boys' chests, but I've had to accept that my daughter needs to learn the signs for herself.

"Men." Her tone is dismissive. "There's a guy in my math class who's started sitting next to me. He's a poli-sci major. We're supposed to go out for coffee after class on Monday. I'm not getting my hopes up."

Diana has the golden good looks of her father. She is slim and lean, but with my hazel eyes and heart-shaped face. Her looks attract attention. Perversely, since she decided she isn't interested in men, she gets far more attention than she wants.

"If you can't muster more enthusiasm, he'll pick up on your attitude. You're dooming yourself from the start."

That I've given up on love while still encouraging my daughter to look for it isn't a contradiction. There has to be a good man for her even if I'll never find one. The way I see it, her odds are better than mine because all the good ones haven't been taken when you're only nineteen. The field is thinner in my age bracket.

"I've been burned too many times to be overly enthusiastic, Mom. If he's so interested, let him chase me."

"I hope you aren't as jaded as you sound."

"Says the Jade Queen herself."

"Oh, come on. I haven't given up on men." At least, I haven't given up on sleeping with them, although this is what my mother would call a "Philadelphia lawyer" defense.

"Yeah, right. Just because you sleep around—and around and around," my daughter pronounces, "doesn't mean you haven't given up on them." Diana has some lawyerly tendencies herself.

"Really. You make it sound like I keep the male version of a harem." Once again, I'm thrown off balance by how astute my daughter is about my inner workings.

"It's not a harem, it is a revolving door," she retorts.

I open my mouth to protest but she holds her hand up, cutting me off. "Do not tell me it's Dad's fault. I admit he's a handful, but if you want me to believe in love after my own disasters, then you have to be willing to do the same yourself, Dad and *Roland* notwithstanding."

I know better than to argue when the subject turns to love. At her age she can't understand my feelings. Diana may compare our experience and see it as similar, but no matter what she thinks, her youth allows her an emotional and spiritual elasticity I lack.

We drive the next few miles in silence. Her conclusion about me blaming her father for my jaundiced view of marriage doesn't make me happy, though of course I do blame him, among others. I've always told Diana that her dad and I weren't compatible. That sometimes you grow apart rather than together. Sharing that he also slept around would serve no purpose except to add conflict to her relationship with us both. It's criminal when parents make their kids choose sides in a divorce. I refused to do it. Although it seems I haven't been as successful at the no-blame thing as I'd hoped. Parenting is definitely a journey of highs and lows.

"So, how's Darius?" Diana asks just when I think the all-clear has sounded.

"We've had dinner a few times, seen a couple of movies, and gone to a museum opening. This invitation to dance was a surprise."

"Who was he seeing before you?" she asks.

"I have no idea." Of course I know, but it isn't germane to whatever is going on between Darius and me.

"That's exactly what I mean." Diana shakes her head in disgust. "He doesn't matter enough. If he did, you would have checked him out. Mom, you stay away from anyone who could have real potential. At least I friended Marc on Facebook to see if he *could* matter."

"It isn't that Darius doesn't matter," I protest, heartened to hear she is a little interested in her math boy. "We've gotten together a handful of times so far. I enjoy his company but I hardly know him. If a relationship is in our future, I'm sure he'll share his romantic history."

"Hmmm." Diana sniffs.

"Which you might consider, honey. If you like this boy, take the time to get to know him before you hand him your heart."

"Excuse me?" Her tone is pure outrage. "As if. Did you not hear anything I said?"

I continue, ignoring her ire. "And don't jump into bed with him after the second date."

"Mom, I'm not an idiot." She jerks her pocketbook onto her lap and rummages, pulling out a packet of gum. "Didn't I tell you I'm not expecting anything to come of it?" She pushes a piece of gum into her mouth and chews aggressively. "*God*. We're just having coffee. Don't you think I learned anything from Cameron?"

Cameron was the only guy she's seriously dated since high school, the one who saw her as a challenge to subdue. Young and inexperienced, she allowed him to mold her into a clingy shadow of her wonderful snarky self. It's taken months for her to find her footing again.

"You aren't stupid," I agree, glancing over at her. "And I don't have to tell you how smart you are. But you are also at an age when hormones can and do get in the way of good sense."

"Right. Maybe you shouldn't let your hormones get in the way of your good sense, either," she mocks. "You are using condoms and having safe sex, right?"

"Geez, Diana!" My daughter is a master at winning an argument by putting me on the defensive. C., the perfect example of my lack of good sense, flashes to mind. My mouth twists. "I'm not having any kind of sex with Darius."

"Yet. Come on, Mom. You're going dancing with him. I know how you feel about dancing. Sex standing up," she taunts. "You're staying in the same room. Add it up."

"It's not a room, it's a suite."

"Whatever."

I sigh. "Can we change the subject? There's something really icky about discussing my sex life with you."

Diana rolls her eyes. "You're such a Victorian."

"No, that's your grandmother."

She laughs. "True."

We drive in silence for a few minutes, eventually falling into more agreeable conversation about Obie's antics and our plans for the Thanksgiving leftovers party we hold every year.

CHAPTER 11

DARIUS AND I drop Obie at Diana's place in Winooski, a suburb of Vermont's biggest city, Burlington, close to the university campus. Obie is having a sleepover with Diana tonight. Darius and I are staying at the Water Mill, a luxury hotel located on a lakefront promontory in downtown Burlington. Our suite is on the top floor with unobstructed views of Lake Champlain. I walk to the windows while he tips the porter. The lake shimmers in the clear late-autumn sunlight. The Adirondack Mountains, more craggy and majestic than the gently rounded Green Mountains to the east, rise on the far side of the water, rolling into the distance. High white clouds with gray underbellies dot the sky, but a bank of altostratus on the horizon promises rain.

I hear the door click shut. Darius joins me at the window. "Would you like to pick a room?" He throws his arms out, indicating the doors at each side of the central living room.

I hope separate bedrooms are where we're starting out, not where we'll end up. I contemplate how I'd like the evening to go, but instead of seeing Darius in my bed, I see C. lounging naked against the pillows. As pleasant as this vision is, it also illuminates the age disparity between the two men. I've never slept with a man fifteen years my senior. Ironic—or maybe not—that C. came to mind. Perhaps I should phone him for insights, since he's the one who's already slept with someone old enough to be his parent.

I stare at the view. There are men like C. whose bodies are an overriding attraction, and then there are men like Darius, whose fuckability is about the sexiness of his mind. Darius has a very, *very* sexy mind. I smile at him before turning to check out the nearest bedroom.

✳

The bedrooms are mirrors of each other, with upholstered head-boards, king-size beds, and minimalist midcentury furnishings in a soothing neutral color palette. As in the living room, floor-to-ceiling atrium windows march across the wall overlooking the lake. I choose the left bedroom for no particular reason except that it's the last I entered. Darius insists on carrying in my overnight case and garment bag. When he leaves, I unzip the bag to begin readying myself for the evening.

When I return to the living room, he is waiting, elegantly attired in an European evening suit, French cuffs peeking from his jacket sleeves. His eyes move slowly down my body to the pointy toes of my dancing shoes. The shoes have thin straps wrapping around my ankles. Lifting two fingers to his lips, he tosses me an appreciative kiss and then pushes away from where he's been standing by the windows.

Some women are turned on by a man in uniform. My temperature rises for a well-tailored suit. I've been known to swoon for pinstripes. Just contemplating Darius in his elegant black evening suit ignites a warm burn between my legs.

The suit is an iconic garment, one that traces its origins to the Prot-estant Reformation. The severe black garments topped by a stiff white ruff symbolized virtue to the Roundheads. Over the past three hun-dred years, the meaning of this enduring fashion statement has shifted to indicate a seriousness of purpose rather than virtue, evolving from ruffs to collars and from doublets to jackets.

This is the dichotomy that arouses me: Even in Cromwell's day, the men inside those austere Puritanical costumes never measured up to its moral design. Human evolution has never tamed male flesh and blood and brain. There is a wolf lurking inside all of that finely woven worsted wool. Though resistant to civilizing influence, I hope that, tonight at least, this wolf will not be immune to my call.

"Would you mind if I take a picture of you the way you were when I walked in? You looked so debonair, like a movie star in the golden age of Hollywood."

Darius shrugs and resumes his stance by the window. I fetch my camera.

"Think what you were thinking when I came into the room," I suggest. He stares pensively into the darkness.

I snap a few pictures, wondering about his thoughts, knowing it is futile to ask. "Perfect. Thanks for indulging me." Setting the camera aside, I walk toward him.

His eyes are bright as he takes the hand I extend, turning it over to rub his thumb lightly over my palm. His eyes meet mine as he slides his thumb away and replaces it with a kiss. Then, as if we were already on the dance floor, he pulls me into his arms. "Lovely," he murmurs, his lips finding the curve of my jaw. "Thank you for agreeing to accompany me tonight."

My heart skips a beat. Growing up a generation and a world apart from American cultural norms may be responsible for Darius's approach, which resembles more of a garden stroll than race to the finish line, far different from how most of us define twenty-first-century courtship. I've found our almost two months of chaste dates a long wait for consummation, while Darius appears to have been content with teasing touch and innuendo.

Not that his tempo hasn't had its pleasures, as well as being instructive. If I'd had Darius's example twenty-five years ago, I would have spent more time getting to know Dan before committing to him. If so, I might have noticed Dan had taken the "if it feels good, it is good" message of the generation before us too much to heart—as well as lower down on his anatomy.

Not that Darius did any better at marriage, from what he's implied. Yet, if he was heedless once, the man holding me in his arms tonight has learned his lessons well. This Darius is always cool, always in control. Maybe a little too in control.

I slide my palms up the front of his elegant tuxedo jacket. The evening is turning into a heady cocktail—one part elegant man, one part gala evening, two parts anticipation about how the night will end.

With a delicate brush of his lips to my forehead, Darius releases me. Opening the door, he gestures with a small bow, the kind an orchestra conductor makes when he is modestly acknowledging his audience. I precede him down the hall.

＊

The room where Waltz Night is being held is a study in white and gold. Huge white chrysanthemums, roses, and orchids are arranged in polished urns atop pillars that stand between the French doors to the balcony. Crystal chandeliers glitter above our heads. Gilt opera chairs surround tables with cut-glass goblets, gold-banded china, and white pillar candles set among white flower centerpieces. White tablecloths pool onto the floor. The room is as splendid as a ballroom out of a fin de siècle painting.

As we search for our table assignment, I begin swaying to the exuberant, sexy rhythm of a salsa. Waltz Night is a benefit for the symphony. Darius introduces me to guests who hail him as we move toward our table. Vermont is a small state, so chances are, most of the people here know someone I know. It's only a matter of discovering the degree of separation between us. Two of the couples we talk with turn out to be people I've shot at weddings in years past. Another couple are the parents of the groom from a wedding last summer in Rochester, a tiny town situated in the mountains between the Killington and the Sugarbush ski resorts, where my father lives.

I set my evening bag on our table. Darius leads me onto the polished parquet. If I'd thought about it at all, I'd have bet his formal manners and private sense of self would make him a stiff dancer. But he is a musician and dances with the natural grace of a man who feels the music to his bones. This observation leads to another: Men who are loose on the dance floor are loose in bed. Desire dances through me to the beat of a sultry rumba as Darius pulls me into his body.

The rumba is a flirty dance, with an easy, sexy combination of swaying hips and relaxed box steps. It's a sweet slide into sensuality, teasing me with what I hope will transpire between us later. Darius knows all the variations, adding quick little twists and underarm turns, as well as a strutting four-count promenade. I laugh, delighted by his skill. He twinkles in return.

We dance through the rest of the Latin set. A series of fox-trots follow, set to classic tunes. The set ends as dinner is served. Once we've returned to our table, Darius hands me his monogrammed handkerchief. I dab the dampness around my hairline. When I'm finished, he curls his fingers around mine and takes the slightly limp cloth to use on his own forehead.

Another preconception bites the dust. Apparently he is not as fastidious as I thought. How might this revelation relate to his performance in bed? Another wash of arousal has me ducking my head as if to examine the cutlery, lest anyone at the table observe the thoughts I'm likely telegraphing. Yet, when I look up, sure enough, the sharp eyes of a woman sitting across the table are watching me. Her husband, sitting at her right, is an insurance broker. Darius introduced us earlier.

I pick up my fork. The cuisine at parties like this is rarely great—I should know, since I cover so many of them—but a taste of tender scallop in the artfully dribbled orange glaze defies my expectations. I realize I am hungry.

The other diners seem to know each other and chat as they eat. Darius's hand brushes my thigh under the table and rests there, telling me I am in his thoughts, although he is conversing with the man to his left. The purr of sexual awareness, present since we arrived at the hotel, rises several notes higher. Finding it hard to keep still, I shift in my chair.

Perhaps Darius misconstrues my restlessness because his hand withdraws. To correct him, I rest my own hand lightly on his leg. I stroke to his knee before retreating to resume eating. His hand returns, though he continues to talk with everyone but me. I'm not sure what to make of this, although there is something sexy about him touching me beyond where others' eyes can see, while to the table at large, it would appear he is ignoring me. It is a perverse little game and it excites me. I decide the passive approach I've taken with Darius has been the right one; I can't imagine him interested in someone who chases.

Working weddings, I've learned how to start conversations with strangers. I begin conversing with the woman on my other side. She tells me she is a lawyer with a specialty in intellectual property.

The musicians begin to tune up as the main course is cleared. They launch into that tired old chestnut, "Moonlight in Vermont." Few couples take the floor. Everyone must feel the same way I do about the tune, which bores me except when Willie Nelson sings it. We're all much happier with the next number, "Don't Get Around Much Anymore." Darius and I dance. When the tune shifts to "Bewitched, Bothered and Bewildered," I throw my head back and laugh, entirely in sympathy with the title.

When the tune is over, we return to the table for dessert. The chairman of the symphony board takes the microphone, thanking us for coming. He is gratifyingly short-winded. Once he steps off the podium, the orchestra begins a Strauss waltz.

Darius pushes his chair away from the table and stands. He puts his hand out for mine. I shake my head.

"You don't waltz?" he asks incredulously.

He looks so appalled that I laugh. "Not Viennese." I rise and cup my hand against his ear to whisper, "I've never learned to spot, so I get dizzy. Four years of ballet and I never mastered the spot turn."

He shakes his head in disbelief. "This is a great tragedy."

"I think so, too." I pat his arm consolingly.

He rests his palm against his cheek, looking perplexed. "You will not mind if I find another partner? I love this waltz."

"Please," I say and sit to watch him approach a table farther down the room. He stops next to a woman with silver hair. She is speaking animatedly to the people around her and breaks off to greet Darius. He bends to address her. She turns to the man at her side, and then stands. Darius follows her to the dance floor. She is almost his height, with a narrow silhouette. When they spin and she faces me, I see she is younger than her striking hair indicates.

It's fun to watch Darius and his partner twirl through one quicksilver spin after another. The way they move makes me think this isn't the first time they've waltzed together. I wonder what *their* story is. I decide I don't need to know. Darius's past doesn't have a bearing on the future, since we don't have one. Which is as it should be. That's what The Rules are for, to prevent emotional entanglements and preserve me from heartache, as well as jealousy.

The waltz whirls to an end. Darius raises his partner's hand to his lips, a gesture that he is adept at. It feels straight out of a romance novel. Darius returns his partner to her table. The man, who must be the woman's husband, rises and wraps an arm proprietarily around her waist. Like Heather and Jerry, the couple I photographed last February when I ran into Roland, this pair seems an uneven match, if only because the woman is beautiful and the man is tall but not the least bit handsome.

This thought is judgmental so I don't pursue it. Sleeping with a boy twenty-two years my junior has made me sensitive to how often I judge other people's choices. I squirm, reminding myself that many women, and I'm no exception, find humor, kindness, and intelligence sexy enough to endow even the homeliest man with his own brand of attractiveness. The couple with Darius has an easy way of touching each other that speaks of a good relationship. I thought I'd found that kind of connection with Roland.

I want it again.

This revelation almost knocks me off my chair. My stomach clenches. I look down at it, as if I'll be able to see if the metaphysical hole Roland carved into me has shrunk. Realizing how stupid this is, I return my attention to Darius. The silver-blond is listening to her husband. She laughs, giving him an affectionate peck on the cheek. Darius laughs with her. He shakes hands with the husband before taking his leave, weaving his way between the tightly packed tables. His progress is slowed by exchanges with other attendees.

The yearning I've been feeling as I edit wedding pictures twists inside me a second time in as many minutes—a sudden, sharp pain. I rub a hand over my heart. Having a relationship, not having a relationship, wanting the kind of connection that couple seems to share and not wanting it—sometimes plotting a course through my own labyrinth of emotions is too damn difficult.

"You look grave, *ma chérie*," Darius notes as he takes his seat.

"I'm fine," I chirp.

A raised brow indicates Darius's belief in the veracity of my answer.

"You have a sensitive truth-o-meter," I observe.

"A what?" The same eyebrow lifts again.

"An interior gauge for telling truth from fiction."

He offers one of his eloquent shrugs. "Experience and intuition only." Changing the subject he asks, "Shall I fetch you another drink?"

"I'll stick with water, thanks, otherwise I'll be too tipsy to dance."

As Darius reaches the bar, the orchestra launches into a tango. I love the tango and the way the music dives and sways, swelling toward crescendo, hesitating, then surging onward once more. The music pulls me into the present and away from my darkening mood.

Darius pivots and returns to the table without his drink. He holds a hand out for mine. This time I take it and rise.

On the dance floor, my body makes contact with his as he spins me close. "So you dance the tango," he says into my ear.

When I nod he asks, "Argentinean or Ballroom?"

I'm delighted to have the choice. "Argentinean, please, but remember—I'm incapable of fast multiple turns. I'll end up sitting on the floor."

He pulls me closer. His right hand opens, warm on the skin of my back. "Where did you learn?"

Wise to the way he operates, I decide two can play the mystery game. "Where did you?" Pressing into his hand, I tilt my upper body into his.

"Argentina," he says, sliding his fingertips slowly across my bare back until they wrap around my side.

I shiver. "Ah. Another story for another day."

"Two stories," he says. "A woman who has lived most of her life in New England and dances the Argentine tango must have an interesting story to tell."

"Not really. I spent my college years in California, where I learned many things, the tango among them. Also, I have a friend who used to teach dance at Ashburton College. I take an occasional lesson to keep the tango inside my body even though it's been a long time since I've had a partner who could dance it with me."

In ballroom-style tango, a man and woman begin the dance joined at the pelvis, upper bodies apart. He looks in one direction while she looks in another, as if unwilling to admit what their bodies are simulating below the waist.

In Argentine tango, the couple begin cheek to cheek, upper bodies close, lower bodies denied contact. No matter the style of the dance, sex is acknowledged and flaunted, yet also suppressed.

My daughter was not entirely wrong: If you are attracted to your partner, the tango is as close to having sex in a room full of witnesses as you can get unless you work in the porn industry or have other, seriously exhibitionist tendencies.

I rest my forehead against Darius's chin, our disparate heights preventing us from dancing cheek to cheek. He holds my right hand out and away from our bodies, elbow bent. My left hand has to reach to cup the back of his neck.

The tempo of the tango the orchestra is playing is lazy, a boon to partners who have not danced the intricate steps together. This dance can be dazzlingly complex; it can also be simple.

We start with simple. Darius guides me into a walking step, or Kakinada, counted in a pattern of eight, then spins. He repeats the promenade a second time, allowing us to assess and adjust to how we move together. At the beginning of the next eight count, he pushes me away. I take two gliding steps backward, my arm sliding from his neck down his arm, hips slightly to the left of his, until I'm at the limit of the distance our joined hands allow. I add a little flourish when he holds me there, twisting left, then right, with sharp little kicks.

Swivel stepping forward until we are lock together once more, Darius swings me around to put my back against his chest. He rocks, spinning me out and back in.

The music is insistent and teasing—the hallmark of tango. In sensual glides and syncopated hesitations it drives us toward each other and then away. My left leg crosses in front of the right—Cruzada—and I shift my weight to the ball of my foot. Darius spins us in a quick quarter-turn and reverses it just as quickly, sending my skirt flying.

Two beats later he sets his foot against mine and presses in, lifting my leg with his own—Cucharita. We pivot. My right leg wraps around his thigh—catches—and slides slowly to the floor. He holds my arm high for a spin and winks, his palm rolling across my ribs, the signaling a spin, and then another. His next cue is a figure eight—Ocho. Our glances hold as I pivot left and right until the pattern is complete.

Playing with embellishments, Darius adds his own flourish, kicking his foot behind him. As he passes to the left, the front of his body brushes my hip. I use the contact as an invitation to misbehave. The music soars. I can't resist. Instead of waiting for his lead, I lean into him, taking the lead for myself—an absolute no-no according to the alpha-male rules of this dance.

Understanding what I desire, Darius graciously forgives my trespass and hugs me to his body as he takes three steps back while I stand in place. Our upper bodies meet, mine at a slant, one leg is bent loose behind me, the other braced against his thigh. He rocks with a hard thrust, his arm banding tight around my back to pull me upright again. We join, hold, and disengage as the music surges once more.

I feel the sweep of his smile where my check rests against his chin. A little growl rumbles from his throat as the hand at my back guides me into the next pattern.

Arousal acts as a sensitizing agent. I am aware of the silk of my blouse sliding against my skin and the heat radiating from Darius's body. The spice of his cologne mingles with my perfume, the scratch of his goatee rasps against my cheek. His hand presses the bare skin of my back, slightly moist.

I want more—more skin, more smells, more him.

When the music stops, we gaze at each other, still touching, breathing hard. His eyes have turned a flat dark gray, desire and intention staring back at me. I smile. We have, I believe, come to an understanding.

Another tango is starting. We dance the entire set. When it is over, Darius lifts my hand and kisses it before leading me from the dance floor. He heads toward our table, stopping only long enough to pick up my evening bag. He nods and smiles at friends who hail him as we pass, but doesn't slow his passage toward the exit.

CHAPTER 12

THE AIR IS SO THICK between us that I can't turn my head to look at him once the elevator doors slide shut. Conversation is impossible. Words would only burn up in the heat between us. The walk down the hall is equally silent. Pulling the key card from his pocket, Darius slides it quickly in and out of the lock. The green light flashes. Inside the suit, the soft glow of a table lamp is the only illumination.

As the door swings shut behind us, Darius pulls me into his arms and walks me into the shadows. When I meet the wall, there is no preamble—we preambled on the dance floor and during our months of chaste dinner dates. Our mouths meet hungrily. He invades with his tongue. I revel in the desire he has finally unleashed and look forward to him demonstrating more of it with his mouth and hands and cock.

He shapes warm fingers around my breast. I unbutton his jacket and pull his shirt out of his trousers. I am burning with want. Happily, what I want is only a trouser hook away. As I release him, he reaches into his jacket pocket and pulls out a condom.

We break the kiss so he can tear the packet open. I take the rubber. Holding the fullness of his erection in my hand, I roll the condom on. The visual is fleeting, though enough for me to know that if navy pinstripes and skin can excite me, eveningwear framing elemental male anatomy is even hotter. He pulls up my skirt. I push my loose tap pants aside to allow him access.

He is thick and alien and exactly what I need. My leg wraps around his hip. He puts an arm under my knee and lifts, opening me wider.

He pumps once. And again. The sensation is divine, but I can't get any purchase in this position. We keep at it but he slides out twice. Finally, by unspoken agreement, we give up. He kisses my forehead.

"Sex against a wall is much easier in theory then in practice," I say. We look at each other. "Bed?" I suggest.

"The sofa is closer."

To spare him the indignity of his dishabille, his pants unzipped, the condom on, I precede Darius across the room. I stare out the window at the dark water of the lake, giving him time to position himself on the sofa. When the rustling stops, I pivot. He has dispensed with his coat. His shirttails cover his erection. He motions for me to join him. I reach beneath my skirt to wiggle out of my underwear.

The fine black wool of his trousers rasps against my stockings as I lift one leg over his, the chiffon skirt flutters around us, spilling onto the cushions. This is a new aphrodisiac—fucking in full evening dress, as if the animal hungers we sublimated into the patterns of the dance remain veiled by the civility of our clothing—cloaked in black wool and blood-red silk.

Curling my palms into Darius's shoulders, I lick the seam between his lips. He licks back but doesn't open his mouth. Turning my head to rest cheek to cheek, I rotate on the tip of his cock, sliding slowly down.

Our adventures against the wall have cooled my blood enough to savor this sweet slide and acceptance of Darius's length and thickness. His hands clasp my hips. Less patient or more interested in control, he thrusts, filling me. There is nothing like the warmth of a man's cock in the first seconds of penetration. Even gloved in latex, the sensation is almost an orgasm in itself.

Darius's body has relaxed into the couch, yet his eyes are intense, focused on the distinct points visible through the silk of my blouse. The cutaway back makes it easy for him to push the blouse off my shoulders, revealing my breasts filling the sheer red lace bra. He studies them for a moment before lifting his gaze to mine. He rolls his thumbs over the thin lace.

Heat blooms along my collarbone and throat. Darius pushes the bra away to pinch the sensitive skin he's been teasing through fabric. My head falls back, my spine bows, and I moan, contracting around him once and then again, expelling a harsh breath as a wash of moisture completes the connection where we are joined.

When he removes his hands, I offer a mew of distress, squeezing him tight, making my preferences known. Instead of giving me what I want, he goes measuring with his fingertips, lightly tracing my nose, the curve of my brow, the shell of my ears. A delicious chill shivers up my back.

Flexing his hips, Darius prompts movement from me. When I don't comply fast enough, he thrusts again, more forcefully this time. I rise and fall, delighted to be impaled by his lovely thickness. The angle is exactly right, stimulating the tender spot inside me where awareness coalesces. My eyes close as he brushes a thumb across my lips. I capture it, biting. I suck him deeper into my mouth.

Under the puddle of my skirt, I drive down, making contact with the base of his penis. He expels a harsh breath. I hum with pleasure and glance at where we are joined, but the fabric of my skirt obscures what we're doing.

Darius begins pushing the skirt up my thighs, exposing stocking tops and garters. "*Très jolie,*" he says gruffly, insinuating a finger under one stocking. His other hand continues to tunnel. My only visual is the pristine white of his cuff disappearing beneath layers of black chiffon. Not an explicit view but sexy nevertheless. I begin to burn.

His hand, so close to where I need it, teases away to play with my garters. I whisper, "Please," and he complies, rolling the slick hard bud of my clit. "Ohhh," I breathe. "Perfect."

"Voluptueuse," he murmurs. "Juicy." He uses his other hand to cup my head, at last kissing me properly. Yet he flicks my tongue away when I try to engage with him, turning his head. A few seconds later, he kisses me again. Surrender seems to be what he wants, so I let him lead. It is the right choice because I get what I want; he keeps kissing me.

I should have anticipated he would not relinquish control during sex any more than he does in other aspects of his life. Yet even as I allow him to do as he wishes, I speculate about breaking such steely control, although I continue to follow his cues.

The reward is plunder.

The man can kiss. This is my last thought because thinking gives way exclusively to feeling as Darius feeds pleasure into my body and lethargy into my bones.

My eyes close. The room fades. He fades. I curl into him, disengaging from his kiss, gasping. Time condenses and then expands as pleasure separates me from my body and for a few exquisite seconds, there is no me at all.

I rest my head against his shoulder and sigh with contentment, fighting awareness, not particularly interested in returning to myself. I relish the silence between us, as luxurious and darkly impenetrable as the fathoms-deep lake outside the window.

Yet, a minute later, conscious of the scratch of wool against my thighs and the ache in the muscles of my splayed legs, the room re-forms, night pressing in at my back. When I lift my head from where I'm nestled into the spicy sandalwood-scented curve of Darius's jaw, his heavy-lidded eyes meet mine.

I kiss his throat below the neat line of his beard. His skin is damp from our exertions. He came, too, though it happened while I was gone, leaving me not entirely clear about the particulars. This is my biggest complaint about condoms, the loss of that lovely spurt of cum, to say nothing of the loss of heat and sensation.

Holding on to his arms, I leverage myself up and off. My legs complain. He holds on to the condom as I lift myself away. Under his shirttails, he pulls the sheath off in a practiced move and makes it disappear.

I flip to my back on the cushion next to him. One leg bent over his, I yawn behind my hand. Darius chuckles. He bends to kiss an exposed breast. The nipple is tender from his ministrations and sensitive to touch. I hum happily when he kisses it again, this time with teeth.

"What time is it?" I sigh, attempting to pull my clothes into some semblance of decency when he lifts himself away.

A vintage Rolex emerges from the crisp French cuff of Darius's shirt.

"After midnight."

I manage to sit up. "Will you join me?" I gesture toward my room.

"Alas," he says.

Any other straight man uttering "alas" without the tiniest note of irony would be ridiculous, but Darius manages to sound truly saddened by his inability—or lack of desire—to share my bed.

"I am a restless sleeper," he explains, softening his rejection. Getting to his feet, he holds out a hand to help me rise. When I'm standing, he hugs me to his chest. "Thank you, ma *chérie*," he whispers in my ear. "May I come to you in the morning?"

I nod, relieved.

He walks me to my door.

The sex has left me keyed up—not my usual response. After the dancing and a fantastically satisfying climax to the evening, I should be dead tired. I'm not. An anxious motor is running. As I take my makeup off and apply lotion to my face, I review the last few hours in my mind's eye.

A new man is always exciting, but, no matter what he says about wanting you in the moment, there is after. Once satiated, his ardor often cools. That's when the other head, the one on his shoulders, begins calculating. It's not unusual for it to come to a different conclusion than his more impulsive partner below. By my own calculation, the first time a man has sex with you, once the orgasm fades, it takes less than a minute for Mr. X-Y Chromosomes to make a decision about whether you will be part of his past or part of his future—immediate or otherwise.

In this case I have no need to worry. Darius has indicated he wants to join me in the morning. For the rest of the weekend, he's mine. Beyond tomorrow shouldn't concern me. Darius is charming, generous, and thoughtful—with privacy walls around his heart I certainly won't be penetrating. Since this isn't exactly news, I have no clue to my agitation. My own walls are as thick as his; we are not in conflict with each other, and our affair—if this is the launch of it—will close before the year is out.

I climb into bed and switch off the light. Staring into the dark, where I can't see my own hand, let alone the answer to my disquiet, I wait for a solution to write itself in the air. After an hour of waiting for either an answer or sleep, I sigh. Clicking on the light, I reach for the novel I brought along should the need arise.

CHAPTER 13

I WAKE TO the steady drum of rain lashing the windows. Throwing the covers off, I pull the curtains open. Small waves are kicking up whitecaps, rocking boats moored along the piers. In the park across the road, the trees are darkened by rain and devoid of leaves. They toss restlessly, as if blown from the pages of the dread-laden Daphne Du Maurier novel I finished when I couldn't sleep.

Yawning, and slightly depressed by the weather, I head into the bathroom, where the mirror indicates full makeup will be required. After a shower, I cosmetically correct my sleep-deprived face. I am reaching for the hair dryer when I hear Darius at the bedroom door. I call out to enter.

He bids me *"Bonjour"* with his glittery, dapper surface in place. Unlike the gothic-novel homage the trees are doing, Darius is channeling a *Thin Man* movie, wearing pressed navy pajamas and a shawl-collared paisley robe, his feet encased in leather slippers. He places a tray with a coffee carafe on the dresser.

My wet hair is curling in too many directions and I'm dressed in only my robe, but I *"Bonjour"* him in return, pleased with the tray and its carafe as well as a basket of muffins and croissants. "I thought we might enjoy *un petit déjeuner*," Darius says, looking me over. His sparkling bonhomie flattens. Having learned what it means when his eyes lose their light, my body heats.

He wraps an arm around my waist and draws me close. Pushing a damp lock of hair behind my ear, he murmurs, "Might I request a pre-breakfast treat?"

"What do you have in mind?" I ask, tilting my head to the side to give him better access. The kiss he bestows on my cheek is warm, with a new familiarity I enjoy. His breath smells of peppermint.

"Will you do something for me, ma petit colombe?" he whispers into my ear. "Would you put on the hose and belt you wore last night? I didn't savor them as I would have liked."

"Just stockings and a garter belt? Nothing else?" It is always interesting to discover what raises a particular man's temperature—and other body parts, too.

Darius's glance falls to the black kitten-heeled mules I wear when shearling isn't quite the thing. A hint of a smile lifts his lips. "Perhaps the slippers as well?"

I like the old-fashioned decadence of Darius's fantasy. Retiring to the bathroom, I put on my spare pair of sheer black stockings. Spraying the air with Yves Saint Laurent's "Paris," I walk through it. The perfume seems appropriate to the man and the moment.

No doubt Darius's expectation is for me to return clad in stockings, garter belt, mules, and nothing else, but our affair is too new for my inhibitions to have dissolved entirely. I pull my robe closed and tie the belt before walking into the bedroom. He is sitting on the bed the way men do, his legs open, knees splayed. I step between them. He unties my sash and pushes the robe aside.

So much for inhibitions.

His hands trace my hips, rounding over my belly and the stretch marks to each side.

"A gift from carrying Diana," I say, moving his hand away from the silvery streaks.

"They bother you?" He seems genuinely puzzled.

"They're not beauty enhancing."

"*Non,*" he says, smoothing his hands over them a second time.

I think he is agreeing with me, but I'm wrong.

"They tell me you are a fertile woman. That you can—and have—borne a child. They make you more desirable." He looks into my eyes, then glances down, cupping my mons. He places his other hand at the curve of my waist, pulling me closer.

Tomorrow I may decide I've never heard a more ludicrous pickup line, but something unlocks inside me and for an instant I'm afraid. A hand rises to my throat.

Pulling it away, Darius kisses the palm. The gesture is tender, as if he can read my state of mind. With my arm no longer obscuring his view of my breasts, however, his attention shifts. He strokes his thumbs over my nipples.

I experience a deep, velvety wave of arousal, my nipples puckering. Darius notices. His thumbs roll the sensitive tips a second time. A fizz of sensation, darkly electric, runs from where he strokes to where I need his touch. I hum low in my throat. Brushing his hands away, I kneel at his feet. I need to draw a similar response from him. Pushing his robe away, I stroke the fabric at his fly. He firms under my hand. I love knowing I have this power, that I can make a man—this man— rise to my touch. I run my fingers up his length.

Tipping my chin up, he bends to press his lips to mine. As he did last night, Darius will kiss me deeply only if I don't chase. I continue to stroke him, my touch light. If he wants to make this about control, I'm happy to be his opponent. Placing his hand over mine, he holds me fast, pressing himself into my palm. I let him do as he pleases, but a few seconds later, I slide my hand away to unbutton him. He leans back to support himself with his hands and watches.

His penis is handsome—large without being scary, the head uncircumcised. I flick the tip of my tongue into the indentation at the tip. He grunts, studying me from under heavy lids. Dropping my eyes to my work, I'm not surprised when he lifts his hips, giving me a "let me in" nudge. I open. He pushes into my mouth. With one hand wrapped around him, I use the other to cup his balls, as yet hidden by his pajamas.

My teeth tighten under the hood of his cock. He doesn't tense as I graze him, a mark of trust that gratifies me. Growling, he pumps, pushing himself so far into my throat that I gag.

I pull away to recover. He mutters a soft, "*Je suis désolé,*" and rises

"You will keep your arms above your head as I've arranged them."

This plan suits me fine, making our game more balanced, the bondage by agreement, not by force. "And if I don't obey?" I ask.

Darius doesn't immediately reply. He reaches into his pocket to extract a small pink box. Shrugging his robe off, he rounds the bed, positioning himself at my feet. Dropping my bent knee, he climbs over me and presses me into the mattress, whispering against my ear, "A little light punishment will be inflicted if you don't stay as I've arranged you." He punctuates his statement by biting my ear lobe.

I shiver. "The punishment?" I whisper back.

"I invite you to find out, *chérie*." He raises the little box, about the size of an index card. "I sensed you might enjoy this sort of play and chanced buying you a little gift we might enjoy together. I hope you do not find this too . . ." His eyes go flat for a moment. Dropping the box onto the bed, he kisses me. If I were to guess, his gift isn't earrings or cologne.

Whatever it is, his cock is excited by it, which excites me. I lift a leg and curl it around the back of his thigh. Breaking the kiss and my hold, Darius rises to his knees. Lifting my right leg, he brings it parallel to his body. He pulls the slipper off and let's it fall to the carpet, kissing the arch of my foot, running his palm the length of the sheer black stocking. When he finally moves his eyes from the top of the garter to meet mine, I say, "Consider the stockings my small gift to you."

"A pretty gift." He rubs his cheek against the inside of my knee, his hand sliding past the top of the stocking. He strokes his fingers over my clit. I moan, wanting more. He moves to lie beside me. I wait impatiently for the real fun to begin.

The pink box is laid on my stomach.

My hands are tied but not immobilized. I could bring them down to open the box. I don't, preferring to see what Darius has planned.

Tucking a couple of pillows under my head and shoulders to give me a better view of the proceedings, he lifts the lid. Inside a sleeve of pink tissue that rustles as he unfolds it, a pair of small chrome objects shaped like tweezers embellished with teardrop-shaped pearls gleam. The cupped ends are covered in gray leather and joined by a length of chain.

Not earrings, or even jewelry—at least not the sort one wears in public. This is a presumptuous gift, but I'd be lying if I said it isn't sexy. Darius has bought me nipple clamps.

"You have played with such things before?" he asks.

"No," I say in a flood of heat. "But they interest me." In truth, the clamps are repellant to my inner Victorian. The rest of me, however, finds them exciting. They will be the first sex toy I've owned. I don't even have a dildo, preferring the warmth of my own hands when I'm pursuing singular satisfaction.

Kissing me lightly on the lips, Darius pushes my robe open. My nipples have already reacted to his games and are puckered tight. He tongues one areola then bites, pinching the nipple between his teeth. He tugs. I moan. Smiling at my response, he moves far enough away to place the curved, leather-sheathed ends of one clamp against the nipple. There's a small oval-shaped ring around both legs of the device. Darius uses it to draw the clamp tight against the sensitive tip of my breast.

"It is good?" he asks.

When I nod yes, he inches the ring incrementally higher and tighter. The sensation is very much like his bite only it doesn't let up. A line of heat spreads, trailing fire from the clamp to the place between my legs where I'm literally dripping with anticipation. Darius flicks a finger across the pearl to make it swing. The pearl must be weighted, because it's heavier than a real one. The sensation is exquisite. My eyes close as I savor the slightly painful pinch and sway.

"Not too much?"

I don't speak. I can't. I expect my moan is descriptive enough.

"So very pretty." He attaches the second clamp. His mouth comes down on mine when he's finished. His kiss is hungry. Predatory. He cups one breast, twisting the clamp with his thumb. I am not prepared for the scale of sensation that radiates from this small bit of flesh. My mind empties inside a dark haze of want. My hips rise. I need him to touch me. There. But he has other ideas and pulls away.

"Now," I suggest, a little breathlessly, lifting my pelvis. "I want you now."

Darius makes that tsking sound of his. "*Non*," he says. "You will be happier if I don't."

I narrow my eyes and growl. In response, he reaches for the chain joining the clamps and tugs. "Ummmm," I breathe. He isn't touching my body, only the chain, but I'm so aroused I think the second he does touch me, I'll come. He tugs again and I gasp.

Finally—finally!—he pushes two fingers inside me. Arousal coalesces into something solid—a wall of pleasure I must climb to reach the climax waiting on the other side.

When I think about sex, I fantasize about being teased past sanity. But this close to release, I want to arrive as quickly as possible. "Kiss me there," I breathe, moving restlessly against his hand. The words are barely past my lips when I realize I've forgotten whom I'm dealing with. Darius drops the chain. His fingers withdraw.

It turns out punishment can be inflicted by omission as well as action. A fast learner, I keep my disappointment to myself and wait, lying completely still except for my excited breathing as I anticipate his next move.

A moment later, I'm gratified to learn he isn't a sadist. He gives me a little, but not all, of what I want, kissing and nipping his way from breasts to navel. He inflicts further punishment via the speed of his journey, or, more precisely, the lack thereof. His touch is light. Too light.

Obediently, if a tad impatiently, I submit. Outside, the wind rattles the windows. Inside, Darius rattles my composure. The rustle of his clothing as he moves over my body is the only sound other than my shortening breath. When his fingers finally enter me again, the sensation is so painfully intense, I groan as I thrust into his hand.

His mouth joins his hand, and—*oh God!*—the heavy slide of his tongue as he circles my clit is exquisite—smooth as velvet, dark as night—yet my climax remains just out of reach.

I think Darius knows exactly where he's taken me. I suspect he plans to hold me there, because he slows down when I need him to speed up. Only when I can't take anymore, when I'm two seconds away from lowering my hands to solve the problem for myself, does he finally quicken his stroke.

"I need you inside me," I pant, once again forgetting who's in charge.

He doesn't change his rhythm, he doesn't do as I ask, but he does reach up to twist the chain connecting the clamps.

"Yes," I groan as the tug on my nipples joins the pleasure he's inflicting with his mouth. "More," I breathe. If I can't have his cock, this will do. Darius's fingers slide faster. Harder. And his mouth—

Perfect. Perfect. PERFECT. "Ohhh," I breathe. And then I can't breathe. Time expands and contracts while I dive, down, down, down—and I'm gone.

It's hard to move after your bones have melted. Eyes closed, I return to awareness, feeling liquid rather than solid. The bed depresses at my side. Darius strokes damp curls away from my forehead.

"It was good?" he asks, as if he doesn't know. It's an effort to turn my head toward his voice. I force my eyes open. I hum *yes*. We contemplate each other. His expression is interested . . . present. I probably look drugged. My eyes feel heavy. They aren't quite focusing. Nor can I speak. I bring my hands down to be untied. My shoulders protest. The movement jiggles the pearls on the clamps and a small aftershock shivers through me.

Darius studies the knot, lifts his eyes to mine, and says, "*Non*." He levers my arms over my head once more and then licks the shell of my ear, making me shiver. "Turn, Leezbeth," he murmurs, adjusting the clamps so they don't twist, which would cause real pain as I roll to my stomach.

I'm not happy about remaining tied. I want my turn to touch him. I want him to take his turn as the supplicant, although I'm beginning

Wrapping it around me, I plump the pillows, and slide beneath the coverlet. Darius fetches the tray and sets it between us. Inside the thermal carafe, the coffee is miraculously hot. Better yet, underneath the basket of pastries is a fat Sunday edition of The *New York Times*. I tug it out while Darius settles himself against the headboard and picks up his mug.

I yawn. "I suppose I should call Diana to arrange Obie's pickup."

"No need to rush. Does 1:30 sound acceptable to you?"

"Maybe we can meet her halfway, in South Burlington somewhere, and take her to lunch?"

"Perfect," he says, choosing a section of the paper.

CHAPTER 14

SETTING MY OVERNIGHT BAG by the door of the suite, I walk to the windows for a last look at the view. The crisp beauty of yesterday is long gone. Under the heavy gray sky, the landscape is painted in winter colors, the mountains a faded purple, the lake a dark slate green. Tracts of evergreens dot the newly bared mountainsides, adding welcome color. My photographer's eye calculates the temperature of the light. It seems to have cooled overnight from the warmer tones of autumn.

Although I've always disliked the coming of the winter, this year I can hardly bear it. I've always lived in the northeast, except for those four years of college. Well into my fifth decade of cold and ice, I've had enough—not that I can do anything about it.

"A majestic panorama," Darius says, joining me.

I swivel to face him. "You would think I would have made my peace with New England winters. Instead, as I mentioned before, I can no longer abide the cold."

"You told me you had a good year, Leezbeth. You should go somewhere warmer until spring. Do you remember the possibility I mentioned? I spoke with my friend. He lives in Georgia." Darius pats his pants pocket, nods to himself, and reaches inside his jacket.

"Georgia?" I say, scrunching my nose. I have a few typical Yankee prejudices about the South. Aside from visiting relatives in Maryland and a couple of long weekends in Florida when Dan and I were together, I've never spent concentrated time below the Mason-Dixon line.

"Coastal Georgia is very beautiful. You will love the light. The landscape is flat, with wide river channels, golden marshes, and live oaks draped in moss. *Très pittoresque.* And best of all are the sunny skies and warm temperatures."

I remain unconvinced. "But it's so . . . conservative down there, isn't it? I'll be afraid to open my mouth."

"You do realize Vermont is the whitest state in the country?"

"I'm being judgmental." I sigh.

He pats my shoulder, looking amused. "Southerners tend to be very hospitable. But if this matters so much to you, I believe my friend shares your political views." He hugs me, and then pushes me to arm's length. "What have you to lose by exploring the idea?"

"I don't know . . ."

"There is no commitment in hearing what Christopher has to say." He hands me the card he's pulled from his jacket, a piece of cardstock upon which he's scrawled, "Christopher Couper, Esq.," and a number beginning with a 912 area code. When I take it from him, Darius grins. "So brave," he says, leaning in to kiss my cheek.

Although he has described these small observations about my behavior as offered wisdom, and I don't doubt he sees them as such, or that I should as well, they are beginning to irritate me. My ire is an excellent example of why not having a life partner has its upside—little irritations like this will never become big ones.

He gives me a playful shake. "Tsk," he clucks. "Come, Leezbeth, what is so difficult about hearing him out?"

"Nothing," I mutter. "Nothing at all."

*

A week and a half later, Darius's card sits on my desk waiting to be used. I'm not sure why I haven't dialed the number. The idea of spending the winter exploring a new environment has begun to intrigue me. In the last couple of days, I've done some cursory googling of the Georgia coast. As Darius promised, the landscape is gloriously, expansively open, unlike the mountainous confines of southwestern Vermont. I'm excited about what my camera and I might find there.

But what if it doesn't work out? What if this Christopher Couper person hasn't found me a house I can afford? I'll be disappointed. Really disappointed. Maybe that's why I've been putting the call off.

I replenish my coffee. Returning to the office, I pick up the phone, punching in the number from the card.

"Hello," says a rich baritone voice, a few ringtones later.

"I'm looking for Mr. Couper."

"You've found him," the voice cheerfully notes.

"Darius Barbari gave me your name, Mr. Couper. I'm Lizbeth Silver. I believe Darius mentioned I might be looking for a place to spend the winter?"

"Ah," he says. "Give me a minute." I hear some muffled noise in the background, managing to make out the words, "I'll call you, dahlin'," before he speaks into the phone again. "Ms. Silver? Still there?"

"Yes."

"Great. And before we get to the particulars, please call me Kit, all my friends do."

"All right. Thank you," I say, although his joviality puts me off. Maybe I haven't had enough coffee yet. Coffee is my cheerful drug.

"No thanks needed yet, Ms. Silver." He laughs. His laugh is as attractive as his speaking voice. "You might not like what's on offer."

He's too flirty and way too cheerful for 10:00 in the morning. But his laugh is infectious. Its husky, sexy timbre melts me a little. "My friends call me Liz," I say. It would be awkward to call him Kit while he refers to me as Ms. Silver.

I'm not a morning person. It takes a lot of really good coffee or really good sex to perk me up before noon. Unfortunately, I've had one cup so far and Darius is not delivering on the sex. We've had a couple of pleasant dinners and attended a local gallery opening since our trip to Burlington, but no repeats of the adventure with the pink-boxed jewelry.

A regular side of sex is what an affair is all about. Based on his lack of action in that department, I'm guessing Darius is a sexual snacker, comfortable with big gaps of abstinence in between feasts. After the intensity of that first experience, I expected more of the same, but it isn't what's happening. Another Darius mystery. I haven't challenged him. This new predilection of mine for subservience is more unnerving than the lack of sex, although I tell myself to enjoy the novelty because it has a finite run.

As for "Kit," if I were to guess about his proclivities, I'd say he's a player, if only in his mind. I know his type; regardless of his marital status, he can't help turning on the charm when it comes to women, even if a thousand miles of fiber-optic cable stand in the way of proximity. I remind myself I don't have to like the guy to do business with him.

"Darius said price is important, otherwise I'd put you in touch with one of the agencies down here," Kit says. "Unfortunately, for the number he quoted, I'm not sure I could find you a closet to rent."

At least he's honest, even if it smarts. "What number did he mention?"

"A thousand or less."

I sigh. Darius got the number right. "Honestly, Mr.—" I stop myself and start again. "Honestly, Kit, I don't know if I can swing this, no matter how reasonable the cost, but I'm open to suggestion, so when Darius insisted I could actually get away from the cold—and not just as an escape fantasy inside my head—I thought, it couldn't hurt to look."

"I like a woman open to suggestions," Kit says, and then adds, "We should all be open to new adventures," a comment that may hold some level of innuendo, but then again, it might not.

"Sounds like this is a lost cause."

"Not true. My brother and I own a piece of property. What's left of the old family farm. There are a couple of houses on it. I live in one and the other is my brother's summer place. Sam is a lawyer like me, only he works for the State Department, diplomatic corps. We just got news he's being posted overseas. That means his place will be empty for the next couple of years." He pauses. I wait for his offer, because I can see where he's going.

"When Darius told me he had a friend who needed something special, I gave Sam a call. He was amenable. We figured you could pay the utilities. There's electric heat if you want, or you can use the wood stove.

The wood is harvested on the property so using the stove wouldn't cost a thing. I can teach you how to use it."

"Wow. That's a generous offer. And for the record, I'm a Vermonter, Kit. A fair number of us know how to use a wood stove."

"I stand advised." He laughs that lovely laugh of his and continues, "The WiFi was shut down when Sam left. I'm going to buy a booster for mine. That should allow you to piggyback onto it. So, maybe the cost per month would be $250."

"And the rent?"

"The same. Guess I didn't make myself clear. This is a housesitting gig. Paying the utilities is all that's required."

I'm so flabbergasted I pop from my chair. Staring out the window, I watch dry leaves scuttle across the lawn. It hits me I could do this. "I don't know what to say." I wonder if Kit owes some sort of favor to Darius and this is how he is repaying it. I make a note to ask.

"I always like hearing a lady say yes," Kit responds.

I ignore that one. I've got his number at this point—flirting is as natural to him as breathing. "Your brother knows about my standard poodle, Obie?" I ask, making sure we cover the details.

"Darius mentioned your dog. Believe me, he can't do worse than Dick and Jane, Sam's Labs."

"For the record, my dog has never damaged anything other than his chew toys."

"I stand advised," he says again, amusement apparent in his tone.

I begin to believe a sunny, moderate winter could be a reality. "Let me think about it," I say. "I had resigned myself to shivering through the winter up here and I need to consider the ramifications of leaving."

"Ms. Lizzie, thinking is highly overrated. Just say yes. You don't want to be walking that big dog of yours in snow and ice. You know you don't."

"Well . . ." I hesitate, even though I believe a new adventure is just what I need. "I guess I'll say—"

"Yes," he interjects.

"Yes!" I smile at my reflection in the window, suddenly giddy with excitement. Whatever the ramifications, they will be handled.

"Great. So, now that you're committed, I should tell you the not-so-good parts."

"What could possibly be bad about a practically free house in a warm climate for the winter?"

"Not much, really. Most people, however, like to be on St. Simons Island because of the beaches. Willing—that's the name of our place— is on the mainland, a few miles below Darien. That's a good twenty-five minutes from the island. We front on one of the channels of the Altamaha River, though. Any of this a deal breaker for you?"

"Willing?" I ask, struck by the fact that his property has a name. I envision Tara.

"The land has been in the family since a little bit after the Civil War. In the old days it was the custom to name your farm—plantation is the old English word for a big ol' farm."

"I'm still seeing Tara."

"Believe me, it's definitely not Tara. No columns. No wrought iron. No ladies in hoop skirts. Although it was once a rice plantation, the land was used for dairy farming by my ancestors, who started out as city people from Boston and Savannah."

"Thank you for enlightening me." His ancestry sounds interesting. My curiosity about people kicks in. I suspect a story and hope I'll have a chance to hear more about his antecedents.

"You're okay about not being on the island? You can drive over there if you have a craving for beach time. What Willing offers is open fields under some really old live oaks, plus nice trails through the woods and access to the river."

I can hardly complain about not being on an island when until a minute ago I didn't know where I'd be located. "A river vista is as beautiful as an ocean view. Each has its charms," I say honestly.

"You'll enjoy the place. Guaranteed."

"Kit, this is an unbelievably gracious offer. Thank you so much."

"How 'bout you check your calendar and get back to me with your arrival date? Let me have your e-mail address and I'll send you some photographs."

"That would be terrific." I give him my address.

"Got it, and happy to be of service."

There it is again, that little overtone of innuendo. Maybe he and Darius became friends when they bonded over the ability to say two things at once, although Mr. Couper keeps his double entendres light, while Darius's often have an edge.

"I'm looking forward to having a neighbor. See you real soon." He disconnects.

My hand rises to rest on my head, so it won't float away. I plop to the chair. What a stroke of luck! I can't wait to tell Arielle. And Darius.

Later, as I post some of last summer's images to my website, I think about the lawyer almost as much as the winter adventure. Although he irritated me at the beginning of our exchange, I kind of liked Mr. Couper—Kit—by the end of it.

Assurance, when not combined with snobbery or conceit, is an attractive commodity in anyone. I try to imagine the man who belongs to that infectious laugh and charming demeanor. I decide patrician, with that easy Southern charm. I picture Kit as average height or a little taller, blond, with a golf tan. Not my type. And yet . . .

I shake my head, doing my own censoring without help from my mother or her internalized doppelgänger. Mr. Couper is not important, as fun as it is to imagine what he looks like and what he'd be like in bed. I decide on naughty, with a little kink.

Okay, that's enough. I don't even know if he's married. But the self-admonishment isn't working; instead of continuing to work on the website, I open another browser window and try to pinpoint Willing on Google Earth. Without coordinates, I can only give it a general location. I see the Altamaha River with a grid of old rice fields clearly visible among the marshes. As the concept of escaping winter takes root, I imagine how much fun my camera and I are going to have exploring the wide expanse of sky and sea my research indicates. Laughing, I realize I just gave my camera human feelings, the way Arielle gives feelings to her pots.

I call her, making a date for a walk later in the afternoon, saving my news until then. After I hang up, my thoughts drift back to my soon to be winter landlord. I wonder again if he's married and decide to ask Darius about his particulars. He shouldn't be on my radar. I'm just curious. Oh, to be out of the cold. Irresistible!

CHAPTER 15

"YOU'RE GOING WHERE?" Arielle exclaims, walking a few steps up the path before pivoting to face me. "Georgia? What are you going to do in Georgia?"

We have climbed to a high meadow with a view of Ashburton nestled into the valley to the southeast, the mountains closing in around the town. The day is mostly sunny and surprisingly mild for this time of year, although scattered clouds move swiftly overhead, driven by a brisk northeasterly wind.

"Darius suggested it. I was complaining about how much I hate winter and he had this idea to call a friend of his on the Georgia coast. It was that easy." The wind tugs my scarf over my shoulder. As I gather it in and stuff it inside my jacket, I say, "How could I resist?"

Arielle looks at me blankly for a second. "Is this related to the conversation we had about feeling unsettled?"

"I think so. This could be my opportunity to shift gears. I've done some research. The area is gorgeous. I can't wait to go exploring with my camera. It's been a long time since I've had that feeling, which is pretty exciting! I'm leaving right after Christmas."

"Amazing," Arielle manages, but I can tell she isn't as thrilled as I am.

We both contemplate the view as I wait for her to process my news. "Those clouds are moving fast," I note.

"Just like you," she snorts, turning to appraise me. "I'll miss you, but you know, this is good. You need a change."

"I think I do. And I'll miss you too. But maybe you can visit? I'd love that."

We walk down the far slope of the hill, circling toward the parking area. Obie tugs on his lead, heading for a large clump of leaves at the side of the path. I can tell from the kind of sniffing he's doing and the angle of his head that he's about to rub himself in something disgusting. Pulling him away, I stoop to examine what he found so enticing.

"Since when did you develop a taste for noxious mushrooms, you silly beast?" I steer him toward the opposite side of the trail.

"How long will you be away?" Arielle asks.

"From the beginning of January through the end of March."

Arielle's reaction is making me question, and not for the first time, whether leaving home for three months is wise. A roll of anxiety flips my stomach. I'll miss Diana, and Arielle. They are some of the logistics I had to consider. I've decided we are all grown-ups. We can manage a few months apart. There is Facetime and Skype, and if any of us needs to communicate in person, there are cars and airplanes.

"You should visit,"

Her mouth twists. "I have to be away for the show. And there's Mom to consider."

"I talked to Diana. She is planning to come home that week; it's during her winter break. She plans to visit a couple of friends who will also be in town for the break. She says she will be happy to visit your mom."

Arielle's face relaxes. "That's so sweet of her, but I'm sure I can get some of Mom's friends to visit."

"Diana wants to help, but do what you think is best."

"I'll let you know. And of course I'd love to visit you in Georgia. I just don't see how I can work it out."

"I'm sorry. It was selfish of me not to think about your mom." We walk in silence for a few minutes. "Oh no! I won't be here to take your show pictures." I curl my palm against my mouth, trying to think of a solution. "I'll come back to do it."

"That's ridiculous. I'll get by without new photos or we'll take them later."

"I'll come back."

"Liz, that's . . . what? A thousand-mile drive?"

In front of us the woods form a dark line against the electric green of the meadow. It is the middle of November but the weather has been so mild that the grass has produced one last burst of bright growth.

"Do you have anything ready now?" I ask.

"A few pieces."

"So how about we shoot those? I can refresh the site from down there. I know—I'll call in a favor and get Vanessa Egan, Tim's wife, to shoot for you. She's good, you'll like her."

"Honestly, I can figure it out."

"Please?" I say.

She walks ahead. I don't try to catch up. Eventually, she stops and turns. "Let's shoot what I've got and then see."

"Deal."

"And, Liz, really—this is going to be so good for you, I know it is."

※

"What was the final price of those Art Nouveau tables? I've lost track."

"The pair came to $2,200, plus the tax," Darius answers.

We are returning from an auction in Saratoga. The contents of a home owned by the same family since the late 1800s were on the block. On our way into town, Darius pointed out the huge old ginger-bread-encrusted Queen Anne among the many huge Victorians lining Broadway. The self-important grandeur of the architecture remains remarkable. It strikes me that these houses were the McMansions of their era. "And you will sell the tables for—"

"Around $4,500 for the pair."

"Not a bad profit for a few hours' work."

Darius's only interest at the auction were the sidetables, so we were able to leave after he successfully bid and made payment arrangements.

"They were an excellent find at a very good price. You must have a customer in mind to purchase Art Nouveau. It is not in vogue at the moment, so not a thing to buy on speculation."

"You have a customer?"

"Of course."

The car is not warmed up yet and the weather has turned cold, right on schedule for mid-December. I shiver, adjusting my scarf higher on my neck. Darius turns up the seat heater for me.

"I can't wait to be out of the cold. As soon as I've cleaned up after Christmas, I'm on my way to Georgia."

"I'm delighted I was able to facilitate the trip for you."

"You said Mr. Couper is a client? How is it that you do business that far away?"

"The fine antique world is small. Some mutual friends recommended me to him. He was hoping I could locate a piece of furniture and negotiate its purchase."

"Forensic antiquing?"

Darius chuckles. "It happens more than you might think."

"What was the piece?"

"A chest of drawers built by a cabinetmaker enslaved on the property, though Christopher's ancestors did not own this cabinetmaker slave. My understanding is that the property was purchased after slavery ended."

"A piece of furniture made by a slave at Willing. Wow." I sit with the idea for a minute before saying, "Your friend said his family is from Boston and Savannah. Some of those Southern ancestors must have owned slaves. I can't imagine such a legacy."

"A legacy is only history. I don't believe in carrying sins that are not mine. What I'm responsible for is right here—" His hand rolls in an expansive gesture. "The present and the future are my concern, not the past."

Another slice of Darius wisdom. Sound wisdom, although I'm fairly sure his past has produced some baggage he continues to lug around. Maybe the distinction is about not carrying *other people's* baggage, whether those people are one's ancestors or not.

There is a lot of my own history I've already stuffed away and wouldn't mind putting up for auction, so I don't argue.

"Did he have to pay a lot for the chest?"

Darius nods. "It seemed very sentimental to me. I could have sold him something with more value for the price."

"Being sentimental and valuing your history are not the same."

He offers his philosophical French shrug. "Sometimes right or wrong, people want to live free of the past."

"What about the concept that history repeats itself if we do not learn from its mistakes?"

It occurs to me that Darius may deal in large antiques instead of small ones not only because of an expanding market, but also to avoid the ghosts haunting the flotsam and jetsam of the more personal items I poured over at the auction preview, including a box of vintage photographs. The photographs made me melancholy. Someday my pictures could end up in the same situation—cast aside by a new generation who shares Darius's philosophy about sentiment, or without any family left to value them at all.

He tsks. "Leezbeth, You know I do not mean we should forget the past, or stick our heads in the sand. But taking on the weight of what is immutable is foolish."

I don't think Darius and I are going to agree on this one, so I ask if he is looking for anything in particular while he is in Europe. With my encouragement, he talks about furniture, antique markets, and his contacts in France, Belgium and Germany until we are a few miles outside of town.

I am musing about what clothing I want with to take with me to Georgia when he says, "You know, you and Christopher have a great deal in common. You will enjoy each other." He twinkles at me in a way that implies a particular kind of enjoyment.

A devil on my shoulder can't let the innuendo—or whatever it was—stand. "Enjoy each other how?" I challenge.

His brow creases. "I suppose I think that you will hit it off. You are both smart, witty people."

"And that's all?"

"What do you mean, that's all. What more could there be?"

"I'm not sure. That's why I asked."

Darius blows out a breath but otherwise doesn't respond as he negotiates a curvy stretch of road.

I don't know why I'm riled. Maybe because I don't want him lining up my next bed partner, which is my interpretation of his remark. Of course, my reaction is hypocritical since I've already had fantasies about Mr. Christopher Couper, Esq., of the easy laugh and possible double entendres.

Shouldn't I be pleased that Darius sees a similar trajectory for me and his friend? Instead, I'm feeling rejected, as if I'm some tragic nineteenth-century courtesan whose beloved patron has passed her on to one of his chums.

God. I hope my winter relocation to Georgia offers a new perspective on these moments of . . . I don't know what they are. Ennui? That sounds so self-aggrandizing, but what else to label this spiritual malaise, the sense that I have lost my way and can't find the road home?

I consider sharing my feelings with Darius—for about two seconds—before deciding that in his inimitable way, he will only tell me to buck up and move on. He wouldn't be wrong, but I want sympathy, not tough love, even if it would be better for me, so I stay mum.

Darius pulls into my driveway.

"Thanks for inviting me along," I say. "I enjoyed myself."

I wish he'd stay the night. My need for human connection and distraction hasn't diminished in the last few minutes, and sex would be an acceptable form of both. That need compels me to ask, "Would you like to come in?"

There has been no repeat of the incendiary Waltz Night, although Darius was no less controlling on the two occasions we've had sex since. What remains the same is that I haven't seen him without clothes. Most men, no matter their shape or weight, are happy to get naked. Apparently, not Darius.

"It is late," he says, shifting toward me. His smile is rueful.

He knows I'm not inviting him in for a cup of tea. I want him to fuck me and he's refused. I don't understand this man, although I'm working on a few new theories to explain his behavior. One is about control turning him on more than sex. Is he punishing me for being too direct? I've been as subtle as I'm able. I suspect sleeping with someone requires a level of intimacy Darius can't abide. Theory number two is that he is only a restless sleeper should another human invade his bed—not that this has anything to do with why he doesn't want to fuck me. I would, after all, be willing to wait until morning.

My mood darkens. It isn't as if he has trouble getting an erection. On those rare occasions since Burlington when we slept together, he hasn't had performance issues. Usually an affair like ours burns hot for at least a couple of months before it burns out. But maybe for him, the kindling burned but the fire didn't ignite.

"Perhaps," he says a beat too late, "you and Obie might come to me instead?"

Obie is allowed to visit as long as I keep him with me so that that he can't roam among the antiques at night.

"I'll go on. Join me when you are ready." He lays a hand on my arm, presuming I'll agree to his plan.

The car heater is blasting but suddenly I'm as cold as when we first drove away from Saratoga. I suppose he wants to end up in his own bed, as well as to take control of the invitation. Is he placating me, since this is the first time I've made it clear I'm annoyed with his disinterest in sex?

"Perhaps you're too tired after all," he comments, when I haven't articulated what I want.

Knowing the right answer is, *Sure, meet you in five,* my devil asks, "Tell me why you changed your mind."

His eyes narrow.

I don't care whether having his control challenged annoys him. I'm annoyed by his need to arbitrate all that we do and when we do it, although his insinuation about me and his buddy also has my dander up.

Does Miss Manners include etiquette in that thick tome of hers about how to discourage your lover from recommending you to another? The Rules don't cover it. They were meant to keep my transactions with men simple and my heart safe. Five years on, however, they seem to be failing me.

"Leezbeth, really—what is it that you want?" Darius sounds as out of patience with me as I am with him.

Perhaps what we need from each other is too different. And perhaps what I want from him has changed in the months since we began our affair. Maybe it should end now, not a couple of weeks from now.

"When you don't want to answer a question, you ask one in return," I observe, strengthening the odds of the end coming sooner than later. "Do you know you do that?"

He shakes his head with a dismissive sniff.

"Okay. Fine." I hit the door handle. Looking over my shoulder at him, I say, "Don't dismiss what I need. I've never done that to you." I want to add, *And I'll pick my own lovers, thank you very much,* but I refrain.

I swing my feet to the ground, just as Darius grabs my arm.

"Leezbeth—" He leans in to kiss the corner of my mouth, a surprisingly sweet kiss. "You mistake what I want."

Startled by his tenderness, I don't know how to respond. His kisses me again, this time with more passion than I've felt from him since the beginning. His hands rise to cup my face. I pull him closer.

When we break apart, he brushes a thumb across my lips. "Collect the dog, *s'il vous plaît.* I will wait."

✳

"It was good?" Kissing the inside of my knee, Darius rises to his feet at the side of the bed.

"Fishing for compliments?" I respond languidly.

"Diving, ma *chérie.* Diving for compliments." His eyes glitter with amusement and then drift slowly down my body, coming to rest at the apex of my thighs where his mouth just worked some potent magic. Little aftershocks of pleasure are still shuddering through me.

"I think the usual term for the act is *eating*," I say.

"You taste of sea and salt, not of earth. One cannot eat the sea."

"Hmmmmm," I respond, too relaxed to quibble.

I am naked, while as usual Darius is not, although he is barefoot—very daring for him. I still can't get my mind around us never having lain skin to skin, and time is running out.

Is he self-conscious about his little potbelly? I'm rather fond of it. In all other ways he's slender and strong, I assume from moving furniture.

The good news is that keeping his clothes on doesn't interfere with my enjoyment—or his. A distinct bulge mars the drape of his gray gabardine pants. I raise a leg from where it dangles over the side of the mattress and press my foot lightly against him. He pushes it away.

Unfastening his belt, he lets his pants and boxers drop. A bright clang heralds the belt buckle hitting the floor. From Darius, this lack of fastidiousness is almost bizarre. Rolling on a condom, he enters me on a swift upward thrust.

I groan, my back arching. He shoves my legs farther apart, pushing himself onto the bed. Our mouths meet. I taste of toothpaste; he tastes of me.

We are not making love. We are screwing. Making love requires an exchange of feeling. Darius isn't interested in feelings.

He is, however, interested in pleasure. Syncopating his rhythm with a twist and grind, he is offering up the extra stimulation I need to orgasm a second time. I may grumble about how controlling he is, yet the man rarely puts a foot wrong—or any other body part—no matter how I categorize what we do in bed.

During the time between entering my house to pack an overnight bag and returning to the car with Obie, I decided I had to let go of my irritation with Darius's all-give-and-no-take proclivities. Why not focus on the lovely slide of his penis inside me and the equally lovely friction of his thumb slicking over my clit? I need to forget the rest?

That he enjoys screwing me and I enjoy the orgasms he supplies has to be equitable enough.

Except, as much as I want to stay in the present, I'm in an odd mood, and, no matter the logic I attempt to apply to the situation or Darius's artistry, my mind continues to churn.

He seems not to have noticed, which is fortunate, since I feel like I forced myself on him this evening, no matter that he also seems to have decided I'm what he wanted, after all. Sliding his arms under my knees, Darius aligns my legs in front of his body, stroking his hands down my calves—once, then twice. My eyes close. He hilts and twists. I purr approval.

"You are so wet, always so wet for me, *mon trésor. Très beau.*" His next thrust is deep.

I moan, my head falling back. The pleasure he's evoking is lovely, yet the melancholy that began in Saratoga murmurs through my mind. I may have decided to let my irritation go, but some part of me—possibly my heart—remains focused on injustices past and present. The result is that the attainment of a second orgasm is receding with every disgruntled second ticking by.

I'm ready to suggest to Darius that he finish without me, when it happens—an explosion of sensation, my mind's nattering is at last silenced, overwhelmed by pleasure.

I'm not finished savoring my liberation when Darius says, "Open your eyes, Leezbeth. *Sois avec moi.*" I think this is French for *be with me.* I translate it to mean, stay in the moment. When I don't react, he slaps my ass. Maybe he means pay attention.

Meeting his gaze, I clench around his cock, holding him tight. "Do it again," I breathe, challenging him.

I enjoy watching a man come, although Darius's desire for me to be present as he finds his release seems oddly personal for a man who can't take off his clothes when he fucks. His request adds another unusual detail to tonight's proceedings.

"*Chérie*," he says through gritted teeth and slaps me again.

A few seconds later, he comes, eyes squeezing shut at the end, his breathing harsh and open mouthed. He collapses on top of me, turning his head away to luxuriate privately in his orgasm.

I walk my fingertips down his spine. The fine cotton of his shirt is silky under my hand. He smells of the cologne he wears—an earthy blend of rosemary and sage and oakmoss. Lying under him, my view is of his nape, the strong column of his neck disappearing into his collar, which is pulled away from his body, untidy and un-Darius.

No matter a man's age, his youth lingers in that sweet curve of muscle between hairline and shoulder. In the moments after release, this visage evokes tenderness in me, a feeling close to love. But it isn't love, and never will be.

Smoothing his collar, I lay it neatly against his body. This act of care makes me inexplicably sad. I attach the emotion to the lost potential C.'s youth represents; to Dan and Roland, men I adored and lost; and to Darius, for whom I've become more fond than I would like.

I shove at Darius's chest, suddenly panicking to be out from under his weight. As he lifts himself away, I roll to the side, covering my face with my hands. Tears fill my eyes until, unable to control myself, I am out and out sobbing.

Darius sits up and lets me have at it.

"I suspect one orgasm too many, *mon coeur*," he comments as the maelstrom thankfully ebbs.

I brush at my eyes. *God, I'm a mess.*

Darius kisses my cheek.

"This is too weird," I choke out.

"Orgasm can release more than pleasure, do you not find it so?"

I nod, having once had a similar experience with Roland, although I attributed those tears to the intensity of our developing love. Love doesn't have anything to do with what Darius and I have been up to, so the theory doesn't hold.

"I take it you've made woman cry with your skillful"—I can't call it lovemaking, so I settle for—"ministrations." I want to make light of my little crying jag, no matter how unsettled I feel.

"Not often, but it is not so unusual," Darius says, ignoring my attempt at humor. He strokes a knuckle lightly across my cheek. "To release this sadness is not such a terrible thing."

"Easy for you to say." I sniff.

He brings his face closer to mine and his voice stern, says, "Do not belittle my experience or your own."

I sigh. "I'm sorry, I do know." Or, more accurately, until this evening, I only suspected. I don't have a clue about the details, although I'm fairly sure his ex-wife smashed his heart to pieces.

He says, "I wish I could give you what you want, you know that, do you not, *chérie?*"

I frown. "Is this about my wanting more give-and-take during sex?" I scoot up the bed against the pillows and cover myself with the coverlet.

"*Non,*" he says, as if my need to reciprocate, to give him pleasure without playing *Darius, may I,* is irrelevant to him. It is a measure of my state of mind that I can't dial up the usual irritation. I simply stare at him, waiting for further enlightenment.

"You want more than *this,* Leezbeth. You want to be in love." His accent has thickened, something it does when he is excited by an idea. "I think you desire such intimacy very much, only you refuse to accept this is so. *Je suis profondément désolé,* but you are making yourself sad."

The breath I've barely recovered whooshes from my lungs. I struggle for words, while Darius retrieves his clothing, giving me time to consider what he's said. When he's buckled and buttoned, he sits down next to me. He pats my hand. "I never meant to make you unhappy, Leezbeth. I had thought we enjoyed each other."

"We have. Our time together has been lovely." I pull my hand from his and press the palm to my forehead, unable to sort my feelings.

I followed The Rules when I chose Darius, but something has gone very wrong. More precisely, *something is wrong with me.* I want to believe the problem is that my heart is finally healing. Anyone who has broken a bone can attest that the knitting is painful, but without it, you will never regain use of your limb. Perhaps the same is true of a broken heart. Perhaps, as well, the creation of health where there has been only illness is unbalancing.

"I'm in a strange mood," I say, needing time to absorb what I'm feeling—the sadness, my little emotional cloudburst, Darius's ideas about me, all of it—without him offering further observations or guidance. "I'm tired. You must be, too." I yawn, emphasizing my point, although I swing my feet to the floor. I need to let Obie in.

My dog greets me, receives his treat, and saunters over to Darius who bends to pet him. Greetings accomplished, Obie begins a sniff around the room. Darius walks to where I'm standing near the door. He gives my shoulder a consoling pat.

If—and when—my heart is finished healing, will love once more seem worth all the pain it has caused me?

"I am satisfied with this sort of affair, Leezbeth. You are not," he declares.

"I *am* satisfied." This is only partially true, a reflexive answer. My thoughts about satisfaction and love and what I want are a jumble. I wish he would let the subject drop.

"You are of a generous, loving spirit. Give yourself to someone who shares these traits. You want more, I tell you. This is why you are unhappy. You wish for a loving relationship. Why can you not admit it?"

I cross my arms over my breasts. Literally and figuratively. I'm too naked for a conversation about my deepest yearnings, theoretical or otherwise. I wonder if Darius will drop the subject if I tell him I'll only discuss it if he strips, so he's as naked as I am.

A more realistic solution is to put on some clothes. I walk to the chair where I've draped my shirt and pants.

"I have all the intimacy I need," I say, picking up my top, a tunic that drapes to my thighs. I'll feel less exposed once I'm in it.

"You consider what we have been doing intimate?" he asks.

I hear derision or maybe incredulity in his tone.

"You don't suppose it takes a certain amount of intimacy, not to mention trust, to allow someone to tie you up?" I query, equally incredulous. The shirt is inside out; I stick a hand into a sleeve to turn it.

"Such a thing is merely the calculation of probable outcomes. Will this person hurt me or deliver pleasure?" Darius tsks. "Don't confuse intimacy of the body with intimacy of the heart." He walks over and reaches for the shirt.

I pull away and count to ten. After which, I manage to soften my tone as well as what I have to say. "If we're going to split intimacy into parts, then I'm focused on the mind and body parts. I'm not interested in adding my heart to that equation." Am I telling the entire truth? Maybe not, but it is as much truth as I can stomach at the moment.

He looks skeptical, as if I've announced I prefer glass shards to sugar in my tea.

"Let's focus on the present, not the future, okay? The way I see it—or at least, the way I've seen it for the last five years—*loving* relationships acquire baggage that gets in the way of intimacy. But, when two people come together for the short term, there are no expectations, except of pleasure, and more importantly, no time for resentments to form. I find the lack of those complications refreshing."

My problem isn't that I want to love you, Darius. My problem that I didn't like your lack of reciprocity in bed, but our affair is almost at its end and so your proclivities are no longer an issue—a perfect example of the point I'm trying to make. But Darius has already focused this discussion on me, and I won't defend myself by shifting it to him—a classic underhanded technique for winning an argument. The trick was a favorite of Dan's.

Clutching the shirt to my chest, I say, "When a relationship is defined as temporary from the start, there is a purity of purpose and understanding almost impossible to attain when your other purpose is *until death do us part.*"

He shakes his head and opens his mouth as if he's going to argue. I forestall him.

"Don't try to tell me I'm wrong, because I lived this truth with my husband. I have also been involved in enough love affairs to know I'm right. You might prefer another kind of intimacy, but mine is working for me."

This short commentary could be the mission statement for my Rules. And, if my feelings are changing, and maybe they are, they are too new and vulnerable for me to expose them to Darius. I'm having trouble exposing them to myself.

"I hate when you lie to yourself." Darius pulls me to his body, trapping the shirt between us. He lifts my chin, forcing me to meet his gaze. "Having nothing to lose is hardly compensation for what you are denying yourself. When you rise above the banality of everyday to be engaged with your lover, accepting his faults as well as the possibility of loss, of rejection—" He breaks off, his grip on my shoulders tightening. "Love is dangerous, Leezbeth. I understand not wanting to leave yourself so defenseless. But it is the only path to the sort of intimacy that means anything, that means everything. To trust your lover, to hand him this terrible power to hurt you and hope he never will, this is the only way to nourish the heart."

"Right now it's enough for me to nourish my mind and body. Two out of three will have to do." I blow out a breath. Pushing against his chest, I add, "Whatever is in store for me in the future, I'm not going there tonight."

"This is no joke, Leezbeth. You disappoint me."

"I object to being told what I *should* want. It's patronizing." I break his hold. "Why is this so important to you, anyway? Can't we agree to disagree and go to bed?"

My feelings may very well be changing, but that doesn't mean I can imagine falling in love the way Darius has suggested. My heart flutters at the idea—with fear.

He shakes his head.

"I'm being realistic about what I can endure. I know my boundaries and my limits, *and* I'm allowed to protect them. Maybe I'll change my

mind eventually, but I know what I'm capable of *right now*, so please—
you need to stop." I stare at the tunic clutched in my hand. I've only
ever shared these feelings about love and loss with Arielle. Admitting
them to Darius, I feel overexposed, an irony since his heart and mine
are not engaged in the intimacy he's recommending, although there is
plenty of a danger in what we are discussing.

Suddenly queasy, I pull air into my lungs. I take a deep breath, and
another.

I care a little too much about what Darius thinks of me, or I wouldn't
be so irritated, nor would my heart be pounding as if it is not just my
body that is naked. Taking another deep breath, I remind myself Darius is armed only with opinions. I slide the shirt over my head.

"*Mon petit colombe*," he sighs. "Do not deny that love nourishes
your soul. Do not pretend you prefer a life without it." He tugs me back
into his arms.

I stand stiffly within his embrace, telling myself he means well. For
all of the times I've resented how controlling he is, Darius is generous
and kind. I force myself to relax against him. "You are a dear to want
the best for me," I say, resting my forehead on his shoulder. "But, love
isn't best for me, at least not right now. The same way, I presume, it
isn't best for you."

If he's going to insist on honesty, I want the same from him. "I
have Diana and many loving friends, as you have Christian and your
family. Those relationships are plenty nourishing. Why do you feel it's
so important for me to seek romantic love when you won't?"

"Because I cannot." Sounding exhausted, he sighs, smoothing his
palm down my back. "But you? You must stop wasting yourself on
men like me."

This is a little too melodramatic, although it doesn't stop new tears
from filling my eyes. "You are not a waste," I say.

He cups my face, wiping way the tears from the corners of my lower
lids with his thumbs. "*Écoute-moi, s'il vous plaît*," he says. "I want you
to be happy. To be loved. Can you not open yourself to this possibility,

Leezbeth?"

I shake my head in denial. "And who is your candidate for the man on the white horse?" I ask. "We can agree, I'm sure, that he isn't you." I move away to sit on the bed.

Darius follows and sits next to me. "He will come along once you stop distracting yourself with these little affairs," he says, squeezing my hand.

"Oh really? And you? Don't you deserve love? I find you imminently worthy." I squeeze his hand in return.

"We all need to be loved." Darius shrugs. "But needing and having are not always compatible, *n'est-ce pas?*"

By denying the richness of a loving relationship, Darius hasn't sentenced himself to loneliness exactly. Like me, he has family and friends, but he seems to have chosen a life without the soul-nourishing splendor of a shared journey with that one person who is your mirror and responsibility, your sustenance and joy.

My heart thuds heavily in my chest. I think, Darius has looked squarely at the consequences of cutting himself off from such a possibility and accepted it as his fate. As for me, I've been so intent on defending my heart from harm, I'm not sure I have fully considered the long-term ramifications of that choice.

In the years since Roland, have I ever asked myself, *Is it still true? Is my heart still too damaged to try again?*

I ask the question now.

The answer is—*I don't know.*

I suppose I don't know is better than an outright no. Discovering that the question needed to be asked, and wishing the answer were yes, seem like significant developments.

I don't have time to react to this revelation, however, as Darius pins me with his glance. "I cannot survive what I ask of you," he says. "But Leezbeth, for you, I wish love very much."

I don't believe Darius intended to reveal himself to this extent. I recognize it is an honor to receive his confidences, yet it is also unsettling—a substantial rending in the Darius firmament. I begin to shake. Whether from fear or desire, sometimes, in moments of intense stress or excitement, I experience a surge of adrenaline so powerful it almost shakes me apart.

"Let me warm you." Darius misunderstands my trembling, or maybe he understands and has decided I've finally had enough emotional reckoning for one evening. He motions for me to slide under the covers.

Feeling hollowed out and fragile, I scoot over to make room for him. He arranges the blankets over us. I close my eyes, hearing the soft click as he switches off the light.

Wrapping an arm around my waist, he pulls me close. I add this to the other firsts of the evening, though I'm not foolish enough to believe he's changed what he wants.

"Shhhhh," he says, as if I need comforting, which I suppose I do. His warmth seeps into me. "Shhhhh," he says a second time, stroking a hand hypnotically up and down my arm.

After a few minutes I begin breathing deeply, feigning sleep. I need to be alone. I must be convincing, because, careful not to disturb me, Darius eases himself away.

Once he's left the room, Obie jumps up to settle at my side. I bury my face in his warmth, not entirely sure I am capable of confronting life without the defensive boundaries Darius is encouraging me to tear down.

"He might be right," I admit to my dog. "Even if I'm not ready to admit it."

Realizing I'm in bed in my top, I throw off the covers. As I pull my nightshirt out of the overnight bag, I think, a trifle fantastically, that Zeus isn't finished with me, that Darius and C. are evidence of his diabolical plan to test my resolve against love.

Once more under the covers, I lay a hand on Obie. I have had enough tsuris for one night, and my brain is blocking any more serious thinking with a steady stream of fatalistic nonsense.

I ask Obs, "Do you know if Cupid uses arrows these days?" As if my poodle has a clue. "Maybe he's into modern weaponry and carries a gun."

I conjure a picture of a chubby naked baby with wings packing a hunting rifle. Revising the weapon, I reimagine a chubby naked baby brandishing a spear gun, the kind a scuba diver might use. I smile. Although I'm obviously not thinking straight, at least my sense of humor didn't wash away with those crazy tears.

Unfortunately, my levity quickly sinks under a biblical sense of doom, weighing down my silly mood. I think, it hardly matters what kind of weapon Zeus's baby bad-boy is packing if he's already set his sights on me.

✸

"So, you are away to Georgia after Christmas?" Darius asks.

I nod as I slide fresh linguine into a pot of boiling water. We have come together for this "last supper" before going our separate ways. Darius flies off to Europe next week. Ending the affair on the tremulous note created by our argument wasn't sitting well with me. Also, I have a parting gift for Darius and wanted to see his reaction to it. Setting my wooden spoon on the counter, I turn toward him.

"I'm out of here as the weather allows. I hope you are flying before the weather dumps more snow on us. I will enjoy imagining you in Prague and Paris."

"And I will imagine you happy in the sun."

"I would love to see Prague someday." I stir the pasta to make sure it doesn't stick together.

"Prague is beautiful, though like all cities on water, it can be raw in winter." He hands me a glass of the Cabernet. "There is plenty of antique-shopping where you are heading. Mostly for the small things that interested you at the Saratoga auction. And you should also visit Savannah, which is about an hour away. A very beautiful city."

The water has returned to full boil. I count to ten and drain the pasta, then toss it into the bowl from Arielle's last shoot. After mixing the linguini with my homemade puttanesca sauce, I walk the bowl to the table.

"So you're ready to leave?" I ask as we sit down.

He flips his hand. "I have a few sales to close first." He helps himself to the pasta, adding shaved Parmesan. "I will be with Christian and his family in Cannes for the holiday, and then off hunting for the shop, but I return to Paris twice before flying home in March. I will see the rest of my family then."

"Cannes." I sigh with envy. "Perhaps one day I'll visit there, too. Your plans sound lovely." I push the breadboard toward Darius, encouraging him to tear off a piece of the crusty baguette I picked up this afternoon.

We dig into our meal.

Darius salutes me with his glass of red. "I will send postcards."

But nothing of you, I think. "How nice," I say.

I'll send postcards is akin to *Let's have lunch,* a proposition meant to ease partings rather than a predictor of get-togethers to come.

"In return, you must send many photographs of Georgia."

If he sends postcards, I'll send photographs, providing I take any that are worthy of sending.

After dinner, Darius says he has a surprise and goes out to his car to fetch it. He returns with a carpet folded into a bulky parcel about the size of a small ottoman. He props it inside the entry. Ducking out a second time, he hauls in another similarly folded rug.

"When I was in the city for Thanksgiving, I saw these and thought they were exactly right for you." He peels off his jacket and lays it on the arm of the sofa.

From his pocket, he produces a small pearl-handled folding knife. He uses it to slice through the twine holding one of the parcels together. Maneuvering the rug to the center of the living room, he kicks it out.

A six-by-nine rectangle reminiscent of a Klimt landscape, in gold and salmon and several shades of blue, unfurls at my feet. The design is intricate, a geometry of stylized flowers. Darius's painter's eye has chosen colors and tonalities that harmonize perfectly with my living room. It's a beautiful rug.

He looks at me expectantly.

"This is amazing," I gasp.

"A Kerman," he says, smiling as he regards the carpet. "From Persia. The design is called millefleur, because of the overall floral pattern. It isn't very old. Early twentieth century." He points at a lighter blue in the weave. "You do not see this shade in an older carpet, when plant dyes were used exclusively."

"Oh Darius, it's exquisite, but—"

"Let's look at the other," he interjects.

The second rug is rolled on top of the first. The colors are similar, though there is a yellow-green in this one not found in the Kerman.

"A Khotan. Probably made in the last fifty years, but handsome, oui? Even though the pattern is more geometric, the two work well together. You could use this one in the dining room?"

I nod because he's right. I'm also calculating that these carpets are worth $2,000 or more apiece.

I bend to skim my palm across the lustrous surface of the Kerman. It is satiny to the touch, the short wool pile giving it body. I feel a hot uncomfortable burn in the pit of my stomach at such an extravagant gift.

"Darius . . ." I sigh. "These are lovely."

"They are perfect for your home, are they not?"

"Yes. And maybe a little extravagant."

"I suppose," he says, smiling, "the level of extravagance depends on your measure. If you place the value on cost alone, I paid what I could afford. The dollar amount exchanged is immaterial to me. I do not see why it should be a concern to you."

"They are lovely. You chose perfectly." I should not have been quite so honest about my feelings because I've bruised his.

"For myself, I value a gift by the enjoyment I hope the receiver will take in it. If I were to measure the pleasure I've found with you, these rugs are too small a gift. But, perhaps, the designs do not please you?" He twinkles, daring me to argue.

"They are lovely. You are very generous." How can I say anything else after such a gratifying as well as arm-twisting speech?

"*Bon.*" He lifts his brows. "*Ma petit colombe*, a piece of advice: When a man wants to give his lover a gift, a smile and gracious thank-you are the desired response."

I open my mouth to say . . . I'm not sure exactly. That I hate it when he calls me his little dove? That he's patronizing me again? He is expressing what is true from his perspective.

Waiting for a response, his brow furrows. "I hoped to delight you. I am selfish enough to want you to think of me with some fondness, not to forget." He gestures at the rugs.

"We are having a misunderstanding. The rugs are lovely. Thank you."

"I don't understand why you are unhappy. You say the right words, but I can see you are not pleased."

With Darius, what I think is complicated isn't, and what should be easy is the opposite. This may be a simple transaction for him, but it isn't for me.

Not that I'm sure it's all that simple for him, either. His gift is certainly generous—extremely generous. Yet knowing him the little that I do, I suspect a level of ego in his choice. He doesn't want an intimate relationship with me, or, from what I can tell, with any other woman, but in absentia, he has chosen to become a continuing and constant presence in my life, literally putting himself underfoot until the rugs wear out, a very long time from now.

Since our chat a week ago, I've thought a lot about what he said. He can't know how afraid I am that he is right.

I suspect that the end of our affair marks my exodus from the safe but meaningless sexual adventures I've enjoyed for the past five years, about to toss away my Rules to seek . . . more.

Seeking more means stepping into the unknown, a place where

hearts can spill over with love one minute and be shattered by loss the next. When I walk across these rugs for the first time, I won't merely be appreciating their color and how they enhance the beauty of my home, I'll be leaving the safe little prison I've fashioned for myself, exchanging it for an uncharted wilderness. I could be swallowed whole by some rapacious beast before I find my way to safety, because make no mistake, love is a monster—obsessive, unheeding, and deaf to reason.

I do not share my thoughts. I take Darius's hand. "You are right. It gives me immense pleasure to accept the rugs. Thank you. Thank you, so much." I rise on my toes to kiss his cheek.

"You must learn to be greedy and make no apology for it," he admonishes, apparently stuck on my initial reaction. "Take everything offered to you, *chérie*. Life does not gift us with all that much."

I recognize another of his absolutes, no doubt acquired through painful experience. A Darius Rule, perhaps.

"Shall I help you shift the furniture?" He is using his most formal tone as he gestures to the rugs.

I feel terrible that he thinks I'm ungrateful. "Thank you, but my neighbor has a strong son who can lend a hand tomorrow."

"Then I should go." He leans over to pick up his jacket.

"Stay for coffee," I suggest. "Please." I don't want to part on yet another awkward note.

He touches the end of my nose affectionately, making me feel a little easier about the last few minutes. "I had best go. I will see you when we return from our travels. You will visit to admire what I bring back from the Continent, and I will exclaim over your new work." His eyes twinkle.

"I will hold you to it," I say, glad to see his mood recover. "But wait just a moment. I have something for you, too."

He cocks his head in question. I hold up a hand, gesturing for him to wait.

I am not as sad that Darius won't stay as I would have predicted. Probably because I don't do confusion well, and these rugs have me flummoxed. Not that I'm not already flummoxed by C., and Darius, and the creative funk I've fallen into. I can hardly wait the few weeks until I head for Georgia where the solitude will help me figure all of this out—at least that's my hope.

In my office, I pick up the bound album I had made for Darius. The pictures inside are from our time together, beginning with the snapshots at the Water Mill and ending with the images I took at the auction in Saratoga. I've been looking forward to giving it to him.

"What is this?" he asks, when I present the album. He flips the pages. His hand stills halfway through, and then pushes the album fully open. The photograph Darius is studying shows him relaxing in his favorite chair. He is reading a letter from his sister with tenderness in his eyes and amusement in the soft upturn of his lips. It was obvious to me how much he loves her and was the only time I saw his feelings nakedly on display—until our *big love* discussion.

I didn't take the time to frame the shot carefully lest his expression change. Serendipitously, Darius is in sharp focus, while the low light and open aperture softened the background, resulting in an atmospheric portrait.

He studies the photograph for a few seconds more before snapping the book shut, beaming at me, his annoyance dissipated. "You have a great talent, Leezbeth. You see so clearly." He cups my cheek, offering a tender kiss.

Putting a little space between us, he adds, "Your wedding pictures don't allow you to express the fullness of your art. I will cherish this very fine gift."

"I'm glad you like it." Pleased by his delight with the album, I nevertheless feel the kick imbedded in his compliment. Really. I'm not imagining that, in his eyes, I'm not living up to my creative potential. This is already known to me. A hope for Georgia is that the trip will kick my creativity back into gear. Hearing what I already know voiced aloud, however, is depressing. No doubt Darius believes that while I see others clearly, I'm blind to my own desires.

One more time, he has knocked me sideways with his uncanny

knack for offering a steadying hand while simultaneously shoving me toward difficult truths.

Darius shrugs himself into his coat.

"Do not forget—I expect to see some very fine photographs in the spring." He folds his scarf against his throat and picks up the album. "And you must please give my best to Christopher."

My heart pounds as I see Darius to the door. After he drives away, I clip Obie to his lead for a turn around the perimeter of the house. The smell of wood smoke and decaying leaves scent the air. Cold bites my bones despite the heavy coat I'm wearing. I send up a little prayer to any god who may be listening: Please send clear weather at the end of the month, so my dog and I can deliver ourselves to a warmer climate immediately after Christmas.

After I've cleared the dishes and cleaned the kitchen, I return to the living room. Going to my knees, I roll up the rugs. They remind me too much that my affair with Darius has run its oddly dissonant course and left me with a lot to think about. I shove the bundled rugs under the sofa, out of sight for the time being.

"Obie," I say, motioning to come with a tilt of my head, "bedtime for people and dogs."

Curled in his favorite spot—a corner of the sofa where a dog can survey his kingdom from both the front and side windows—Obie manages a sleepy tail wag. Otherwise, he ignores me.

"Dogster—I'm not kidding," I say sternly. "One male desertion a night is all I can handle." He gives me a hard look. We face off. Reluctantly, he drops to the floor.

As I climb the stairs with Obie leading the way, I tell myself that no matter the depth of involvement, the end of an affair is bittersweet. "I don't know, Obs, I think maybe I wasn't as successful with Rule Number Ten as I should have been."

Rule Number Ten: If your heart won't stay out of the equation, it's time to leave.

My poodle looks over his rump at me. He could care less about anything except that I'm following, since I was the one who insisted he move himself from sofa to bed. Brushing my teeth, I speculate that Darius only ever wanted Julianne and can't move on to love someone else. This isn't new information. I intuitively understood it that first afternoon when coffee turned into drinks and then dinner. Yet, as I slide into bed, Obie curled at my feet, I have a blinding flash of the obvious: Just like Darius, I haven't been rejecting love so much as refusing to love anyone except Roland.

My heart stutters. Ever since Roland, I've behaved like Charles Dickens's Miss Havisham. After being jilted at the altar, she spent the rest of her life denying herself any further chance for love and happiness. Instead of washing her hands of the man who broke her heart and living life to the fullest—the best revenge, if you ask me—she remained willfully stuck in time, feeling sorry for herself, surrounded by the moldering trappings of what should have been her wedding feast. But haven't I behaved similarly, refusing to move on, while Roland has a new wife and child?

I sit up and place a hand on Obie's back. He raises his head in alarm. "It's okay," I say. Only it isn't. I can hardly breathe as the heavy weight of this new truth settles over me. I considered myself a brave women when I came up with my Rules and defended them to Arielle, Diana, and my mother as a courageous new frontier. But what if the opposite is true?

The idea so radical, as well as frightening, that I pull the covers over my head. Huddling inside their protective warmth, I decide to do a Scarlet O'Hara, and think about this tomorrow, or two weeks and a day after tomorrow . . . in Georgia.

PART THREE
~ KIT ~

CHAPTER 16

CONSULTING KIT'S INSTRUCTIONS, I exit I-95 at Darien, Georgia, and make my way to Route 17, the old highway that skirts the shore, a two-lane until it reaches the outskirts of the town, where it widens before returning to its former width to cross a long concrete bridge spanning the Altamaha River. The Altamaha is one of an expansive system of waterways running from Virginia to Florida. This close to the sea, the river flows into channels, some wide, some narrow, creating small islands and vast wetlands as it spills into the Atlantic.

Fields of wheaten winter marsh grass bracket the swiftly moving water, tinted pop-art pink and turquoise by the low-slanting early-evening sunlight. I consider pulling off to capture a particularly spectacular vista, but our eighteen-hour drive is almost over. By Kit's calculation, his home is less than ten minutes away. I stay my course.

A few miles later, the watery landscape gives way to pine and oak woodlands. A whitewashed paddock fence appears, indicated by Kit's directions to be the boundary of a local historical site and my cue to slow. Checking Obie in the rearview mirror, I see he is sitting up. The change in the car's speed tells him we will be stopping shortly. Obs is more heartily sick of traveling than I am.

"Here at last," I announce as I turn left, also as instructed, at the second road after the park's fence. New Field Road, once I bump onto it, is less road than unpaved sand track running into the woods. When I spy brick pillars guarding an open wooden gate tucked into the oaks, I turn again. A small plaque reads, "Willing, 1761."

We crunch onto a crushed-shell drive. Past the gate, the trees thin and the view opens to manicured pastures enclosed by white fencing of the same type we just passed. The driveway curves around massive live

oaks cloaked in Spanish moss. The trees form a living archway overhead, the moss swaying in spooky slow motion as we pass underneath.

A house comes into view. As Kit asserted, it isn't Tara but a
well-maintained, moderate-sized clapboard farmhouse with clean lines
and two single-story side extensions. I presume the raised foundation
is a precaution against storm tides. A deep screened-in porch runs the
length of the marsh-facing, just visible as the drive curves to the left.

Trade the broad overhanging oaks for maples, lower the foundation by half, and the building would integrate seamlessly into a Vermont hillside. A small red barn sits at our right. I turn into a parking
area between barn and house.

Obie leans over the front seat, tail wagging. I clip him to his lead. A
light comes on in the house's extension closest to the parking area. My
feet hit crushed shell. The air is warm enough for my sweater to be all
the insulation I need against the evening chill.

Pushing past me, Obie jumps to the ground. He shakes himself,
prances a circle, woofs with delight, and circles again with his nose high,
sniffing the air. It is hard to know who is more pleased to have arrived,
me or my dog.

"Handsome animal," my landlord remarks with a smile as he
bounds down his back steps.

Christopher Aiken Couper is not what I expected. I had envisioned
one of those men who looks like a boy forever—Johnny Carson gone
slightly to seed. But Kit is neither beefy nor blond. His hair is wavy
salt and pepper, his facial features angular. There are laugh lines at the
corners of his brown eyes, and nothing about his body is past its prime.
The man is tall and slim with wide shoulders and the privileged athletic
carriage I associate with the Kennedys and their ilk.

To complete the stereotype I had worked up in my head, I'd dressed
him in a pastel sport shirt and those odd patchwork slacks golfers sometimes wear. Where I get these ideas is anyone's guess.

Kit is dressed in a T-shirt that shows off his broad shoulders and
trim torso, paired with jeans thinning at the knees. I guess him to be

about my age or a few years older. He is also far more attractive than I anticipated. I offer up a broad smile. Sometimes I'm delighted to be wrong.

"Liz, welcome—welcome."

My shoulder receives a hello pat. I wonder if it would have been a hand shake if I didn't have the dog lead in one hand and a poop bag in the other.

"I hope my directions were useful?" Kit asks.

"Perfect."

"Glad to hear." He holds out a key attached to a leather tie. "I turned up the heat over there. It's been colder than usual these past few days. Brought some wood in as well, should you want to fire up the wood stove."

"Thanks. That's really thoughtful." I transfer the poop bag to the hand holding the leash to take the key.

Kit smiles again. Lines at the corners of his eyes crinkle attractively.

"The temperature out here feels great to me. My daughter texted to say the mercury never moved past the single digits in Vermont today."

"I feel cold when the temperature dips into the low fifties." Kit rubs his forearms, looking amused. "You Yankees are made of stern stuff." He tilts his head toward the other side of the drive. "Sam's place has a quirk or two you might want to know about, but maybe you'd like to settle in first? The quirks aren't life threatening and can wait until tomorrow, if you'd rather."

In the quickly descending darkness, it takes me a few seconds to locate the renovated barn I will be calling home for the next few months, hidden inside the shade of two enormous oaks. Unlike Kit's house, this one is tabby, a natural cement made from ash, crushed shells, and sand. But like its clapboard neighbor across the way, the porch is deep, wrapping all the way around to the back.

"I'm beat even though it's barely 5:30," I admit. "The tour sounds good for tomorrow. My plan is to empty the car, have a snack, and go to bed."

"You've got it. Can I help you unload?"

"I won't refuse," I say gratefully. "First, though, Obie needs to do some sniffing around. Should I knock when we're finished?"

"Do you think he would be okay with me? You drive in. Obie and I will follow."

"Sure." I hold the lead out to him.

"The parking area is on the other side of that big oak." Kit points at the far side of my winter abode where there is a tree with a trunk a good eight feet around. He takes the lead but refuses the bag. "I'll take my chances," he says, his mouth quirking at the side.

Yikes. He's show-stopping when he smiles, his eyes crinkling attractively into well-established laugh lines. I return his smile, telling myself I'm in photographer mode, not pheromone mode, as I try to justify my notice.

With my landlord's help, the car empties quickly. By the time we're finished, I'm way too tired to unpack. Or have a conversation with Diana. I had promised to let her know when I arrived, but she'll want a level of description I'm incapable of providing at the moment; so, once my landlord departs, I text her and Arielle to announce I've arrived and promise more intel in the morning.

On the way down yesterday, I stopped at a BI-LO grocery store, a chain we don't have in New England, where I picked up a few provisions. In the kitchen, I discover Kit has stocked the fridge with sandwich fixings along with milk and eggs. A box of coffee cartridges sits on the gray stone counter. I need to remember to thank him for his hospitality. My plan for peanut butter and crackers morphs into a more sustaining turkey and Vermont cheddar sandwich.

I don't believe for a minute Kit chose that cheese by accident. Already inclined to like him, my heart squeezes and my eyes begin to tear, a regular occurrence since saying good-bye to Darius. I plop onto a stool at the counter where I've already set my sandwich.

During the trip, alone with the road and the past, I accepted that I never finished grieving over Roland. Instead, I shoved my grief into boxes and deep-sixed them inside my subconscious. The Rules kept the feelings locked away—until they didn't. Which leaves me, five years later, not so much trying to get over a man I should have left behind years ago, but mourning all of the time I've lost in the process.

I dab at my eyes with the corner of a paper towel repurposed as a napkin. Setting it down newly crumpled, I pick up the sandwich and bite. Since tearing up is my new normal, it doesn't stop me from other activities, like eating. While I chew, I decide that basing tender feelings for my landlord on his purchase of my favorite cheese indicates I'm punch drunk with exhaustion.

Obie, who has finished licking out his dinner bowl, pushes his weight into the side of my leg. His eyes roll to mine.

"It's okay," I tell him.

But as usual these days, it isn't okay. He doesn't, however, need reasons to be a sad doggie wreck when his human has the job aced.

❋

Stretched out beside me, Obie offers a lazy tail wag when I leave the bed the next the morning. This bedroom, the only one on the ground floor, faces the marsh, which is why I picked it, although the traditional decor isn't to my taste. Padding across the oriental carpet, I open the plantation shutters over the doors to the back porch. The view is of flat pasture, a sliver of marsh, and the vast cloudless sky—far more sky than our mountains allow in Vermont. The temperature is balmy when I push a door open to test the air.

"Obster," I say, "we are going to like it here."

Once I'm dressed, Obs takes me on a meandering morning pee-promenade to the front gate while I do a mental review of the day's projects. First on the list: unpack and set up my home-away-from-home office. When that's done, I need to drive into Brunswick, the nearest big town, for a serious pantry stocking.

The unpacking goes smoothly until I can't open the bedroom closet doors to store my hanging clothes. The doors aren't locked, but they nevertheless refuse to open. After several ineffective yanks, and wary of breaking the antique pulls, I give up. Betting the problem is on the house's idiosyncrasies list, I make a mental note to ask my handsome landlord about it.

Trailed by a large black Obie shadow with a his tail drooping, I head into the den that will be my office for the next few months. I think Obs is worried that if he takes his eyes off me, I might disappear.

"Come here, beast." I bend to wrap an arm around him. He rests his snout on my shoulder. "No more long car rides. That's a promise." I give his ribs a last thunk and enter the office, home to some serious man-toys, including a gargantuan television and an impressive iPod dock shaped like a futuristic football. The furniture includes a glass-topped desk, a Knoll desk chair, and a pair of modernist wood and leather lounge chairs with matching ottomans, a sleek side table between them. Though the room is furnished sparely and overwhelmingly modern, the sisal rug, wood-plank walls, and ceiling open to the rafters give it warmth. Light pours thorough large double windows on one wall. The view is of pastureland to the west. On the opposite wall, more windows face the marsh.

By the time I've configured the equipment and turned on the computer, noon has come and gone. The WiFi password left on a sticky note does its job. I download my e-mails and deal with a couple of booking inquiries, leaving communication with friends for later.

On the way into Brunswick, I put in a call to Diana.

"I'm loving the landscape. It's so different from home. And the temperature is a balmy sixty-four degrees," I say after we greet each other. "How are you?"

"I'm fine. Enjoying the break. Marc is home in Clarendon, but he'll be back at the end of the week. I can't believe he lives only an hour from Ashburton and our paths never crossed."

As Diana's mother, I'm *very* interested in meeting Marc, the math-class boy, especially since my daughter was so dismissive of his chances. Yet three months after their coffee un-date, they are still seeing each other.

"That's nice." I hope a low-key response will prevent Diana from going off on a rant about how I'm projecting a future she's not sure she wants. "Any fun plans?"

"Nope. I'm tired and saving my energy for next term."

"You're too young to be so tired."

"And you're too old to have *so* much energy."

We laugh. It's an old joke. Long ago, my daughter and I accepted our energy outputs aren't the same. Hers is more like her father's, with peaks and valleys. Mine is a more of a steady high-pitched hum, like my mother's, although hers is so righteously purposeful. I want to believe mine is more practically purposeful.

"Call me next time something interesting happens, Mom."

"You do the same," I tell her. With love-yous, we sign off.

✳

Obie and I return with a week's worth of groceries. Once they are stored behind assorted kitchen cabinet doors, I wander from room to room. I have no other activities planned for the day, except to relax, which isn't easy for someone with purposeful energy. Humming energy or not, I am tired from the drive. Negotiating around Washington fried my rural-girl brain, not to mention the speed of the traffic all the way down here and sheer number of cars on the road. Acclimating myself to unfamiliar surroundings, along with the uncertainty about whether I did right by coming here, only add to my après-travel jitters.

Exercise is always good therapy, and I need to get into my lapsed habit of carrying a camera wherever I go. Grabbing the point-and-shoot camera, I attach Obie to his lead. Obs has to be coaxed outside. He thinks he's in for another ride, but once I get him past the car, he prances ahead, happy to go exploring.

I'm a lot mellower an hour later. Obie is cheerful, too, tail held high as we reenter the house. Nothing like chasing bird shadows and squirrels—and dragging me along—to make a dog happy. Between draggings, I managed to snap a few promising photographs as the late-afternoon light shimmered through the oaks.

Past documenting a specific moment, photography is about the way light describes an object, whether the object is a person, thing, or landscape. This may seem obvious and simple, yet manipulating a camera into capturing what the eye sees is more difficult than it might seem. As a teenager with my first camera, I snapped an atmospheric black-and-white of a foggy ocean view. Imagine my surprise when the developed film delivered a perfectly sharp image of waves and sky. I've learned a lot since then, and this afternoon the camera and I were one.

Downloading the shots to the Mac, I feel a glimmer of creative hope as the thumbnails populate the screen. The photographs are good, although no better than any other competent photographer could accomplish. However, I refuse to be disappointed. The mere fact that I was inspired to snap those pictures is a step forward after years of standing in place.

What a change three days can make! Vermont is all mountains, hills, and valleys. I haven't seen a hill since I drove through North Carolina, never mind a mountain. As far as the eye can see, the landscape is low and flat with more sky than anywhere I've visited outside of the high plains of Texas.

Here, instead of frigid temperatures and white snowfields, the only white on view is the paddock fencing and high, fair-weather clouds. A brisk breeze lifts the Spanish moss, which sways so slowly that it seems to defy gravity. Even the shadows are different here. At home, the maples create dappled shade; at Willing, the shade is streaked by the moss.

The differences don't end there. Back home, the brush along roadsides is home to slim grape vines. Here, whatever it is climbing the oaks—jessamine, and other flora I haven't yet identified—is as thick around as a strong man's arm. There is something horror-movie spooky about those vines snaking into the trees. The resurrection ferns, though tiny, add another level of strange. When I drove in yesterday, they were shriveled into dry little claws. I didn't hear rain in the night, but the ferns told the story. Today, when Obie and I took our morning walk, they had unfurled, bright green and vigorous.

If the weather is nice tomorrow, I plan to explore the area south of Darien where the views tempted me on the way in. I'll take the Nikon. It weighs more and is bulkier to handle than the compact Sony I took with me today, but the lens and high pixel capacity give it superior capabilities.

Returning to the kitchen, I open the refrigerator to contemplate the contents. Not in the mood to cook, I pull out the carrots and hummus.

"Well, Obie," I yawn, dipping a carrot stick, "here's to the engines of industry restoring themselves in the next couple of days." I hold the carrot high to salute Darius, because I wouldn't be here if not for him. I suppose I should also thank him for making me face the truths I have been avoiding but decide to hold off on that one until I see what good it does for me.

I wonder if I'll receive a postcard from him. This thought is a reminder to arrange for my mail to be forwarded. I'll have to ask Kit for Willing's mailing address. I add the note to my mental list along with the sticky closet door.

✳

A few hours later, Obie and I leave the porch for his last pee of the day. He tows me up the drive past the reach of the porch light. Hoping we're not on the trail of southern wildlife with big teeth, I cautiously follow him into the darkness. On the far side of the barn, Obs gives an unassuming fence post special attention. I wait while he decides if it's worth spritzing. He's still deciding when headlights appear at the gate. Flashing in and out of the oaks, they move toward us.

Kit offers us a wave as his silver Audi cruises past. My poodle snorts, decides the post will do, and sprays the dirt in front of it. Business done, he prances after the car, ears and tail held high.

"Hey, Liz." Kit unfolds himself from the sedan with the lovely smile that crinkles the corners of his eyes.

"Evening," I hail.

My landlord ambles in our direction looking really good in a tux.

He is obviously returning from a fancy social event. His wavy, silver-streaked hair has been tamed away from his face, accentuating high cheekbones and the hard line of his jaw. He looks sleekly elegant from the top of his head to the tips of his polished black shoes—Italian, if I'm any judge.

"Who knew you'd clean up so nicely," I purr, then cringe. Exhaustion adversely affects my ability to keep wayward thoughts inside my head where they belong. Tonight I'm having my usual reaction to a handsome man in a suit—and this one is especially handsome, as is his eveningwear. Working so many weddings, I recognize couture when I see it.

Kit is not offended by the remark. He throws his head back and laughs, a wonderful husky sound that would do something naughty to my insides if I weren't chagrined by what I just said. Sure, compliments are great conversation starters, but this one was a little too flirtatious for this stage in the game, particularly since flirting isn't on my prescribed list for this Southern sojourn.

"If I'm not mistaken, you're wearing Tom Ford." I hope the observation will distract both of us from the previous one. Kit's eyebrows rise in surprise.

I explain, "In my line of work I've become something of an expert on formal wear."

Not a lot of men can wear Ford because he cuts so close to the body. You have to be in really good shape and, even so, the styling favors trim, long-muscled men like Kit—my favorite kind. I feel a little sizzle where I shouldn't, not if I'm going to stick to the plan to do a great deal of serious thinking before I do more jumping . . . or backsliding (pun intended).

Obie tugs us forward, intent on greeting Mr. Tuxedo, who bends to give him a scrub behind the ears. "My mother will love that you recognized her designer of choice," he says, straightening.

"Your mother?"

"I imagine you are thinking that a man who is about to hit the half-century mark shouldn't allow his mother to influence his clothing choices." He turns his palm out, three fingers raised Boy Scout pledge style, and earnestly swears, "This is the only sartorial choice she's been allowed to participate in since I was a child."

"I sense a story," I say with a laugh.

"Isn't there always a story?"

"I suppose. Though a good raconteur is required to make it entertaining."

He grins, one brow lifting. "Is that a challenge?"

"Why not?"

"I like challenges. Care for a nightcap and a story?"

"Sure." A little flirting doesn't mean we'll end up in bed, I assure myself, even as the thought of him in bed sends a happy shiver to places that should remain shiver-free—not that a little fantasizing is going to harm me.

"Oh darn." I frown. "I'd better take another rain check. I'm not comfortable leaving Obie alone in the house yet, especially if he senses I'm close."

Maybe this is for the best. I should probably keep my fantasies focused on an outlet for my creativity rather than on my charming landlord.

"Bring him along," Kit says.

"You sure?" I'm a little too pleased my better instincts are being thwarted. I suspect I'm about to enter the flirting ring where all bets are off about how many rounds I can go before I am KO'd by lust.

We turn toward his house.

"I wanted to stop by this morning but I had an early closing and figured you might be sleeping in after your drive." He tilts his head toward his brother's abode. "Everything okay over there?"

"Great. And, so far, I've encountered only one quirk—the closet doors of the master bedroom refuse to open. They aren't locked. I checked."

"Probably swelled while the house was closed up."

"My theory as well."

He stops walking. "How about we relocate our nightcap so I can take a look?"

"I'd love you to have a go at those doors, but I haven't put in a liquor supply yet."

"I happen to know where my brother keeps his stash and have no compunctions about raiding it."

I nod. "Okay. I'll restock as needed."

Obie takes the lead, prancing in front of us as we reverse direction. Kit lays his palm low on my back.

I love the courtliness of this gesture. I liked it when Darius used it, too. But as the warmth of Kit's hand begins to travel through the fabric of my shirt, a dangerous little switch trips. My heart hesitates a beat, my skin tingles, and the planet seems to spin a fraction slower—enough slower that I notice the sweet dark scent of Willing's soil and the distant hoot of a barred owl. Overhead, I swear, the stars begin to multiply inside the heavenly depths.

Kit's hand falls away as we reach the porch steps. If only my intense awareness of him had fallen with it. I tell myself to put a damper on the magical realism. And, I curse the Tom Ford suit.

My broad-shouldered landlord holds the door open. Inside, he aims us in the direction of the living room. Easy in his body, he strides to the built-in cabinets between the French doors to the porch. I veer toward the seating area.

Needing a distraction, I admire the painting hanging behind the sofa. The artist has depicted a sliver of marsh against a broad coastal sky. I would love to shoot an image of similar impressionistic beauty.

I glance at Kit. He has a cabinet door open, revealing a selection of liquor, along with bottles of spring water and mixers. Pulling two highball glasses from a shelf, he reaches for the Jack Daniel's. "What can I get you?" he asks, pivoting toward me.

"The same," I say.

A minute later, he walks over with a tumbler in each hand. There is an inch and a half of amber Kentucky whiskey mixed with a splash of water in each glass.

"Have you had a chance to make ice?" he asks.

"I'll fetch it." I take the tumblers, careful not to touch him.

"Why don't I get that closet door unstuck in the meantime," he offers. Not waiting for a reply, he ambles down the hall. Obie, the traitor, ambles after him. I fantasize about following, although with a different purpose, wanting Kit to open me up instead of those doors.

Get a grip! I pivot toward the kitchen where I attempt to drop some metaphorical ice on my libido while dropping the real thing into our glasses. I usually love having such an immediate response to a man, but tonight I could do without it.

Obs is lying on the carpet keeping an eye on our guest when I walk into the bedroom a couple of minutes later. Kit is contemplating the closet doors. A frown creases his brow.

"See what I mean?" I motion to the doors.

He grasps a door knob with both hands. "They just need a good tug," he says through gritted teeth. Putting a shoulder into it, he lifts, yanks—and voilà—the door springs open.

"Well done," I congratulate.

He closes and opens the doors a couple of times, noting there is still a little bit of resistance.

"Why is it," I say, "that some objects require a dose of testosterone to make them behave? I tried the same move without your success."

"Maybe you greased the way," Kit suggests diplomatically.

I hand him his drink. "Or maybe it's magic. The male touch is 'open sesame' to stuck doors, overtightened bolts, and cars that won't turn over." Although I'm joking, I've noticed the phenomenon enough times to take it seriously. "I suppose the truth is, dads teach their sons about mechanical things but don't always do the same for their daughters. Whatever the reason, my testosterone theory has legs." And other significant body parts, I think, but manage to keep this thought to myself.

"I give thanks every day for the few things left in this world you gals can't do for yourselves. Makes me feel useful."

I consider all of the ways I could reply and decide it's best that I don't, although I can't suppress my acknowledging smile. One corner of his mouth quirks. I turn, retracing my steps to the living room with Kit behind me. Obie brings up the rear.

"You might want to run some soap across the top tomorrow," he says, waiting for me to seat myself before he collapses into a club chair and stretches his long legs out with a contented sigh. "I could plane it a little, but I'm betting after a week or so with the heat on, the problem will disappear on its own." He takes a healthy swallow of his drink.

"In Vermont, if soap or duct tape won't solve the problem, the other all-purpose solution—bag balm—probably will."

Kit salutes me with his glass. "Here's to folk wisdom."

Here's to brawn—another thought I keep to myself. Unfortunately, even if I am keeping a few of my more wayward thoughts to myself, I'm way too interested. "Was the door on the idiosyncrasies list?" I ask.

"Nope. But there is a key and the lock can be difficult, so I was going to tell you not to lock that closet. Also, I've been meaning to glue one of the kitchen chairs. Don't sit in the one without a cushion; it won't end well."

"Got it. Anything else?"

"Please turn the thermostat to fifty-five degrees or so if you leave overnight. And watch the kitchen faucet. The handle has to be pushed down and to the right or it may drip. I don't know why Sam hasn't replaced it."

"I will manage, now that I know the trick."

We sip our whiskey. My companion doesn't launch into the story I'm waiting to hear.

"So," I prompt. "About that suit . . ."

He smiles. "Isn't much of a story. I confess to angling for your company. I thought a tale or two might help."

I raise my brows at his player-boy smarm. "Sadly, you bought my company with the promise of a good story. Pony up, Mr. Couper."

"Sadly, dahlin', I'm thinking you didn't read the fine print."

"Why are you stalling?" I'm enjoying his banter way too much.

"Negotiating, not stalling." He winks, finishes off his whiskey, and rises to fix himself another. "You have to promise a story in return. Then, I'll tell you about this ol' suit."

I roll my eyes but say, "Sure. What do you want to hear? The Three Little Pigs? Goldilocks?"

"A true story. Something from your life. Maybe a small secret like I'm going to tell you."

"Not Bluebeard, then?"

He shakes his head. His mouth quirks. "I'm suggesting a small secret, not a dark one, but hey, your choice."

"I'll work on it." I can't think of a single interesting story from my recent life that I'd want to share except maybe the one about the time Obie got into the cupcakes while I was out and stored a half a dozen of them around the house for later.

Kit reseats himself and tugs at his stiffly starched shirtfront. When he's arranged himself to his satisfaction, he says, "Okay. First, you need to know, I don't like clothing that draws attention to itself or to me. And second, I'm a fan of wearing clothes 'til they fall apart."

"Interesting details, since the suit you are creasing is of recent vintage and definitely shouts 'look at me.'"

Kit responds with a grimace and begins stripping off his jacket, no easy trick when it's as fitted as this one. I rise and motion for him to hand the jacket over once he's done wrestling his way out of it.

While I have photographed brides and grooms and their entourages wearing thousands of dollars' worth of wedding attire, it isn't often that I handle clothing this fine. Kit's jacket has a heft and construction all about the good things money can buy. Carrying it over one arm, I smell his cologne, some sort of spice with a hint of musk. I reach inside the entryway closet for a hanger and carefully suspend the jacket from the cornice above the door.

In my absence, my landlord has made himself more comfortable. His shirt collar was open when he drove in, his bow tie loose. Since I left the room, he has removed his tie, and gold knot cufflinks. His sleeves have been rolled, exposing angular wrists and forearms roped with muscle.

I wonder what he does for exercise. Men who do a lot of lifting have bulkier bodies. Maybe he's a runner. If so, that's not all he does, not with those shoulders. Wanting to get him talking as well as to distract myself from his anatomy, I offer a theory. "Is it possible this story is about two suits?"

"One of the things I like about you already, Ms. Lizzie, is you don't miss the subtext."

How true, I want to tell him, but I'm determined not to add another distraction or clear a path to more flirting, even if flirting has definitely become the evening's subtext.

"My previous formal attire was perfectly serviceable no matter that it was purchased the year after I graduated from college."

"Are you telling me you've worn the same size for almost thirty years?"

"Granted, the Brooks could get a little snug at times, necessitating the waist be let out. Other times I had to notch my belt tighter, but sure, it still fit."

"Amazing. It's a wonder the termites didn't eat it."

"You mean moths."

"I mean termites. That suit must have been petrified after three decades of wear."

He laughs. "Nah, Brooks Brothers makes clothing to last. Besides, how many times is an evening suit worn after those first few years after college when your friends all couple up? I don't think I wore mine more than once a year after I hit thirty, and not even that when the boys were young. It's only in the last few years that I've attended more charity events and required formal attire on a regular basis."

"How many sons and how old?" I ask, knowing people usually enjoy talking about themselves and their families, which suits me because I'm interested in learning more about him—another ominous sign.

"Noah is twenty-two. Levi is three years older." He pauses to take a sip of his drink. "Darius mentioned you have a daughter."

"I do. Diana is in her second year of college and a force to be reckoned with."

"Good for you for bringing a strong woman into the world. We need more of them."

"We do," I concur, pleased by his opinion. I'm curious about the women in his life. Not just his mother, but the mother of his children. He is living alone. Where did a wife enter and exit the picture? I'm sure he's willing to say more about his sons—what proud papa wouldn't?—but like ex-husbands, ex-wives can be a conversation killer. Either the guy clams up, or, as my lawyer pal Elliot so aptly demonstrated, he'll talk about his divorce and his grievances to a disturbing degree, so I have no plans to find out about Kit's wife, since his marital status shouldn't concern me anyway.

Feeling more virtuous about the goals of my stay, I say, "I look forward to trading more information about our families, but you promised me a particular story and I'm waiting for it." I lean forward, setting my glass on the coffee table between us. "We have established the prehistoric tux had some wear left in it—by your estimation. So, how did your mom influence the purchase of a new one?"

He shakes his head. I smile, curious about his suit story, his family story, whatever he wants to talk about. The twists and turns of people's lives never fail to fascinate me. Even though landscapes are my first love, I enjoy portraiture and my sitters relax under my genuine interest in their lives. Taking a good picture is easier when the person in front of the camera is not hiding from it or from me. Kit would make a good subject.

"Just a guess," I say. "Your mother didn't see eye to eye with you about the Brooks Brothers tux."

"Correct. Dad died four years ago and since then, as the oldest of her men and the closest geographically, it has fallen upon me to escort my mother to various social engagements. But she declared my services subpar. Not because of any action on my part, mind you. Nevertheless, I was accused of not upholding the family values."

"I'm sorry to hear about your dad."

Kit rubs a palm over the back of his neck. "Yeah, it was a hard thing." A beat of silence tells me he isn't going to elaborate and it's still a hard thing.

I know from experience that big grief requires a long recovery. If he's anything like me, four years is just a start.

"What your mom said? It's such a textbook Jewish-mother comment," I offer.

Kit chuckles. "Funny—the Jews in the closet are on the other side."

"You're a member of my tribe? I'm shocked. Jewish Southern white boys are not something I've come across before, although they are rumored to exist." Traditionally, Jewishness is traced through the mother's line, but I'm not going to disagree with Kit if he wants to claim his heritage.

"I would hazard a guess that Great-Great-Grandpa Jarrett's Bostonian family—he's the founder of the Willing branch of the Couper clan—felt the same. Jarrett was one of Sherman's officers. Did some looking around for opportunities when the War ended. That's how we established ourselves down here."

My eyes widen. "I definitely want to hear that story, too."

"Let's save it for another day. I'll trade it to learn what it's like to be Jewish in Vermont. That can't be the usual, either."

"Only nine other Jewish kids in town when my daughter was growing up," I say, "and one African-American family. I grew up in Massachusetts. But back to you—an interfaith marriage right after the Civil War, especially in the South, had to be a rarity. Did the bride's family disown her?"

"Not at all. My theory is that with so many dead sons of the Confederacy, when the guns stopped firing, a good man of any stripe wasn't turned away." He points at me. "I'm thinking we're two little Jewish fish swimming upstream in our own individual ways."

I laugh, imagining fish, probably carp, in yarmulkes.

"Let's return to the suit story. We left off with your mom enjoying your company. That's lovely. I have no idea whether my mother enjoys my company."

"And for her love, I spend way more nights gadding about than pleases me."

"Come on, it can't be that bad."

"Depends on the food," he quips.

"Food is important. So is dancing. I work a lot of weddings, and men who know how to jitterbug, never mind waltz, are getting thinner on the ground. Too bad, since they definitely have more fun than their dance-impaired pals." With the curtain down on Darius, it would be nice to know if there might be another dance partner in the vicinity, even if it's only a vicinity of three months' duration—in the aid of gaining theoretical knowledge only—of course.

"A Southern gentleman knows how to dance," Kit says.

"Aren't you painting with broad brush?"

"But true."

"Even if I were to believe you, there's a distance between knowing how to dance and enjoying it." I picture Kit as my new tango partner. This conjures where the last tango led me. I try to erase the idea from my mind but it won't leave.

"Depends on the lady the man has in his arms." Kit winks and the side of his mouth pulls up in the lopsided grin I'm beginning to recognize as pure mischief.

Oh boy. It's obvious we have chemistry. It's also obvious he's a player—with a capital P. Flirting is like breathing to guys like him. I remind myself that his interest isn't personal, that he can't help himself. *That he's kind of like me.* Or, like me for the last five years. I haven't a clue what *like me* means today, which is why I shouldn't be contemplating our chemistry, or dancing.

"So your mother got tired of seeing you in the same old suit, and . . ." I make a circle with my hand, encouraging him to continue.

"I suspect her reasons were more complex. Not that reasons matter. Let me tell you, a true Southern lady is exceedingly skilled at getting a man to do her bidding, particularly when the lady is his mother begging the favor." He leans toward me, resting those lovely forearms on his knees. "My mother is the quintessential flower of Southern womanhood, born and bred in Charleston." He looks seriously into my eyes, although the glint in his own suggests he's laying it on thick.

"I've always wondered how that's done," I say, playing along. "We Northern gals tend to come straight out with what we want—an imperfect technique, although it works well enough with a frying pan in your hand."

Kit chuckles. "The other half of the equation generally doesn't respond well to brute force. The key, dahlin', is to make your man feel protective. When a fella can ride to your rescue, he's bound to do as you ask and feel good about it, too."

"I suppose it isn't polite to point out that your theory is sexist. But, your theory is sexist." My nose wrinkles. I find his ideas both fascinating and repellant.

"Men are a primitive bunch, Ms. Lizzie. Trust me, I have inarguable experience."

"Too much subterfuge for me," I say, with a lift of my brows. "I don't have a manipulative bone in my entire body, although to be honest, I admit there are times when, as repellent as I find the kind of games we're discussing, I wish I knew how to play them. It's good to have a wide variety of tools in one's arsenal for all sorts of reasons."

I suppose there are women who could find my ethics a little too flexible, but I'm a practical woman; I don't think we're going to overthrow thousands of years of sexual politics anytime soon. Sighing dramatically, I throw a palm to my forehead. "Perhaps I should consider tucking a few magnolias among my frying pans?"

"You should," Kit says, ignoring my theatricals. "We're talking about a reciprocal exchange. The gentleman is flattered and feels important; his lady gets what she wants. Everyone wins." He presses his lips together. Deviltry brightens his eyes. "I'm sure my mother would give you lessons if you ask politely."

I harrumph again, though I'm delighted by our banter. "The key here is how long she'd been trying to talk you out of that old suit. Exactly how long was it?"

He squints at his glass for a second before pronouncing, "Three years, give or take."

"Then I'm not sure about those lessons. The 'Southern Belle's Gentle Art of Persuasion' is not all that effective if it took three years to yield results." I reach for my glass.

"See, that's the difference between the North and South right there. Most Southern ladies of my acquaintance wouldn't share that observation, even though they might think it, or considerably worse." His mouth quirks at the corner again. "Or maybe you're just less patient than my mother."

"Should I apologize?" I smile sweetly. "I'm sorry I maligned your mother by suggesting she's not all that successful at wrapping you around her little finger."

"Now, now. In Mom's defense, I'm a hard case. She can cite any number of instances from my childhood when she was sure I'd end up a delinquent because I never let on that her reprimands made any impression. If you listen to my mother, it's a wonder I eat with cutlery and not my fingers, never mind that my mailing address isn't one penitentiary or another."

I laugh. "I'll look forward to hearing a few particulars if I ever cross paths with her."

"I have no doubt you will."

How did we get from stuck closet doors to meeting his mother? Voicing this question, however, will only suck me deeper. "Okay, Kit, about this suit story already?"

His face lights. "Nothing to it, really. My mother found a way to twist my arm—the leverage will not be disclosed—and off we went to buy a fancy new suit."

"I'm siding with her." I wonder if I'll ever be privy to the specificity of the arm-twisting, mentally commending the woman for getting her boy out of that ancient out-of-fashion garment and into one that turns him into such a swoon-worthy peacock. I'm betting she drags him to all of those events hoping he'll attract another wife. Then again, he's entirely too charming as well as too attractive not to have women swarming all over him no matter what he's wearing, which is, I'm sure, how this player-boy likes it—another reason to keep my distance. I've never enjoyed being part of a swarm.

"Yes, good for Mom, but feel a little sorry for me," Kit says. "There I was, totally at the mercy of Mr. George and his assistants, who, with my mother goading them on, decided this . . . this . . ." He trails off and pats his shirtfront, his brow wrinkling. "It took three fittings to produce the glorious vision you see before you."

Lest I take this last bit of puffery too seriously, he adds one of his mischievous smiles.

If we are going to spend the evening spouting stereotypes, why not lay out a few more, so I say, "I imagine the belles of your acquaintance are not unhappy with your transformation. Not many men of 'a certain age' can carry off couture with quite your . . ."—I search for the right word—". . . savoir faire," I conclude with a little twirl of my index fingers.

He scowls again. "I miss that old tux. Good Lord—I'm assured this is a perfect fit, but it's hardly comfortable."

"Now you know what the fairer sex goes through to look good for you boys. Just do what those of us with matching chromosomes do—suck in your stomach, shimmy into some spandex, and suffer for fashion."

"Unpleasant," he says.

"Me or my philosophy?" I ask, taking a sip of whiskey.

"Oh, definitely your philosophy. And this getup. I want the ol' tux back. Though for the record, I have a new appreciation for women who eschew tight anything for loose and comfortable clothing."

"As you should," I concur, taking stock of my own outfit, a loose knit top with an asymmetrical hem and boot-cut jeans with plenty of spandex in the weave.

Leaning back in his seat, Kit crosses his arms behind his head and arches his shoulders in a stretch that pulls his shirt taut across his chest.

He really is a lovely specimen.

Finished stretching, he downs the last of his whiskey. Thankfully, he seems not to have noticed me smoldering across the coffee table from him. He says, "I'm done for. That last drink will finish me off in about three minutes. Best get out of here while my dignity remains intact." He rises smoothly from the chair, evidencing no signs of intoxication.

Walking to my side, he offers a hand, curling his fingers around mine.

The second his warm hand meets mine, a fire ignites low in my belly. I stand helpless as it spreads to more dangerous places. He squeezes my fingers and pulls me to my feet. "Ms. Lizzie, I thank you for your hospitality."

"Mr. Couper." I manage to offer him a curtsy-ish dip.

Kit motions for me to precede him into the foyer. "Next time the drinks are at my house," he says, pulling his jacket off the hanger.

I'm happy to take him up on his invitation and say so. Actually, I'm a little too happy. "With your family owning this place for over a century, you must have a few more good stories. I'd love to learn about Willing. And the Jewish connection."

"How about a tour? It's a good way to get the picture. Willing's history is reflected in the landscape. I could show you and Obie a nice trail through the woods. Would Saturday afternoon work? And how about this—afterward, I'll introduce you to the best fried oyster joint around." His forehead creases. "You aren't so Jewish that you don't eat oysters, are you?"

"I love oysters."

"Great. Can't live around here without enjoying shrimp and oysters." He slings his jacket over his shoulder. "I'll see you on Saturday. Let's make it around 2:00." Surprising me, he drops a farewell kiss on my forehead. It isn't romantic, more like the kiss you bestow on a favorite relative. He bends to pat Obie.

"And don't forget that story you owe me," he tosses out as the screen door swings closed behind him.

I decide that if flirting were an Olympic sport, Kit would take home gold. My body heats in the usual places.

Nope, I say to myself. Not going there. *No.* No. NO. He's my landlord. Best to remember that little detail. I'm not complicating my winter living arrangements, arrangements I'm enjoying just fine.

Turning off the porch light, I call Obie to follow me into the bedroom. As I slide my nightgown over my head, I review the evening, realizing that I let Kit call me Lizzie. I should have found it presumptuous. Instead, just remembering the way he said my name, I go a little melty inside—dahlin'.

CHAPTER 17

DURING THE NEXT FEW DAYS, I update my website, taking old images down and adding newer ones. Next, I work on my expense records in preparation for sending them to the accountant who does my taxes.

By Saturday morning, I'm feeling virtuous about the progress I've made on both fronts, so I take the rest of day off until Kit shows up, amusing myself by poking around in the living room cupboards. The discoveries are not unexpected; the window seats hide board games and sports equipment. The built-ins surrounding the television store the liquor supply and bar glasses as well as CDs and old copies of *Southern Living* and *Garden & Gun*.

I leaf through the magazines for a while before deciding to bake some chocolate chip cookies to thank Kit for his help with the closet and for the fabulous living quarters.

A little before 2:00, I'm about to pull the last batch of cookies out of the oven when I spy him through the kitchen windows as he crosses the drive between the houses. He has a backpack on his shoulder and looks way too handsome in an open barn coat, a dark blue T-shirt clinging to the hard planes of his chest. The shirt is tucked into his worn-in Levi's.

I call out for him to enter. Kit appears with his nose angled high, doing an inadvertent Obie imitation, sniffing the air. "Lord," he says, "do I detect chocolate chip cookies fresh from the oven?"

"As if you don't have eyes at the front of your head," I tease, transferring cookies from the pan to the cooling rack in front of him. "Help yourself." I gesture toward the cookies.

He studies the selection for a moment before choosing one crammed with chips. Taking a bite that reduces it by half, he hums with approval. "I'm in love," he states, putting the rest of the cookie into his mouth.

"Good to know your weakness, Samson." I hold a bag of cookies out for his inspection and begin adding more from the rack. "These are for you to take home. A token of appreciation for unsticking the door and also for this winter, although there is no way to adequately thank you and your brother enough for letting me stay. I already know Willing is a very special place."

Kit beams his craggy smile. "Now that I know you make great cookies, I may never let you leave." He selects another, setting the bag too close to the edge of the counter.

"Obie loves chocolate and he's sneaky," I say, pushing the cookies out of my standard poodle's reach. "We've made a couple of trips to the vet after past chocolate escapades."

"You and I share a chocolate addiction, fella," he says as Obie leans into him, likely hoping for a share of the partial cookie that remains in Kit's hand. When the rest of it goes into his new pal's mouth, Obie looks at me, cocking his head beseechingly, pink tongue lolling.

"Yes. I have cookies for you, too." I offer him one from a separate stash. "Whenever I make cookies for humans, I make him some, too, substituting carob drops for the chips, and mixing oat flour with grated carrots to sweeten them without sugar," I tell Kit.

We watch Obie trot into the dining room in order to savor his cookie in private. No matter how many times I've told him otherwise, he believes it's best to leave the room with a particularly yummy treat. Obs is certain that if he stays, I'll insist he share.

"You mentioned your family acquired Willing after the Civil War," I say as we step off the porch a couple of minutes later.

"Let me clarify something," Kit says. I'm holding the lead, but my dog is prancing along at Kit's side. "Down here, we refer to that particular war as the War Between the States, although, I should probably warn you, some continue to refer to it is the War of Northern Aggression."

"You're serious?"

"Yes, ma'am."

"Wow. I've only read the term in books. I've never heard anyone use it. What about how Willing got its name? In Vermont, houses and properties are rarely given names like the ones here. In Vermont you might find a Cozy Nest, but no New Hope or Rice Hope, names I saw on historic markers coming down Route 17."

"I imagine the original owners hoped the land would be *willing* to grow rice and make them rich. But after the War, the economics of rice didn't add up. When my great-great-grandfather bought the property, he bought it for dairying."

We stroll beneath the same majestic canopy of oaks that Obie and I passed under during our constitutional yesterday. A brisk wind is blowing, swaying the Spanish moss into a sunlit alley of dancing light and shadow beneath our feet.

"So you come from a family of farmers?"

"Not entirely. Jarrett, the Bostonian, was on the farming side. He bought Willing with money he saved from his pay and a bit he inherited. His Jewish father-in-law, Simon Halevy, bankrolled a herd of cows to start the dairy."

A cascade of almond-shaped leaves loosened by the wind pinwheels to the ground, adding a clickity-clackity accompaniment to Kit's words. Obie halts on the path in front of us, one front leg bent up.

If I'm any judge of how his doggy brain works, he's wondering if there's sport in chasing minuscule brown, leaf-shaped creatures. Deciding the challenge is beneath him, he starts off again, nose to the ground.

I consider asking Kit if any of his ancestors owned slaves, but I'm clueless about how a question like that would be received. I decide to save it for another time.

Most people don't realize that even though the Northern states prohibited slavery, we were involved in it right to the end. The North–South divide is complicated. Most of the banks that financed the slave trade were in New York and Boston. Jews weren't exempt, either. The

mighty and colossally rich Rothschild family financed slave ships. And
Brooks Brothers, practically an American institution, found its first
success supplying slave traders with clothing for their cargo.

But that was then. Right now, schools and neighborhoods are no
less segregated in most Northern cities than they are here. The real difference is probably that here, people may be more openly racist than in
other parts of the country.

What I know for sure is that the topic is hard to talk about. I've
never been in a position to ask someone with direct ties to slavery
about their own relationship with family history. I'm interested in that
opportunity—I just don't think this is it.

Kicking a slippery pile of leaves out of my path, I ask instead,
"When did the dairy go out of business?"

"My great-aunt, known around here as Miss Addie, kept the dairy
until she retired in the late 1970s. Sam and I used to visit her for a
couple of weeks every summer. We ran wild down here in a way we
never could in Savannah. After she passed, my granddad became the
sole owner of the property."

"And then your dad inherited?"

"Dad bought out his sibs and put the land into a trust Sam and
I inherited when we reached what he considered the age of reason,
which happened to be forty."

"Seriously? I wish I'd known your father. He was obviously a wise
man." I gesture at the gorgeous landscape. "It's amazing that Willing
has been preserved intact."

"As we say down here, *we are blessed.*"

Kit and I walk for a few seconds in companionable silence, until he
says, "Okay, I'm tired of my stories. I'm ready for yours."

"Sorry, this is your story hour. And don't forget I'm toting a big,
though invisible, frying pan."

Kit laughs. It starts low, a deep rumble, bubbling up and out in a
joyful expression of mirth.

Something low and deep inside me responds. For me, the admiration of an attractive man is one of the most potent aphrodisiacs on the planet.

Obie turns his head to look at us. *Enough carrying on,* his expression says. *We have exploring to do!* Kit gives him a consolation scratch behind the ears before heading us north to the edge of the pasture where the woods are dense with palmettos under tall water oaks. Finding a break in the undergrowth I can't see, Kit pulls away palmetto fronds to expose a hidden trail. A few yards in, when I look back, the meadow has disappeared behind a thicket of green.

I feel as if I've entered an enchanted world.

Before we changed paths, the color palette was the brown of fallen oak leaves, blue sky, silver moss, and the straw yellow of dormant winter grass underfoot. The wood is deeply green—dark-green oak leaves and mossy-green bark, contrasting with the limey green of the palmetto fronds. The ground underfoot smells of loam.

Overhead, a cardinal flashes in and out of the canopy, a brilliant streak of red. Other birds trill songs I don't recognize. A light breeze adds to the soundtrack with a soft whir as it moves among the oak branches and clatters against the palm fronds. Small trumpet-shaped yellow flowers drift onto the path in front of me, falling from jessamine vines overhead.

Obie pushes past Kit, too excited to display good manners, pulling me after him. Kit jumps a narrow stream. Obie powers through the shallow water. Holding a hand out, Kit helps me across. His hand is large and warm and I pull mine away as soon as I've safely crossed the water. Climbing the shallow bank, focused on the echo of his touch, I miss a protruding root and stumble.

This display of klutziness doesn't prevent a further stumble because I do learn from my mistakes, so I'm watching my feet, which means I'm not watching the man in front of me. I collide with his back.

"Oh—" I breathe as he pivots to steady me. Embarrassed, I look past him, utter another startled "Oh!" and stare in wonder at the clearing we've entered. "What in the world?"

More like out of this world! I grin at the improbability of what is before me: an oak grove where the bark on the trees is speckled with vivid pink splotches. From about knee high to just past my head, the trunks look like victims of a pink paintball party.

"I thought you'd like it." A smile lights Kit's face. "You're looking at the lichen, *Cryptothecia rubrocincta*, more commonly known as blood lichen. As you've noticed, it's pink."

"Very, very pink," I say in wonder, beelining for the nearest tree to take a closer look, tugging Obie along with me.

"It grows in coastal areas. I've tried to research it online, but there isn't a lot of information out there. And nothing about why it grows in such profusion in one spot and not another."

Tickled by the oddity of trees with hot-pink bark, I snap a quick close-up before returning to Kit's side. "I read about a tabby slave cabin on St. Simons Island covered in this stuff," I comment.

"You probably also read it no longer exists. The owner of the property demolished it. He took so much flak for tearing it down that he ended up rebuilding the cabin on the same footprint. He used historically correct materials, but the lichen never grew back."

"Why did he tear it down in the first place?"

"He wanted a tennis court."

"Unbelievable," I sigh. Studying the clearing, I think about how to photograph it. Turning back to Kit, I ask, "Would you mind holding on to Obie while I take a few more shots?"

The photos are for reference. I'll need to return at other times of day to watch how the sunlight moves through the trees so I can take a picture that will do the place justice.

We continue down the path after I retrieve Obie's leash from Kit. The pasture reappears. Kit aims us toward a gate in the post-and-wire fencing at the marsh's edge. Holding it open, he says, "The entire acreage is fenced. I should have said so before. Sam usually brings the family's horses down for the summer, but they are being boarded until the family returns from Spain. If you want, you can let Obie run."

"Obie isn't perfect about returning, which makes me nuts, although he does come home eventually."

"He can't get off the property. The fencing is solid. I walk it regularly. I'm betting he'd love to run for a bit."

"He would. Thanks. Maybe later." Obie dances ahead of us, his lead fully extended. I think he understands what Kit has offered and can't wait for his chance to go exploring.

The ground has become soggy, but farther on, it dries into a gravel road wide enough for us to walk abreast. At each side there's a steep drop into a marsh stubbled with dry grass.

"We're walking on an old levee Sam and I restored," Kit notes. "Do you know anything about rice cultivation?"

"Not a thing except it grows in water."

"Actually, it grows in fields that are alternately flooded and drained during the growing season. You can see more fields off that way." Kit gestures north.

I squint into the distance but the landscape is too flat or I'm too short to see past what is left of the next levee. "It seems miraculous the fields are still here. They've been abandoned for, what—more than a hundred and fifty years?"

"It's a testament to how well the levees were engineered that even broken by storm tides, most of them remain—although not in usable condition. When in use, sluice gates drew in fresh water riding above the heavier salt water at high tide and drained it when the tide was low."

"To me, the building of those levees seems as impossible as building the pyramids."

"I know," Kit says. "Hard to imagine."

As we move closer to the river the wind picks up, slapping our clothes against our bodies.

"Tide's coming in," Kit notes.

We zip our jackets against the chill. A heron glides low, landing among the reeds.

"Ashburton is entirely surrounded by mountains," I say. "There is so much more sky here. The expansiveness of the landscape is a great attraction for me. I love the light. It's so different from home."

Kit cocks his head in question.

"I'm sure you've noticed how at dawn and at sunset here the sun's rays seem to come almost from below the horizon," I explain. "I call the effect *beach light.* In Vermont the sun is high in the sky when it rises and sets over the mountains. We never get that lit-from-below-glow you see here."

"I remember some pretty dramatic winter sunsets at Dartmouth where I spent my college years, when the valley would already be in shadow but the peaks were lit up."

"I'm not saying the mountains don't offer their own dramatic vistas, just that I'm enjoying the difference."

"I guess I've noticed that difference but never thought about it. No wonder you are the photographer and I'm not."

We have reached another levee. This one runs along the river's edge. A long wooden walkway, perched on pilings and wide enough for a golf cart, extends out from it.

"That was an excellent explanation, by the way. You're a good teacher," Kit says.

"I am."

"And not overly modest."

"Not about my work."

He grins at me. "I admire that in a person."

"Are you a good lawyer?" I ask.

"Absolutely. Good at a few other things as well." He winks.

I lift my brows, knowing he wants me to ask about those other things. Wiser, I decide, not to take his bait. At least, not yet.

"You went to Dartmouth?" I ask, hoping to push the conversation sideways.

"From all over. I ended up there because my father told me that getting out of the South should be part of my college education."

"He sounds doubly smart."

"How about you?"

"CalArts."

"Also far from home?"

"I was attracted to the lack of winter rather than the lesson in cultural differences, though I got that, too."

The planks of the boardwalk make a pleasant clomping sound as we tread our way toward a boathouse. A flock of pelicans flaps a line across the sky, traveling from north to south. Although we have herons and the occasional egret in Vermont, we don't have pelicans or anhingas. The pelicans thrill me. I turn to watch them pass behind us, noticing how small Kit's house looks from here. We are farther out than I realized.

A few seconds later, we reach the end of the walkway. Kit swings a wooden gate open. We step onto a platform where a square boathouse with a hip roof is surrounded on three sides by a deep railed deck.

"What's the distance from the house out to here?" I ask.

"A bit over a tenth of a mile, give or take. When there hasn't been rain for a while, the creek can drop a couple of feet. My brother and I have a boat we keep at the marina in Darien because there isn't enough draft here for a sloop. We kayak on the creek."

Kit puts his hand on my back to steer me toward the water. The frisson of awareness I experienced the last time he touched me reignites. His palm trails higher, until the tips of his fingers brush the skin above my collar. I shiver. Our eyes meet. His are aware—assessing. He offers me that cocky bad-boy grin. Just a guess: He felt my little quake and knows it wasn't caused by the breeze. He confirms my supposition when he says, "I can't tell you how delighted I am that our mutual friend called me about you."

I hear the echo of our mutual friend saying, *You will enjoy him.* I remember at the time being very irritated about what I read between Darius's words. Today, I'm downright thankful, happy with the sunshine, the temperate weather, the amazing landscape. And maybe, I'm a little too happy with Kit. My brain flashes the caution light, reminding me to stick to my newest rule—the only rule I have at the moment, since I've ditched the rest—about not playing around until I've done some extensive soul searching.

Unfortunately, and as usual, my body could care less about what my brain thinks is best.

A gull standing at the pinnacle of the boathouse roof flaps into the wind, cawing hoarsely as it rides the current into the sky. Kit's hand settles on my shoulder. I sizzle.

The wind is stronger on the river. It's colder out here, too. A gust flattens my clothing against my breasts and belly and thighs, producing goose bumps. The only place I'm warm is under Kit's hand. If I turn into that warmth, what might happen? Would the press of the wind transmute into the press of his body into mine?

Why not find out? Lust and its geometry—two bodies coming together for the sheer exploitation of physical pleasure—is simple in a way love will doubtless never be for me. This recognition pours some needed cold water on my libido. I break contact. Crossing the deck to the far railing, I lift my face into the sun.

Mr. Irresistible catches up to me almost immediately. Leaning his forearms on top of the rail, he stands close enough for his sleeve to brush mine. He appears perfectly at ease while I'm strung as tight as a bow. Am I imagining his interest? *Not likely.* I'm rarely wrong when desire is in the air, and guaranteed, his touch was more than friendly.

I study the dock below us, accessed by a metal stair, currently retracted. I consider that Kit owns a sailboat that requires deep water. Adding up the rest—the rebuilt levee, the walkway, the boathouse, the couture evening suit—I conclude that the money I'm paying for utilities is inconsequential to Kit or his brother. The scope of Willing's acreage, its water access, and the property's pristine condition should have alerted me before now that neither Couper brother needs my money.

So why am I here? I never asked Darius if Kit is paying him back for a favor, although the reason I've been allowed to stay could be as straightforward as Kit indicated when I first called him.

My host pulls a key out of his jacket pocket and crosses to the boat-house. "Come inside," he calls over his shoulder. He unlocks the door and holds it open. "There's a bench across the back. It's a nice place to sit when the breeze is cool like today."

The interior is warm and, as Kit noted, protected from the elements. I seat myself on the long navy-striped cushion atop the bench built into the back wall. Obie stretches out at my feet. Clustered against the right-side wall, white wicker porch furniture waits to be set outside. Four brightly colored kayaks are tied to the rafters overhead.

"I like walking out here in the evening as dusk comes in," Kit says, fiddling with the door. He folds it back against the other screened-in panels until the front of the building is completely open.

"This seems like the perfect spot for summer parties," I observe, enjoying the view of the river from my perch. Obs lies on the floor at my feet, and since Kit reclosed the gate at the top of the walkway, I unclip him.

"Indeed. The extended family converges for the Fourth of July weekend. It's a fun time." Sitting down next to me, Kit opens his pack. He hands me a water bottle and twists the cap off his own. "Need a cookie?" He pulls out the bag he'd insisted we take along.

I shake my head as Obie scrambles to his feet, looking expectant.

"Then I'll go ahead and replenish some energy." Kit does his two-bites-and-it's-gone routine and gives Obie the last piece, free of chocolate. He reaches for another.

"Our big summer shindig is on my birthday in August," I comment as he crunches. Obie, who inhaled his treat, watches Kit's every move in hope of a second share.

"I throw the party more as a celebration of my friends than of the day I was born." I look out at the creek, enjoying the warmth of the sun bathing us in light and the sound of the water lapping the dock.

"So you're a Leo. I should have known."

I twist to meet his glance. "What's that mean?"

"That I'm not surprised you were born under a bold sign."

"Do you believe that stuff?" I ask, challenging him but also pleased with how he sees me.

"Nope. Just making conversation." Kit grins. We both laugh.

I lean into the cushion, looking out at the view. "This weather is grand. I can't believe it's the first week of January. My daughter texted this morning to say it was six below when she got out of bed." I lift my feet into the warm light slanting through the window behind us. "Thank you for bringing me here. It's glorious."

"Happy to do it." He closes the cookie bag.

Obie, his dream of a second treat thwarted, nudges my water bottle. Spying a plastic pail near the porch furniture, I get up and pour half the bottle into it. He sidles over and gives the pail a careful sniff. I'm certain he's worried I'm trying to poison him. The sniffing is instinct, but not all dogs are as suspicious—or as well loved. Satisfied he'll live another day, Obie lowers his head to drink.

"When I was a kid," I say, returning to the bench, "we lived on the edge of farmland where we were free to roam. You must have had that same sort of experience here when you were young. My daughter grew up in town. I've regretted Diana didn't have the same freedom I enjoyed."

Nodding his understanding, Kit studies the water, affording me a few unobserved seconds to admire his profile. Catching me at it, he smiles.

"Willing is a special place," he says.

"It must have been lovely for your boys to grow up here."

The light leaves Kit's eyes. His mouth hardens. His gazes fixes on the water.

Until now, he has been entirely cheerful about his family stories. I guess I've hit a sore spot.

The silence goes on long enough to be awkward. I try to figure out how much responsibility to take for shutting Kit down. His silence is my fault, even though I don't understand how a harmless comment about his kids set him off. Maybe he divorced when the boys were young and it was one of those acrimonious splits. Willing could have figured into the mess. I bend to pet Obie, giving myself something to do, sorry for injecting discord into what has otherwise been a delightful afternoon.

Kit heaves a deep sigh, his gaze fixed on the horizon.

"The boys did all right," he says, "but losing their mom made their lives a whole lot less than carefree. If there was any magic in their childhoods, it was black magic." He rubs his hand over the back of his neck. "Eleanor was sick for about fifteen years, so . . ."

My back slams into the cushions. "I'm so sorry. God, that's terrible."

Boy, did I get him wrong! I assumed he was divorced; rather, he lost his wife and lost her far too young. She can't have died all that long ago, either. No wonder her loss is painful for him to talk about. Added to the death of his father four years ago, I can understand why he needed a moment to regroup.

Kit's gaze remains fixed, his voice gruff as he answers what I haven't asked. "It's been eight years." He finally meets my eyes. "Darius didn't tell you?"

I shake my head.

"Well—for the record, you're right. Willing is a magical place, but all the magic in the world can't cure grief."

"Cancer?" I ask. Sometimes I jump to conclusions. Should I ask about Kit's wife, or take his lead and not try to delve into what is obviously a tremendously painful segment of his life?

"Yes," Kit says, but doesn't elaborate, making it clear which way he prefers to go.

How long does it take for grief to lose the power to knock you to your knees in a situation like his? For five years, thinking about Roland made me feel like a weight was pressing me into the ground, but after the first couple of years I no longer felt I was going to suffocate under it. But then, I didn't know Roland for very long. What's it like when you've spent half your life with someone you love and have to watch them fight a painful battle they will ultimately lose?

I decide Kit's feelings are a testament to the quality of his marriage. Roland professed to be brokenhearted after Laura died, then rushed out to replace her. At the time I thought, How sweet, he loved being married so much, he wants to do it again right away. But when I didn't tidily fit his parameters, he abandoned me. Then, immediately found someone who was a better fit. As my vision has cleared over the months since we met at that wedding, Roland's behavior during our courtship seems more desperate than genuine.

I don't expect Kit to say anything else about what happened to his family, but I rethink the idea of changing the subject. Waiting him out is probably the best way to respect his privacy and his loss.

I join his study of the water. The current appears slow but I'm guessing that like the man next to me, looks can be deceiving. As the silence yawns again, I reconsider offering a topic shift. I could ask about the ecology of the river, or if he's heard a weather report for tomorrow—anything to put us into an easier frame of mind.

Lost in these deliberations, I jump when Kit touches my arm. He says, "Children can be amazingly resilient."

It takes me a second to catch up, and to agree.

"I became a single parent when Diana was barely five years old," I say. Obie, sitting on the floor, is basking in the sunshine. He climbs to his feet. I stroke his head. "Being divorced is obviously different from losing a spouse, but it taught me that balancing work and taking good care of a child on one's own can be a road of hard choices. No matter how much I loved my daughter, right after Dan and I split, I wasn't winning any best-mother prizes."

I did better after Roland, but that's only my opinion; I've never asked Diana for hers.

Kit rubs the back of his neck. If he really is a player, I'm betting he didn't start out that way. I'm betting it happened the same way it did for me. The kind of loss he suffered would make it impossible for me to risk loving again, lest fate deliver more of the same. I know all about how that works. So does Darius. Obviously, Kit does, too.

I consider confessing that when Dan and I split up, the work of supporting and taking care of Diana didn't allow me time to grieve, let alone the space to heal. It occurs to me that this may be why I locked my grief for Roland away. I was doing the best I could to survive it. Too bad I didn't understand the collateral damage I was inflicting.

"We were fortunate my mother and father joined us for the first few months after Eleanor died," Kit says. "Then Agnes rescued us. Thank God for Ags."

I wait for him to say more about the rescue and to acknowledge what I told him about my divorce, realizing this conversation has offered a lot to think about.

"Agnes Postelle is my neighbor," he says, hitting one mark but missing the other. "She's one of the most capable women on the planet. Lucky for me and the boys, Agnes lives just up the road on Needwood." Kit smiles for the first time since we entered the territory of his loss. "At various points in their youth, my sons spent more time with the Postelles than at home."

"Where are they, now?" I'm relieved the conversation has moved on to less uncomfortable territory.

"Levi is teaching at a private school in Atlanta. He is beginning a master's in education this fall. He wants to be a headmaster someday. Adam is studying computer science at Tulane. Matt, Levi's best friend and Agnes's oldest, is in his first year at the University of Chicago's medical school. Jordan, the Postelles' other son, is a year younger than Adam. He's a master electrician and works for his dad."

"It's nice your sons had good friends close by."

Kit's narrative hasn't included a single word about his own experience as a widowed parent or how it felt to become a widower at a young age. As presented, his transition from happy family life to widowed fatherhood was doable—no sweat—because of his parents' and a kind neighbor's support.

Since he didn't reject my personal facts, which were just as thin, I don't reject his, though I'm sure I'm hearing an abridged version of his story. Smiling my understanding I wait for what he'll say next, noting the shadows have lengthened.

Kit must have noticed, too. He shoots his cuff. We both check the time on the slim watch banding his wrist. Actually, he studies the watch while I admire his musculature.

"Almost five," he remarks, collecting our water bottles. He rises, holding a hand out to me.

I place my palm in his. As he did two nights ago, he tightens his grip and pulls me to my feet. This time I don't tingle. Just as well. We all have our issues.

Kit didn't acknowledge mine, offering not a word in reaction to what I told him. His lack of reaction is kind of standard for a guy, but disappointing, nevertheless.

What is also true is that I can be hypersensitive in my assessments of men. Kit did explain his reaction to my remark about his boys enjoying their lives here. Their trauma somewhat excuses his lack of response to mine—but still. I walk out of the boathouse to wait at the rail as Kit locks up behind me.

Walking toward shore, neither of us comes up with a conversation restarter, or maybe, after the previous discussion, neither of us has the energy for one. At the pasture gate, Kit is the first to speak, suggesting I let Obie run.

No less anxious about my dog being off lead than I was before, I know I'm reacting like a hover mother, defined by my daughter as overprotective to a fault. In other words, I'm feeling the stirring of Super Jewish Mother overconcern. I bend and unhook Obie's lead.

With an arf of pure canine delight, he zooms away, trailing more excited yips in his wake. Kit and I exchange a smile. He says, "That dog has a gorgeous gait."

I relax a little. Obie is indeed a sight to see. At a run he resembles a trotting horse with his high graceful stride. Remaining in sight for the time being, he sniffs his way toward three immense oaks shading the yard on the far side of Kit's house.

I flex my shoulders in an attempt to roll away the tension I'm hold-ing about Obie's run and, in larger part, the stilted exchange with Kit at the boathouse. The way his demeanor went from sunshine to full eclipse was startling.

He rubs his nape, a gesture I'm beginning to associate with trouble. He says, "I'm sorry, about your divorce."

Surprised as well as pleased he was listening after all, I say, "I really hate the adage, '*You're never given more than you can bear*,' because even if it's true, which I doubt, what you're given can make you totally miserable and include dismal long-term consequences."

He looks away, his expression both smile and grimace.

I think, *Okay, time for a less fraught subject. The guy has experienced a lot of heartache, and forcing him to discuss it isn't necessarily some-thing he's going to thank me for later. While this isn't one of my Rules for Romance-Lite, deep emotional territory explored too soon can be dis-tancing rather than friendship-inducing. I'm not feeling anything but sad about what Kit has revealed about his wife, but sharing more than you intend can leave a bad taste in your mouth no matter how it is taken, so I'm all for switching to a less traumatic topic. And, I remind myself, he is my landlord, no matter how compelling I find him. It would be smart to dial down on the intensity level.*

"I've never seen trees resting their branches on the ground like that," I say, the weather and flora and fauna all being time-tested top-ics for innocuous conversation. I gesture to where Obie was standing before he disappeared behind the house. One of the trees has spread its branches onto the lawn.

"The oaks grow as wide as they are high and their branches droop like that when they're very old," Kit responds, seeming to welcome the subject change. "We have a painting of the house from the early 1800s with that tree in it, already fully grown. There's a saying around here that live oaks spend a hundred years growing, a hundred years living, and another hundred in decline. It's a neat concept, except that tree is estimated to be six hundred years old."

"Wow. Think of the history that tree has lived through."

"And a few hurricanes, besides. Luckily, none of the big storms have done worse than to take out a few trees in the woods. Hurricanes tend to miss us due to the way the coast is tucked in here."

Having covered the weather, I decide to try history next, since it is a topic we've already touched on without any trouble. I say, "From the sound of it, some of your family has been rooted in America almost as long as that tree. My own came through Ellis Island in the 1880s."

"The Aikens go back to the mid-1700s here. In England, we trace ourselves to a French knight who fought at the side of William the Conqueror."

"What about the Jewish side? When did they emigrate?"

Before he can answer, Obie bounds out from behind a great oak and streaks toward us. Skidding to a stop, tongue lolling, he leans not into me but Kit, who gives him a ruffling and a couple of hard pats. The traitorous dog grins, I swear, he actually grins. Shaking himself out, he ambles off in search of further adventures.

Kit's eyes follow Obie as he moves with tempered exuberance toward the pasture at the marsh's edge. "We go back to the beginning, to the Carolina Charter," he says, moving his attention to me. "The wilderness of the new world probably seemed a better bet to Spanish Jews than being persecuted in the Inquisition."

"You really do have papers, don't you?" I quip.

Kit laughs.

I love the sound of his hearty amusement and laugh with him, relieved we have escaped the Emotional Danger Zone and returned to the easy rapport we shared before the boathouse conversation. "No genteel Sephardic blood in my veins; I'm full-blooded Russian rabble," I comment.

Spanish Jews are called Sephardic Jews. They were among the first Jews to emigrate to America. Like the Ashkenazi of Germany and Austria, the Spanish Jews—Sephardim—consider themselves superior to the peasant stock that spawned me.

Kit lays an arm across my shoulders. "Russian rabble is the best kind." He gives me an affectionate squeeze. I melt, glad that what I'm beginning to think of as Kit's "Kit-ness" has returned.

"My only claim to fame is my cookies," I mumble, joking to gloss over the way this show of camaraderie is affecting me. My brain registers that this is exactly what Darius objected to—that I can't genuinely accept a compliment. But it's a relief to move past the recent awkwardness, and Kit's touch is warming me in all the right places, although they're all the wrong places if I'm going to stick with the plan to go entanglement free for a while.

"As far as I'm concerned, good cookies are more important than good genes. Not that I don't already know there is more to admire about you than your cookies." Kit offers a suggestive rise of his brows that has nothing to do with what he says next. "I've checked out your website, you know. Pretty impressive."

His admiration finishes me off. I'll have to gird my loins, whatever that means—something to do with wrapping up one's private parts for safekeeping before heading into battle—to withstand a regular onslaught of his charm. I have a sudden vision of him in the Tom Ford tux, the way it hugged his body—including his loins. Swoon-worthy, indeed.

"Thank you," I say, because I have to say something and my brain has seized.

"I'm looking forward to learning more about your assets." Kit's grin is the flirty crooked one. "You're really talented. I wish the boys were around so you could do their portraits."

"What a lovely vote of confidence. I would love to do that, should either one of them show up during my stay."

In the distance, I hear a bark. More follow in quick succession. From their tenor, I can tell Obie is frustrated. A squirrel has likely eluded capture. I call him without the least expectation he'll come. That dog has his priorities straight whether I like them or not; he loves freedom more than he loves me or my cookies.

A minute or so later, I'm pleasantly surprised when he trots out of the deepening gloom, his sprinting energy used up. The three of us promenade home at a sedate pace, although I don't take a chance on his energy returning and clip him to his lead.

In front of Sam's house, Kit says, "How about I meet you in a half hour and we'll head to B&J's for oysters?"

"It's a deal." I wave him on. Obie and I turn up the path to the house as I work to combine the two Kits I met this afternoon—Mr. Closed and Mr. Open—but they won't quite mesh.

CHAPTER 18

A LITTLE TIME goes by before I hear from Kit again. Because our schedules are different, I don't see him coming or going. There was a little too much intensity to our boathouse conversation, so it's no surprise that he's making himself scarce. No matter how much fun we had at the oyster place, I'm betting the emotional wallop of our exchange put him off. But late the following week, a few minutes after his car headlights flash in the front windows, he knocks.

"Hey there," he says when I open the door. "I saw the lights on and presumed you were up. I'm hoping you might like to join me for the nightcap I owe you."

He is dressed formally, although in a business suit, not his tux, for which I say a quick hosanna to the gods of fashion. Since I last saw him, I've gotten my libido under control, although his eveningwear could cause a relapse.

"I'd be delighted."

"Bring Obie. Your dog is the secret handshake."

I laugh, telling him I'll take Obie for his last out and stop by on our return. I'm absurdly pleased that Kit likes my dog. A number of men of my acquaintance view poodles as sissy dogs and not the bird dogs they've been for centuries.

A few minutes later, I knock on Kit's door. He ushers me into his mudroom, a narrow beadboard-paneled room open to the rafters.

Unclipping Obie, I set his lead next to Kit's squash racquet on a long bench under a set of windows. A canvas coat and a gym bag hang on wrought-iron hooks close by.

"I love your blue ceiling," I say, looking up.

"That blue was the color of the earliest layers of paint we found when we did a little renovating."

"Is it Haint Blue?" I ask. "I know the color was sometimes used inside slave cabins, but I don't know why. The word *haint* suggests it has something to do with ghosts." When he looks surprised, I add, "Stray facts stick in my head. Maybe I remembered it because I enjoy the sound of the word."

"We think this part of the house might have been a slave cabin. People used to move buildings around, way more than they do now. But about your question: The blue paint was meant to mimic water. Haints—bad spirits and the shades of the dead—don't have the ability to cross water in some African traditions, so the color was applied to trick bad spirits into staying away. Supposed to be where the tradition of painting porch ceilings blue originates as well. As for this ceiling, when the boys were young, they were keen to keep bad spirits out, so we restored the blue up there."

I smile. "Sweet." If I were a child with a sick mother, keeping bad spirits out would make sense to me, too.

Kit gestures for Obie and me to precede him up two steps into a wide hall running the length of the main house. The hall ends at a set of double doors.

"I've noticed the house faces the water, not the road."

He nods. "When Willing was built, the roads around here were no better than rutted tracks. Most folks arrived by water." He walks toward the stairs where his suit jacket is thrown over the newel-post and picks it up. The staircase is old and narrow with an oriental-style runner. Through a doorway on the same wall, I glimpse a dining room with a massive mahogany table surrounded by chairs with graceful claw-foot legs. Oil paintings of venerables who look like righteous Puritans hang in gilded frames along the back wall sternly guarding the table.

In the hall, on the wall opposite the staircase, five long rows of uniformly sized black frames display family pictures that look to date into the distant past.

Seeing where my attention has been drawn, Kit waves a hand toward his photo gallery.

"I'd introduce you to my illustrious ancestors, only it would take all night. At present, I hope you don't mind if I run upstairs to change into something more comfortable. I didn't want to be up there where I might not hear your knock."

"Isn't that business about getting more comfortable supposed to be my line?" I quip, although I should keep a lid on the flirting.

"You look pretty comfortable already."

I look down at my loose sweater and pants. "You have a point."

Kit crosses in front of me, bending into a doorway on the same wall as the photo gallery. He clicks on a lamp. "Have a seat. I'll be right back." He bumps my shoulder as he passes. I can't tell whether the bump was deliberate or not.

It isn't easy, but I manage not to watch his great butt as he runs lightly up the stairs. Okay, I watch a little—and then, ignoring the suggestion that I hang out across the hall, I head for the photographs.

Beginning with the bottom row, I study a distinguished young man in a Union uniform staring rigidly out of his frame. I'm betting this solemn youngster is the great-great who bought Willing at the end of the War. Hanging next to him is a family group. The husband wears a skullcap. Likely these are great-great's Savannah in-laws.

A couple of rows up, I notice a boy wearing a mortarboard and gown. He looks a lot like Kit. From the proud parents' clothing, as well as the sepia tone of the image, this is probably his dad. The athletic teenager with wide shoulders captured on Kodachrome in the next row is recognizable as Kit. The boy next to him must be his brother. Sam is built more solidly than his sibling. I can't tell which of them is older.

A few snapshots farther along the row, a petite woman in an honest-to-God Chanel suit, with the de rigueur chain belt and ropes of pearls, smiles into the camera. She is standing with an older, slimmer version of the sepia-toned graduate. A couple of frames away, I find the wedding photo that proves these are indeed Kit's parents. Kit inherited his honey-brown eyes from his mother. The rest is of him a clone of his dad, minus the man's narrow physique.

The top rows are dedicated to Kit and his sons, from their toddler-hood through young adulthood. One is dark-haired and solidly built, like his uncle Sam. The other is fair with the lanky grace of his father and grandfather, and, I presume, the fair coloring of his mother.

The fair son reminds me of C. Not for the first time, I consider exactly how young C. was when I took him to bed—around the same age Kit's sons are now. With a shiver, I tell myself all is well. C. and I have both moved on.

Blowing out a calming breath, I return my attention to the photographs, scanning the rows for signs of Kit's wife, Eleanor. She isn't in the pictures with Kit and the boys. On a hunch, I reverse direction and head toward the mudroom entry to the main part of the house. I swing the door closed. The corner is devoted entirely to Kit's wife. I wonder if it is too much for Kit to see these photographs every time he passes by—the best explanation for hiding them behind a door that I can come up with at the moment.

Eleanor was an ethereal beauty. As I suspected, she bequeathed her golden hair to her blond son, as well as her delicate bone structure. My attention settles on a snapshot of her beaming at a baby in her arms, looking too thin and wearing a headscarf. The baby's older brother clutches her skirt, laughing into the camera.

I try to imagine how it would feel to know there was a high proba-bility I wouldn't live to see my children grow to maturity. I think about Diana and my heart breaks for Kit's departed wife, as well for her sons and her husband, deprived of this visibly effervescent woman.

With a lump in my throat, I scan the rest of the images. Kit and his wife were the quintessential Brahmin couple: long boned, athletic, and good-looking. I can't help noticing that in almost every shot, whether they are posed in front of a boat, eating with friends, sitting at a side-walk café, or playing with their children, they are touching one another.

Their wedding photos are in the next-to-last row, above images of Eleanor as a child. She was married in a dress that complemented her slim, elongated figure, her hair elegantly styled in a loose knot at the base of her neck with a camellia tucked into the knot. Baroque pearls dangle from her ears.

I hone in on a shot where the photographer caught a particularly interesting moment. Eleanor is looking at Kit with affection. Kit has pulled his new wife into his body, but he faces the camera, his expression triumphant, as if he'd won the grandest prize of all. It takes me a minute to remove my glance from their shining faces to notice that he's wearing a tux with wide lapels—no doubt the late lamented Brooks Brothers suit. With new understanding of his reluctance to part with it, I straighten.

"Taking the tour without me?"

I startle. Immersed in the meaning of the Couper family's visual history, I was deaf to Kit's approach. A few feet away, Obie scrambles to his feet, tail wagging. *Geez,* I silently admonish my dog, *some watchdog you are.*

"Hey." Kit lays his hand on my shoulder.

At his touch, the usual fizz begins. *Damn*—so much for having this attraction thing under control. I turn toward him, at the same time returning the door to the way it was positioned before Kit went upstairs, hiding the photographs.

"Your gallery is wonderful." Setting aside the addendum to the suit story for processing later, I add, "I hope you'll be willing to introduce me to everyone." I motion to the lines of black frames.

"It's an extensive tour. Let's have that drink, since no one out here is going anywhere."

"I have a weakness for family photos," I say over my shoulder as I proceed him into what appears to be both office and den. More traditional than his brother's man-cave, it too has leather chairs but Kit's are the classic club variety. There is also a chesterfield couch, a cluttered library table that looks like it's used as a desk, and a wall of white-painted bookcases. I don't see a television. If there is one, it must be hidden, maybe inside the mahogany cabinet close to the seating area.

"Why did you choose wedding photography?" Kit asks. "Do you

enjoy documenting family dynasties in the making? Or are you a closet romantic?"

"I enjoy the optimism of weddings, but weddings are how I earn my bread. The choice is as unromantic as that. Landscape photography is my big love. I enjoy portraiture, as well. Weddings come in a distant third, although first in income."

"I'd never know that from your website. You do a great job with those weddings."

"Thank you. I'm curious as well as nosy, which is a prerequisite for taking good people pictures and also the reason I'm looking forward to your tour. Give me a choice between chocolate cake, my other great love, and family snapshots, and I'll go with the snapshots every time."

"Duly informed." He chuckles.

He's changed into a loose crewneck sweater and jeans. I get a hit of his cologne as he walks by. I resist the urge to close my eyes to savor it. Aiming for the cluttered library table in front of the bookcases, Kit switches on a lamp sitting on the table. He also turns on the lamps bracketing the couch and the one between the club chairs. That one looks like a genuine Tiffany, with a hand-blown glass shade in a mosaic design of narcissi.

"My aunt updated the electrical system in the house but never installed wall switches except in the hall," Kit grumbles, gesturing for me to sit. "Make yourself at home. I'll get our drinks. Jack for you?"

"With water, please." I sit on the dark leather couch.

Kit opens an Empire armoire. It has been repurposed to hold his liquor supply among other bits and pieces including a small freezer. I assume the freezer and cabinet's interior light are wired through a hole in the back of the cabinet somewhere. As Kit mixes our drinks, I tell him the lack of wall switches is charming and period authentic.

"Not so charming when you smash your shins into furniture trying to find a lamp in the dark. Then it's just a pain in the period ass."

"Interesting visual." I laugh. "Would it be too forward to ask why you never installed those switches?"

"Although I grumble, I like the house's little discomforts. They remind me of my aunt and the past."

"So *you're* the closet romantic."

He shrugs. "Never looked at it that way, but maybe so. Promise you won't tell anyone?" He offers his lopsided grin.

Be still my heart!

Obie jumps up to sit beside me. I make a shooing gesture, but my dog, like most poodles, is both an intuitive and logical thinker, so my attitude perplexes him. He knows couches are for dogs and can't figure out why I don't love him anymore. He lowers his head, his tail drooping between his legs.

"Leave him be," Kit interjects, rescuing Obie from the ignominy of having to make himself comfortable on the carpet. "Believe me, that couch has seen worse treatment than one lone dog can dish out. My boys were wild things. Obie is fully domesticated in comparison."

It's true that the brown leather sofa is creased and gouged in a few places. I motion for Obie to lie down. Looking relieved, he complies, resting his head on my thigh.

Kit hands me my whiskey. He gives Obie a scratch behind his ears then seats himself in a club chair across from me. The Tiffany lamp bathes him in amber light. Swinging a leg onto the long tufted ottoman between us, he sips from his tumbler, offering up a contented sigh.

I take a sip of my own for courage. "Your wife was lovely," I say once I'm fortified. Kit has made it pretty clear he doesn't want to talk about Eleanor, or can't, but I can't ignore that she died too young or that he found me studying her photographs. Better to offer up the usual civilities and let him decide where he wants to go with them.

"I'm charmed that my family snapshots were so engrossing that I startled you." He offers a brief and very different smile from the last one.

It is hard to say whether he's charmed or not. At least he didn't freeze the way he did on the river, though he does glide past the subject *oh so neatly*. Knowing how to roll smoothly around the hard stuff is a skill I can appreciate. I give him an additional credit for weaving his redirection into a compliment for me.

I don't press. It wasn't as if he was all that interested in what I had to say about my own experience. My guess is that for Kit, flirting is the object; learning about the hard stuff—not so much. If we end up in bed, a nice superficial surface skim is the way to go even if the idea of romance-lite depresses me a little—another clue that Darius was probably right about what I'm yearning for.

But Kit isn't the right guy for yearnings. Number one, I can already tell his baggage is as big, if not bigger than, mine. Number two, he lives a thousand miles away from the place I call home. Better to help change the subject than moon over him. I ask, "Did you frame and hang all those snapshots yourself?"

"The boys and I put it together when they were home for Christmas a couple of years ago. I bought the frames and had a shop size the images that were too big to fit, and then we assembled everything."

"May I borrow the idea? I really like the way that looks."

Kit salutes me with his whiskey. "Borrow away."

We sip our drinks. From what I can tell, he's comfortable with the silence. I'm less so. To keep myself from studying him too avidly, I gaze around the room, taking in the bookcase stuffed with folders and law books and novels. James Lee Burke's latest mystery rests on the ottoman. The richly appointed room with its heirloom antiques is messy and lived in and warmly comfortable. The windows are covered with white plantation shutters rather than curtains, the same as in his brother's house. On the sage-green wall behind Kit hang old-world vistas of the Venetian lagoon and St. Mark's Square. The oil paintings are not new, nor are they reproductions.

My glance returns to my host. Our eyes meet.

"Tell you what," Kit says, twirling his glass against his sweater. "How about a game of twenty questions?"

"What kind of questions?"

"Haven't you ever played this game, Ms. Lizzie? That's for me to know and you to find out." He offers a smile. This one is part challenge, part genial amusement. "After all, you owe me some stories and I'm thinking it might be fun to hear them in revealing little bites."

The look I give him is one Diana refers to as my dagger eyes. "I assume I get to ask my own questions?"

"One question to my two." His mouth quirks.

"One for one or no deal," I counter.

He leans into the chair as if he's pondering pros and cons. "If you must," he finally decides. "But I go first."

I roll my eyes. "Go on, then." I'm pleased he's interested in discovering more about me, although I should put a lid on my enthusiasm. Kit is probably going to speculate about my favorite color. Or, propose a couple of preposterous scenarios I'll have to choose between and explain why.

He sips from his tumbler, eyeing me from under long lashes. How is it I haven't noticed those luxuriant lashes until now? Setting his glass down on a coaster, Kit drawls, "Why aren't you attached? I'm thinking a glorious woman such as yourself should have been snatched up a long time ago."

"Ha!" I exhale. This isn't what I expected. "I was married once and have a lovely daughter to show for it. But once was definitely enough."

"Never been tempted a second time?"

I shake my head. "Nope." This isn't quite true. Roland tempted me and I said yes—for all that was worth. I'm not, however, divulging this technicality. It's personal and complicated and not light entertainment. It's on the same level as the revelations Kit hasn't shared about his life after Eleanor.

"I'd think you'd have men beating down your door," he says.

"Speaketh the man who hath women falling all over him?"

"Hey." His mouth turns down in an effort to keep from laughing. "I have the floor, not you."

"Where did it say you get to ask all of your questions first?"

"You have to start reading the fine print, dahlin'. You're missing the itty-bitty qualifiers." His grin says, *Go ahead, try to outwit me.*

I heave a long-suffering sigh, secretly tickled by the picture he's drawn of men piling up on my doorstep. "You've spent time in the North among us Yankees. Have you forgotten what it's like up there?"

"Is that an answer?"

"Kind of. Don't you know smart opinionated woman of a certain age are not in fashion with the opposite sex?"

"Oh, come on. That's not true." He sips his drink.

"In a small and predominantly white Vermont town, I haven't found a guy in the market for an opinionated woman except as a buddy. Ego stroking isn't my forte, which means I'm seriously handicapped in the relationship department."

Kit makes a face. "That's simplistic. And I don't find you opinionated."

"Having spent, what? Maybe all of eight hours in my company?" I scoff, though I give him points for defending me. "Stick around for a while and you'll see."

"I like strong women."

"Maybe that's your Jewish blood talking. Our culture respects strength in both sexes. Then there's your other culture. The stereotype is that Southern gals are tough as nails, or so I hear, though they cloak those nails in pretty pink polish. But you're the expert, not me." I offer him my own challenging look.

"I won't dispute there is often some truth in stereotypes, but also plenty of exceptions. Not that this is material to what we're talking about. I don't see you walking around in armor bashing everyone who gets in your way. If you believe that, I would argue you don't see your-self clearly."

For a second, I flash on Darius telling me the same thing, insisting my ideas about myself are distorted. *Weird.* This is the second time Kit and Darius have offered similar conclusions about my inner workings. I add this observation to the string of worry beads I keep for gnawing on when I can't sleep.

It is tempting to offer him a cute thanks for his latest compliment, something like, *"Oh, you do say the sweetest things, Mr. Couper"*— except I'm too invested in making my case.

I argue, "No matter the longitude or country of origin, there are men who like powerfully independent women, but I believe many of those same men prefer their powerful women clocked in fashionable femininity and the pretense that they are the weaker vessel. Isn't that the Southern belle's modus operandi?"

"You are overgeneralizing."

"And you are the man who said his mother is a Southern belle, then offered an example of her technique."

"Tell me you don't enjoy it when a guy takes care of you."

"Tell me you don't want a helpmate." I'm enjoying Kit's willingness to spar with me. "Wouldn't you rather be with a sweet woman who makes it her exclusive business to care for you and your home, than with an opinionated woman who goes to work like you do and is too tired afterward to cook or tidy, also like you?"

"I have a cleaning service and the restaurants around here are excellent. We're talking about you, dahlin'. Answer the question."

I set my glass on the side table and cross my arms. "I love being taken care of, though not to the extent it is assumed I can't do for myself." I pause, trying to find a way to describe my philosophy. "I think it's okay to do a little leaning on your partner from time to time. But not all the time. And, I don't believe support has to be from a man to the exclusion of all others."

"You prefer girls?"

"I'm being serious," I growl. "You asked, I'm giving you an honest answer."

Not the least put off, he responds, "Come on, most women want someone to take care of them. You just admitted you do, too."

"I said I wanted support. There's a difference between support and what you're talking about. I want someone to dust me off when I fall, not someone to coddle me so I never fall. There's no learning in that.

I enjoy earning my own living and take pride in providing for myself. What I do appreciate is sympathy after a bad day. A lot of men don't know how to give it. In my experience, men are too solution focused." Picking up my tumbler, I salute Kit and take a sip.

"That's one way to have a relationship," he says, his mouth drawing into a line.

"But not your way?"

Sitting forward he swirls the liquid at the bottom of his glass and regards me for a long second. Finally he says, "You must have had an interesting marriage. I'm sorry your husband didn't know how to do his own heavy lifting. Or have sympathy for yours."

"Thank you." I am touched by his empathy and his intuition.

"Like you," he adds, "I think self-sufficiency is important. But sometimes we need to be carried. Sometimes there isn't any choice and you might be glad to have the help. And, for the record, my commiserating skills are pretty good, or so said my wife. If anyone should know . . ."

He doesn't finish his sentence. Instead he swallows some whiskey, and, sounding gruff, finishes, "I hope I carried my weight and that I always will."

It dawns on me that Kit wasn't freezing me out last Saturday; he was trying to keep himself together. My face heats but I hold his gaze. "I'm sorry. I wasn't thinking." He's probably carried more weight for his dying wife and grieving sons than most people will ever shoulder. "You're absolutely right. Sometimes you have to let someone carry you, and it's okay."

"It is more than that. It's an honor."

My throat tightens with shame as well as longing. How is it I've never considered this sort of caring or carrying? Maybe because I've never experienced the kind of love Kit and Eleanor seem to have shared—or not for long enough to matter. My heart lurches. I feel sorrow for Kit, as well as respect.

He rubs the back of his neck and smiles, but with little zeal. "About the Southern-girl mastery of men we were discussing? For argument's sake, I think you underestimate your expertise."

I'm guessing that, like me, Kit recognizes our conversation has veered down an emotional dark alley and is making an attempt to pull us onto a better-lit path. Although the transition is a little abrupt, I'm relieved and change direction with him.

"Where's your evidence?" I ask.

"For one thing, you stroke my ego just fine."

Is he referring to what I said the other night about his tux? Unbeknownst to me, a Southern belle—or her haint—takes up residence inside my head. "Why Mister Couper, you're joshing me," she says.

"I'm dead serious, dahlin'. I get a little electric kick from your company and I like it more than fine."

The next bump in the road is easy to see. I'm wracking my brain for how to avoid it when Obie the ESP dog climbs to his feet and sticks his nose in my face. He's probably feeling the sexual charge in the air. I certainly do.

I ruffle his hair. Reassured, he circles a few times before plopping back down at my hip, while I pray that the absence of a response from me has altered Kit's direction.

No such luck. He's still heading merrily down the path he's chosen.

He says, "What about a little ol' lovemaking if we're talking needs? You like to be self-sufficient, but I suspect you're a woman who enjoys herself in bed. How do you get around that one, if needing a man isn't part of your equation?"

The charge in the air is stronger. The tingle up my spine proves it, along with a burn much lower down and more to the front. I say, "Oh, sex is a need, but needing sex isn't the same as needing a man, is it?"

His eyes light with merriment. "I like sex, too," he says confidingly. "Although I prefer having mine with a woman. It isn't nearly as satisfying on my own."

I widen my eyes. "Overshare?"

He winks. "I thought I should make note, seeing as we're being honest."

There are many ways to go from *here*. The most direct one is to bed. *Without him.*

"All this honesty is delightful but exhausting, don't you think?" I respond. "I'd better get some sleep. I can tell I'll need to sharpen my wiles if I'm going to keep up with you." I stand. "Thank you for a stimulating evening, Mr. Couper."

He guffaws, the sound so irresistible I want to vault the ottoman and land in his lap.

Yup, definitely time to go.

With raised brow, Kit says. "Lizbeth Silver, it's my opinion that your wiles are plenty sharp already. Any sharper and there's no telling what could happen."

Oh boy. I'm thinking even a storefront psychic could pull a prediction out of her crystal ball about where we're heading.

Obie jumps to the carpet with a soft thump, interrupting this last wayward thought. I follow him into the mudroom.

Behind us, Kit props his shoulder on the doorframe. I walk to the bench and clip Obie to his lead.

"This Tuesday is Cookbook Club. I'd be pleased if you would join me," Kit says, shoving away from where he's leaning. He steps down into the mudroom.

I straighten. "What's Cookbook Club?"

Obie trots toward the door, ready to go home.

"It's a monthly gathering of folks who buy an agreed-upon cookbook and sample the recipes. We use the same cookbook for three months and then switch to another. I'd love for you to come along." The smile he offers is so innocent, I could have imagined what came before. "Be my guest, Ms. Lizzie?" He steps in front of me, standing a little too close.

I have to look up, way up, to meet his eyes. "Why Mr. Couper, I think I will."

When I get to Sam's house, I'll perform an exorcism to offload the Southern belle who's decided to share my body.

"What time should I be ready?" I ask.

"Would leaving for town at 5:30 suit you?"

"Sure 'nuff."

I decide I'd better burn some sage as well.

Kit grins and holds the door for me.

The lead playing out, Obie bounds into the night. Kit bends to kiss my forehead before stepping away. "Thank you for your delightful company, Lizbeth."

There is a side of me that finds this forehead-kissing business charming. The other side wishes he'd aim a little lower.

CHAPTER 19

THE COOKING TIME for Kit's entrèe wasn't exactly as the recipe suggested. Because of the extra fifteen minutes the scalloped root vegetables spent in the oven, we are among the last to arrive at the bookstore in downtown Brunswick where the Cookbook Club meets.

Kit hands his food contribution to the bookstore's owner and helps me off with my jacket. We walk between a row of shelves to an open area filled with tables and chairs. There's a bar counter behind the tables where the food contributions wait to be served. A side table closer to us is strewn with blank name tags and pens. We write ourselves in and slap the labels onto our chests.

A man wearing khakis, a short-sleeve blue golf shirt, and the buzz cut of a retired military man, joins us at one side of the food counter where several open bottles of wine await our selection. After the usual pleasantries are exchanged, he engages Kit in conversation about a business dispute. Kit hands me a glass of red wine and squeezes my arm, acknowledging the conversation excludes me. When the fellow, labeled Walter, continues on without a pause we could use to switch to a more inclusive topic, I take myself over to the appetizer table.

Engaging in idle conversation is part of a wedding photographer's job, so I say hello to the two women and single man standing at the round table with a bowl of dip and basket of chips sitting at its center. Off to the side is a platter holding one lonely tomato bruschetta toast.

The man, with the faded hair of an aging redhead, helps himself to a chip, smearing it with dip. As soon as the chip is in his mouth, he snatches the last toast. His name tag reads, "Hello, I'm" printed in red across the top; below that, in chunky block letters, he's penned, "Dean." Dean munches, looking past me with an unfocused stare. He is either very shy, very drunk, or has way too much on his mind.

I pick up a chip. The woman closest to "Hello, I'm Dean" glances at my name tag, then at me. "Pretty necklace. Where did you find such a unique piece?" she asks.

Before I can answer, she slaps her hand to her own tag. "I should have introduced myself. I'm Rhonda."

"Hi, Rhonda, nice to meet you. I'm Liz, but you know that already." I pat my tag and tell her the necklace is made from vintage Bakelite and glass beads by my friend Evie. "It's fun, isn't it?"

Dean reaches for another chip, acknowledging only the food and the wall of books behind my left shoulder.

Unlike her partner or date or whatever he is, Rhonda is one of those women who practically vibrates with energy. She's wearing an electric-blue cardigan over a green-and-blue top with touches of coral in the print. Her jewelry, which is as gold as her hair, doesn't appear to be costume. When she leans in to get a better look at my necklace, her perfect coif doesn't move.

"Evie collects vintage beads and uses them in her designs. She's on Etsy. If you want to see more of her work, her shop is called Circa Beadazzled."

"Oh, thank you. I'll have to look her up." She gives me a bright smile.

At home, I feel arty and fashionable in the outfit I chose tonight, the Circa Beadazzled necklace worn with a forest-green top and my favorite knee-length black skirt. But here, among women in bright tropical colors or pastel versions of the same, my ensemble seems less arty than funereal.

"It's so nice to have you join us for Cookbook Club. Are you a snowbird?" Rhonda asks.

I'm betting my outfit gave me away. "I wish we had a Cookbook Club in Vermont where I'm from," I answer. "It's such a fun idea."

"Pretty foliage up there, although I don't think I could abide those cold winters." She gives her shoulders a shiver at the imagined deep freeze.

"You are absolutely right about the cold. It chased me away." I realize that although I haven't quite matched Rhonda's drawl, my normally crisp New England diction has softened like butter left out too long. This is not the fault of the phantom Southern-belle body-snatcher who made her appearance last Thursday at Kit's house. This is because I pick up accents too easily. When I toured England right after I graduated from college, my hard Vermont A's moved to the back of my mouth. I found myself saying things like, "Cahn you tell me where I cahn find the nearest tube station?" Similarly, as Rhonda and I talk, my vowels stretch and I lose my consonants—*suga'*.

With a little circle of one coral-tipped finger, Rhonda gestures toward Kit. "I saw you come in."

I glance in his direction. He and Walter have been joined by a couple of other men, all in animated conversation. Kit throws me an *Everything okay?* look. I nod that I'm fine.

Rhonda doesn't miss our silent exchange, which compels me to say, "We met recently through a mutual acquaintance." Kit may have told his friends I'm living on his property, but there is a scary gleam in Rhonda's eyes I don't want to encourage.

"How sweet," she replies, drawing out the *eeeeeet* so it has extra syllables. Taking a step closer to me, she says, "I hope you don't mind me asking. It's just that he's been a member of this club for years and never brought a friend along before." The way she emphasizes *friend* tells me I haven't succeeded in discouraging her.

"The area is new to me. Kit has been helping me find my way around," I clarify. Then, I can't help doing a little fishing of my own. I lead off with, "He's so nice."

As hoped, Rhonda runs with it, taking another step closer. "Kit's a charmer, for sure. But"—she leans in to say—"havin' a woman on his arm isn't the same as dating." Lowering her voice she confides, "As far as I know, he's never been partial to anyone since his tragedy." She nods, as if confirming this fact for herself, and then beams at me, giving my arm a congratulatory pat.

The significance she's heaped on Kit's arrival with me in tow is a teensy bit thrilling, yet even as I match Rhonda beam for beam, I can't help wondering why she is sharing this information with me, a total stranger. Is she cruising for gossip to carry back to her garden club, or wherever she trades confidences? Is she warning me not to get my hopes up? Or did she just nominate herself as captain of my cheerleading team?

"The Lord is surely with us tonight," Rhonda says. Another comment I can't interpret. She tilts her head at Dean, and the two of them share their own silent exchange. He grabs another chip. Without once acknowledging me or the other woman who has been watching her converse with me, Dean trails after Rhonda's brightly plumed personage as she sails toward a group of couples on the other side of the store.

I'm not used to the Lord entering a conversation unless his name is taken in vain or used in worship. Since I spend barely two days a year in the synagogue during the High Holidays and go with body-centric curses, I'm nonplussed by Rhonda. Did she just offer her blessing for me and Kit to date?

Huh.

The silent woman who completed our foursome introduces herself. She is slim with short frost-tipped hair. Her name tag says, "Lydia Jane." She notes that the evening has become a bit nippy and rain is forecast. We trade observations about the weather and the beauty of the Golden Isles—the region's moniker—until Kit collects me a few minutes later, after the store's owner has announced it's time to gather for the pre-dinner recipe review.

✳

"Thank you. That was fun," I tell Kit as we drive through Brunswick, heading home.

"Glad you enjoyed it. Do you have a favorite recipe?"

"I wouldn't mind copying that cornmeal orange cake from your cookbook."

"I can take a picture with my phone and send it to you. The flank steak got my vote."

"That's because you haven't tasted my barbecue sauce yet."

"I love barbecue anything. It's in the Southern genetic code."

"Would you care to try a Yankee version?"

"There's an almost perverse idea." His mouth quirks. "Imagine that. And yes, I believe I would like to try it."

"Very open-minded of you." I laugh. "Next week?"

"How about this week? Should I bring something? A salad? Cole-slaw?"

"Sure. Either one. Would Thursday work for you?"

"Thursday it is. I have some Yeunling in the fridge. I'll bring that, too."

We continue our conversation about the recipes we sampled as well as some of the other cookbooks the club has used, but as we wait for the light to turn at the intersection of Route 17 and the causeway to St. Simons Island, I decide it's time for another game of twenty questions. The car is a perfect staging ground, since Kit is stuck with me for the next ten miles.

"Don't think I didn't notice you asked all the questions the other night," I begin.

"You didn't stay long enough for it to be your turn," Kit responds, his lips compressing into a tight line, but he loses his battle not to smirk. His lips pull up at one corner.

"If you want to keep those points you've been collecting, you need to ante up."

"I've been collecting points?" he drawls. "Isn't that fine." The last word is elongated—*faahn*. He stops at the next light and throws a glance in my direction "Dahlin', I'm an open book, fire away."

Sure you are, I think, wishing I didn't find his genteel Southern drawl as appealing as the rest of him.

When we played this game the other night, he asked me why I wasn't married. I've considered asking the same of him, except asking might lead back to Eleanor, which will only get him circling his wagons. Better to come at the question sideways.

"Let's assume you're a man who enjoys women, since you said as much the other night."

Kit accelerates away from the light. I see mischief sparkling in his eyes.

"I also respect you ladies, but you know that by now." He glances in my direction. "Respect you and enjoy you in all kinds of ways."

This is going to be fun. His craggy smile is warming me from my head to my toes, including significant areas in between that I continue to believe would be better off cold.

"I'm also guessing you're not interested in long-term companionship," I continue. "And that women are falling all over themselves to get at you."

"There you go, flattering my ego again. Damn, I'm enjoying this more than I would have thought." He reaches over to pat my leg. The gesture is more jocular than flirtatious. "But that wasn't a question, was it?"

Based on Rhonda's intel and his late nights in fancy suits, I ask, "How many big charity events did you attend last year?"

"This relates how?"

"Answer the question, Mr. Open Book."

He thinks for a minute. "There was the Georgia Symphony Ball, the Friends of the Library Table of Contents Dinner, the Marshes of Glynn Reception, the Museum Heritage Gala, Art Association Soiree . . . Chili Cook-Off . . . I don't know, maybe twenty in all? Something around that."

"And how many of these did you attend with your mother?"

"The symphony ball, the literacy dinner . . ." He thinks for a minute before adding, "The Museum Gala here, several others in Savannah."

"Which leaves a dozen events you attended with . . . ?"

"Friends."

"Who are female."

"Is that a question?"

"Actually, the question is how many different woman accompanied you to those events."

"Jealous?"

"I'm trying to make a point. How many?"

His brow wrinkles as he considers. "I think, five."

"You don't know?"

"Five," he says more definitively.

"And how many of those women do you sleep with?"

"I can't divulge that and consider myself a gentleman!"

"Which, by default, must mean I'm not a lady for asking," I push back.

"Don't be ridiculous, of course you're a lady."

"Maybe not. And maybe that's why you like me."

He laughs. "There's no right answer to that one, so I'll keep my own counsel."

When he stops chuckling, I say, "My guess is you enjoy 'benefits' with them all." I'm checking his answers off against my list of desirable characteristics for short-term men. I have no idea what I'll do if he meets them. Since that night with Darius, my plan has been to throw The Rules out. Kit probably won't pass, anyway. First and foremost, I already know that keeping him at arm's length is impossible. Then there is the significant detail that I want him close, which means I'm already cruising in the danger zone.

His brow furrows. "I don't understand how this relates."

I can't tell whether the displeasure I'm reading in the hard line of his jaw is for real or part of the game.

"My turn. You've been asking all the questions," he says.

"Oh, no you don't. It's still my turn," I say with exaggerated patience. "And I'll take that as a yes. You sleep with them all." I shake my head in mock disbelief. "Christopher Aiken Couper, *you* are a player."

"Ms. Lizzie, I've got a feeling we're two peas in a pod." Offering me a speculative once-over, he declares, "Tables turned, dahlin'. Let's see if I'm as right about you as you are about me. First question: How many *friends* did you make last year? Six?"

"Oh, so it's six for you, not five?" I volley back, trying to retake control of the game.

"Five for you, too?" He smirks.

"Gentlemen don't ask those questions."

As soon as the words leave my mouth, I realize I'm going to eventually answer, since he did . . . sort of.

"We're not talking gentlefolk here. We're talking you and me. Sisters," he suggests fatuously, "under the skin."

"You're hilarious." I harrumph, giving in. "Last year, it was two. The year before, one." I don't count C. One-night stands don't count, I decide, wondering if this is like former President Clinton's oral sex defense when his affair with his intern became known.

"One? Were you ill? Did you break something? Your libido, maybe? That's not normal!"

I roll my eyes, although he can't see me do it since he's watching the road. My interest and accomplishments in changing partners a couple of times a year brands me as promiscuous in my mother's eyes. Clearly, Kit disagrees. As do I.

"I'm going to assume that one lover in an entire year was a weird anomaly," he declares. "Two or three is exactly what I figured. I don't see you as a jezebel, so you probably work up to your affairs. No jumping into bed in a hot flash for you." He chuckles at whatever this image conjures for him. "You aren't the type of gal to see a comely set of shoulders from across the room and need immediate possession. I see you wanting to be seduced—and if I am any judge of human nature, I say you also like to do the seducing. So, you need a little time, maybe a month or two, to enjoy building the tension before going for the climax." He grins, pleased with his wordplay and in all likelihood offering a map for the route he sees an affair between us traveling.

"The thrill of the hunt and all," he concludes, taking his eyes off the road for a second to throw me a speculative glance. "After that, I see another month or two going by once you hit the sack with the lucky man of your choosing. That leaves another month or so to disengage before beginning again."

"Is this a page from your book?" I ask. I'm not happy that he's pegged me, but then, I've pegged him, too.

"I don't have a book," he says. "And, I don't sleep around any more than you do. I have a number of friends with needs similar to my own."

"So, your lady friends are happy with this 'eenie, meenie, miney, mo' system of yours? At least I'm a serial monogamist."

He laughs. "I'm honest about my intentions. In my experience, given enough development time, the other half of the equation will self-select out if the terms aren't agreeable. I'm assuming you're as honest within your own system."

"This is the first time I've heard anyone describe his love life as if it were a series of contract negotiations."

"I would agree with you if we were talking about my so-called love life. But this isn't about love—this is about mutually satisfying physical gratification. I assure you, I don't get complaints."

I can well imagine. A naughty "book" opens in my mind with an illustration of him doing . . .

I tell myself this rush of feeling is only lust, but my heart skips a beat as a shiver runs up my spine.

"Apparently I was correct about how you manage your own . . ."— Kit's hand strokes the wheel in a pantomime caress—"friendships."

I grimace, trying to understand the intensity of my feelings. The feelings are a problem. How to cool them down is a bigger one.

"Hey, dahlin', you started it," Kit says, misinterpreting the look on my face. "I'm only taking advantage of the opportunity to learn more about you." He meets my eyes for an instant. "We're a lot alike, is how I see it. Maybe scarily alike." He stays focused on the road, adding, "Truth to tell, I'm fascinated."

I see the dare he is throwing me when he meets my eyes.

A little panicked by that dare, I try to add up the sort of alike he thinks we are. Are we alike because we admit to having managed our needs for physical gratification and companionship in similar ways? Or is it because neither of us cares to expose ourselves to the kind of hurt we've experienced before? Or all of the above?

He's moving a little too fast, or maybe only too fast for a woman who doesn't know what she wants anymore. What if I'm no longer the woman I'm obviously still projecting? Do I want an affair or something more permanent?

I gaze out the side window. In the darkness, the details are missing. I can make out little more than the outlines of houses, cinder-block churches, looming oaks, and matchstick pines as we speed past.

A man can be too seductive, too much like a drug. And since men are my drug of choice, I'd do well to be wary of Kit.

The car crunches off the highway onto gravel and Willing's gate appears in the headlights.

"There are some things I don't ever want to do again," Kit says as he rolls the car to a stop.

I swivel to look at him.

"I'm betting we have the same 'don't' at the top of our lists," he declares enigmatically. Dropping his hand over mine, he holds my gaze for a second. Then he nods, and presses the gate's remote.

The car eases between the pillars. Kit says, "Nothing precludes us having some fun as long as we're stuck on the planet living out our days, does it, dahlin'?" His tone is contemplative. "While there's breath in my body, I'm all for no strings attached, good safe fun."

With this final utterance, one that makes *fun* sound a lot like waterboarding, he drives us the rest of the way home.

My plan had been for a game of verbal ping-pong with a soupçon of truth-or-dare thrown in to keep things interesting—the same game Kit played with me. Instead, I feel like my ball has bounced off the table into a thicket of sawtooth palmetto.

Unfortunately, I understand what he's alluding to: Kit is up for an affair, but no more than that.

Fine, my head argues. He's too hung up on his dead wife; he lives too far away from Vermont; and he's an admitted player who has no plans to change his stripes. He is massively flawed, a Rules man to the core. I should be overjoyed.

It doesn't bode well that I'm not.

In his parking area, Kit switches off the ignition. I have my door open before he rounds the car. He offers his hand. This time the tingle feels dangerous. He smiles, squeezing my fingers. We disengage and start toward my—his brother's—house. Only when we are close enough to hear Obie's excited barking does Kit say, "Well, dahlin', I enjoyed myself."

We step onto the porch. Veranda. Whatever.

"Likewise," I reply, which is mostly true although I can't exactly categorize the last few minutes as enjoyable. Revealing, yes. Also a little weird.

I fumble the house key from my purse. Kit bends to brush my cheek with his lips. He's quick about it. As I push the key into the lock, he backs to the edge of the porch, ready to be on his way, although he's too much of a gentleman to leave before I'm safely in the house.

The lock turns. Kit waves and heads across the drive.

Inside, Obie dances around me, sneezing. Actually, sneezing is my interpretation of the noise he makes when he's so excited he can't contain his happiness. Distracted by his exuberant greeting, it takes me a second to realize Kit moved his good-night kiss a lot closer to where I want it, which is also where I shouldn't want it.

God. I've known the man for barely two weeks and he's already reeled me in and tied me in knots. I lift a hand to touch my cheek, looking toward his house. The light has come on behind the den shutters, although I can't see him moving around.

The only non-mercurial male in my life, Obie bows low, tail wagging.

It's a comfort to be loved unconditionally, if only by my dog. His happiness is easy to provide; all he needs is affection, food, a soft bed, and the occasional ramble. I wish my needs, as well as those of my neighbor, were as simple.

CHAPTER 20

"LIZ!" ARIELLE CHIDES after I've carried on for a few minutes.

I needed confirmation that I wasn't imagining the subtext of what Kit said in the car, so I called Arielle for a reality check.

"Why are you so worked up? Isn't this business as usual? I hate to say it, but you sound more like a pouty teenager than an experienced woman of the world. What gives?"

"Am I imagining that he warned me off?" I ask, ignoring her question. "Wasn't he also saying, *And if you are interested in more than a good roll in the hay, you need to modify your expectations?*"

My poodle and I are seated on the sofa, where we ended up after I took Obs for his last out. As I wait for Arielle's response, I stroke the big soft head resting on my thigh. Obie sighs and closes his eyes.

"Maybe Kit was warning himself off? Being a guy, if he's as big a commitment-phobe as you are, instead of figuring out what the problem is within himself, he might be blaming his response to you, on you."

"I don't know. He seems pretty aware. And I'm not a commitment-phobe. I'm . . ." Unable to decide what I am, I mutter, "Okay, here's what concerns me. What if I'm not as done with love as I thought?" My heart speeds, terrified and also thrilled to admit this possible change in philosophy.

There's a second of silence at the other end of the line. Finally, Arielle says, "You want more than he's offering? That's a cosmic shift, Liz. I say good for you!"

"Hold on! Even if I wanted *that*, my focus needs to be on my work. I don't have time to fall in—" I stop before uttering the forbidden word, modifying it to, "infatuation."

I wish I believed this statement as fervently as I've claimed. "An affair is not a good idea in terms of the time and brain-space it would consume. And what if it doesn't work out? That would be awkward. Imagine living next door to your landlord and former lover for another couple of months."

"Well, there's your answer. Problem solved."

Arielle calls out sharply to her cat, explaining Miu-Miu has an exciting new sport—climbing the curtains.

"He's a small but fierce maniac."

"That he is."

"Maybe I'm having one of those nights." I rub my stomach, wondering if indigestion can spin your brain out of control. "What seems best to my head doesn't seem best to my body. And here's another thing. Kit and I can't keep things light the way people only interested in no strings attached fun should. Whenever we're together we start off light, but somewhere along the way, we veer into heavy. The worst example was when I offered him my latest theory about how relationships should be conducted. Kit disagreed and used his own life to illustrate why I was wrong. When he was done, I felt more like that immature teenager you compared me to than the grown-up I think I am."

"You are not immature, any lapses notwithstanding. But this is interesting. Exactly what did he say?"

"It's complicated. Here's the condensed version: I told him I didn't think it was fair for anyone to carry their partner in a relationship. Kit said sometimes you don't have a choice about needing help and it's a gift to be allowed to support your spouse. He said he was honored to be there for Eleanor when she was ill. His wife died after a long, debilitating fight with cancer." My voice trails off, throat clogging with the grief that rises so readily these days.

I feel sorrow for Kit, but also for myself—I'll never be loved the way he loved his wife. I rub my eyes.

"I'm beginning to like this guy," Arielle says. "Maybe you should stop thinking so much and see what happens."

I moan. "He's got that perfect combination of sexy brain and sexy body and he's genuinely nice. How often does that happen?"

"I wouldn't know. The last time I fell in love it was with a slinky black kitten."

"The young curtain-climbing demon," I say, happy for the subject change.

"All men are trouble, even in cat form. Miu-Miu believes the way to my heart is to leave mice at my feet."

"At least the little beast gets your blood flowing."

"And Kit does the same for you. Although I hope he's into better surprises than half-dead mice on your doorstep."

"Remains to be seen." I sit, thinking. "I need to stop projecting and stay in the moment, don't I?"

"Have you tried that?"

I flop onto my back. Obie's head falls off my knee. He gives me an accusatory look as I throw a pillow behind my head and offer another to him. Ignoring the conciliatory gesture, he moves to the far end of the couch, facing away from me. I'm being given the doggy cut direct.

I roll my shoulders and hear little popping noises. "It's a life-force charisma thing," I tell Arielle. "Kit's got it in spades, as well as the male beauty-vitality thing. You know how I go for those glittery eyes. And I'm a sucker for good hands. Muscular, artistic—" I exhale. "He also has a wonderful laugh along with the rest of what he's got. You should see him. What's worse is that his mind turns me on. *Really turns me on.* I'm forced to stretch my own to keep up with him. Not to mention that he gives great affirmation."

I can't stop gushing. "You know our theory that a lot of men don't actually like women, even though they want one? They may be attracted, fascinated, et cetera, but deep down they don't trust us? Kit isn't cut from that cloth."

"Whoa!" my friend says. "If your goal is not to get involved, you need to consider, and I quote, that in your world 'men come in a wide variety of pleasing shapes and sizes.' Generalize, don't personalize."

"The same way you like cats?" I suggest, because Arielle isn't into men—or women, for that matter. She is very private and doesn't have a lot of friends of either type. I feel honored to be in that select number.

"Let's leave cats out of it. Dogs, too. I'm trying to make a point about men, the kind who walk on two legs and carry a big stick . . ."

"Ha ha ha! Good one."

"*That stick*," Arielle emphasizes, "is your attraction to them."

I swing my legs to the floor and reach across the couch to pet my dog. "You always put things in perspective. I guess I need to work harder on the one-day-at-a time concept."

"Definitely. Though it's never been your specialty and could use some work regardless."

"Is the weather bad?" I'm once again ready for a new topic. I doubt I can pull off anything approaching a go-with-the-flow philosophy about Kit, though I recognize we've flogged my *to-do-it or not-to-do-it* question to death.

Arielle tells me the usual pattern of snow followed by rain freezing into ice is unchanged. "The sidewalks are like a town-wide luge run," she says.

"I can't describe how thankful I am to be out of all that. I'm enjoying the weather here. And the cultural differences."

"Speaking of travel, Diana and I talked yesterday. You were right. Her help will be a boon. Thanks for setting that up. It'll be great to have her visit Mom. You know how much Georgie adores her. Diana said she'd be happy to stay with Miu-Miu, too. I'm going to pay her extra for that. God knows what that cat would do if he were left to his own devices for four days"

"What you pay her is between you and Diana, although you know she will protest payment. So, is Vanessa taking the last of the pictures? You haven't said."

"Yes. And she insisted on trading, the way you do."

"Are you surprised? Your pottery is amazing."

"I'm grateful you arranged it. But if you end up leaving next winter, I'll get my act together earlier so you can do all the shots."

"Deal," I say.

CHAPTER 21

"**FANTASTIC DINNER,** but I'm repeating myself." Kit dabs his mouth with his napkin as I rise to remove our plates. "Will you share the recipe? The boys would enjoy it."

"Absolutely. The flank steak is even better cooked on a grill, but I didn't want to drag your brother's huge contraption out of the shed."

"It's the party-size model," Kit says. "I have a smaller one. Next time, we'll grill at my house."

Kit called yesterday to confirm dinner plans for tonight, barely sixteen hours after our truth-or-dare session ran amok. If making such quick contact is any indication, he doesn't mind the way our conversations teeter between comedy and pathos without much middle ground. As for me, I'm attempting to go with the flow—the new Zen flow I'm hoping to master.

"Dessert?" I ask. "I found strawberries in town that smell like the real thing. They inspired me to whip cream and make biscuits."

"I'll be doing additional laps if I keep eating like this. I'd love to take you up on the offer, but the sad truth is I'm too full to down another bite."

"You're a swimmer?" That explains his sleek build.

"Since high school. Won a few medals in my time. Do you have a sport?"

"I ski, but I wasn't on the school team. I've never been a good team player. I spent most of my time in the darkroom when I wasn't on the slopes with friends."

"All that practice paid off."

"Like you, I won some awards, including a free ride at college."

"Good for you."

He rubs his stomach. "What do you say to an intermission, since

I'm willing to do those laps once I make room for more food?"

"How about we take a tour of your photo gallery?"

"Sure." Kit sets his napkin on the table and rises. "Let me help with the cleanup and we'll head over."

✳

During the tour of the family photographs, Kit identified his father and mother and the boys as well as friends and relatives but didn't say a word about Eleanor. Perhaps, having found me viewing her photographs last time, he felt no need to identify her. More likely, he just didn't want to go there.

For all of my ranting about Kit's plans the last time I spoke with Arielle, he doesn't seem inclined to move in one direction or another. My body, ever the glutton, is frustrated. My mind, split down the middle about whether I can handle an affair with Kit or not, has decided to let fate, or those rascally gods, make the decision for me, not that the wait isn't stressful.

Completing a review of the morning's e-mail, I call Obie. He hangs out on the living room couch while I'm working because I won't let him sit in the Eames chairs. He prefers a soft perch to the sisal rug in the den. "Common, doggerel," I say, "Let's go for a ride!"

We've been here long enough now for Obs to find this suggestion agreeable.

I am hoping to be inspired to take a few pictures. I could return to the blood lichen clearing. I've been back a few times. In the shot I envision, the light needs to glow yet also be defused, which will intensify the color of the lichen. My guess is that dawn may deliver the light I'm looking for, but I'm not an early riser, so I haven't confirmed the theory yet.

After loading Obie onto the back seat of the car, I load myself and the camera bag in the front and head out.

✳

When Kit drops in for our nightcap a couple of nights later, he's wearing his tux, returning from another of his fancy-dress charity events. He mentioned where he was going, but the sight of him in the Tom Ford getup short-circuits my brain.

Peeling off his jacket as he walks into the house, he breathes a sigh of relief. No such relief for me. This particular man in that particular suit is like mainlining arousal. Desire singes my toes, never mind what it's doing to more critical parts of my anatomy.

I imagine wearing him on my arm at a glittering party like Waltz Night.

As is his habit, Kit drapes his jacket over a chair on his way to the liquor cabinet, removing his cuff links and rolling the crisply starched sleeves of his shirt along the way. The breadth of his shoulders is emphasized by the brilliant white of the shirt winging from the low taper of his waist. I stop salivating long enough to pluck his coat from the chair. Warmed by his skin, it smells like his cologne as interpreted by his body—Eau de Kit. I don't lift the jacket to my nose for a heady whiff until I'm in the foyer where he can't see me do it.

In a different and more established relationship, one based on the cumulative pleasures and frustrations that arise when two people spend their lives in close proximity, the notice of Kit's coat-toss might become irritation and then exasperation over his inability to hang the jacket for himself. At this stage, I'm merely charmed. Yet, even as I'm enjoying the sweet fantasy of domestic harmony his toss and my pickup implies, I am reminded of what Darius said about how these small details and conflicts are the stuff of true intimacy. It seems as if Darius, although very much alive, is turning into my resident haint, his observations echoing too often and with more truth than is entirely comfortable. At least C. doesn't float into my thoughts the way Darius does, forcing me to face that what I've written in stone may be less durable than I'd like. When he shows up in my head, he doesn't evoke fear anymore, and sometimes alone in bed, I make pleasurable use of him.

Returning to the living room, I remind myself that Kit and I are friends of the moment. We will not be establishing long-term rituals, frustrating or otherwise.

Mr. Irresistible ambles to my side, whiskey on offer. By now I've learned to stock the ice bucket in the drinks cabinet. I take a substantial taste before clinking my glass against his. As he brings his glass to his lips, my eyes rise to the line of his throat as he swallows and hums satisfaction at the taste. Kit has shared that he limits himself to a single alcoholic beverage at the events he attends, preferring to drive safely home where he can savor his whiskey in private. My focus moves to the plump fleshiness of his bottom lip where the rim of the glass presses.

I manage to look away, but he's caught me watching. I don't think I'm imagining the assessing look he's giving me. I decide not to be embarrassed caught ogling him, since it's clear I'm not the only one whose sexual radar is on alert this evening.

He raises his brows and his mouth quirks—acknowledgment of what we're likely both thinking but not doing just yet. Since I know what is holding me back, I wonder what holds him. He clinks my glass a second time and gestures for me to sit. In his well-mannered Southern universe, a gentleman never sits until his companion has seated herself.

"So, Ms. Lizzie," he says once I'm settled, "how was your day?"

"Actually, Mr. Couper, I had a productive day. I not only fielded a couple new booking queries, I also took some pictures that pleased me." I can't help grinning.

"Can I see?"

"Sure, but tomorrow. I'll show them off after I've done a little work to them."

"What are the subjects?" He backs up a step to sit in what I consider his chair.

"I was meandering on the back roads along the Altamaha River when I saw an old house—more of a ruin, really—overtaken by vines snaking up the porch pillars and in and out of what was left of the window frames. The sky was clouded over, which gave the image a spooky effect—Southern Gothic at its best. I think the vines were wisteria. I have to find out if the wisteria will bloom before I leave, because the same image with those vines in bloom will be even more amazing and strange."

"It usually begins blooming at the beginning of March."

"Great. I'll be able to see it."

Kit takes a sip of his drink, and then says, "I need a favor, Liz."

When he doesn't elaborate, I say, "I hope I can grant it."

"I expected to attend a gala for the Garden Society with my mother, but of all things, she double booked herself, promising a friend giving a speech in Savannah that she would be her on-the-spot support." He shakes his head, taking another sip of whiskey while the teenager inside me, the sulky one Arielle lied about me not owning, anticipates that finally, almost thirty years after the boy I had a crush on did not ask me to the senior prom, this is it. I sit up a little straighter.

"Mom hasn't missed the gala since Dad passed away," Kit remarks. Setting his glass on a low table between us, he looks not at me but at the couch cushion to my right, although I could be imagining where his glance is falling.

My inner teenager slumps with dejection. The forty-six-year-old me tells Miss Immaturity to stop sniveling.

Kit begins talking—to my shoulder. "So I'm hoping you will do me the honor of attending the event with me."

This is a Kit I've not met before, unsure of his reception. I have an inkling of why he isn't meeting my gaze. "But?" I ask, deciding not to come to his rescue, a form of payback for the fact that while he isn't looking at my shoulder anymore, he's not meeting my eyes. Plus, he's making me crazy with anticipation. I feel he should suffer a little for that, too.

"But," he sighs, "after our discussion on the way home from Cookbook Club, I am uncomfortable about asking because I don't want you to think you are one of . . ." He trails off again and shame on me, I'm enjoying his discomfort. This observation guilts me into offering him a hand with his dilemma. Sort of.

"So, what you are suggesting is that you want me to go to this party with you but you don't want to sleep with me afterward?" Or maybe he wants to sleep with me afterward and that's his problem?

"Yes!" Kit says, relief clear in his voice. And then he immediately says, "No!"

At *yes*, he met my eyes. But with *no*, he hangs his head, giving it a shake before he looks up again, his brow furrowed. His mouth twists into a rueful grin and he rubs his hand through his hair.

I laugh, although I'm not sure I find the situation funny. "How about we don't go there?"

Kit sits back, taking my comment as a rebuttal.

I clarify, "Oh, I don't mean the gala; that would be fun. I'd love to go. You can fill in the details later. What I mean is, let's erase this piece of the tape."

"I owe you an explanation—"

"Nah, honestly, you don't. Which isn't to say we won't go there in the future." *God, why did I say that?* Knowing him the little that I do, I already know he's going to put his own spin on my words. He lifts one expressive brow and grins, spin accomplished.

It occurs to me that Kit has come back from all of his charitable evenings looking dapper and not as if he's picked himself up from some woman's bed to return to his own. Except for the time he was in Savannah visiting his mother a week ago, he hasn't driven in later than midnight, or been gone overnight.

Maybe I'm putting two and two together and adding it up to sixty-nine, but I think this indicates he hasn't been sleeping with his "benefits" since my arrival. A wide smile lifts the corners of my mouth practically to my eyelids.

"What?" Kit asks.

"Oh, umm, I'm excited about your invitation. And, as it happens, I'm in a great mood because the pictures I took today were more than special." This is a dodge, a way to pour a little water on the flirting flames and give us each space to cool off—if that's what we want to do. I decide to go for a little more space and tell him about why I'm excited about today's images.

"It isn't only these shots. Do you remember a few nights ago on our way to dinner, the way the sky was thick with moisture-laden gray clouds and the marsh was beginning to shift from winter gold to spring green? I shot out the car window. The wind must have gusted as I snapped the shutter. When I downloaded the images, the grass was blurred, the sky sharply defined. The result looks more like an impressionist painting than a photograph."

If I hadn't lived the last couple of years of creative drought, I could imagine they'd never happened. That photo is as good as the painting over Sam's couch. So are the shots of the house buried inside the wisteria vines.

"That's great. *And*, I am holding you to the promise of a look at what you've shot." He salutes me with his drink.

"Will there be dancing?" I ask at the same time he says, "That's great."

Reverting to Southern gentleman mode, he doesn't pursue his demand. "There will indeed be dancing, although the floor will not be ballroom size."

Saluting Kit with my own drink, I say, "Cool beans, and yes, you will see the photos as soon as I've edited them." I take a celebratory sip, delighted that Zeus has put a second dancing man in my path less than three months after the first. I'm also delighted by my creative output. I shout a silent *yes!* to the bevy of deities who may have lent a helping hand.

Returning to the subject he'd been pursuing, Kit says, "You have been elusive about letting me see your work, so now that I have your pledge, I'm holding you to it."

I nod okay.

Relaxing into the chair, he sips his whiskey. After a few swallows, he says, "This evening, some old friends I haven't seen for a while invited me to visit. I'm thinking that could be a nice outing for us if you have time this Sunday."

Us. A nice outing for us. I grin.

"It's a pretty place. You might want to bring your camera," he prompts.

"Sounds like a plan. Where do your friends live? And when do I need to be ready?"

Kit sits forward, resting his swoon-worthy arms on his knees. "Late afternoon is the best time for what I want you to witness. Let's leave here around 3:00 to give ourselves time to wander. We can hit Coastal Kitchen for shrimp and grits afterward. Deal?"

"Deal. But you forgot to mention where we're going. Are we going to St. Simons Island?" It's a reasonable assumption, since Coastal Kitchen is in a marina about a mile from the island end of the causeway.

"It's a surprise. One you'll enjoy."

"Okay."

"Just like that? No questions?"

"I like surprises. If you think I'll enjoy wherever it is you are taking me, I'm sure I will."

Kit flashes a grin. It lights his face, crinkling the corners of his eyes and bracketing his mouth with deep creases. It also makes him even more attractive, if that's possible. He stands and crosses to me, offering his hand. In my present state, the contact of his warm palm on my own makes me dizzy. He squeezes my fingers, holding on a few seconds too long after I'm on my feet. With an upward quirk at one side of his mouth that I have decided communicates amusement and speculation, he releases me. Was Kit thinking I should have pulled him closer while our hands were joined? Or that he missed his chance? *Damn.* I wish I knew.

CHAPTER 22

THE TIDE IS HIGH as we travel over the Torras Causeway toward my big surprise. The Intracoastal Waterway's many channels reflect the ethereal robin's-egg blue of the cloudless winter sky. The day is mild, and the water's surface is as smooth and reflective as glass. Tall palmettos stand unmoving in the still air on the island's banks. Pelicans glide overhead, coming to rest atop pier posts on the south side of the waterway where there is a marina. Cormorants are already in possession of several posts, drying their outstretched wings. The island's historic lighthouse, visible above the tree line, is brilliantly white, reflecting sunlight slanting in from the west.

Obie isn't with us. He is being tended to by Michella, the daughter of Kit's friends the Postelles. My dog took one look at Chella when she arrived and pranced away to fetch a toy, which he promptly dropped on her feet, his highest honor.

"Before the War," Kit says, "the island produced cotton and lumber. Have you heard of Sea Island cotton? The area was famous for it."

"I have." By now, I don't need to ask which war he's referring to. We've been heading up island for the last few minutes. Toward the northern end, we turn onto a dirt drive. Stately oaks arch overhead. "I thought the only oak alley was at the Sea Island Golf Club."

"That's the only one on public view."

"Ah. I see." Late-afternoon sunlight slants in soft streaks across the sandy drive. A cultivated landscape emerges as we move toward the water, the vista opening to sea and sky and a rambling house sitting high on an authentic tabby foundation. Kit parks in front of a freestanding barn. Victorian in style, it was clearly built long after the house.

Too excited to wait for Kit to hand me from the car, I grab my camera and jump out, eyes wide. "It's antebellum, isn't it?"

He nods, grinning. "I need to take you to Savannah next. Old houses aren't an oddity there."

"This is wonderful!" I exclaim.

"And only part of the surprise, although Little Hampton dates back to the late 1700s. Most of the additions are later, though all are ante-bellum."

Like other area plantation houses I've seen in archival photographs, this one is nothing like my idea of a planter's mansion. As simple in design as Willing, it has a few more wings and an extra story. Also like Willing, it faces the water.

"Is that the Atlantic?" I ask.

"The Little Hampton River. Hence the name of the property. The ocean is out that way." Kit points southeast.

A deep, broad porch—a *veranda* as the Georgians call their porches—extends across the front of the house. A huge live oak offers shade at the river's edge. There is another tree of similar size at the back of the building, arching over a terrace bordered by budding azaleas.

A slim patrician woman steps onto the terrace and waves at us.

Kit lifts his hand in answer. "I don't know why I didn't think of bringing you out here before when we had that conversation about fires and termites," he says turning to me.

"How did this place survive?"

"Dumb luck? The family that originally owned the property had financial problems and sold out before the War. The Tisdales' ancestors were New York financiers. They bought it for the forests, not for cotton. You've probably heard that the wood for 'Old Ironsides' was either from St. Simons or Sapelo. Oak from the islands was highly prized for shipbuilding."

This gives me pause, reflecting on Vermont's forest. The state is presently eighty percent woodland, but it was eighty percent pasture-land during the latter half of the nineteenth century as the population grew and needed to cook and heat their homes.

"Does that mean the huge trees in the woods here aren't that old?"

"Probably none more than a hundred and fifty years, except for the oaks around the house." Kit gestures at the giant in front of us.

We've climb to the terrace where our hostess is waiting. I guess her to be in her seventies, with the barely lined complexion of a woman who has always had access to the best skin care products.

"Christopher," she enthuses in a mid-Atlantic accent that doesn't locate her on a map as much as it suggests a life lived on multiple continents. She gives his arm a squeeze.

"Pamela, so good of you to invite us." Kit puts his arm around her shoulder and leans in to kiss her cheek.

"My pleasure," she replies with a tinkling laugh. "How's your mother, dear? I can't believe we were so busy talking about local politics the other night that I never asked."

"She's suffering from a slight cold, but otherwise her usual busy self."

"Will she be down for the gala?"

"Unfortunately, she double booked. Liz has consented to fill in on short notice."

"These things happen as we get older." She tsks. "Marshall says if I didn't act as his social secretary, he'd constantly be in one place when he should be in another. But I'm sorry to hear Maddie won't be attending. I was looking forward to seeing her." She sighs philosophically. "I'll have to check the calendar but I think I've got to run up to Savannah next week. Maybe your mother and I can have lunch."

"I'm sure she'd love that."

"Well, then," our hostess says, "must I do the honors, young man, or will you?"

"I have forgotten my manners," the fifty-ish young man standing next to me replies. "Liz Silver, meet my dear friend, Pamela Tisdale."

"Welcome, Liz. It's so nice of you to visit us. Kit tells me you have an interest in local history and architecture."

"Kit didn't give me the slightest clue where we were going this afternoon so you can't imagine my excitement when I saw your beautiful historic house."

"Would you like a tour?"

"Would I ever!"

Pamela laughs, glancing at Kit. "I believe our friend is eager to show you his surprise, so we will be quick."

As good as her word, she leads me upstairs. The wide oak staircase is intricately carved with swags of flowers. We begin with the attic, which Pamela notes was used as a ballroom during the house's antebellum heyday. On the second floor, we poke our heads into six good-sized bedrooms off a wide hall. She tells me the armoires lining the hall would have stored clothing and linen until the turn of the twentieth century, when the dressing rooms were reconfigured into closets and bathrooms.

Returning to the first floor, I meet Pamela's husband, Marshall, chatting with Kit in the library. Our last stop is a great-room kitchen, remodeled from an in-house storage room and a separate cookhouse. In the colonial South, if you could afford it, you kept the cooking fires away from the main house. That way, if the kitchen went up in flames, which happened far too often, the house didn't go with it. The original fireplace of the cookhouse, no longer used for meal preparation, is the width of the room.

"I love the way you've integrated old and new," I tell Pamela. "Sometimes, in homes as old as yours, the furnishings are so 'of the period' the effect is more museum than home. You've done a lovely job of holding on to the past while including creature comforts."

"Thank you! I've attempted to make the place livable while showcasing the family antiques." She gives me a warm smile. "We so love when Kit visits and brings his friends. It's been far too long since he's been out here."

She throws him a speaking glance. "When was the last time you came just for fun?" Not waiting for his answer, she confides, "He attends our parties, but I think it's been ten years otherwise."

"Life gets away from us, doesn't it?" Kit comments. "I don't think I've seen Tolly in a score of years." His elusiveness confirms my guess he hasn't spent much time here since Eleanor was alive.

"My son is as busy as you, dear. We do the traveling these days—the mountain to Mohammad." To me, she explains, "He's pitched his tent on the Washington State coast."

As we stand in the vestibule conversing, Kit begins running one knuckle idly up and down my spine from midpoint to waist, sending small electric sparks zinging from my brain to darker regions. There is something so trancelike about the motion of his hand that I'm not sure he's aware of what he's doing. As for me, I'm having trouble focusing on anything else.

"At least I see my grandchildren on a regular basis," Pamela is saying. "I love a house full of young people. Sammie and Ben, Tolland's brood"—she clarifies for my benefit—"are staying the summer starting mid-June. I can't wait." She brings her palms together over her heart in a gesture of delight, while Kit's hand drops to his side, exponentially improving my ability to think straight.

"Family is the greatest gift." Our hostess's eyes widen for a second. She throws a worried glance at Kit. I guess she's afraid she's said the wrong thing.

He doesn't react except to say, "The boys will be down for a couple of weeks in June as well. Maybe we can all get together."

Pamela smiles, crisis averted. "Let's make a plan closer to June. Right now I'm keeping you too long. You'd better get out there before the light goes."

"Out where?" I ask.

In on the secret, our hostess smiles serenely instead of answering the question. Holding open the door to the front veranda, she says she'll see us later for cocktails.

Kit and I follow a herringbone brick path through extensive gardens. The bottlebrush trees are not yet flowering. Pansies, able to withstand some cold, are mulched in along the path. Kit steers us toward the river's edge, where a wide sand trail swept clean of leaves takes us into the woods. Overhead, songbirds tweet the late-afternoon news and a mockingbird launches into an extended aria of other birds' hits.

"Can you identify any of the mockingbird's fragments?" I ask Kit a bit breathlessly. Usually he's conscious of the difference in our strides, but today he is too intent on wherever we're going to remember to slow down.

He listens for a moment as I catch my breath. "There's some cardinal in there. And maybe warbler and robin. Here that *tweetweet-tweet, tweetweet-tweet*?" he asks, mimicking the rise and fall of a robin's song.

"I do!" I respond, pleased he can identify birdsong. Normally I rely on Arielle to answer my questions about the natural world.

"Prepare to be amazed," Kit announces as the path moves uphill, curving out of sight behind a stand of water oak. I don't see anything amazing about it, although when Kit slides a hand down my arm, his warm palm tightening around mine, I feel amazingly fine. He takes the lead.

At the top of the rise, the trees open into a clearing. A small chapel, no larger than a one-room schoolhouse, is perched at its center. "Oh my," I say after I've stood speechless for several seconds. "This is indeed incredible."

Kit grins. "Better than my grove, which is pretty damn special."

In front of us, the trunks of the trees are pink with lichen. More extraordinary than at Willing, however, is the tabby chapel. Old whitewash shows through, but most of the exterior is covered in blood lichen.

Past the glory of the vibrant pink lichen, the building is modest in design, with tall windows at each side topped with Palladian arches. The windows reflect the sunlight, long pink-toned rays that increase the intensity of the building's coloration.

"The entire hilltop looks like someone doused it in pink dye," I exclaim.

Kit laughs, delighted with the awe he hears in my voice. "It's been like this forever. Marshall says his grandfather told him it was no different when he was a child."

I walk around the building, shaking my head and marveling. "*I love it!*"

"I knew you would."

Pulling the cover off my camera lens, I hit the On button.

Kit's hand comes down on my arm. "I debated whether I should bring you out here. I knew you'd want to take pictures, but the family doesn't allow photography of the chapel exterior. In the end I wanted to share this place with you badly enough that I made a selfish decision to encourage you to bring your camera without letting you know about the restriction. I hope you can forgive me. Nothing else at Little Hampton is off-limits, inside or out."

"Why the chapel exterior?" I ask, hardly registering the rest of what he's said.

"The building is a cherished island secret. Marshall is afraid that if the location were to become generally known, if images ended up online where people could pull coordinates out of the metadata, trespassers might invade. Not only would that be a nuisance, it could potentially upset the ecology here, which is delicate."

It doesn't matter to me whether I print these shots or not. But I need to take them.

"What if I promise never to publish what I shoot?"

I'm almost hopping with anxiety. I can wipe the geographical data, but I'm not telling Kit because I don't want him to consider why that would be important if I'm not publishing the pictures. He could decide I'm lying. I'm not, and I would never show them to anyone except Arielle and Diana, and only on my computer screen.

The sun is dropping lower with every second Kit hesitates. The angle of the light could change in the next instant. The chapel will cease to glow, the lichen will lose its astounding intensity, and I'll lose the picture. I need to shoot now, not when Kit is finished deliberating.

"Trust me?" I plead, meeting his eyes. "I swear, any picture I take of the chapel will be exclusively for my personal collection."

"You're putting me in a difficult position."

"Not if you trust me. You said the Tisdales don't want the chapel publicized. So be it. It's enough for me to take the photographs as a memento of a perfect surprise on an afternoon when I was feeling completely in harmony with the world."

That's one reason I have to do this. The other is that these photographs could be the best I'll ever take. I'm humming with creative energy, excitement, and the kind of passion for my work I haven't felt in a very long time. I need these pictures.

Kit looks away, running his hand back and forth over his nape. As I anxiously anticipate the light illuminating the chapel changing for the worse, he heaves a sigh and raises his palm in surrender. I lay mine against it.

"I swear," I say.

"Okay, dahlin'. I trust you."

"Good. Because you can."

I raise the camera, adjusting the focal distance to bring the hill closer. I want the chapel to loom a little. Glancing at the light meter, I make my calculations, find the f-stop I want, and click.

"Can you pull the tripod out of your pack, please?" I ask as I refocus and vary the stop again.

Kit hands me the segmented aluminum tripod. It weighs less than a pound so it's perfect for trips like this, allowing me to use a slower shutter speed than if I'm bracing the camera in my hands. Both the lens and shutter speed affect what is in focus. I want the building crisp while catching motion in the trees when the moss is swaying in a light breeze that is beginning to pick up.

A photograph captures a single magical second otherwise lost to time. I love anticipating the perfect infinitesimal moment for my click, before time slides past, lost forever.

Native peoples had an innate understanding of the sacredness of such moments, and when first confronted by cameras believed a photograph could capture the soul.

I don't think they were wrong; a good photograph communicates the soul of a particular moment, whether the moment is inhabited by an organism or an object brought alive by light. That's what I hope to

on inside his own head. Another second goes by. He blinks, pats my shoulder, and turns away, retreating down the aisle before disappearing past what I can see of the porch.

I drop onto the nearest bench. Have I been rebuffed? Or did he think I was asking for release? Have I been reading his signals wrong? And what about me? Am I using him, as I have used other men, to distract myself from feelings I don't want to acknowledge? I drop my head into my hands.

My motivation is more of a blank than it should be beyond my attraction to him. His feelings are as opaque as ever. It's Kit's move now. I'm officially kicking the ball into his court.

Scanning the benches for where I left my camera, I note that the miraculous light has faded, although the peace intrinsic to this place is as present as ever. Too bad my internal self is too roiled up after what just happened to allow much peace to penetrate. I climb to my feet, and, picking up the Nikon, start toward the door.

I've taken only a few steps when I stop to stare at what is front of me. Framed in the doorway, I see river and sky but without trees or riverbank or porch floor. The illusion their absence creates is of the chapel floating in midair, as if it is hovering above the river. I reverse direction. Two steps back, I see only sky. Two steps beyond the point where I saw the building float, the porch floor appears to anchor the building in place.

I set the tripod on the sweet spot and look through the camera's viewfinder. I may be confused about Kit and his intentions, but I'm clear about the excellent photograph waiting for me.

Emerging onto the porch a minute later, I find Kit leaning against one of the side railings. Pushing away he says, "Sit with me?" He folds himself down, extending his feet onto the steps. Twisting toward me, he extends a hand. I set the camera next to his backpack and join him. We sit quietly for a minute or two. As out of balance as the last few minutes have been, I was wrong about the chapel's magic. It seems to linger between us, a spell neither of us wishes to break.

"I used to come here with Eleanor when we were courting," Kit says.

"I can see why. This place is lovely. More than lovely." My stomach flips because his admission points to Eleanor as the reason my attempt at seduction failed. I press my palms into the warm porch floor.

"Loving someone to distraction probably isn't healthy, but that is how I loved my wife."

This is not what I expected to hear next. I expected that having shared something private, he'd retreat inside himself. He has repeated that pattern since our walk to the river, which makes what he says next fairly mind-blowing.

"I'm pained to admit I was jealous of Levi as soon as Eleanor told me she was pregnant. I'd watched what happened to my friends' relationships when they had children, so I was primed to resent the attention I felt sure she would lavish on the baby, though he hadn't arrived yet."

I swivel to glance at him. "I don't think yours was an unusual reaction to a first child. As a mom, I didn't love the way I disappeared inside new motherhood, when I finally found a few minutes to assess the situation. And, like you, Dan resented how totally focused I was on Diana."

Our hands rest next to each other, not quite touching. I adjust mine the tiniest bit to brush his. After my failed seduction, I'm feeling cautious. He can choose to understand my touch as an accident and move his hand away . . . or not.

"Well, I didn't stop feeling it. Don't mistake me, I love my boys. But loving them didn't prevent me from resenting that our lives were no longer exclusively about me and Eleanor. So, when she got sick during her pregnancy with Noah, I felt sure I was being punished for those feelings. The hormones meant to nurture the life of our gestating child were feeding a cancer with the potential to kill my wife."

"Oh God," I gasp. His hand shifts to cover mine. Afraid to move, afraid to startle him out of his telling, I risk a glance at his profile. His eyes are fixed on the water, although I'm guessing he sees only the past.

"The tumor couldn't be removed while she was carrying, which was bad because the cancer was aggressive." His runs a hand through his hair. "They took Noah early, a risk we agreed to, so Eleanor's treatment could begin. We reasoned that the sooner treatment started, the more chance there would be that Noah and Levi would have a mom to help them grow up."

Kit rocks once, twice, and then once more, his head bowed. "I can't imagine how it must have been for her, even though I was living through it, too. I was terrified, but Eleanor refused to acknowledge her fear. She believed fear would feed the cancer and while Noah was inside her, harm him, too. She was so damn brave." Kit heaves a deep sigh and turns to look at me with red-rimmed eyes.

I splay my fingers. His twine with mine. The wind picks up as it often does at tide change, whirring through the trees, the sound of a thousand ghosts calling.

Kit pulls our hands into his lap. "After Noah was born, Eleanor endured a mastectomy and radiation. She lost her gorgeous hair. God, she suffered so," he whispers, his grip tightening. "Eventually, the horrific side effects of the treatment let up and she began to recover."

I squeeze his hand in sympathy, understanding that I'm hearing a false happy ending. I could tell him how sorry I am, but I sense this isn't the time, and what does my sorrow mean compared to his?

"I loved Eleanor when she was fighting the cancer even more than before, although it hardly seems possible." Kit's voice is rough. "Her initial suffering through radiation and chemo bought us eleven amazing years." He sighs. "By then, we had a clear bead on what's important and what isn't." He shakes his head, his free hand raking through his hair a second time. "Three years almost to the day we got the news the cancer had returned, Eleanor died."

There are no adequate words. I squeeze his hand again.

"When you told me your daughter helped keep you afloat after your divorce? Levi and Noah were my life preservers after Eleanor died. The boys are her legacy. I don't believe in heaven or an afterlife; our children are our afterlife, our gift to the future. I couldn't fall apart. I had to keep Levi and Noah safe for her."

His grip on mine is tight enough to hurt. He blows out a breath. "There are times when one of the boys moves a certain way, particularly Noah, who looks so much like his mom, or an expression will pass over his features, or Levi's, and I see her again." He releases my hand to lean forward. "It's wonderful and also terrible, you know?" His breath shudders. "For the first few years after she died, those little glimpses of her in the boys would just about kill me." He jaw tightens. "But my sons kept me going. In truth, they were my only incentive."

"Children can coax you back to life from whatever your heartache," I respond, my own voice rough around the edges. "They are so full of love and the joy of discovery. The world is a wonder to them. And you feel a responsibility to keep it wonderful, to hide the bulk of your grief because it's destabilizing for them, and they are grieving too. Gradually, eventually, their life force creeps into the darkness inside your heart and light dawns for you, too."

"That's exactly it."

He twists to look at me. "I don't seem to know how to move past that point."

I return his gaze. Adrenaline kicks my blood pressure up a few notches. I imagine Kit can see the color rising in my face. I hug myself. I made a choice inside the chapel to accept Darius's truth. I want free of the boundaries I set to keep my heart safe, but freedom is easier in theory than in practice.

Sitting with Kit on the sun-warmed chapel steps, I feel like I'm on a boat tilting precariously into the waves without a handhold to keep from falling overboard. Kit is obviously still in love with a woman who died eight years ago, and also traumatized by what they went through before she died. I certainly understand his feelings. But I also understand he is too hung up on Eleanor and too scarred by experience to be a candidate for anything but a good time, which, come to think of it, is exactly what he said about himself when our game of twenty questions veered off course.

Paying attention to what men say about themselves is Rule Number Seven. It is a rule I'm not throwing out. In my experience, women often make deprecating statements about themselves they don't entirely mean. It is "being nice" behavior that we use to prevent us from appearing too bold or threatening, to seem likable. Men, on the other hand, unless they're blowhards or politicians, tend not to say much about themselves, but when they do, it's smart to pay attention, which is why I can't ignore that Kit has said he is only interested in fun, even if he is currently distancing himself from the concept.

I begin to shake. Not again! A limitless supply of adrenaline must have been a plus when our ancestors were being chased by savage beasts or defending their turf from the marauding tribe the next valley over, but in the modern world, the kick of this primitive hormonal spike only magnifies the clash between what I want and the reality I'm living. At the moment, I'm all too aware of the difference between what my heart desires and what Kit can offer.

"Are you okay?" He stands to reach his backpack. Pulling out my sweater, he sits and drapes the sweater over my shoulders. He pulls me into his side, which makes the shaking worse. Kit rubs a hand briskly up and down my back. I suppose I should be glad he doesn't understand I'm shaking because my equilibrium just shattered.

When the tremors finally subside, he asks, "Better?" At my nod, he sits forward. "Have you noticed how you can think you're okay, that you've moved on, and then something happens and—boom!—all the lights blink out and you're groping around in the dark without any idea of where the floor ends and the abyss begins, never mind how to find a light switch?"

Yeah, like right now, I think, realizing he absorbed everything I said that day at the river.

"If your next question is about how to willingly open yourself to love and the possibility of more loss after your heart has been torched, scorched-earth style"—I squeeze his arm—"I'd turn the lights on for both of us if I knew where that switch is, believe me."

"So you want to?"

Do I? "Maybe. Sometimes I think it's better to stay in the dark. That way, you can't see the monster hiding behind the door." I'm not entirely joking.

He smiles. "Lizbeth, that makes no sense."

"Sure it does." A flash of insight lights my brain, but this one is about me: It doesn't matter why I've been on my particular path these last five years, what matters is that even if a monster is behind the door, I have to face it, win or lose. If I don't, I'll never move forward.

Amending what I just said, I tell Kit, "I suppose I do want the lights on, even if the monster finds me before I figure out how to defend myself."

This time Kit plays along with my metaphorical fancy. "It is against my dragon-slaying ethics to let monsters carry away Yankee women I like, so you're safe with me." He grins and wraps an arm around my shoulders. "Ms. Lizzie? You know what? I adore you." He chuckles, punctuating his adoration with a vigorous buddy-buddy shake to my shoulders. "Who else but you would think imaginary monsters are germane to a conversation like this and make me think so, too?"

A conversation like what? I guess he can't say a conversation about love and loss and how to surmount it. But then, I can't say it, either. Nor am I sure how to react to the claim that he adores me, and I don't have the time to figure it out—at least not now—because Kit says, "It's getting late. We'd better get going," and climbs to his feet.

I separate the tripod from the camera while he locks the building. I hand the folded tripod to Kit to put in the backpack.

As we turn down the path to join the Tisdales for drinks, I consider what I know:

1. We shared an intense spiritual moment in the chapel.
2. We shared Kit's deflection of my advance, before I was more than halfway to making it, which might have been deliberate on his part—or not.
3. He shared his heartbreaking story about Eleanor, a story sure to haunt me for a very long time.

4. He's admitted he's as lost in space as I am. (I mentally underline this point.)

5. Although he said he adores me, his delivery makes me feel less like his next lover than his best friend's cute little sister—when she was ten.

I can't add it all up. Especially number five. When a man says "I adore you," isn't the next act in the sequence supposed to be a passionate kiss? In the interest of transparency—hey, here's a new guiding principle, if not a rule—I admit I don't have a clue about where Kit and I are heading. All I know is that all of a sudden we're sharing a lot about ourselves, and that means *something*.

CHAPTER 23

GEORGIA IS TUCKED so far under the northern mass of the continent that its longitudinal alignment is with Ohio, which means that even though it is fully dark in Vermont at this hour, it's only dusk here.

Our return to the house has been companionable in a buddy-buddy way, not a guy-and-his-gal way. For most of it, Kit entertained me with stories about his childhood visits to the island and Little Hampton.

When the house comes into sight, I ask Kit for the car key. I want to put the camera away, thereby avoiding the possibility of an awkward show-and-tell. "Do you want me to take your backpack?" I ask.

He offers to do the camera run, but I tell him to join his friends and I'll meet him on the veranda. Keys in hand, I hoist the backpack and veer toward the barn.

It's a lot darker a few minutes later when I reverse direction. At the shore, it always seems to take the sun forever to drop into the horizon, and then—poof!—it's gone.

The oil lanterns hanging from the veranda roofline offer a cheerful beacon as I round the house to the sound of Kit's laugh and Marshall's deep rumbling voice.

There isn't a power line or telephone cable in sight. The home's interior shutters mask any telltale glare of electrical wattage. The vista can't look very different from a similar evening two hundred years past.

During one of our Jack Daniel's chats, Kit and I discussed the concept of pentimento, which is the trace of an earlier painting under the surface of the visible painting. We applied the definition to time. I mentioned that to me, time seems thinner here. I have felt, walking Willing's fields or taking a backroads drive, that I could return to the house to find myself in 1814 instead of 2014. Tonight, I feel that same alchemy in the air. Nothing feels solid or sure.

A melancholy hyperawareness of my own mortality falls over me.

The sages of many religions agree that life is eternal if you are fully present in each moment. Today brimmed with perfect eternities, which, I suppose, explains why I regret it drawing to a close.

Pamela greets me as I mount the veranda steps. She asks what I would like to drink.

"White wine, please."

She moves to a wicker table where bottles have been set out on a silver tray. I join Kit and Marshall, who are standing at the other end of the porch, sipping their whiskey.

I hand Kit his key ring. He slides it into his pocket. Marshall is speaking about a recent Nature Conservancy purchase on the island. While he's talking, Kit takes my hand and strokes his thumb softly against my palm.

Desire practically tips me over the balustrade, although somehow I manage not to squirm, swoon, or otherwise give away what I'm feeling. Pamela returns with my drink. I smile my thanks. And then I can't stop smiling. Not because the wine is great, although it's quite nice—but because I no longer feel like that cute little sister.

✳

"Perfect day," I comment as we roll to a stop beside Kit's house. "Today was as perfect as days come. Thank you so much!"

"I'm glad you enjoyed yourself," Kit says. "I did, too." Handing me from the car he says, "How about we gild the lily with a nightcap? After all, the day doesn't officially end until midnight."

Because I was careful not to over imbibe at the Tisdales' or during our scrumptious shrimp and grits dinner overlooking the Intracoastal Waterway, I nod my agreement. No surprise, I'd like to gild a couple of other lilies as well, hoping Kit will make good on what his thumb maneuver at the Tisdales' promised.

"Shall I download the photos so we can take a look?" I ask. "They are going to be even better than the last batch I showed you."

"Sure would!"

I wish he'd stop smiling at me so I could breathe.

We step into the house to the accompaniment of Obie's ecstatic yips. Too excited to be greeted, Obs gallops through the house a few times before pouncing on Kit. I'm not pleased when Kit encourages his bad manners. Obie is allowed to prop his front paws on Kit's chest, from which position man and dog commune. When they're done, my disloyal poodle condescends to offer me a tongue-lolling lean. Better manners, but still.

"I'll start the computer," I tell Kit, giving Obie a final pat.

"Obs and I will do a quick visit to the 'water' garden."

The download is done by the time Kit walks in with our drinks. Obie settles near the door where he can keep an eye on us.

Since I'm sitting in the desk chair, the only other seating that will fit the desk is an ottoman. I push one over. Because he's tall and the ottoman is low, when Kit sits, our eyes are on the same level. I usually look up at him. It is surprisingly intimate to be eye to eye.

"Almost done downloading," I say, shifting my focus to the computer screen. I'm definitely wound tight with anticipation, which is better than shaking with it. But, hey, the night isn't over. I reach for my drink, hoping a little whiskey will ease my jitters.

"Wow," Kit says with a rattle of the ice in his glass. "I know you're good, but damn." He studies the image thumbnails filling the screen.

"Years of practice." I make a valiant attempt to pay attention to the screen rather than the flex of Kit's shoulders as he leans his forearms onto the desk.

We study the images in silence. The light is spectacular in the interior shots. In the outside images, the chapel shines in all of its pink glory. The slight blur of the Spanish moss caught in motion evokes a ghostly timelessness, exactly as I hoped.

"That one," Kit says, pointing at the shot I've already decided to star. "But they're all magical. You have absolutely captured the spirit of the place."

His admiration is as heady as the whiskey I'm sipping.

"They'll do," I say.

"Oh, come on. Why not admit how good these are?"

I shake my head. "For the last few years I haven't been inspired, so while I'm thrilled with what I'd done here, I'm hesitant to congratulate myself. I'm afraid to jinx the creative surge I'm experiencing."

"Well, I'm not afraid, so indulge me."

Kit offers a high-sign. I hesitate for a second, then meet his palm with my own.

The gesture is too percussive to be anything but comradely.

One minute he's my pal, the next, he's flirty, and then he's my pal again. I really don't know what he's up to. Or if he's up to anything.

Pointing to one of the exterior images, Kit says, "Can we see that one blown up?"

"You have a good eye." I open his selection.

"The clarity is incredible. I can practically feel the texture of the lichen."

"The miracle of a twenty-megapixel camera and a superior lens." Enhancing the image's clarity, I decide to open the midtones and punch up the reds. Sitting back, I study the results. The lichen appears as intense as I remember it.

Kit and I contemplate the photo. He says, "Looks great to me, but was that cheating?"

I laugh. "Photographers have been manipulating images since the very beginning. Digital software has simply added more and better tools to our arsenal."

"That shot is amazing. The adjustments you made are so subtle, but hugely effective." He squeezes my shoulder. "Can we look at the rest?"

My shoulder burns where he touched it. I scroll through the rest of the interior images and what I've dubbed the floating pictures. Kit and I agree on the best ones in each series. I star our choices for editing later.

"It's a shame Pamela and Marshall will never see those exterior shots," Kit remarks.

"Wouldn't an oversize print be great in their living room? If it were me, I'd hang it on the long wall behind the piano—that wall is crying out for art." I reach for my tumbler. "What about a triptych? I can see the exterior, interior, and the floating view hanging together."

"I can, too." Kit tilts his head from side to side, stretching his neck. "Here's an idea. Since pictures of the view aren't off-limits, nor did they say anything about the interior, what if I show Pamela and Marshall those two?" He points to a photograph of the water framed in the doorway, and another of the light pouring into the chapel. Narrowing his eyes, he considers. "I could say you would love to photograph the exterior just for them, a thank-you for our visit. If Marshall and Pamela say yes, you could return to Little Hampton, ostensibly to take the pictures you've already taken."

"Now who's cheating?"

"It's okay to cheat for a good cause." We both laugh at the right and wrong of his statement.

He bumps his shoulder against mine. "What do you say, dahlin'? Deal?"

"Deal," I agree, sealing the deal with a yawn.

"Looks like I'm keeping you up past your bedtime."

I could say, *You are, and why don't you join me for bedtime?* I would if he weren't looking so bright eyed. It isn't the look of a man waiting for an invitation. So, I say, "Nah, probably not enough oxygen in the room."

"Am I being accused of stealing it?" Kit asks.

"The house is stuffy from being closed up all day," I say primly, then ruin the effect by laughing. Of course he's stolen all the oxygen in the room. I'm ninety-nine percent sure he knows it, too, no matter the look on his face. Opening the window in front of the desk, I make a show of enjoying the cool night air—not that it has any effect on the inferno burning inside me. I take another swallow of whiskey before remembering that alcohol fuels fire, rather than dousing it.

Kit drains his glass while I close programs. Reaching over my head, I arch against the chair, attempting to stretch away my nervous awareness of the man beside me. I risk a glance at Mr. Trouble. His honey-brown eyes hold an altogether different look than a minute before. One corner of his mouth lifts. Our gazes lock. Neither of us looks away. A second ticks by. One single, weighty second, and I think, *This is it.*

With a bright flash, the computer screen goes dark, the whir of its cooling fan ceasing abruptly. Kit blinks and glances away.

My stomach flips. *Damn, damn, damn!*

A wave of light-headedness hits me as I stand. "Let's sit in the living room where it's more comfortable." My suggestion sounds like a come-on . . . and it is.

Kit unfolds his long frame and rises, without a yes. He reaches for our whiskey glasses. Mine is as empty as his. I finish a drink once in a blue moon, and didn't notice doing it just now.

I turn off the desk lamp. The moon may not be blue or totally full tonight, but its silvery illumination provides enough light to navigate our way out of the room.

Pivoting, I aim for the hall. The room shifts. Grabbing for the desk to steady myself, I stand in place, recalibrating. I hope Kit didn't see me reel, but I don't dare look over my shoulder to check because there's no guarantee I won't pitch sideways again. Hell, maybe I should. If I swoon, maybe he'll catch me. More likely, he'll think I'm drunk.

Drunk is an offense to my dignity. Kit's as well—as many nightcaps as we've sipped together, I've never seen him past his limit. So, I don't pitch or swoon. I take a cautious step, and then another, relieved the floor has decided to steady itself.

With one hand doing a balancing skim along the wall, because I may be a tiny bit alcohol impaired, I aim for the living room sofa. Kit continues into the kitchen with our empty glasses.

When he returns, he says, "As loath as I am to leave your charming company, I had better go. Busy day tomorrow, even if it is Sunday. I'm working on a time-sensitive contract and need to conference with my client first thing in the morning, which means I'm swimming early."

The hall clock chimes midnight, the witching hour as well as the end of my perfect day, although it isn't ending as perfectly as I had hoped. "No rest for the weary," I say, using humor to deflect my disappointment.

"No rest for the wicked," he corrects as we make our way to the foyer.

"Ah." I nod. "That would explain why I haven't been sleeping well these last few nights."

"You've been wicked without me? I'm wounded." He throws a hand over his heart. "Lizzie, dahlin', you know I'm saving all my wickedness for you."

His playfulness throws me off balance for about the hundred billionth time today. Honestly, I can't figure out what he wants. I feign exasperation—actually, it's real this time—as well as being a good fallback response to Kit's shenanigans. "You're awfully full of the Irish blarney, for a Gentile-Jewish Southern Gentleman," I say, reaching for the doorknob.

"That would be baloney I'm full of. Possibly kosher." He grins and bends toward me. Anticipating his gentlemanly good-night peck, I present my cheek, but that isn't where his kiss lands.

There is no lead up to the combustion. Kit's lips meet mine and—*whoosh!*—up we go. His mouth is hot with desire and sweet with whiskey. My hand splays out behind me for balance as the force of the kiss pushes me into the wall. My free hand opens against Kit's chest. His nipple pebbles under my palm.

Tracing the line of my jaw with his fingers, he brushes a strand of hair away from my cheek, clasping the back of my neck to keep us aligned. I moan, circling my arms around his waist, drawing myself more tightly against him. Dizzy with desire that's been smoldering for way too long, my balance deserts me. I move my hands to Kit's shoulders, as much for the delight of touching the broad plains of muscle under my palms as to hold myself upright.

I want him so badly I can hardly breathe.

And this time, unlike when I made the same move in the chapel, Kit doesn't pull away. He nips at my lips. I chase after him, the aggressor now. Unlike Darius, he enjoys the pursuit. When he lets me catch him, he smiles into my mouth. We kiss some more. His kisses are better than divine.

To tease me, Kit pulls away, angling his lips over mine. He shifts one way and then another, as if he's searching for the slant that offers the deepest penetration. He finds it and we both groan. But it's not enough. Not the kiss. Not the touching. Not the embrace.

The kiss becomes rougher, hotter, taking on a rhythm that's a lot like—

A sliver of reality resurrects itself. Or maybe it's the lack of oxygen— for real this time. We break apart.

"Jesus," Kit says as my mind churns ineffectively, trying to explain what just happened. That was more than mere lust.

Backing away, he puts a couple more feet of entryway between us, meeting my eyes before quickly looking away. His fingertips smooth over his bottom lip. "That was—" He doesn't finish. His lips are red and slightly swollen with what burned between us. Mine must look the same.

I nod in agreement with his wordless assessment.

"Mmm . . ." Kit tries again. Once more, nothing follows. He looks . . . perplexed.

My brain, flooded with endorphins, conjures pictures of where we might have ended up if we hadn't come up for air. In my bed. Or on the floor in front of the door.

With a shudder, I gaze restlessly around me as the silence lengthens. For all of his wit and charm, Kit doesn't seem to know any more than I do whether we should move together or apart.

While I'm considering the options, Kit takes one. I look up to see the screen door swinging closed. His shirt catches the light as he turns to wink at me. "I'll see you tomorrow, okay, dahlin'?" He doesn't wait for my answer. Before his lovely broad shoulders disappear past the light's reach, he waves.

The night swallows him. I stare dumbly into the dark until Kit is inside his house for a full minute. Retreat is definitely one option. Probably the best option. Maybe we should pretend nothing happened, but I'm pretty sure that isn't going to work.

Obie nudges my hand.

"I'm okay," I say, reaching down to pat his head, offering reassurance, but, as is often the case these days, I'm not telling him the truth.

CHAPTER 24

A GLOWING MIST is hovering low in the meadow when I look out the windows the next morning. Grabbing my camera, I slide my feet into flip-flops and unlatch the door to the wraparound porch. I'm still in my nightgown and groggy after a night of little sleep, but it's now or never if I want the picture. Besides, who's going to see me in my dishabille? Willing's squirrels? Kit must have set out hours ago for his swim and then to work.

My bones melt a little at the thought of him. I woke up every couple of hours with an endless kissing loop whirling through my head, which was entertaining, unsettling, and, ultimately, exhausting.

I snap a couple of shots at a distance, then move closer to the wispy, glowing cloud and snap a few more. Mission accomplished, my brain in its own glowing fog, I shower, walk Obie, and down a first mug of coffee.

Refill in hand, I settle into an Adirondack chair on the veranda to enjoy cup number two. Staring at Kit's house, I work up a new set of conclusions about him that are the same and different from yesterday's.

MORNING-AFTER KISS LIST

1. I'm not sure either of us is ready for the feelings that hit us last night. AND—
2. I like Christopher Aiken Couper a little too much for my own good. Oh, who am I kidding—I like him way too much for my own good.
3. A guy who says playing around is his current mode of operation, and then, a few weeks later, tops that statement off by admitting he doesn't know how to unlock his emotions for more, is not

ready for a serious relationship. Considering my own track record, I would be stupid to be optimistic about finding love with a man who claims his desire is for "fun."

4. If I could be content with a good fuck, because there is no way a man who kisses like that isn't one, and leave it at that, I wouldn't need this list.

My old Rules were all about steering clear of losing propositions. Wanting more when less is on offer is a losing proposition. Yet here I am, trying to logic myself out of getting involved with Kit when I know I've already hit the override button and I'll be doing it anyway—that is, if he hasn't changed his mind.

I pick up the phone I conveniently brought out with me and dial Arielle.

"Greetings from the tundra," she says, sounding groggy.

"Damn. Am I calling too early?"

"If you need to ask, it's too early."

"I'm sorry. I know you sleep late on weekends, but I figured 10:30 would be safe."

"I'm up. And giving you a hard time because I can. I've been trying to talk myself into some cleaning and decluttering." She yawns. "So a distraction is plenty welcome."

What am I doing? This is stupid. As if Arielle will have the answers I don't. "The show is next weekend, right? Are you ready?" I ask.

"Postcards out, e-mails out, calls made. Pottery packed. Booth inspected and checked. Diana is staying the night before I leave, so she can ask any questions that occur to her. For the first time in weeks, the weather is predicted to be balmy. And, with the aid of a spray bottle, I've convinced Miu-Miu not to climb the curtains. Life is ducky."

"Good. I'm glad." I pause, looking for another topic.

"So, Liz," Arielle says into my ear, "Do I need to remind you how long and well I know you? Are you going to tell me what is bothering you, or are we going to make small talk for the rest of the morning?"

"That wasn't small talk." I sigh. "But I do need your advice." What the hell, I'll test out my theories and see if she agrees with them.

"Let me pour another hit of caffeine to up the chance I'll have advice to offer. Hold on a second." The phone clunks to the counter.

While she's gone, I try to figure out where to start.

Picking back up, she says, "If I'm allowed to guess today's topic, I guess 'man.'"

"You always guess man. It's kind of depressing to reach the august age of forty-six and have trouble always be about a man."

"Or you could go with a more positive story. How about, your daughter is fine; your dog is fine; your parents are fine? Even your work is fine from what you said last week. And I'm fine, too, just so we're clear."

"The mood you're in, let's do the not-about-a-man news first. Drum roll, please. My creative logjam is definitely over! I can't describe how good it feels to find great images everywhere I look. I'll send you some shots so you can see why I'm so excited."

"I can't wait and I'm delighted for you! So, if the only rough spot in your world is a man, then—pffft—life is good, right?"

"I knew you could put this in perspective."

"Glad to help. Have we solved the problem?" She pauses for a sip of coffee.

I tap my fingers on the chair arm. "Not exactly. Remember the Zen business I was supposed to be practicing?"

"I love you, Lizzie, but I feel compelled to point out your track record set the odds for the 'I just want to be friends' plan pretty low. Whether the issue is basic chemistry or some kind of spell you unwittingly cast, when a man catches your eye, it's a foregone conclusion you and Mr. Of-the-Moment will end up in bed."

I groan. "Not true."

"Is true. And from what you've reported, your Southern friend is attractive, charming, smart, and unattached. You already know I like the idea of you seeing where this leads, rather than prequalifying him for failure, so please explain why we are discussing him again."

"He isn't the problem; I'm the problem." I come out of the chair and pace to the end of the veranda. Obie whines from behind the screen door. "All he did was kiss me, but I'm as jittery as if last night was my first kiss ever." I pace out to the gate at the end of the walk, lock it so Obie is confined to the enclosed front garden, and let him out.

"You have been kissed before," Arielle says. "Except—"

"Except, I'm not sure I've been kissed like this before." I take a breath and blurt, "You diagnosed the problem the last time we talked. I like Kit way too much, but he's on the fence about wanting a relationship." Unable to keep still, I work my way to the far side of the veranda, Obie at my heels.

"Lizzie," Arielle says crisply, "you know I'm rooting for you to get serious, but if this doesn't feel right, trust your instincts. Say no."

"But I want to say yes," I moan. "Of course, as soon as we came up for air last night, Kit made his retreat. I don't think he knew what to make of that kiss, either. I'm telling you, it wasn't a normal *let's-have-fun* kind of kiss. It was a let's-become-one, heart-and-soul kind of kiss. I'm saying to myself, okay, ignore that aspect, since he probably will. Kit's charming, he challenges me intellectually, and I want him. Even if I were dumb enough to fall in love, I couldn't possibly fall so irreparably in love during the remaining two months before I head home that my heart would be put in serious jeopardy, could I? A few weeks of post-affair moping might ensue, but nothing like what happened with Roland, right? So why am I so jittery?"

"Because emotions aren't logical?"

I plop into a chair and prop my head in my hand. "I won't survive having my heart broken again," I say, contradicting my previous statement. "God, I can hardly stay inside my skin over one stupid kiss. Imagine what is going to happen if sleeping with him is as intense?"

"Liz, it's okay to change your mind about what you want. It's okay to want a relationship. You don't know he absolutely doesn't want one, do you?"

I think about what I know.

"Either he's the one," Arielle continues, "or the universe sent him for you to practice having real feelings for a man without dying from them."

"Huh. I need to think about that concept."

"The way I see it, you like the road straight and absent conditions you can't anticipate. But relationships are not straight roads, are they? Hence your problem. And the need for practice."

"You'd think I've never done this before."

"You haven't."

I wrap my arm around one of the porch pillars and lean into it. "What are you talking about? I've fallen in love—and unwisely—as you well know."

"You haven't fallen in love when you knew so much about the pitfalls. Maybe that's why most people do it when they're young and ignorant of the consequences."

"You could be right," I say morosely.

"But consider that you are tougher than you used to be. And hey, on the bright side, you could be wrong about Kit and he's already falling in love with you."

"How often has happily-ever-after been delivered to me?" I push away from the pillar, too agitated to stand still. "You're right about my feelings on the subject of love." I rub my temples where a tension headache is building. "What the hell am I doing? I might as well be Little Red Riding Hood, because the wolf is about to eat me," I mutter, giving my monster form.

"I'm lost. Come again?"

"You aren't lost. I'm the one who's lost, lost in the woods, and this love thing is like the big bad wolf stalking me. I'm going to be eaten alive if I don't run in the other direction—and soon."

"Lizzie, you are confusing your fairy tales. The big bad wolf belongs to the three little pigs. And Little Red wasn't lost. She knew where she was going. Granted you have a point about including a wolf, except love isn't your wolf. Your wolf is the lock and chain around your heart."

"Even better." I pace toward the other side of the veranda. Obie backs up. He sits, eying me with concern.

"Liz," Arielle says in her most soothing tones, "you can do this— whatever 'this' turns out to be." She pauses a beat then adds, "And while I beg your pardon for the morning's mixed metaphors, I'm pretty sure you don't have a choice; your emotions have left the station and they're steaming down the tracks. All you can do is hang on for the ride."

"And fall off and be crushed under the wheels," I whine.

Obie arfs, startling me. I drop the phone as he launches himself off the porch. "Leave it!" I shout as he goes after a squirrel, my command having as much effect on him as logic is having on my emotions.

Picking the phone off the porch floor, I say, "You still there?"

Obie sniffs his way around the oak, trying to figure out how that furry varmint eluded him.

"I'm still here," Arielle says.

"So, my choices are to wimp out or ride the train to the last stop?"

"With an open heart and mind," Arielle confirms.

I hit the speaker button as I walk into the house to get a dog treat to lure Obie inside. "I'm just a little self-involved today. I haven't asked about your mom," I say.

"Don't add me to your list of feel-bad-abouts. Georgie is fine. Oh, wait. I do have a bit of other news. I talked to Anna last night. She thinks I should collect everything that isn't mine in the house, except for the furniture, of course, and store it in my parents' bedroom. Her theory is that with all of it put aside, by the time she shows up in July, I'll be clearer about what I want to keep. She also said we'd sort it out together."

"That sounds like a great plan. If I can be any help in the meantime, once I'm home, please don't hesitate." I blow out a breath. "I really miss you."

"Same here. I'll call after I'm back from the show."

CHAPTER 25

"OH, COME ON. You're female, of course you want to talk about it." Kit grins, carrying our drinks to the coffee table.

"Can you back that with statistical data?"

"Empirical." He laughs and salutes me with his drink, having arrived an hour earlier than his weekday schedule allows, which makes sense since it is Sunday.

"Geez, aren't guys supposed to be better at avoiding the relationship topic?" I ask, sounding peevish. I'm still not sure this is a good idea.

As for what Kit wants, if his good cheer is anything to go by, he's all for passing Go and collecting on the promise of last night's kiss. He hands me my whiskey, but instead of sitting in his chair, he takes a seat on the couch, his oh-so-kissable body settling a seat cushion away. I look at my drink.

"Lizzie," Kit says, eyes lit with amusement, "guys only ignore what they don't want to acknowledge. Even if I didn't want to admit what happened last night—and believe me, I do—we would still have a mighty big gorilla plonked here between us." He pats the cushion for emphasis.

I think about my monster. Whether it's a gorilla or wolf hardly matters. Either creature has its own form of menace. "Maybe the gorilla is a sock monkey with a giant shadow," I say hopefully. "Let's stuff him back on the shelf where he belongs." I take a swallow of my drink.

Kit throws his head back and that wonderful laugh, the laugh that turns my resolve to mush, rumbles up from his belly. "Delightful," he says when he's done chuckling. Taking a sip of his own whiskey, he salutes me. "But you're disappointing me, dahlin'. Show some of that Jewish Yankee girl spunk." He takes another swallow, bright eyes focused on mine. "I admit I was a little surprised—as well as entirely pleased—by how hot that kiss was. Practically blew off the top of my head; other body parts, too." He winks. "Common, Lizzie, you know it was bound to happen. Last night impulse finally led to action, is all."

"Impulse led *you* to action," I clarify.

The brow over Kit's right eye rises.

"Okay, okay. I participated."

The eyebrow rises again.

I raise a hand in surrender. "Yes, I wanted you to kiss me."

"And sent up a few smoke signals."

So he got those after all. "I don't want to screw up a good friendship." I wince at how much this statement leaves unsaid as well as my word choice. I promised myself I wouldn't do this. Too bad Kit ran away last night. I was ready then.

His brow wrinkles. It isn't exactly a frown, more like he can't quite figure me out. I'd help him, but I can't figure me out, either.

"First off, you know how to keep that from happening and so do I," he says. "For good or bad, we're two of a kind. You and me, Ms. Lizzie, are experts at this sweet dance. Second, since our gorilla has reared its big ol' head, it ain't goin' nowhere until a little action is taken, and I don't mean stuffing it back in its cage. I mean letting it loose." He crosses his arms. The look he tosses me says, *Admit you've been outreasoned.*

Kit dispenses with the one-cushion distance between us and reaches for my hand. "Lizbeth, sweet dahlin', you know how this goes. We're gonna have some fun until we decide we've had enough, and after that we'll go on being friends." He begins swirling his fingertips in a slow circle around my palm. "Not that there isn't a chance we'll like what we're doing so much we won't want to stop. I think we owe it to ourselves to find out."

I close my eyes. The highest concentration of nerve endings anywhere on our bodies is in our hands. They are our advance warning system for danger as well as our best conduit for pleasure. Kit is serving up pleasure now at an intensity that makes it hard for me to breathe. I really am a wreck, caught between relief that he sees us having a "fun" affair, and disappointment that's all he sees, except for that last comment. I don't know what to make of it and don't want to hope. I pull my hand from his.

"Lizzie," he says patiently, "we're not getting past this without getting into it first."

I open my eyes.

"You could look happier," Kit remarks, lifting my hand from my lap. "Dive in, dahlin'. The water's warm. Why are you resisting?"

Isn't that the thousand-dollar question? He's right, I tell myself. We are both experts at this game. *Yet to dive in . . .* The warmth of the water isn't what has me worried. It's the depth and swiftness of the current. I dare a glance into his warm brown eyes.

He gives my hand a reassuring squeeze and leans in, brushing a lock of hair away from my cheek. "Lizzie, Liz, Lizbeth," he breathes, touching his lips to the curve of my jaw, skimming sensitive skin to whisper into my ear. "Say yes . . ."

Oh God. "Yes," I breathe. "Yes." *Because no matter where this goes or doesn't go, I can't resist him.*

His lips take mine.

This time, I anticipate his sweet whiskey taste. A smile lifts one corner of his mouth as my arms encircle his neck. Ardor rises around us, as bright and mysterious as this morning's mist. We kiss and kiss and kiss.

Without his mouth leaving mine, Kit works at the buttons of my shirt. I reach for the hem of his, sliding my palms up his muscular back. His skin is as smooth and warm as the muscles beneath it are hard and unyielding. Our hands roam, learning each other's contours, punctuated by little moans and growls as Kit discovers a few of my sweet spots and I find his.

Beyond our touch, beyond the sofa where we lie and the room surrounding us, beyond what I want and what I fear, day fades into night without our notice, the world shrinking until it holds only the two of us.

At last, Kit breaks away. He stands and tugs me to my feet. Yet, whatever his plan, our bodies refuse to separate. His fingers tangle in my hair. He pulls me in for another of his befuddling kisses. I push into his erection. He rubs himself against me, his hands skimming down my back to shape the curve of my ass. I hum approval into his mouth. He growls in response.

The way he touches me, the way his strong body surrounds me . . . it's as if I've never been desired before. Fear knifes into me. This is not how I felt with Dan, or Roland. I pull away, bowing my head, trying to understand what is going on inside me. Kit tilts my chin up so our eyes meet. He runs a thumb across my bottom lip. His eyes are tender, his voice husky as he asks, "Still yes, dahlin'?"

I tell myself that the hotter a flame at ignition, the quicker it burns out. I tell myself this one will burn out quickly because my heart is already on fire. I nod. His mouth turns up in a smile filled with heat. He looks so boyishly pleased with my answer that the fear inside me dissolves. I smile and muss his hair. He laughs. Capturing my hand, Kit tows me toward the bedroom. Docile as a lamb, I follow.

At the door, Kit says, "Call me old-fashioned, but I like privacy when I'm making love to a woman, even if the voyeur is a dog." With my approval, he closes us off from Obie. Having had the experience before, my dog knows there will be special treats when the door reopens.

Kit prowls up to me and pushes my shirt down my arms. I let it fall to the carpet as he moves in to nuzzle the curve of my neck. "God, you smell good. Spicy," he adds, "with a hint of something sweet."

He licks just below my ear, having already discovered a few of my instant arousal switches, like the one he's teasing. I purr, reaching up to wrap my arms around his neck.

"Grapefruit?" he guesses, sounding puzzled.

"And ginger." I kiss the lovely angular spot where his jaw meets his neck. A little shiver runs through him.

His voice is a tad rougher when he says, "Ms. Lizzie, you're the first woman of my acquaintance who smells like food instead of flowers." He licks again.

I moan, disgustingly delighted to come in first in any category among his women.

"Why does you wearing perfume that smells like food make sense to me? I'll tell you why," he answers himself. "It's because I've been thinking of you as a woman-sized snack since the first time I kissed you."

"Yesterday?" I finish unbuttoning his shirt, a project I started in the living room. I let it drop to the floor to join mine. I've waited for what feels like an eternity, though in reality is a little over a month, to explore the splendors of Kit's chest. My palms slide over sleek muscle and a light smattering of hair lying against his skin. Either he's into male grooming or he doesn't grow a lot of hair. Whatever—I like it just fine.

I'd love to photograph him shirtless, only not right now.

"No, ma'am," Kit says as if I'm a slow learner. "You've been driving me to distraction since the night you invited me to unstick that closet door."

This surprising fact goes unremarked as he turns me to unclasp my bra. Unremarkable although demi-cupped, the bra joins our shirts on the floor. I spin to press myself against him, but he holds me away with one hand and slides the other up my ribs, to my breasts. He flicks one nipple with his thumb. We both watch it contract. A small sound of longing hums in my throat.

I cup him through his jeans, gratified by the similar noise he makes. He bends me back to tongue my breast, tugging the sensitive tip into his mouth. I clutch his shoulders. Arousal pulls me tight and unravels me at the same time. I guide his face to mine and kiss him.

We begin a conversation without words—a curling question at the tip of his tongue, a darting response from mine. A dare is tossed between us, our tongues arguing it back and forth. Alternatively aggressive and seductive, we duel until urgency overtakes us and Kit topples me onto the bed.

I study him where he kneels above me, noting his beard shadow, the angular bones, strong jaw, and nose that is a little too large yet perfectly fits his face. Eyes intent, he does his own study of me, desire glinting under luxuriant lashes. He strokes the back of a hand down my cheek, holding my gaze a little too long.

"What?" I can't help asking. He looks a little sad. I wonder if he is thinking of Eleanor. I reach for him.

He resists but smiles, his expression brightening. He says, "You know, I like you a lot, Ms. Lizbeth Silver."

Is this a step above adoring me? Or a step below? Before I can say I like him, too, he leans in and bites my nose.

While I squawk and grumble about ill usage, he divests me of the rest of my clothes—shoes, socks, pants, and panties.

"Geez, what was that? Some kind of weird hazing ritual?" I frown at him as he strips me of my underwear.

He winks. "Only for the especially tasty ones. It's your own fault for being so delicious." His eyes roam appreciatively over my body.

"I'm buying a flower-based perfume tomorrow."

"Squeamish about a little love bite?" Kit offers me a glance of mock surprise as he falls partially on top me, his body pressing me into the mattress.

I wiggle against him, happy with the skin-on-skin contact and the bulge pressing against my thigh. I'll be happier when the cause of it is no longer inside his jeans.

"You seem to like it when I bite you here," he says, angling his body so he can tug at a nipple.

I hum with pleasure, confirming his supposition.

"Maybe I'd better do some reconnaissance. I should know which parts want to be bit and which don't." He sinks his teeth gently into my earlobe. "How about here?" he asks when he's finished.

"Umm. Yes, there." I turn my head to meet his gaze. "Your research is promising, although more exploration, not to mention practice, never hurts, does it?" I'm enjoying his game. "I can think of a few other places where you could hone your technique."

"Really?" He looks perplexed, although the sparkle in his eyes gives him away. "I wonder where, exactly?" He locks his arms, giving me a serious once-over, from the top of my head to my belly, where he is pressed against me.

I don't need to employ the same scrutiny to know I'm not as beautiful or finally sculpted as Kit. I do, however, possess curves where a woman should have them; my waist is trim enough, even if my hips flare in a way that twenty-first-century fashion appreciates less than it should, although the Kardashians are doing their best to return hourglass shapes to fashion. Luckily, Kit seems to be a traditionalist, or to have broad tastes. Finished with his perusal, he offers a sexy curl of his lip in pure animal approval.

"I'm off to do some experimentation, dahlin'," he says, backing off the bed. "Got to figure this biting thing out." He kneels on the floor and pulls me toward the edge of the mattress until my legs bend over the side. "Let me know if I'm on the right track, will you?"

"Your instincts are excellent so far," I say.

He plants a soft kiss on top of one knee. A nip follows, a sharp pinch between his teeth. He rubs the sting away with the side of his cheek, his jaw stubble pleasantly textural. I'm content to lie still and appreciate the slow trail he's kissing and nipping toward what I'm hoping will be his ultimate destination.

"Yesssss," I breathe, as he plants kisses incrementally closer to where anticipation is making me slick. To encourage him, I stretch, tilting myself open.

Inching toward his goal, Kit aims a swift puff of breath at the swollen bud between my legs. I tense, an electric jolt of arousal lifting my pelvis toward his mouth. When I'm capable of breathing again, I lean up on one elbow to watch his progress.

Kit lifts his head, meeting my eyes. "Should I do that again?" As if he doesn't know the answer.

I rest a foot on the mattress and let my leg fall open. The view should make the answer obvious. "Oh, why not," I say, just so there are no misunderstandings.

He resumes his slow tease, coming oh so close and then retreating, inching his way toward his target too many times to count. I think, *Yes. Finally. Yes please,* only to be disappointed once more.

When he finally licks his way over my clit, the sensation is so intense that I gasp. A lovely, elemental growl rumbles from his throat as I push myself into his tongue. He lifts my legs over his shoulders.

With a final savoring lick, Kit raises his glance to mine, his expression knowing, mouth turned up at one corner. And then his eyes harden as he watches his thumbs spread me open. He flicks his tongue, wetting his lips. I contract on a flash of arousal before he even touches me, heat rolling up my body as I collapse onto the mattress. I have to remember to breathe when his tongue laps my clit at the same time that he massages me with his thumbs.

A man who enjoys his work and does it well is a miracle.

"Mr. Couper, I think you've found the best spot of all," I gasp.

"I couldn't agree more." He slides a finger inside me and then another, as good with his hands as he is with his tongue.

Inner and outer pleasure-points trip electricity up the line. I begin to melt. Kit is throwing one switch after another. It feels so good, but I would rather come with Kit inside me. Twisting away, I reach for him. He eludes me, climbing to his feet. Not willing to be denied, I use the gap at his waist where his erection has pulled his jeans away from his body to bring him closer. He allows me to unzip his fly and slide jeans and briefs down. A drop of juice decorates the tip of his cock, which is as sleek and well-muscled as the rest of him. He backs up to push off his shoes and socks, pulling a condom out of his pocket before he lets his clothing drop to the floor.

Kit is as beautiful as I imagined, his body cut with lean elegant muscle. Ripping open the packet with his teeth, He drops the rubber disk into my hand. My fingers close around it. I hate condoms, but I don't want to break the spell so we can have "the talk," although I do want a little more time to savor the visual before we move on to the finale. "Come here," I say.

Unlike Darius, Kit doesn't appear to mind taking orders. He brings a knee onto the bed, putting himself close to my mouth. I lean in to lick away that enticing droplet.

"I'm betting *you* know exactly how hard to bite," he says, stretching out on the bed and pulling me down next to him. I resume my explorations. The musky scent of male arousal makes my mouth water. Wrapping a fist around the base of his cock, I close my mouth around him. He goes down sweetly, as smooth as the whiskey he loves.

"Liz," he rasps as I suck, dipping to savor a second droplet pearling there. Hardening my tongue, I slide it across the sensitive undercurve of his cock. Kit groans and rakes his hands through my hair as he thrusts into my mouth.

I love what I'm doing and how much he likes it, yet a minute or two later, need overrides patience. Although I crave the luscious heat of his naked cock inside me, I work the condom over him. Once it's on, I touch him again, tracing a finger up one thick engorged vein. "Top or bottom?" I ask.

"Top."

It's always good to start simple and work your way up. I roll onto my back. Kit kneels between my legs. In a single sensual twist, he is inside me.

My eyes close as I savor this first lovely second of connection. I breathe in, humming happiness on my exhale. We are a snug, slippery fit. Perfection. I clench around him.

He thrusts. We groan in unison.

Neither pulling out nor driving deeply, Kit rocks against me. Opening my eyes, I tilt, tugging him into the hungry wet heat of my body. Eyes closed in concentration, he arches, exposing the strong graceful curve of his throat.

Everything about him thrills me, from the taut lines of his body to the way he uses it. A primal sound—more beast than man—grinds out of him as he finds my sweet spot and slowly rubs his cock over it.

There is no whoosh of flame, no instant incineration as with our first kiss, but incrementally, Kit sets me on fire, arousing my senses and my body, igniting sparks, lighting one conflagration after another.

Yet he remains a marvel of control. A little too like Darius. I want him to feel as out of control as I do. The question is how to get him there.

Withdrawing until only the very tip of his cock remains inside my body, Kit's eyes glint as I growl in frustration. I hook one leg behind his thighs and tighten around him, hoping to encourage him to change his plans. It works. He pumps once, twice, three times.

Yes, yes, yes!

Smiling sweetly, he winks and pulls his little in-out trick again. Kit is a terrible and terribly enthralling tease.

I buck to signal my impatience. He smirks, mouth curling, and returns to his torturously slow tempo. Under the sweep of his lashes, his eyes sparkle with mischief as he sets out to slowly drive me mad.

The sky outside the windows has deepened to a translucent indigo, stars glittering, the moon full, gilding Kit in silver, caressing the firm line of his jaw, the breadth of his swimmer's shoulders, the smooth taper of ribs into waist. He is built like a Greek kouros, those lovely idealized statues of athletic young men associated with the worship of Apollo. Like C. in his proportions, but older and more substantial, Kit is tempered and solid yet lithe. Moving above me and inside me, he is my ideal of male beauty: broad shoulders, trim waist, narrow pelvis flowing into powerful thighs curving gracefully into his knees. Kit is built for efficiency, for slicing through water, and, as it turns out, for fucking me.

My hands follow the moonlight caressing his shoulders, tracing over his biceps, well-defined pectorals, and the light pelting of hair on his chest. I find a small male nipple and I flick my tongue over it.

His response is a satisfying grind and pleasured groan, as well as a more urgent rhythm.

It seems I've found the correct switch. I nip and suck, alternating my attention between those sweet little disks as Kit finally pounds into me.

Having attained what I wanted, I collapse onto the bed although I can't stop touching him. It is a wonder after Darius to be with a man who enjoys my participation.

Kit's stomach is a hard plane over supple skin. I follow the line of hair that starts a few inches above his belly button to where it thickens and curls. Insinuating my hand into the tight space between us, I close thumb and forefinger around him. His rhythm slows. He pulls away to watch himself move through the ring of my fingers, his cock glistening with our comingled juices.

Pleased and reassured that Kit gets off on the give-and-take of pleasure, I release him to give his balls a gentle tug. He expels a sharp breath. The weight in my palm contracts.

Releasing the velvety sack, I purr low in my throat, which, perversely, Kit takes as a sign to slow, creating a literal point of contention as he holds me captive with his tantric games.

This time, it is his hand that pushes between us. He massages my clit. I'm already so aroused that in seconds I'm close and begin to pant. He thrusts in micro increments, inching in and out. "Please, Kit," I beg. "Harder."

He does as I ask. The orgasm begins to gather.

And . . . he stops moving.

Hot, ready, and frustrated—I clench my fists in the coverlet. "Fuck!" I say and close my eyes in frustration.

"Oh yeah," Kit agrees with an erotic little twist.

I begin where he left off, touching myself, watching for his reaction. He focuses on the wet slide of my fingers doing what he won't, eyes narrowed, his fleshy bottom lip dropping as he expels an excited breath. I slide into a suspended place of waiting, the orgasm close and yet just out of reach.

And then, as always, mysteriously and without warning, lush and silky and dark, it begins.

Which is when Kit, my prince of sensual torture and emperor of delight, fine Southern gentleman in all other ways—the sort of man who should be speeding me the last little distance over the edge—tugs at the hand I've been using to stroke myself and carries it to his lips.

The sound that grinds out of me is equal parts outrage and desire.

Kit ignores the outrage and makes a show of sniffing my fingers. And then he closes his eyes and licks.

"You taste exactly the way you smell," he murmurs, his eyes opening on mine. "Spicy. Tart-sweet. I could have eaten you all night, but"— he gives a dramatic sigh—"dahlin', we're going to have to work on your store of patience."

I'd be offended if his eyes weren't alight with amusement, his lips curling in a telltale smirk. Dropping my hand, he finally gives me what I need so badly. He thrusts and thrusts again, picking up speed. Holding himself up on one arm, he rolls his thumb over the hard bud of my clit.

The orgasm rises once more. This time, he doesn't stop me from rising with it and I soar. Away from him. Away from myself. I rise until I can't rise higher and fall into the sweet release Kit built for me.

A moment later, I am recovered enough to watch my lover's elegant finesse burn to the purity of in and out. Eyes squeezed shut, he savors the slide, though seconds later his gaze meets mine and holds there. I reach up to caress his cheek. He turns his head and kisses my palm—a tender gesture. Holding on for the ride, I wrap my legs around his waist. He is fierce and beautiful, and for the sublime present, he is mine. Arms locked, Kit's head falls forward and with a final thrust, he arches and roars.

Sheened in sweat, he collapses on top of me. We lay still, catching our breath and savoring the total absence of tension within our bodies. Eventually, Kit pushes onto an elbow. He cups my face in his palm and meets my lips for a last sweet kiss before lifting himself away to settle beside me. His hand finds mine and squeezes.

I love that he hasn't separated himself after sex. My eyes close. I allow myself to drift, deciding Kit was mostly right about how we would be together. Only, the water isn't warm; it's scalding hot. It isn't calm, either, but churns over wild rapids, and although I'm too relaxed to feel any fear, there is a possibility that one day soon, I'll drown in him. I turn my head. Kit is lying on his back, eyes closed, his elegant profile relaxed and soft.

This was more than good sex. I've had enough of it to know. Sex was good enough with Dan, no matter that at the time I had little experience to judge it by. But Dan was never tender. Roland, who was tender, was not a terribly skilled lover, but I trusted him so completely that the intimacy we shared made up for his lack of finesse.

Kit is a master of technique, and also motivated to please me, perhaps more than he wanted to please himself. I try to imagine us getting better with practice, except we're better already. Any better might kill me. I smile at this idea and enjoy how pleasure has emptied my brain, its overfired synapses unable to produce even the tiniest whisper of anxiety.

And then I realize I've forgotten about Obie. I kiss Kit's cheek, tell him I'll be right back, and get up to get my dog a piece of cheese—a favorite treat—and to let him out. When we return, Kit has laid a stack of comforters on the floor for Obs. We watch him settle.

Holding the covers up for me to slide underneath, Kit shifts to fit himself around me. I say, "Do you want some dinner?"

"Not yet. Maybe later. You?"

"Same." I curl into the curve of his body, facing him. He caresses my waist with his palm. I pull my legs up, so my calves rest against his long thighs. Using his arm as my pillow, I lay one hand against his chest. He places his hand over mine and kisses my forehead. I smile and drift into sleep.

CHAPTER 26

OVER THE LAST two-and-a-half weeks, Kit and I have developed a routine. Way too early for me, he goes off to swim and then to work. I rise later, discuss wedding details with clients, answer e-mail, and attend to the paperwork side of my business, or I drive out with Obie to find photographic inspiration, leaving clerical work for later. If Kit arrives home early enough, we walk Obie to the dock or into the woods as the mood suits us. Dinner depends on the contents of his refrigerator and mine. Sometimes we eat out or see a movie. But our primary entertainment is each other.

Tonight, Kit settles on his back, lacing his fingers with mine. "How can this keep getting better?" he murmurs.

Lying next to him in his glorious rice bed after another amazing session of lovemaking, I think the question is rhetorical, because how should I know? Practice makes perfect? Or, maybe the sex keeps getting better because our feelings are more and more involved, although I don't know if this is as true for him as it is for me. I squeeze his hand considering how to answer, although I wonder whether I just violated my new rule about being as truthful and transparent as possible, especially with myself.

Since we began our affair, there have been only two evenings we haven't spent in each other's company. On the first occasion, Kit attended a golf awards dinner with his guy pals. On the second, he attended a dinner dance with one of his lady friends, arranged long before I entered the picture. Her name is Joan. I appreciated this information, mostly because Kit was so open about it. He also arrived home long before the event must have concluded. I appreciated that, too, and that he didn't smell of perfume or wear any lipstick stains.

I have wondered whether he was equally transparent with Joan about me, the joker in his pack. I didn't ask because it would be possessive, and although I feel possessive, the emotion isn't one I allow in a short-term affair.

This thought skirts the truth, a further break in my recently established transparency code, at least with myself. I like this man way too much, and when we part in a little over a month, I will be way too sad.

"You get better with practice," I tease, leaving out the mental gymnastics my brain went through to come up with this light-hearted answer. I roll into him. He wraps his arms around me and says, "I'm inspired."

"It shows." I close my eyes, feeling sleepy.

"Lizzie?" He brushes a lock of hair from my forehead with a feathery touch. I blink up at him. His expression is serious. Too serious for what we just did. Foreboding sets my heart pounding.

His eyes lock with mine. "I want you to stay."

I relax. "Of course. But I need to take Obie out one more time."

"I'll take Obs out. But you mistake my meaning. I'd like it if you could stay at Willing a while longer. How about it?"

If he'd upended a bucket of ice water over my head he couldn't have brought me as suddenly and fully awake. I push against his chest. "Not in the contract," I joke. I start to shake, adrenaline running away with me for a second time in less than a month.

"There's nothing in the contract that says we can't change the terms." Kit's tone is lawyerly. He shifts to the side, allowing me to sit up. I pull the blanket over my breasts as I twist to face him.

"You, Mr. Couper, are drunk on endorphins." I punctuate the observation with a quick kiss, smiling into his eyes. This idea for me to stay is likely the by-product of a stellar orgasm, one I take full credit for, even if it means his desire to keep me near is afterglow induced. The phenomenon is well known to me. Give him thirty minutes and he'll have that figured out, although I'm flattered he thinks he wants to enjoy a few extra weeks in my company.

Understanding this reality doesn't prevent my stomach from flipping. The idea of staying on is so seductive. I remind myself that he'll regret his invitation—I glance at the clock on the bedside table—in twenty-seven minutes tops.

As if he's read my mind, he says, "This is not an impulsive idea." He pushes up to sit next to me and pulls me onto his lap, rubbing his hands up and down my back. "Why are you shaking?" he asks, understanding I'm not actually cold.

How do I respond? I slide down on the bed. Kit follows. Turning onto his side and propping himself on one arm he says. "Well?"

"Which question do you want answered first?"

"Your pick." He begins circling the tips of my breasts with a fingertip, rolling around one nipple, and then the other. No matter that my nipples are just this side of sore from the attention he's already lavished on them, a banked fire begins to smolder, my shaking notwithstanding.

"I'm surprised," I say. "Sometimes I get shivery when I'm surprised."

"A super adrenaline surge? Interesting. But I don't see why you should be surprised. We've been having a great time together."

"And should probably stick to the contract as written."

His brow furrows. "As far as I know there is no clause set in indelible ink about the length of your stay." His hand, playing with my nipples, urges compliance. "Unless you're tired of me already?" He leans in, our eyes locking.

The question is ridiculous. I'm certain he knows it. With what he's doing to my body, I'm too short-circuited to keep shaking. I'm certain he also knows I can't think past the sparks he's throwing off. Insinuating himself between my legs, he presses us together where it matters most, and holds himself above me.

I skim a leg down his calf. "As if I could be tired of you," I breathe, feeling him stir. We look into each other's eyes for a long unblinking second. His gaze is all earnest intention. Mine is earnest, too—I'm earnestly going to make the case for this being a bad idea.

Not that it isn't a compelling one. The problem is, the longer I stay, the harder it is going to be to walk away. The truth is that leaving him will hurt. No matter when it happens, the hurt will be significant.

Every day, this knowledge grows. I tell myself the pleasurable memories will eventually outweigh the pain of parting. But the pleasure-to-pain ratio will become more out of balance the longer I stay on.

"Lizzie?" Kit leans in, tenderly kissing my brow. "Say something, dahlin'."

Licking the skin below my ear, a personal erogenous zone that sends a lovely tendril of arousal snaking through me, he works his hand between our bodies and rolls his thumb over my clit. Kit doesn't play fair. My breath hitches.

"Think about it," he advises with a grind, pressing me into the mattress. For a guy closing in on fifty, he recovers with amazing speed. "You know you want to keep me around."

I moan—my traitorous body is voting without me. Kit takes the sound as encouragement, lavishing attention on all of my favorite hot spots, presenting me with the shallowest benefit for extending my stay. I'm already crazy about his facile intelligence, his kindness, and his ready clever wit. Not that the way we fit together in bed doesn't have its special delights.

"We aren't done yet," Kit argues, raising his head from my stomach where he's kissing the points of the compass around my belly button. "You told me you don't have a shoot until the beginning of May, so why not stay until then? Why not see what develops? You could lose interest before then. Though I'm certain I won't."

"I could maybe manage until the end of April," I murmur, drugged by the confirmation that he is as entranced with me as I am with him.

"I'll accept that. And then we'll see what there is to see."

Having made this two-part declaration, the one about staying on and the more provisional one about the slightly more distant future, he cups me with his palm and then strokes with his thumb.

Looking up through his lovely thick lashes, Kit smiles into my eyes. If sweet words don't win him what he wants, he's clearly not above applying other kinds of "pressure."

"Lizzie, dahlin' Lizbeth . . ." He blows a breath between my legs.

I'd rather he lick. "Maybe I need to rethink my decision," I say.

He raises himself up, frowning. "But, you already said—" And then he notices my raised brow and laughs. "I can see I need to apply all of the tools at my disposal to prevent any more rethinking."

"Especially that tool," I say, prodding him gently with my toes. "Staying on is a sacrifice, but I'm willing to make it for you." And thus I commit myself, for better or worse.

"Good woman. Your sacrifice will be rewarded."

Ever a man of his word, Kit immediately makes mind-blowingly good on his promise.

※

Light is barely visible through the shutters when my forehead receives Kit's good-morning-I'm-off kiss. He's leaving to swim and from there to work. As his steps fade down the stairs, I breathe in the scent of the bedding, a mixture of Kit's cologne, my perfume, and the musk of sex. Feeling satiated, I stretch, enjoying the arousal that seems to always linger just off stage between us these days.

I must have dozed off again, because when I turn my head, I see Obie is flipped up on his back next to me. I comb my fingers through the hair on his narrow chest, blinking into sunlight streaming through the open shutters. This morning the light is sharp, cutting across the rich patina of the mahogany furniture, delineating the intricate rice motif carved into the bedposts, the rumpled folds of the sheets, the imprint of Kit's head on his pillow.

I want him to be the one. My wanting has the same clarity as the sunlight, but burns hotter. I want him way too much.

With a sigh, I fling off the sheet to begin the day.

CHAPTER 27

"THIS IS GOING TO SOUND like a stupid question to you, but what exactly is a praline?"

"You have never eaten a praline?" Kit looks at me, his expression incredulous. We are walking toward the front gate, on our way to visit his friend Agnes, who lives about a half mile away on Needwood Road. Agnes is the mother of Kit's son's best friends, and of Amina and Michella—Chella—the teenager who looks after Obie sometimes. Agnes is, as well, the woman who offered Kit so much support after Eleanor died.

"Nope. Not kidding. I've never met one in person. All I know is that they're made with pecans."

"As well as sugar, cream, and butter. It's kind of like peanut brittle only with pecans, but softer and richer."

We stop at the top of the drive for Kit to tap the code into the gate's lock and then wait for the gate to swing open.

"The original recipe is supposed to have arrived on this side of the pond with the French. That recipe called for almonds, but pecans were more plentiful here. The cream is another American innovation."

We wait for the gate to swing open.

"How did I know you would have the origins and the ingredients tucked into your brain?"

"Because I live to eat? Why do you think I swim?"

"To maintain your youthful figure and keep the ladies swooning?"

"Ha! That too. But, seriously, Agnes makes the best pralines in the world, so you're in for a treat."

After we pass through the gate, Kit takes another one of his hidden paths. The path spits us out on Needwood, a dirt track bordered by water oak. As we pass a modest, one-story wooden house, my camera strap slips. Kit snags it and transfers it to his shoulder.

"Lucky for you I'm not one of those photographers who is overly protective of my equipment or you'd be dead."

"I promise to give your camera back the second picture-taking lightning strikes." Kit grins. "Come on, admit it's heavy. Why not let me carry it? Another benefit of keeping me around."

I love the Nikon but it is awkward and heavy. "What are the other benefits?" I ask.

"There you go, wounding me again. You Northern gals can be so harsh." Kit smirks. He grabs my hand and laces our fingers together.

"You haven't answered the question, Mr. Couper." Unable to prevent myself from reacting to any sort of physical contact with him, my stomach does a happy little skip.

"Well, then, I'm guessing you might keep me around because I know my way around a grill."

"Nah."

"Your dog likes me?"

"Obie is definitely a consideration."

"How about my witty repartee and clever tongue?"

He spins me into his chest and offers a demonstration.

We are at that sublime stage of infatuation when no amount of sex or togetherness dampens our appetite for each other.

"Ummmmmm. Self-serving woman that I am, that lovely mouth of yours is a definite consideration."

He kisses me again. I wonder if you can OD on endorphins. When we break apart, I say, "You have to stop doing this."

"Kissing you in the middle of the road?"

"Discombobulating me when we're supposed to be doing something else."

"That's a problem?"

"When you *discombobulated* me while I was making dinner last night, we ended up going out because I didn't remember the casserole was in the oven until the smoke alarm went off, remember?"

"You are saying that meeting my friends, you don't want to be thinking about what I'm going to do to you as soon as I get you home. Is that it?"

"Your intelligence is one of your most enchanting traits." But it isn't his brain I'm thinking about and he knows it.

He laughs and gives my hand a squeeze.

I'm going to pay for this happiness. The thought sobers me. I swallow, wondering how many contrasting emotions it's possible to feel at any given moment. I'm thrilled Kit is so happy about us, yet I'm anxious about meeting his friends. My heart is filled with hope because Kit wants to introduce me to them, engaging me in the fabric of his life. Yet I will be leaving him, even if the departure date has been postponed a few more weeks.

I wish I had new and improved Rules to guide me through this affair, but so far, I have only the one: be as honest and as transparent as possible.

What that really means is, be brave and don't hold emotions back for fear of being hurt. To the best of my ability, I'm complying. I didn't run away when Kit asked me to stay. I looked squarely at the situation, recognized it was going to hurt later, and did it anyway.

He's implied on a couple of occasions, including just now, that he hopes we'll outlast the time we have. How wonderful would that be? Complicated, but wonderful all the same. Yet, I have to be honest—I'm afraid I won't be able to cope with how it is going to feel if this is it, just these four glorious, shining months.

Kit lifts our joined hands to point to a house coming into view past the densely wooded area where we are walking. The house is tan brick, with a hip roof and single-story addition on one side. Several cars and a van advertising the family's electrical business are parked in the driveway.

We mount the steps and cross the porch. Kit knocks, and then slings his arm around my shoulders. We wait for the door to open. I try to disengage from under his arm, not sure I want to put our temporary relationship on display. "Stop squirming," he admonishes, without releasing me. "You'll knock the camera off my shoulder."

A woman looks at us through the door's glass panel. Her eyes widen. She probably isn't used to seeing Kit on her porch with a woman pressed to his side, although I could be wrong. Once again, two emotions war: the thrill of being the woman with Kit, and gloom because being with him is temporary.

The door opens. From Kit's description of Agnes's child-rearing skills, I've been imagining an African-American version of Mary Poppins. Maybe she is, but Agnes is way more interesting-looking than Miss Poppins, even if, odds are, she doesn't possess a flying umbrella.

Almost as tall as Kit, his friend has elegant bones and shallow-set brown eyes. Graying at the temples, her hair is tied away from her long face with a colorful scarf. Her clothes are conservatively cut but the colors are bold.

By the time she swings the door wide, she has mastered her expression. "Kitten!" she exclaims. "I'm so glad you could visit and bring our new neighbor." Her gaze shifts to me, eyes lit with curiosity.

Kit says, "Ags, this is Liz," as I simultaneously say, "Kitten?" my voice tight with incredulity.

"Believe it or not," she says, "he was a tiny child and our token white boy when he visited here in his misspent youth." She grins. "Of course, we had to give him a nickname to fit his stature and remind him who was top dog in the neighborhood."

"Was that you?"

"My oldest brother, Aaron."

I can tell she loves razzing Kit. I contemplate my sleek six-foot-something lover as a sweet little kitten and grin. And then I whoop.

"It's not that funny," Kit grumbles, releasing me. His irritation makes me laugh harder.

Agnes stands aside and motions us into the house. "Even though his size changed some," she explains, "his enjoyment of his nickname has not, so you can see why we had to continue using it at every possible opportunity." She grins and pats Kit's cheek. He rolls his eyes.

I admire the Parsons-style couches tossed with bright, Kente-cloth pillows in the Postelles' living room as I continue to chortle about the sulky kitty at my side. "I can think of other sobriquets for you, but that one never would have occurred to me," I say, squeezing his arm.

"If I were you, dahlin', I'd think of me as a big, dangerous sort of cat." He rubs a palm down my back and over my butt, which Agnes can't see, and squeezes before putting his hand in his pocket.

Last night Kit prowled naked up the bed and into me. I expel a loud breath. Kit grins. I'm betting he knows exactly what I'm seeing in my mind's eye.

"Don't think I won't get even for that overshare, Ags," he says to his friend.

Watching our exchange with speculative interest, she shakes her head. "No, you won't, because if you do, you'll never eat another of my pralines."

I grin at the dangerous kitty. "She wins," I say.

He sighs, but his amused expression indicates this sort of back and forth is business as usual between these two, probably since childhood.

We pass through a wide hall, with a staircase rising to the right. Agnes gestures us into a spacious great-room kitchen with a big blond wood table to one side. Past the kitchen proper, a comfortable couch and loveseat are positioned near a bank of windows overlooking the backyard. Agnes motions us to sit.

"Sweet tea?" she asks.

"Here's where you'll know I'm a Yankee if my accent hasn't already given me away," I say. "Do you have unsweetened? If not, ice water would be great."

"Unsweet it is. My girls are always dieting and want unsweet so they can add that stevia stuff." She makes a face, leaving no doubt about her opinion of the natural, calorie-light sweetener. "I don't need to ask you," she says to Kit.

While Agnes attends to the tea, I look around the room, decorated in shades of rust and blue. Kit asks after the boys. She fills him in as she adds our glasses to a tray already prepped with a bowl of her special candies. I ask after Chella. Agnes says the girls are with friends. She tells Kit that Matt is doing well in his medical studies; Jordan is on a service call. Picking up the tray, she sets it on the rough-hewn coffee table in front of us.

Kit grabs a praline. I envy him his swimming, although not enough to take it up. I choose a smaller candy and bite.

"Wow. This is divine."

Kit grins and reaches for another. "See?" he says, significantly. "Better than"—he catches himself and finishes—"just about anything."

Agnes glances at him and then at me. I'm pretty sure she hasn't misconstrued the hot look he just gave me. She looks thoughtful. Kit reaches for thirds.

Tall like Kit but built on a more strapping scale, Agnes's husband enters the room.

With a quick swallow, Kit stands. He cuffs Jon on the shoulder the way guys do when they like each other. Then, motioning to me, says, "Jon, this is my friend Liz from Vermont. Liz, meet Jon."

Reaching across Kit, Jon takes the hand I hold out. "Nice to meet you, Liz. I hear you're here for the winter?"

"Until the end of mud season."

He cocks his head in question.

"Until the ground is thawed enough for the danger of mud burying a car to the axles on one of our many dirt roads has passed."

"I'd like to see that!" Jon says. "Well, welcome to our sand spit." He turns to Kit. "Want to take a look at the Giants and Kansas City in exhibition play? The Giants are looking good. You might want to switch. I'm toggling between the game and the golf tournament."

"Lizzie?" Kit says. "Would you mind if I step away for a couple of minutes?"

"Your girlfriend and I will find *something* to talk about," Agnes says, shooing him off. "Most likely, you."

I laugh, though I register the "girlfriend" comment with a small internal twitch. Kit's eyes are merry, as if he noticed the figurative hit to my solar plexus, too, and found it amusing. He raises his hand and pantomimes shooting me before following Agnes's husband out of the room.

Since it's a lovely spring day, she suggests we adjourn to her back veranda. I choose a big wicker chair with a yellow-striped seat and back cushion. She takes the matching chair across from me.

"Kit says this is your first time in Georgia, that he only met you in January." Agnes is cutting right to the chase.

"I needed a break from winter and to work on some creative issues I've been having. That's how I ended up here." I realize I'm not answering the intent of her question.

"Creative issues?"

"I'm a photographer." I lift the camera I brought out with me. "I was in need of inspiration, which I've found here in abundance. I really love the coastal landscape."

"Well, that's a fine thing then." Agnes pushes the pralines toward me. "You know, I haven't seen that man take a real interest in a long time."

It's hard to keep up with her topic shifts, although her track is on Kit. I consider answering, *He's definitely interested and we're having really hot sex. We like each other a lot but I haven't a clue if either of those facts are significant.* Of course I could also go with an enigmatic, *What do you know?*

I say, "Really?" hoping this response elicits a few facts I don't have— in the interest of transparency, of course.

"What he went through with Eleanor pretty much broke him for good. I'm going to give it to you straight, Miss Elizabeth, you're the first woman he's wanted to introduce to me since Eleanor passed away, so don't mess with him. His heart is fragile."

My eyes widen. "Maybe mine is, too. And please call me Liz, it's short for Lizbeth."

Agnes picks up her glass and takes a sip of her tea as silence reigns. She sits back in her chair. "I'm sorry. That was over the line." Setting her glass on the table between us, she says, "What you and Kit get up to isn't any of my business. It's just that I've known him through a lot of heartache and I feel protective."

"Hey, I get it. You're his friend. You don't want to see him hurt. For the record, I'm heading home to Vermont at the end of April. Kit and I are clear with each other about this being a *good-time-for-now* sort of situation."

"Hmmmm," she says noncommittally, although I think what she means is she's not buying my version of the story.

I smile. There is something about this woman that makes it okay to tell her things I only tell Arielle. Agnes is definitely not the kind of Southern lady Kit and I have had so much fun stereotyping. She says what she means, which makes me feel comfortable doing the same.

"I don't know if that's true anymore," I admit. "He's lovely, isn't he? And . . ." I pause, because it feels risky to say what I'm feeling, but I think about Darius and Arielle and their perceptions about what I'm capable of, as well as the new transparency rule. I say, "We've both been hurt, so, as you put it, there's damage on both sides. Where that leaves us, I don't know. I don't think Kit knows either. We're feeling our way."

This, I realize, is the unvarnished truth. Unfortunately, the truth isn't going to set me free. Instead, the anxious little engine inside my brain, the one that's been switched on since Kit asked me to stay, gets louder.

I turn my attention to Agnes's yard, where an old-fashioned wood-and-rope swing, attached to the branch of a big live oak, is swaying in the breeze.

Agnes says, "I can respect that. I hope it works out for the best—for both of you."

We sit for a moment, each of us considering. Eventually, I come up with a change of subject. "Kit didn't tell me you've known each other so long."

"Then it won't surprise you to hear he was always a troublemaker even as a pint-sized child." She chuckles, a pleasing mellow sound that I find as infectious as Kit's laugh. Launching into a story about her and Kit as seven-year-olds, Agnes describes how he instigated a pre-breakfast, potato chip raid on her mother's kitchen. After a few more funny stories, including one about the time Kit dared her to climb higher into a tree than she wanted to go and he had to spend a good part of an afternoon coaxing her down, I ask about what occupies her time now that her children are older.

She tells me that once her boys were in junior high school and the girls in elementary school full time, she got her master's degree. She's a social worker for the Brunswick school system.

The topic of children leads us to the discovery that dealing with teenage daughters is the same no matter where you do it, North or South.

"There were times I fantasized about putting Diana on a boat and floating her out to sea," I admit. "Though she'll be twenty-one in October, she can still boil my blood when it suits her."

"I hear you! And the next minute, I bet she's as sweet as spun sugar and you just want to hug her to death."

"That's true, too."

Agnes sets our empty glasses on the tray and rises. "The problem is, you never know which child you are dealing with—quicksilver is to teenage girls as snapping is to turtles."

We laugh as I follow her inside.

"Thank you for your frankness, Agnes. I've enjoyed this."

She sets the tray on the counter. "And I thank you for forgiving me when I got in your face. Like I said, my excuse is that I really care about that man."

"Me too." I sigh.

She gives me a sharp look, but doesn't press. "Would you like to have dinner sometime? We can leave Kit and Jon at home in front of ESPN with some leftovers."

"I'd love that."

"Let me check the calendar. With Chella and Amina in high school, there are a lot of activities to coordinate."

"I remember those years well. Call, text, e-mail?"

She pulls out her cell phone. I pull out mine. We share our contact information.

"You know," I say as I watch her bag pralines for Kit, "it occurs to me I know Kit's a Bulldog fan when it comes to college football and a Falcons fan otherwise, but which baseball team does he root for? The Braves?"

Agnes laughs. "Nope. But I'm betting you can figure it out. Base your guess on his mischief and not on where he lives."

Just then, Kit and Jon return to the kitchen. "Yeah," Jon says, obviously having heard the last of our conversation. "Don't forget his great-great-granddaddy was a Yankee."

Kit crosses his arms and lifts his brows in my direction.

I think about where he went to college. The Yankees just don't feel right. The answer pops into my head. "The Red Sox."

"Kitten," Agnes chuckles, "I like this woman."

✳

On our way home, I thank Kit for introducing me to his friends. Agnes is a formidable person, which, I decide, may be Kit's definition of amazing, the word he most uses to describe her.

"What has you so far away?" he asks as he opens his gate and we turn down the drive. "You haven't said a word for five minutes."

"Oh, I've just been thinking about the stories Agnes told about you, Kitten," I answer, hedging the truth a little. This isn't dishonest, exactly. I'm merely withholding the facts in their entirety. I've been thinking about Agnes' cross-examination and what she got me to reveal. It was a relief to acknowledge the limbo of my relationship with Kit to someone other than Arielle. Except that now I feel even less shatterproof.

"I don't know why she brought up that stupid nickname," Kit grumbles.

"Because she loves you." I cuff him on the arm.

He harrumphs. "She's a good woman."

"She's a great woman. And you're a great guy."

"Which is why I plan to keep you around," he says. "Behind every *good* guy there's a great woman."

"I'm considering keeping *you* around so I can call you Kitten."

"As long as you stick around, I'll put up with it, although that nickname is a sore trial." He smiles, and then, looking serious, he asks, "Diana's okay with you staying longer?"

"Actually, Diana and I haven't talked about my extended visit. The first wedding on my calendar is the May 8 weekend, which is a week before Diana finishes her sophomore year. She's coming home for a couple of weeks, but the plan is for her to work in Burlington again this the summer and live with her boyfriend and some other friends in a shared apartment, so I don't see a problem, although I appreciate your concern."

We round the bend. His house comes into view.

"Like Diana, Noah, isn't out of school until mid-May, either."

We climb the porch steps to Sam's house. Inside, Obie does his usual gallop around the living room. When the dog can hold himself still, Kit loves him up, saying to me, "I'm sorry we won't be meeting each other's kids, but I'm going to take what I can get and be content."

"Me too." I mean it, although the end of us is already weighing me down.

CHAPTER 28

"WAIT," I SAY, as we walk toward the car. "I need a picture of you in that tux." I run into the house to grab my point-and-shoot.

Kit lifts a brow when I aim the camera at him. I click, loving his amused expression. "Nice. Now, walk toward me would you, and do that brow thing again."

"You're a hard taskmistress," he jokes, doing as I ask. One eyebrow lifts, and then he laughs. *Click, click, click.*

There's a certain déjà vu to this scene, although in contrast to the pensive photographs I took of Darius in his tux, these images are not dark, although they're just as sexy.

I question the gods' choices for me a lot, but the gift of two men who can dance within a three-month period after an almost decade-long drought is a gift I'm simply going to celebrate.

"You can make me pay later," I say. This suggestion adds an additional naughty glitter to his smile. I capture that, too. I'll be leaving in a month. As time shortens for us, I am taking more pictures of Kit, as if more images will offer more consolation after I leave him.

Adjusting the pashmina wrapped around my shoulders, I admire the ombre silk subtly graduating from black to deep green to midnight blue. Kit bought it for me. In what seems to be a never-ending parade of lessons from Darius, this one is about how to accept gifts gracefully. The shawl was a lovely, thoughtful present and I expressed my delight with it, which wasn't difficult since the pashmina didn't have the complex undertones of Darius's rugs.

As we drive onto St. Simons Island, Kit tells me the resort where the gala is being held, The King and Prince, was not named for British royalty, but for a family named King, who owned the Retreat Plantation on the island before the War. Kit circles the parking area rather than use the valet. He finds a spot at the back of the lot. Opening my door, he holds out his hand.

Once he's hauled me out and locked the door, he presses me into the Audi Based on our height disparity, my view narrows to his chiseled jaw and shapely mouth. I think about what that mouth is capable of doing to me and start to tingle. Breathing in, I savor the lemony scent of his cologne. "Who's wearing food flavors these days?" I ask, straightening his bow tie.

"You inspired me. And thanks for doing this."

In my most genteel Southern-girl drawl I say, "Aren't you the sweetest thang." I rest my hand over the polished cotton of his dress shirt. "But honestly, the pleasure is mine."

Kit's eyes narrow.

"Don't do that," I chide, feeling way too hot and not because the sun is bathing us in bright early-evening light. Tonight is our first big public outing. Rhonda's attention, as well as Agnes's reaction to Kit and me as a couple, has me primed for at least a few sideways glances. Still, I'd rather not look singed around the edges upon arrival.

Kit swears he could care less whether people speculate about us. I suppose I don't like the idea of his friends imagining me as his flavor of the month because I want to be the flavor of every single month. Accepting that our time together is coming to an end, that there will be other flavors after me, is difficult. The kind of difficult performing brain surgery is for someone who wields a knife only in the kitchen. The clock is ticking. With a mere three weeks to go, my yearnings grow stronger with each passing day. I wonder if I should start reading medical texts and consider buying a scalpel.

"You look lovely," Kit says, dropping a kiss on my cheek. "The belle of the ball," he adds with a twinkle in his eyes. I hear desire in the dark rumble of his voice.

After I accepted his invitation, I hit the Belk department store, not having anticipated the need for dancing clothes when I packed for the trip. I bought a sleeveless jersey top with a draped neckline sprinkled with opalescent jet beads to pair with my all-purpose gored black skirt. At Goodwill, I found a pair of strappy closed-toe dress shoes. For sparkle, I picked up some dangle earrings encrusted with crystal beads and dark pearls, and a wide cuff bracelet of similar style.

Reaching out to adjust the stole he bought me, Kit rearranges the drape over my shoulder, tracing the silky fabric across my upper arm. His fingers roll off my arm and over my breast. My nipple puckers. He rubs the tips of his fingers back and forth over the hard nub he's raised.

I exhale sharply. "Christopher Aiken Couper, this is a public parking lot. Someone might notice," I say sotto voce, glancing past his shoulder at the walk winding toward the massive old beachfront hotel. Thankfully, everyone is headed toward the building and away from us.

With his eyes crinkling at the corners, his mouth lifts into one of his swoon-worthy smiles. "It's adorable how prim you are sometimes, when I know how not so prim you are at other times." Kit raises one brow, doing his own scan of the lot behind me. He lifts his arm to wave at someone. "Nope. Doesn't bother me," he affirms.

Unable to stop myself, I twist to see who is behind us. The lot is full of cars and conspicuously devoid of humans.

"Not funny," I grumble.

"Dahlin', you have my answer in word as well as deed. No one cares what I do."

I breathe a sigh of the long-suffering variety. "Right. The most eligible bachelor on the Golden Isles walks into a party with a strange woman on his arm and you really believe no one will notice?"

"Sweetheart, let me restate what I just said. *I. Don't. Care.* Why does this matter to you? And you're not a strange woman. You have many singular attributes, but strange isn't one of them."

"Cute, Kitten. But, the problem is, I don't want to be on your all-too-public conquest list." I tug at his jacket front for emphasis.

"Is that what this is about?" He chuckles. "Let me assure you, Lizbeth, you are too singular to be on any list." He puts his arm around me, and before I can offer a response, twists us into a dip. "You're an original." His eyes meet mine for a second before his focus shifts to my lips.

I throw my arms around his neck as he continues to dip me toward the ground. Lucky for me, his grip is like iron. He begins a not so subtle campaign to kiss my misgivings away *in the parking lot.*

Damn, the man can kiss. Still, when we come up for air, I mutter, "A person would think we'd have this out of our systems by now."

Kit seems to find me particularly amusing tonight. As he returns us to a standing position, his deep belly laugh rumbles. I roll my eyes. Then, noticing we've knocked his bow tie askew, I reach up to straighten it. He catches my hand and guides it lower, over his crisply starched shirt, over the firm musculature beneath his shirt. "Why should a person have 'this' out of their system by now?" he asks, pressing my palm to his fly where there will soon be a conspicuous bulge if the teasing doesn't stop immediately.

"Perhaps if that person weren't sleeping with you," he suggests, a master at answering his own questions. "But I am sleeping with you— and dallying, too." He gives his one-side-up grin. "And that seems to make me hungrier as time goes by rather than the opposite."

This stops me in my tracks. He's just admitted he feels the same way about me as I do about him. Or maybe he's only talking about sex. I prefer to believe it's more than that. Going up on tiptoes, I meet his eyes. His cock lengthens under the hand he continues to hold against his body. For an instant I consider how well I've come to know him— in the biblical sense—and wonder where a discreet hedgerow might be located. Half of my brain wants to smack him into showing more decorum while the other half can hardly wait for his next outrageous display.

"I know what you are thinking, Ms. Lizzie," he drawls. "You are thinking very naughty thoughts." He grins, twining his fingers with mine. "Come on, dahlin', time for some public hanky-panky—time for dancing."

Keeping a lid on our "partnership" is obviously a lost cause if the giddy mood Kit is in is any indication. We walk toward the hotel with our hands linked together while I savor the perfection of the evening.

The breeze is light, the temperature is mild, the sky a soft blue, and the man I'm with delights me.

The waves make a lazy slurping sound, slapping the shore on the ocean side of the resort. We take the wide stone entry steps to the lobby. Kit drops my hand and centers a palm between my shoulder blades in that courtly gesture I adore. As he opens a tall wood and glass door, I hear "My Funny Valentine" along with the hum of the crowd.

The ceiling of the spacious lobby is high over our heads, held aloft by a series of Moorish-inspired columns topped with gilded palm-frond capitals. The decor is classic early-twentieth-century opulent. Guests in evening finery mill about the lobby crowding the bar, which has been arranged on a raised platform at one end of the room. Banks of doors open into the ballroom, where long windows offer a glorious backdrop of ocean and sky.

Vermonters tend toward the casual even when dressing to excess. Here, the women seem to relish the chance to dress up, although there are a few like me who didn't get the memo about not wearing somber colors. Most of the ladies shimmer in skin-tight knits or bright satin, some with boned bodices and poufy skirts. I notice a surfeit of gold jewelry, from tasteful to exuberantly excessive. A blinding amount of bling flashes as hands flutter and heads turn.

In contrast, as has been the fashion for the last hundred and fifty years, the men look elegantly dashing in black and white. Among the bow-tied fellowship, a few of the more daring sport dots and prints. I salute their sense of adventure but prefer the classic look Kit wears with such sartorial flair.

He works his way toward the bar. I follow, on the lookout for a man who can outdo him for the perfection of his tailoring. I don't see one. Or anyone as strikingly handsome, although some young waiters look like moonlighting surfer boys with the requisite golden tans and lovely lithe bodies. While they can compete with Kit in the physical perfection category, yet are far too young to possess the lived-in attractiveness he wears so well.

When he returns with my tonic water and lime—no point putting alcohol in my system when I'll be taking to the dance floor—Kit too surveys the crowd. Friends and acquaintances take this as their cue to approach. In short order we are surrounded by a group of elegant couples.

"Liz, let me introduce you to some of the more disreputable company in these parts," Kit says with a grin.

"The man is looking in the mirror again," a fellow on my right quips. Everyone laughs.

"Lizbeth Silver, meet Greg Clairborne, my doppelgänger and law partner." He directs my attention to the man who shares Kit's tall, dark-haired symmetry although his features are more blunt. "And Jillian, his better half," Kit adds.

"Pleased to meet you," says the petite blonde next to Greg. Her coiffeur is disheveled in a way that implies she spent a fortune on its calculated disarray. I envy her ability to carry the look off.

"Meet Barth and Karen Como." Kit gestures to a slightly older couple at the Clairbornes' right. They nod hello. "Barth and Karen own the antique center on Frederica."

"I love that place," I say. I've visited many antique stores during my rambles, though none that can compete with Darius's shop.

"You already know Pamela and Marshall."

I turn my head and smile, acknowledging the Tisdales.

"Lovely to see you, my dear," rumbles Marshall.

I note the speculative glances exchanged by the other couples and suspect that among the questions in their minds is how I'm acquainted with the Tisdales.

"Liz is my friend from Vermont," Kit pronounces, wrapping an arm around my waist.

"I see on the news that New England has been particularly hard hit with snow this winter," Greg says.

"Exactly why I'm here." I smile.

"Have you relocated, or are you a snowbird?" Karen asks.

"Snowbird, though I wish it were otherwise."

Kit squeezes me closer. "She only wishes that because summer hasn't kicked in yet."

"I don't remember you mentioning friends in Vermont, Kit," Jillian says. She turns to her husband. "How come you didn't mention Kit had a friend visiting?"

Interesting probe. I settle into Kit's side, deciding to let him handle what is likely to be a delicate yet thorough grilling.

"Didn't I ever tell you there is an entire town named after us up there? It's called Couperville. Some Boston ancestors on my father's side lit out for the hinterlands about a hundred years before the other side settled here."

The band strikes up "It Had to Be You." Before anyone can respond to his story, Kit excuses us and steers me onto the dance floor.

"Neatly done," I comment, with renewed appreciation of how well he dissembles. Taking my hand in his, Kit rests the other on my back. "Don't think I didn't notice how you never actually answered that question."

He grins.

"And I rest my case, Kitten. You're a catch, so of course they're interested."

"But you're the one who caught me." He spins me under his arm, and then pulls me close, murmuring into my ear, "It's got to be vexing to have a Yankee take the prize." He is teasing about my earlier concerns. "And dahlin'? I have warned you about paying for that Kitten business."

I grin, delighted with the picture he's painted, as well the numerous pleasurable punishment options that await. We've played a few fun games, although unlike with Darius, we took turns being tied to Kit's bedposts. "Yes, dear," I coo.

"Yup," he says, pushing me into a twirl and bringing me back. "I'm hooked and on the line." He dances us across the floor.

"I don't see you flopping around in my net," I say as we settle into a basic fox-trot.

"That's because I'm happy to be there." He slides his palm to my waist and pushes me into another spin, his hand rolling across my rib cage as he guides me out and back in. I don't think it's an accident when his thumb rides over my breast.

I whisper, "Knock that off."

He grins. The tempo shifts into a heavy syncopation, resolving into an up-tempo cha-cha.

Kit releases me to dance away, his fingers snapping with the beat. Returning an instant later, he closes in but moves out of reach again, playfully teasing me with a macho twist of his hips as he goes, capturing the spirit of the dance. The cha-cha is all about swaggering boys and sultry girls on the make.

This is sexy as hell, if a little too overt for my Yankee blood. Then I decide, what the hell, I'm not likely to see these people ever again and I love to dance. I swish my hips and extend my arm in a come-here flick of the wrist.

Dancing in, Kit curves an arm around my waist, twirls us a half turn, and releases me, backing away with his own come-hither command and a raised brow. I cha-cha toward him, flipping my skirt from side to side. He reaches for me. I slide past. He stalks closer. This time I let him catch me. One hand in mine, the other around my waist, he bends low, forcing me to arch over his arm. When he straightens, I push him away and fan myself with the flat of my hand. Enjoying the pantomime, Kit closes in with a broad smile of amusement, grabs me, and the real dancing begins. *Cha-cha-cha.*

In the same way his mind moves with such swift intellectual dexterity, his fluid expertise on the dance floor makes keeping up with him seriously intense. No surprise, really. In bed he is the same—fluid and intense and enthralling.

We need a break. When the music stops we use it to find our table.

"Wow," I say, as we sit down. "Maybe all sons of the South dance, but where on earth did you learn to dance like that?"

"In college." When my brows rise, he adds, "I don't expect you to believe me, so I'd better set the scene. It was the late '80s. Disco was still the thing. Translated by an erudite though slightly arty college crowd, the homogeny of disco wouldn't do. We had to learn the source dances and do them better than they might be done at competing schools like Middlebury or Williams. Plus, Eleanor was a dance major and I wanted to catch her eye."

This is the first time Kit has mentioned Eleanor so casually.

"Why is it that most men don't understand how sexy it is for a guy to dance?" I ask.

"Being the precocious boy I once was," Kit answers, "I'm with you on this one, dahlin'. I haven't a clue why most men don't understand the benefits. But then, a lot of them also don't understand why they should give a woman flowers for no particular reason. I always scored big with flowers *just because*. And, I like giving them."

"The payoff never figured into it?" I ask, thinking about the vase of gorgeous pale-yellow tulips on the living room table at Sam's house.

"Of course not," he says, but his mouth betrays him, quirking at one side.

I made my gratitude for those flowers immediately known. He leans in to whisper, "You need to watch those naughty thoughts. There's no telling where they might lead." I roll my eyes. He squeezes my thigh under the table and then asks, "And where did you learn to dance like that?"

"Same as you. In college. There were lots of fun Mexican dives in California for college students inclined toward authenticity."

A hand with long red nails lands on Kit's shoulder. The hand is attached to several charm-encrusted gold bracelets. I figure there is a wrist under there somewhere. A second later, Kit's face disappears behind a curtain of tawny blond hair. A model-perfect woman busses him on the cheek. When she's finished with her greeting, I see a pretty cosmetically masked face. The woman is wearing a red dress that hugs her gym-hardened body. The dress is very short, ending a few inches below her shapely little bottom.

"Evening, Billie," Kit says, rising with gentlemanly etiquette. "I don't think you've met Liz."

"Oh hiya, Liz," she responds, holding out her hand. As soon as I've squeezed it, she refocuses on Kit.

"Honey, you need to dance with me." She gives his lapel a pat. "You know how much I love to dance." She offers him a sweet little pout.

"As much as Parker does not," Kit affirms.

Billie beams at him. I'm surprised when she says to me, "Kit is such a dear. He always takes pity on me at these events and turns me around the dance floor. I'm telling you, I did not read the fine print when I married Parker. I might have thought twice if I'd realized no amount of coaxing would get him onto the parquet once our wedding waltz was over."

Kit turns to me, his brow raised in question. I'm not sure whether he's asking for permission or rescue. Staying neutral, I shrug my shoulders.

Billie heads away from the table, taking his compliance as a foregone conclusion. Kit bends to murmur in my ear, "I owe you. And dahlin', you'll like the payment plan I have in mind."

This time I'm not acting when I use my hand to fan away the heat his words inspire.

Kit and Billie do a slow rumba. She's as tall as Kit in her black patent-leather stilettos that flash Louboutin red when she kicks up her heels. It pleases me to observe that he holds her at a careful distance, markedly different from the way he holds me. Billie laughs at something he says. I wonder if she is one of the cards in his shuffle pack but decide he is more ethical than to sleep with a married woman.

"Billie's a free spirit and not one to worry about," remarks Pamela, who is sitting beside me. "The problem is that Parker is too old for her." She takes a sip of her drink then adds, "But neither Parker's age nor his lack of skill on the dance floor are in contention, and so far, Billie and Parker seem relatively happy."

"Have they been married long?"

"A few years. I'm a friend of Parker's first wife, Connie."

Before I can respond, she changes the subject. "Kit tells me you took some lovely shots of the sunset when you visited the chapel."

"Yes, I plan to have one printed for you, a thank-you for that wonderful visit."

"How thoughtful, although I'd love see everything you shot."

"Everything?" I ask with feigned innocence, my heart skipping a beat.

Pamela lets the air stir between us as she takes a sip of her drink. Marshall, talking with a man at an adjacent table, takes no notice of our conversation. She puts her drink down, and pats my hand. In contrast to Billie, her wrist is garnished lightly, with three slim gold bangles. "Kit confessed he let you take some pictures of the chapel exterior."

"I'm sorry," I say immediately. "He told me you don't want the chapel publicized, so I promised the pictures would never leave my computer. I know I broke the rules, but I'm a woman of my word and the light was too magnificent. I had to document it."

"If Kit vouches for you—and he does—then I hold you both to the promise not to share those photographs. *And* I want to see them. He says they're quite something."

"Thank you." Surprised by Pamela's vote of confidence, I sit back in my chair. "The pictures are stunning," I say, deciding to go for it. "If I were to print them—which I promise I will not—I would do a triptych, really large."

"Maybe behind the piano?" she says. "I've been looking for the right thing for that wall."

I smile, excited that she and I have imagined the same scenario. "May I stop by? I can bring my laptop. I'm sure the images would be safe uploaded to the site I use for remote viewing, but I'd rather not stray from my pledge."

"Perfect. Have Kit give you my number. I'm busy for the next couple of weeks, but let's make a date for the end of the month."

"Thank you, Pamela."

Waiters enter the room in a stream, carrying trays of plated salads. The band puts their instruments down and the dancers disperse to their seats. I follow Kit's progress as he threads in and out past obstructing chairs, stopping for a casual hello as he moves along. Observing the easy way his body moves, his elegant athletic grace, a switch trips inside me and I can feel his hands gliding over my skin, that first gorgeous moment of penetration, the intense concentration on his face when he comes and the satisfying way he collapses, satiated, on top of me. I take a quick breath, recognizing how completely and utterly infatuated I am with him.

"Liz?"

I take my eyes off Kit to see Pamela studying me. Her expression is a little too knowing. "I thought you might find it interesting that I haven't seen Kit dance that way in very long time."

Somehow I understand she's talking about our cha-cha, not Kit's turn round the floor with Billie. I also intuit her subtext. "Oh?" I hope I sound nonchalant. Then, unable to resist, I ask, "How long might that be?" I wonder why Rhonda and Agnes have all wanted to share confidences about Kit. Pamela is easier to figure out, since she is a friend of his mother.

"Well . . ." She taps her wineglass with one finger as if deep in thought then pronounces, "At least since the boys were in middle school."

I nod, sure I'm translating her correctly: Kit hasn't danced like this since he was married. This news pleases me too much, although I'm granted only a few seconds to process it as Kit slides into his chair. I'm far too delighted with the concept that I am different from the rest of Kit's women. Grinning broadly, I'm also thrilled that Pamela isn't angry about the chapel pictures and wants to see them. "I will call about meeting," I tell her.

"Hiya," Kit greets, reaching for his water glass.

The waiter assigned to our table serves the salad course, the greens garnished with flower petals. Kit converses with Barth and Katherine while I talk with Pamela and Marshall about Little Hamilton's history.

The Union requisitioned the house as a residence for officers when the island was occupied during the War. Apparently, they didn't trash it, maybe because the owners were from the North. As we talk, I continue to think about what Pamela said and grin every time I do. I can't help it.

Kit whispers in my ear, "Your dinner must be tastier than mine from your happiness with it." I let out a bark of laughter as the musicians begin the next set. Kit pulls me up for more dancing. Throughout the remainder of the evening, women stop to say hello and to hint they would be open to a turn around the floor. Kit employs his bonhomie and issues a few rain checks. If any of them are his friends with benefits, the "don't ask, don't tell" policy is in effect and I honor it by not requiring clarification, assuring myself those women don't matter— and, to stay in the present. This, I decide, should be new Rule Number Two: *Stay in the present.* It isn't all that difficult tonight, since Kit doesn't leave my side. The only exception is during a slow waltz, when he taps Marshall on the shoulder and we change partners, to which I have no objection.

My caution about being seen as a couple whirls away on the dance floor, so when Kit laces his fingers with mine as we retrace our steps through the lobby on our way out, I've given up the fight.

"I need to make a little detour." I angle my head toward the ladies' room.

"I'll collect the car and meet you out front," Kit responds.

CHAPTER 29

KIT TAKES OBIE for his last out. His absence provides me with the opportunity to mix our nightcaps, the first time since we began the nighttime ritual.

I hear the screen door creak. Obie prances into the room and jumps onto the sofa. I glance over my shoulder. Kit is idling in the doorway.

He says, "You know, Ms. Lizzie, I'm not sure I've mentioned how much I like the look of you coming and going."

I smile, having surmised this already from the many times his hands have stroked my "going" side as I walk past, though it's always nice when a man puts his admiration into words. I close his drinks cabinet and laugh because the double entendre registered a little late.

"Mr. Couper, I like you *coming* and going, too." I hand him his glass. We clink. Gesturing toward the seating area, Kit waits for me to move ahead of him, a courtesy that might be as much about admiring the view as good manners.

Seating himself in his club chair, Kit relaxes into a contented sprawl, one leg bent, the other stretched in front of him. As usual when wearing a jacket, he has dropped it on his newel-post the same way he drops it on a chair when visiting me. Dressed formally, he usually loosens his tie in the car. Tonight is no different; his bow tie and top shirt stud were tucked into his pocket on the way home. He must have taken his cuff links out while walking Obie because his shirtsleeves hang as he takes his tumbler from my hand. Taking a sip, he lets his head fall onto the chair back with a satisfied hum.

I'm ready to put my plan into action. Pulling a throw off the couch, I gesture for Obie to follow me. In the hall, I lay the throw on the plush oriental runner in front of the picture gallery. "You need to hang out here for a bit, Doggerel."

Returning to the den, I close the door, and then step between Kit's legs. I run my fingers through his wavy salt-and-pepper hair, pushing it away from his forehead. He peers up at me through those killer lashes, looking happy and tousled. My heart lurches. I so want to keep him.

Setting my own tumbler aside, I brace my hands on the chair's arms, leaning in to touch my lips to his. Kit's hand wraps my neck to pull me closer. There is whiskey on his tongue when he kisses me. I feel drunk, not on alcohol but on the taste of him.

Dropping to my knees, I press my cheek to Kit's shirtfront, enjoying the scent of starched cotton, cologne, and sweat—civilized polish commingled with elemental masculinity. One heady whiff warms me in all my favorite places. I tilt my face to Kit's, my hands flattening against his shirtfront. He sits forward to kiss me again.

Sometimes we come together with urgency but tonight we both seem invested in slow pleasuring. One slow pleasure will be divesting my elegant lover of his evening clothes. Since the first time I saw him in this suit, I've fantasized about undressing him out of it.

Breaking the kiss, I extract the remaining gold and pearl studs from his shirt. When I'm finished, Kit holds out his hand. He drops the studs into his pant pocket, managing the little chore without glancing away from my savoring attention. I push the sides of the shirt aside, exposing his muscular chest. The contrast between polished white fabric and sleek animal nakedness quickens my blood. I feel the clench and release of it between my legs.

Tracing across his clavicles with my fingertips, I ask myself when clavicles made my swoon-worthy list. The answer is probably when I pulled off C.'s T-shirt a year ago, but I let the thought slide, my hands sliding with it over Kit's pectorals. Brushing his nipples, I watch them bead a tight rosy pink, the color innocent; my use for them so much less so.

My own nipples peak inside the bra I chose especially for tonight. It is a sheer black demi-cup and was a bit of a worry under my thin jersey top, but the wrap Kit gave me solved the problem.

Kit puts his drink aside to circle a finger lightly, teasing one crest and then the other through the jersey. "Nice," I murmur. Encouraged, he reaches for the hem, and begins pulling it up.

"Not yet." I remove his hands, offering positive reinforcement by worrying one of his pretty nipples with my teeth as I stroke the other and pinch. He growls, his eyes closed.

I lick away the sting. Sitting back on my heels, I admire the tight pink disks glistening with the attention I've given them. "Have you ever thought about how erotic male nipples are?" I ask.

Bestirring himself to raise an eyebrow, he smirks. "Because they're attached to me?"

"That was a rhetorical question, my sweet. Although you might consider yours are not as practical or dual purposed as mine."

He shakes his head but his mind is not on our banter. I know because his hand curls around my fingers in an attempt to renew my attentions.

"I've never researched this, but I'm sure the consensus is that nipple stimulation is pleasurable for women in order to strengthen the primal bond between mother and child." As I talk, I rise to lick Kit's throat and drop kisses under his jaw, whispering, "All that Freudian return-to-mommy business with Oedipal elements attached makes the male interest in female breasts a little kinky, don't you think?"

Kit chuckles and straightens, putting us eye to eye. He nips my bottom lip. "I assure you, dahlin', when I suckle your breasts, I'm not thinking about my mother or her milk and cookies. I'm thinkin' about fucking you."

"So crudely yet delightful expressed." I dart my tongue out to lick his lips. He cups my head and deepens the kiss, but I have more to say, so a few seconds later, I pull away. "That's exactly what I think about when I see these delicious little nipples of yours." I pinch a bewitching pink bud between my fingertips. "I think of you, inside me. But my point is—"

"Oh, good," Kit interrupts, "there's a point other than to drive me to distraction." While his words suggest disgruntlement, a smile curls his lips.

"My point *is*," I continue, "that male nipples have only one purpose—the delivery of sexual pleasure."

"Which leads us here? As far as I can see, men are in most ways not programmed for multi-tasking." He rolls his pelvis, pressing into me, knowing where we are heading—eventually.

I move one hand down to test the hardness under his fly, stroking the firm weight beneath my hand. "Actually, it leads to imagining how uncomfortable it is for us ladies to see a good-looking male chest on public display, those perky little nipples stirring our blood." I stroke into the seam between his legs as I wind up my dissertation. "It could be a college boy mowing the lawn, or, worse, a pack of them enjoying a hot summer stroll. My personal favorite is roofers." I stop stoking him to fan myself. "When the next-door neighbor had her roof reshingled last summer, once the day heated up the roofers took off their shirts. Those guys were built. And totally distracting."

"Guys have never played fair, and neither do women." He presses into my hand.

I meet his eyes and grin. "Yet we women do not walk around with our sexual bits hanging out, certain pop stars notwithstanding." I raise one brow, daring him to contradict me.

He chuckles. "Poor you."

I can tell he thinks I'm joking. "Are women of lesser appetites? I don't think so. I'm only saying that however you choose to justify what you do, the public display of a comely male chest is a sexual come-on. Any gay man will tell you I'm right."

"This is titillating news," he says.

I narrow my eyes. He stares back, trying to look solemn, but he can't help laughing at his own pun.

"I'm serious!"

"Ms. Lizzie. Dahlin'," Kit says with mock solemnity. Humor crinkles the corners of his eyes. He lifts my hand from his trousers and kisses the palm. "I swear to you, I had no idea the only reason I've never been jumped when I took my shirt off at the beach was a thin veneer of female restraint." He gives my hand a squeeze. "Why don't you come up here and let me apologize the best way I know?" With a playful leer he tugs me toward his chest. "Not only to make up for my misdeeds, mind you, but for my thoughtless and callow brethren's shirtless misdeeds as well."

"Oh, no you don't." I pull my hand from his. "I'd rather get even."

He leans against the cushions with a delighted chuckle. "Never say I shirk my gentlemanly duty when it comes to doing what's right. I await your retribution."

If he was going to say more, he loses his words as I lift my top over my head, pausing to let him enjoy the half-moons of dusky areole peeking above the black lace cups of my bra.

"Come here, dahlin'," Kit urges, his tone gratifyingly dark.

"Christopher," I say, tossing the top aside, "stop trying to take charge and accept your punishment like a man." I rub my cheek against his lower abdomen, just above the spot where his enjoyment of what I'm doing is in lovely firm evidence.

His evening trousers, as it transpires, hide another well-tailored layer—striped boxers in the French fashion, yoked and flat-fronted with three buttons where the standard American issue has only a slit. Elegantly sexy, they are entirely frustrating.

Kit tries to help pull off his boxers and trousers, but I stop him with a kiss before pushing him into the cushions. "Remember the business about taking your punishment?"

He grins.

I untie one mirror-polished Italian dress shoe and remove it and his sock, taking the garter that holds up the silky hosiery with it. I massage the arch of one narrow well-made foot, provoking a moan of appreciation. There is nothing more comical or mood-diminishing for me than a naked man wearing only his socks, so I strip both feet before moving between his legs. "Lift," I command.

One tug takes trousers and boxers down to his knees, revealing his swim-contoured thighs. A second tug takes everything off.

Kit sits splendidly naked in the chair, erection framed by his open shirtfront. I take two shallow breaths.

"Lizzie. Come here," he growls. Lifting his tumbler, Kit gestures me closer with it. He raises his glass, sips, and then sets it down. Leaning forward, he beckons again.

I shake my head with a theatrical sigh. "Cold?" I ask running a finger down his leg. I'm boiling hot and all I'm wearing is my bra, skirt, and earrings, and some hardly worth mentioning unmentionables.

Kit's mouth quirks. "If I am, Ms. Lizzie, I'm sure you're plotting to warm me right to the boiling point."

I unclasp the bra and let it slide off. His eyes narrow as I lean in, cradling his cock between my breasts.

Apparently done with asking for what he wants, Kit scoops his arms under mine and pulls me up until we are chest to breast. I hum my appreciation. Twining my arms around his neck, I rub against him. He is warm and slightly rough where there is hair, velvety soft everywhere else. Pressing a hand into the small of my back, he pulls me tighter and kisses me.

A long time later, I lay my cheek against his chest. His heart pounds under my ear. I trace a circle, expanding outward from his nipple, until I encounter the smooth ridge of a rib. Kit presses his lips to the top of my head and runs his fingertips slowly up and down my arm from shoulder to elbow, sending ticklish chills up my spine. This intermission has been sweet, but I'm ready for the next act and slide from his lap.

I kiss his nipples. I kiss the valley down the center of his chest, breathing in the delicious scents of Kit and his new lemony cologne. I kiss my way around his navel and keep going until I meet the head of his cock. I kiss it, too. He holds the hair away from my face to watch me take him into my mouth, groaning with pleasure.

Is there a man on the planet who doesn't like to watch fellatio performed on his person? View a little porn to have that truth literally ground into you. Even Darius liked it, although only at his instigation.

Not that I entirely understand the ease with which much of the male population will unzip for a blow job or how indiscriminate they can be. I often wonder if they truly understand the hazards involved. I'm not talking about venereal diseases, which are bad enough. I'm talking about a lady coughing with a penis in her mouth. And what if she forgets for one tiny second to sheathe her teeth? Attention can wander, particularly if one is not all that into one's work.

None of this, however, seems to matter to the male brain. My theory is that the organ—the one above the shoulders—short-circuits the minute a woman assumes *the position.*

It's a good bet that, straight or gay, part of the heady pleasure—pun intended—is the power fantasy both participants play out no matter which gender you'd rather have bowing before you.

Kneel, my sweet slave . . .

Here's the truth I'm not sure men understand: In this game, the master is the slave and the slave, the master.

I confess—as a younger woman I pretended to enjoy giving head because my boyfriends liked it so much. While I was doing it, I'd try to figure out if there was a switch somewhere on the male anatomy that would hurry things along. I did eventually find more than one, but speeding the action didn't solve the enjoyment problem.

My attitude shifted only when I realized that taking a man's penis into my mouth was not an act of subjugation—at least not in the normal consensual way of things. Fellatio is about power. It's about who controls access to all of that mind-blowing pleasure. It's about teasing and drawing the pleasure out, or delivering it in one heady rush. He may think he's in control of how this all "goes down," but he'd be wrong.

After that lightbulb went on, a craving developed, although how much is about the power I wield and how much is about consensual enjoyment is difficult to separate when Kit thrusts into the wet heat of my mouth.

What I do know is that I love the musky scent of male desire—of Kit's desire—and the almost gagging fullness when his thrusts go deep. I love the taste of the salty-sweet tears his cock weeps so excitedly as I roll my tongue under the sensitive curl of his hood. I love the satiny velvet skin of his glans and the texture of his shaft—like the softest suede—with its ropey veins when fully aroused.

I adore his animal groans of pleasure.

When Kit is in my mouth, his life force is mine, and so is the hot spurt of cream when he comes—mine to control, mine to allow access to this wicked pleasure.

I lift my eyes to enjoy the fierce concentration on his face as he watches the wet slide of my mouth. I assume he is fantasizing about my submission while I'm enjoying his.

"Liz," he breathes. "You have a very talented mouth."

I smile as I lick up his length, sharpening my tongue as I give the underside extra attention. Kit's eyes close and his head tilts back, exposing the strong arch of his throat. I clasp his balls and tug gently. His breath hitches, body tightening. He's close.

Our eyes meet. His glitter under those sublime lashes. My own narrow. I release him and sit back.

"Beg me," I suggest.

"Jesus," he growls. We stare at each other for a second. And then, he drags me up his body.

I didn't think he'd acquiesce. My knees settle against his thighs.

"Lizzie—" he breathes into my mouth, his tongue finding mine. We are starving. Ravenous. Insatiable.

"I need to be inside you," Kit rasps. "And, I need you with me." He works the zipper of my skirt down, then forcing my arms high, he pulls the slithery fabric over my head. Neither of us pays the slightest attention to where the skirt lands.

I watch the surprise I arranged for him to register; I'm wearing a pink garter belt with black satin ribbons, sheer dark stockings, my dancing shoes, and a fine gold chain loose around my waist. The matching pink and black panties came off in the ladies' room before we left the resort.

"Ms. Lizzie, you are going to kill me yet." Kit slides his hands up my legs. He traces the back of his fingers under the garter belt ribbons.

"I suppose you've been punished enough," I whisper into his ear, rubbing myself against him.

"Tortured almost past sanity," he confirms, his fingers opening me. Having had the safety talk some time ago, we've dispensed with condoms. Naked pleasure awaits us now.

We pause to enjoy the sight of his sensual slide, his handsome length pushing into me. In typical Kit fashion, he stops moving after the head of his cock penetrates me. "Kit," I moan. "Please."

I could attempt to hurry him along, but I'm enjoy the slow tease of his lovemaking. Hands rising to grip my waist, Kit at last guides me down. There's nothing civilized about the sounds we make as our bodies join.

"Touch yourself, dahlin'," Kit growls, guiding my hand to where it will do the most good. My eyes close in concentration as my fingers find the sweet spot. He finds the angle of greatest sensation. We move in rhythm. I quickly reach my boiling point.

"I love this," Kit whispers in my ear.

I open my eyes to follow his glance. What he loves is watching me arouse myself. He spreads me to get a better view and says, "You are so beautiful," and brings his thumb in to stroke. "Pretty little pink lips," he adds as I let him take over.

He punctuates the compliment with a powerful thrust. I grind into it. Our eyes meet. I'm so, so close. My lids flutter closed again, my awareness narrowing to what he is doing with his thumb and his cock.

My lack of attention doesn't prevent Kit from continuing his recital of my assets.

"I love your breasts," he says, weighting them in his palms. "So firm, so sensitive." He tweaks my nipples, knowing how the tiny pinch of pain at the right moment can send me soaring. I moan, holding on to his shoulders as he twists into me, the angle just right for the stimulation I need.

"I love your curves. This flare"—Kit shapes the contour of my ribs, his hand dipping in at my waist and out at the hip—"so absolutely female." Thrusting deep, he arches off the chair.

Feeling that a response is needed, I settle for, "I love this, too." I'm not much for talking after a certain point during sex, but so many superlatives from Kit leave me feeling that my four little words aren't quite enough.

Kit slows. I groan. Resting his forehead against mine, he deliberately backs us away from the precipice. He whispers against my lips, "We're good together."

"We are."

Yet my avowal seems to displease him in some way. He stops moving at all, tilting my chin up until I meet his intense gaze. I rise on my knees until he's barely inside me, wanting to tease him out of whatever is bothering him. I want him one hundred percent inside his body—and mine.

He accedes, his hands sliding over my breasts and around my waist. He pushes me down and thrusts up, and then again. I match his rhythm, using my hand to carry myself the last aching distance. I contract around him, the orgasm opening just in front of me.

"Yes, love, yes," he gasps.

I register the words, but I'm past the ability to respond. Kit surges inside me. The last spark ignites. Desire and ardor coalesce. I wrap myself around him, panting his name against his lips.

His mouth covers mine. My brain stutters, yet before the abyss takes me, I think *Kit* my love—

With a hoarse shout, he rears, straining against me. And I—for the eternity of a few exquisite seconds—I do not breathe. My heart does not beat. I am free—shattered and more whole than ever before.

✳

After a few minutes, I gently lift myself away. Kit removes his shirt and tenderly cleans me with his shirttail, and then cleans himself. Climbing to his feet, he pulls me in for a lingering kiss.

Upstairs in the big rice bed, he turns onto his stomach and throws an arm over me. I rise on an elbow to stroke damp curls away from his forehead. He smiles, carrying my hand to his mouth and kissing it, before relaxing into sleep.

I gently disengage and arrange myself flat on the bed. Looking up at the ceiling, I accept that I love him.

One leg bent, Kit spreads his arms under his pillow, totally relaxed.

I'm not. All I can think about is, Does he love me? He called me his love, yet I know better than to trust the chimera of desire. All too often there is little adherence to that sentiment after passion has been spent.

Tears leak from my eyes. I want his words to have meaning—profound meaning. I want Kit to love me. I want him to never let me go. If this was infatuation, it isn't anymore.

Oblivious to my distress, Kit sleeps on. Obie, however, lifts himself from the pile of old blankets on the floor next to the bed. He bows, and then rests his head on the mattress near my head, regarding me with sympathetic eyes. I stroke his soft black head, comforted by this creature who loves me utterly, whom I can trust never to break my heart. If only Kit would prove as stalwart.

Stay in the present, I tell myself. Stay in the moment. It is such a lovely moment.

But I don't find this concept any easier to execute than it has ever been, new Rules be damned.

CHAPTER 30

IF IT WEREN'T SUNDAY, Kit would be off for his early-morning swim and work, leaving me to stew about what he said last night. Part of me, the ever-hopeful part I was sure Roland killed off for good, is walking on rose petals this morning. The other part, also Roland induced, is sure thorns are hidden among the petals and I'd better watch my step.

We're up a little before 8:00. At Kit's suggestion, our plan is to spend some time on the water. I'm groggy after barely six hours of sleep, but a cup of coffee perks me up. We leave Obie in an unused paddock Kit closes off to keep him from roaming. He drops an old horse blanket and a pail of water inside the shade of an oak's spreading branches. Kit wants Obie to have some fun this morning while we're having ours. I ask about chiggers. Kit assures me it's too early in the season. I warned Kit about my poodle's hole-digging proclivities, and sure enough, Obie starts digging before we've closed the gate. He may be in China by the time we return.

It's a gorgeous morning with a bit of night chill as yet in the air, but the sun is warm on our faces, promising a rise in temperature. It's been a couple of weeks since we pulled two of the kayaks down off the boat-house ceiling. We only have to lift them from the lower dock to place them in the water. The tide is low, but Kit reminds me to stay close to shore because the current can be unpredictable and swift farther out.

Mist is rising off the creek into downy clouds that seem lit from within as they dissolve into the brightening sky. I love wandering the marshes in these sturdy little boats. We've done it a couple of times before. My paddles tap and dribble as I stroke upstream enjoying the hoarse call of herons, the squawk of high-flying gulls, and the rustling of the marsh grass in the breeze. It's easier than I would have thought to let worrisome thoughts flow away with the current, my attention focused exclusively on the world around me.

Kit and I are relaxed and windblown when we pull the kayaks onto the dock a couple of hours later. We're also starving.

In the paddock, Obie is covered in sandy mud. I survey the damage: three large mounds of dirt tilting at various angles offer easy clues to the trajectory of their creation.

Kit garners points—adding to his ever-expanding collection—when he laughs at his once pristine pasture riddled with gopher holes the size of Montana. Obie, his muzzle brown with dirt, grins at me but leans into Kit—two of my favorite male animals sharing camaraderie as they survey a job well done.

Proving his chivalrous chops, Kit sets out to rescue his damsel in distress—who would be me—performing the knightly service of hosing off my dog. I wave a fond farewell as he and Obie head around the side of the house to the spigot, while I enter Kit's kitchen with plans to gather ingredients for a substantial breakfast.

The refrigerator yields a few stray mushrooms, some cheddar, an onion, and half a potato from a dinner out. I begin chopping while browning sausage from the freezer. Working on the omelet's innards, I do my best to ignore the sock monkey, the one that figured into Kit's argument to begin this affair. It should be comforting that my pointy-toothed fairy-tale wolf has morphed into a creature that prefers to make a meal of fruit rather than flesh, not that primates can't wreak their own form of havoc.

The damn thing has skulked in from wherever it's been keeping itself. Truly gorilla-like in size, it props itself in the corner opposite the door and goggles at me with the word "Love" written across its knitted chest in big pink letters.

Ugh. Even if the thing is the product of my overly fanciful—as well as fatalistic—imagination, I'm pretty sure that just as before, it isn't going anywhere until Kit and I get around to discussing last night. I try telling myself nothing happened last night, but obviously my subconscious disagrees if a giant sock monkey haunting the kitchen is anything to go by.

When Kit arrives with a clean and towel-damp Obie, we sit down to eat, perusing The *New York Times* delivered every Sunday, God bless the man. As we read bits of particular interest to each other, Kit acts as if nothing important has happened.

I get up to rewarm his coffee. Kit's head stays down. He is working the crossword puzzle—in ink. Returning to the table and the style section, I sip from my mug.

I hear a satisfied grunt. Kit fills in five squares, and sets his pen on the table. Tapping my hand he says, "We need to talk."

I'm sure my blood pressure jumps twenty points as I set the newspaper on top of the other sections. He looks serious. I brace for what comes next, the thought flitting through my mind that he terrified himself with that "love" business last night and is about to back out of the plan for me to stay longer. This wouldn't be in character for the man I know, however, so I tell myself to calm down. I hope he can't hear my heart pounding.

"We need to figure out how we are going to make this work," Kit says, nailing me with his gaze.

My brow furrows. As far as I'm concerned, our *this* has been working just fine, no alterations required. Not sure what to say, because I need to know exactly what isn't working, I wait for him to elaborate.

Kit frowns. "Dahlin', how are we going to make this—us—work when you'll be heading home soon? It's not easy, as far as I can tell, to be in a relationship and live a thousand miles apart."

"You want—?" He wants to pedal closer instead of racing away.

"Do I need to refill your mug?" he asks patiently. "I did put off discussing this until we had two cups of coffee in you. I know you well enough by now to understand that if I want to engage your fabulously inventive brain before noon, I need to fuel it." He tilts his head as if this is a question. When I don't say anything, he reaches for my hand. "We need a creative solution for our near future, since I'm supposing it might be a bit too early for us to consider more distant horizons."

My anxiety level should logically be dipping since I had imagined the "about last night" speech. It spikes instead, although a grin overspreads my face.

Kit gifts me with one of his crinkle-eyed smiles. "I'm tryin' to be a gentleman here, Lizzie, taking the 'ladies first' approach, but—" He picks up the French press I brought to the table and tops off my mug. "It looks like this is a three-cup morning. So while you finish caffeinating, I'll put a few ideas on the table."

Damn right it's a three-cup morning! I'm teetering between elation and fear that history will repeat itself—the last time a man asked me to stick around, it didn't end well.

"So here's what I'm proposing," Kit says as I add milk to my mug and stir. "How about I buy some airline gift cards so you can come down whenever you have time? I know you'll be working weddings most weekends, but not during the week, right? I could get a big monitor set up in den, so all you have to do is bring your laptop to work here. I'll aim to be in Vermont once a month, although it may be trickier for me to take time during the week. Might have to make do with me coming in on Saturdays. We'd be together for whatever part of Sunday you've got free, and then I'll fly out around dinnertime on Monday. I'm hoping you have someone good to keep Obie company when you are away overnight? I don't have a solution for getting him down here with you. I wish I did."

Kit leans forward in his chair, tenting his hands on the table in front of him. "You come down once a month if you can get away that often—more if you can swing it—and I'll fly up when I can." He clears his throat. "So, what do you say?"

"You're serious." I put the mug down.

His expression goes from happy to troubled. "Aren't you?" he asks quietly, extending a hand across the table.

I grasp it. He curls his fingers around mine.

"I'm sorry if I've made you feel you need to ask." This is true, yet I'm scared to hope, afraid this won't last, afraid of how much I love him, terrified he will break my heart.

These feelings must be obvious, because Kit squeezes my fingers. "What's wrong?" He refuses to let me glance away.

Other men have sworn to love me forever and reversed themselves right around the time I began to believe them. It isn't as if Dan or Roland were the only men to make that pledge and change their minds. I haven't been singled out for an extra-special helping of bad luck. Or never ended a relationship myself, although I always tried to do it before anyone's feelings were intensely engaged. It occurs to me that some of the men on the receiving end of my rejection might have been more affected than I believed at the time. I look into Kit' troubled eyes.

He is waiting for a yes. I give him one on a shaky sigh. If I were smart, experience should triumph and I'd do the pedaling away. Instead, I'm going with new Rule Number Three, made up on the spot—*step into the unknown*—trying Arielle's twisting road. That's what I did when I chose to spend the winter in Georgia, and it worked out better than I ever could have imagined—at least for my creative output.

If Kit and I are going to have a relationship, then I had better also activate new Rule Number One and be honest about how I'm feeling.

"I love your idea, but I have a condition."

"Okay."

"You have to be sure of your feelings before we commit ourselves to this wonderful plan," I say to our clasped hands.

"I'm sure." He squeezes my fingers.

"I mean really sure." I shake my head and meet his gaze. "Here's the thing: No matter how it happens, losing someone you love rips out a piece of your heart. I know you understand that." I sigh nervously, and take another sip of my coffee.

"Kit, I haven't told you my entire story. I owe it to you to explain the hesitation you've hearing." I take another sip and set the mug down, twisting the handle a little this way and that, looking for the best photographic angle. Then, realizing what I'm doing, I look up. "First significant point," I say. "My husband left me for a neighbor—literally the woman next door—but she was merely the last in a series of women he screwed throughout our marriage."

His mouth thins with dismay. "I'm sorry, Lizzie."

Kit might end a relationship for a lot of reasons, but I'm sure he'd never cheat.

"Ironically, Dan didn't break my heart, or maybe he did it so slowly that by the time he left, there wasn't much more than a black hole where my affection used to be. The problem was that we were too different. Even though I didn't understand it at the time, in hindsight I realize I could see the break coming and braced for the end before it arrived. That isn't, however, how things went with Roland." My throat closes. "God, I don't want to talk about this," I whisper.

Kit continues to hold my gaze. I'm the one who looks away, focusing on the view out the windows. I have to tell him these things before we can move forward, and, until now, Kit has been a lot braver than I have, sharing his feelings for Eleanor. I've shared . . . well, not much.

I return my gaze to his. He regards me with compassion—one of the many reasons I love him.

"I fell in love a few years after my divorce," I begin. "Roland was a widower, like you." I pull my hand away and rub my temples. "But also not like you in that he'd lost his wife barely a year before I met him." I blow out a breath.

"Six months after we began dating, he swore he was in love with me. He must have said it a hundred times in the weeks after that. I knew he wasn't far enough into his grieving, something you probably understand better than I do even after my experience with him. But, I let Roland convince me he was in love. The truth is, I couldn't resist him. Roland saw me. He saw the good and also the bad, and loved me as he found me." I take Kit's hand again. "Like you, he was kind and compassionate, funny, and really smart. When I was with him, I wanted to be my best self, just as I want to be my best self for you."

"I feel the same way," Kit says. He stands and pulls me up, wrapping his arms around me. "What happened to him? Did you lose him the way I lost Eleanor?" He pushes hair away from my face, his expression regretful.

"No. I lost him after we ordered dinner a year into our relationship, when he pushed his chair away from the restaurant table and announced he couldn't be with me anymore." I offer Kit a rueful smile.

"Oh no," he says, squeezing me tight.

"Unfortunately, yes."

Kit kisses my forehead. My cheek presses against his chest, where I can hear the steady beat of his heart. I say, "The dissolution of my marriage was easier to accept than Roland leaving me. I was intensely in love with him, and up until that moment I thought he was just as in love with me. Roland asked me to marry him a few weeks before he left. Then, he walked out of that restaurant, and . . . and that was all she wrote."

I pull out of Kit's arms and walk into the kitchen, putting the island between us.

"Jesus," he says softly.

"I was devastated."

"God, Lizbeth, I'm so sorry. You had no idea it was coming?"

"I wasn't totally oblivious. Our children were not happy about us dating. Sadie and Rob couldn't understand how their dad could be over their mom that soon after her death, which was their interpretation of his dating. From their point of view, I was trying to usurp their mother's place and he was letting me do it. Diana felt the same way, like Roland was trying to usurp Dan's place with her." I shake my head with a frown. "I could never replace Laura. I wasn't Sadie's and Rob's mother. But I certainly could have loved them *like* their mother. If we took the courtship slowly, I was convinced all of the kids, Diana included, would eventually see reason."

I open the refrigerator and peer inside. It isn't until I feel the cold that I realize I'm holding a jar of strawberry jam. I could be clutching the milk carton or a tin of sardines for all I've been aware of myself once my confession chased me away from the table. I set the jam on the counter.

"Did you tell him what you thought?" Kit asks, rounding the island.

"More than once. But his world was black and white as well as fragile. While we were seeing each other, he'd worry about Rob and Sadie, and I'd try to reassure him. When he left, I felt like one of those metaphorical switches you and I have talked about had been tripped."

I spin the jam jar until the label faces me. Offering Kit a sardonic smile, I say, "He married six months later. He was in the early stages of mourning when we were seeing each other. Grief and sanity are not friends. But I didn't know that at the time, and he broke my heart. It's taken years to mend."

Kit cups my face. "You're afraid I'm Roland all over again, aren't you?" As usual, his perception is acute. "Lizbeth, I've been alone for a long time. I've done my hard grieving, although I don't have to tell you it will never be completely over."

His arms drop to my waist. "For the record, I couldn't get involved with anyone after Eleanor died. It took a couple of years for me to want to touch another woman. Not that I'm a better man because I didn't date right away." He shrugs with a rueful twist of his lips. "That was just how grief struck me. The way I've lived since has satisfied me to a point. That point would be you." He kisses my forehead and then pulls away to look into my eyes. "I think I've figured out how to do this."

I rest my hands on his chest. "I haven't been satisfied with 'up to a point' for a while. But until I met you, I hadn't wanted to face that my feelings were changing." I pat his shirt. "I didn't think I'd ever get over Roland. And no, I don't think you are anything like him. It's just—" This is so hard to admit. I bite my bottom lip. "The truth is, I no longer trust my judgment about men or love. But what I do know is if what happened with Roland happened again, I won't survive it."

"I'm not Roland."

I smile. "You are definitely not Roland. But you and I had a deal to keep this light." It pains me to offer the reminder. I leave Georgia in a few weeks, possibly leaving Kit forever. I judge my current feelings as survivable. If, however, the relationship deepens, if he were to love me the way I thought Roland did, and then we go our separate ways? That would be more than I can bear.

"We had our reasons. Good reasons," Kit affirms. "And now we have other reasons." Emphasizing his point, he does a little side-to-side shuffle, as if he wants to shake his reasons into me. "We are allowed to change the contract, as long as we both agree to the terms."

I smile at this lawyerly pronouncement.

He folds me more securely into his warmth. "Dahlin', you can be sure of me."

"I know. Really, I do."

"With your head."

I shrug and step out of his arms. In fact, he's wrong. It is my all too gullible heart that trusts him. My head is less sure. Picking up our mugs, I carry them to the microwave. He steps into my path. "Lizbeth?"

"You'd better be sure you mean what you say," I advise, dodging around him to set the mugs in front of the microwave. Meeting Kit's eyes, I grab a fist full of his shirtfront for emphasis. "In my experience love comes and goes and there's no predicting the how or why of it."

If golden brown eyes can go cool, his do. "In my experience love is constant even past death."

I digest this statement, not allowing the steel in his voice to dissuade me from sharing a different assumption. "Maybe I'm fatally flawed, then, because I'm not sure I will ever trust an oath of love again." This is too honest, as is the weariness in my tone. "It isn't that I don't want to believe in us, Kit. God, I hope you know that. I just don't trust words anymore. I trust deeds, so as you suggested, let's see what happens, okay?"

His eyes lose some of their frost. He rubs his palms up my arms. "I understand, Lizzie. I'm willing to earn your trust. And I swear, I will."

Oh God. I want to believe him. Decades distant from the green girl

I once was, however, I would be a fool not to be wary, yet my heart, my stupid optimistic heart, desperately wants to believe him.

Rising to my toes, I touch lips to his. Kit smiles into the kiss. While the dog looks quizzically on, I kiss him with as much faith as I can muster. He returns the kiss with the same promise. Yet, I can't help but note he doesn't speak of love himself.

"Okay," he says, with a final peck. "Here's the plan. We're going to finish our coffee and firm up the plans for this summer." He puts the mugs in the microwave and hits the timer.

I smile. "Okay, let's do it."

"There's the woman I know!" Happy with my willingness to believe we have a future past the end of next month, Kit says, "When you come down next winter, who knows, it could be for good."

He's raising the stakes. The microwave dings. He pulls the mugs out and hands mine to me. His brows rise in challenge.

I gulp, then cough as hot coffee burns down the wrong pipe. Time to inject a bit of reality. When I can speak I say, "That could happen." Because it could. "Time will tell."

"The secret is looking forward, not back," Kit says.

"Right." After all, he is right. Except the cynical, reality-based part of me honed by Jewish ancestors trying to stay a step ahead of the next pogrom is skeptical about how long he's lived this mantra. His eight-year lack of committed partnership, as well as his musings at the pink chapel, indicate his interest in anything other than flipping the cards in his deck may be as new for him as it is for me.

I recognize I skew to the cynical, but survivors learn from experience and my experience hasn't produced a lot of positive reinforcement where love is concerned.

I want to be happy. I want to be overjoyed about Kit's believing he's ready for love and that he's chosen to be in love with me. But I feel more like I'm walking a rope suspended above a rocky canyon, praying it won't fray.

We sit with our reheated coffee. We don't, however, discuss our summer schedules. Kit reimmerses himself in the crossword puzzle; I sip from my mug; and behind the pages of the arts section, I alternate between elation and fear that this is too perfect to last.

Half an hour later, working myself back into full-on anxiety mode, I decide staying in the present should not only be Rule Number Two, but Three, Four, and Five as well. Kit puts the crossword down at the same time I fold my pages. He carries his mug to the sink. Saying he'll be back in a couple of minutes, he disappears.

Wondering what he's up to, I gather the rest of our breakfast paraphernalia. Obie follows me, settling himself in a warm patch of sunlight near the windows. The sock monkey reappears, although it takes up less room than before. To my relief, the nasty thing stays only long enough to blow me a kiss before fading away.

I need to calm down. And, I need to believe in Kit.

If Mrs. Shaughnassy, my fourth-grade teacher, were around, she wouldn't offer any stars for how well I'm staying in the present. Rinsing the breakfast dishes, I arrange them in the dishwasher, wash the frying pan, dry it, and put it away. Kit is still MIA, so I wipe down the counters and polish the stainless steel stovetop. I'm rearranging the mugs in the cupboard, handles facing south, when he walks in clutching a handful of paper.

"Your gift cards," he announces, retaining a couple of sheets for himself. "The actual cards should arrive in a few days."

"You work fast," I say with real admiration, even though the definitiveness of what he's done sets my heart pounding. Whatever it is that pings around my stomach when I'm agitated—butterflies or bats—my digestion also takes a hit.

"I've got you sussed, dahlin'," Kit says. "That hyperactive overanalytical mind of yours is already churning away inside your pretty head, isn't it?" He taps my forehead. "Tell me you aren't all worked up and on the lookout for where the trip wires are set."

I open my mouth then close it. "Guilty as charged." I can't help smiling at his knowledge of my inner workings.

"While I admire your mind's quicksilver charms, Ms. Lizzie, sometimes that brain of yours can be a little too tricky." He shakes his head. Eyes glinting with amusement, he bends to kiss the end of my nose and traps me against the island. I have to grab his shoulders or tumble backward.

"Likely you've already come up with fifty reasons why you can't accept these gift cards." He waves his paperwork. "Good thing my brain is as tricky as yours."

My lips quirk.

"You boggle at my brilliance." His expression is full of mischief. "My plan is to null and void contrary arguments proactively. Hence, the immediate gift card purchase. I'm sure I don't have to tell you these are nonrefundable, although if you return to Vermont and decide you can't stand me, you can use them to fly wherever you want."

"I love it when you talk lawyer to me," I say as he hoists me onto the counter. "And for the record, Christopher Aiken Couper, Esquire, I accept." With reservations, but enough of that for now.

"Smart woman. You've got an instinct for the winning side." He spreads my knees and steps between them. "I need to talk lawyer to you more often," he says gruffly, angling his lips over mine.

"I can't resist a good legal brief," I murmur, unbuttoning his jeans. He laughs at the pun, his laugh quickly turning into a groan as my hand finds him. He kisses me, pulling my T-shirt over my head.

"Aren't men your age supposed to need a lot of recovery time?" I tease as I push his pants down his hips.

"Don't tell me I wore you out in the wee hours," he answers, reaching to unhook my bra. I tickle his ribs until he grabs my arms and holds them behind my back, kissing me so thoroughly, as well as satisfactorily, that one thing leads to another and we tire each other out enough to require a nap. Which, no big surprise, leads to another bout of exercise. It's well into the afternoon before Kit has the opportunity to return to the crossword puzzle.

CHAPTER 31

"I CAN'T BELIEVE how nervous you are."

"I'm meeting your mother. Meeting a man's mother is significant."

"Relax. It's only dinner."

"In her home."

Kit steers the car off the exit ramp onto Martin Luther King Boulevard. We are going to spend the day in Savannah touring house museums, after which we're having dinner with his mother.

"When you first arrived," he says, "I wanted you to meet her because I could tell the two of you would hit it off. Now I want her to meet you because I adore you, and you are leaving in a couple of weeks, so—"

I bury my face in my hands. "But I'll be back. Don't you think, maybe, say, next January would be a better time to meet her?"

With one hand on the steering wheel, Kit laughs and playfully pats my shoulder in the gesture of an easygoing victor about to claim his spoils.

Arielle reminded me just yesterday to stop looking for trouble, lecturing me about letting go of what she labels my culturally induced persecution complex. She suggested I'm mindlessly responding to old programming. "You need to start believing you deserve to be happy," she said.

"This isn't about whether I deserve to be happy or whether my ancestors are a winning subset of the population," I responded, feeling obliged to point out that assorted despotic emperors, kings, and chancellors of the near and distant past tried their best to eradicate my people. We survived and prospered anyway, which makes us winners in my book. "The issue is whether a man who spent the last eight years loving a ghost to the exclusion of a flesh-and-blood woman can shift his allegiance in a matter of weeks. After telling me he didn't know how to let himself go, less than a month later, he seems to be doing exactly that. It's miraculous. But what if it isn't permanent? What if he backslides?"

She suggested I wait to contemplate crossing perilous bridges until I'm actually in front of one. "Why do you insist on looking for trouble?" Arielle asked, sounding out of patience. "Maybe you should have more faith in your heart, and in Kit's. Look, Lizzie, you know there aren't any guarantees. Hell, you could return to Vermont and decide on the way home that loving Kit was a temporary madness on your part. You could end up being the one who breaks it off."

We hung up after that. She was right. Sometimes my neurotic side takes over.

Outside the car window, the old city of Savannah appears. The streets are narrow and oak-shaded. Every few blocks another beautifully landscaped square appears. Each one has a statue of a historical figure dear to Savannah's heart at its center. As Kit promised, the houses lining the old squares date as far back as the early eighteenth century. The cityscape is elegant on an old-world human scale. As nervous as I am about meeting Kit's mother, I can't wait to explore the city.

He points out Forsyth Park as we drive along its border. A few turns later, we roll through a set of open wrought-iron gates and down an alley next to the grand dove-gray house where Kit grew up. Glossy black shutters frame floor-to-ceiling windows on the parlor floor, with two stories of verandas—piazzas, as Kit refers to them—enclosed by lacy iron railings.

In the front garden, white double-petal amaryllis bloom in profusion. A mature, waxy-leafed magnolia shades part of the herringbone brick path. We walk up the alley to the street.

"We're not stopping to say hello?" I ask.

"We have houses to see. Plenty of time for visiting later."

"You just want to keep me in an agony of suspense about your mother."

"I'm sure the agony will dissipate by dinnertime." He pats my hand.

"Faint hope." I sigh.

✳

I manage to forget my worry about Kit's mother while we tour the beautiful historic houses Kit takes me to see, but as we cut through the park and turn onto her street, my jitters return and I ask, "Just how many women have you brought home, anyway?"

"Not counting Eleanor and the girls I dated in high school?" Kit hesitates barely long enough for me to notice. "That would be you."

"I may be developing a bad sinus headache."

He quirks his brow.

"Hey, with so much in bloom, it would be a believable excuse to head home early."

He laughs, grabs my hand, and pulls me up the cobbled garden path to the broad stone staircase of his childhood home.

When we are standing in front of the massive front doors with their fancy etched-glass panels, Kit turns to me, a finger poised over the doorbell. "I think we need a secret signal. How 'bout you pull your earlobe if you need rescuing?"

I'm still laughing at the various secret gestures he's suggested when he hits the bell. He doesn't wait for the chime to stop sounding before sticking a key in the lock. I assume ringing the bell was to alert his mom of our imminent arrival. I follow him inside. The hall has a polished checkerboard marble floor. I'm still trying to sort out whether our signal is earlobe pulling or a finger tap to the temple as I take in the grandeur of the mahogany staircase in front of me. A glittering Murano chandelier of fanciful, opalescent hand-blown glass flowers hangs from the ceiling two stories above our heads.

"Dahlin', you ah he'ah!" An elegant silver-haired woman with Kit's warm brown eyes descends the stairs. I recognize her from the wall gallery. After the many times I've studied Kit's pictures, I know she is petite like me. Nevertheless I somehow expected a tall, willowy blonde like Eleanor.

"Sweetie," she says, directing a delighted smile at her son. "I *have* missed you so."

"It's only been two weeks," Kit says good-naturedly, hugging his mother.

He has to bend down, the same way he does for me, so she can buss his cheek. "It's still too long," she sniffs. Pulling away, she looks in my direction.

"Lizbeth," Kit's mother says warmly, "you cannot know how glad I am to finally meet you. Your ears must be ringing with the praises my son has been singing. I am just *so* pleased." She takes my hand and gives it an affectionate pat.

This is a little too effusive for my cool Yankee blood, although a warm reception is far better than the other kind. "I've been looking forward to meeting you as well, Mrs. Couper."

I'm sort of telling the truth and sort of not.

"Call me Maddie, dear."

"Thank you, Maddie. Please call me Liz."

She beams. "Did you enjoy your day?"

"Yes. This is such a beautiful city."

"There isn't a city I like better," she says, then amends, "well, maybe Paris."

Maddie lays a hand on her son's arm. "Sweet boy," she says, "why don't you make the drinks?" With that, she leads us into a living room approximately the same size as my house's entire first floor.

A hour later, dinner is served in a smaller room overlooking the back garden. I can see why Kit's mother chose this more intimate setting. The mahogany table in the formal dining room seats sixteen, and that's without added leaves. Maddie serves crab cakes picked up from a gourmet market around the corner. The side dishes are green beans and corn pudding.

"I'm not much into cooking anymore," she volunteers, "but the pudding is one of Kit's favorites so I put on my apron when he said you would be visiting."

"It's new to me," I say between bites. "I can see why Kit enjoys it so much. He's turned me on to other Southern specialties like shrimp and grits, and pralines. Thank goodness I don't live here year round or I'd be a few sizes larger."

Kit says, diplomatically, "You'll learn to pace yourself."

His mother throws him a glance accompanied by a couple of eye blinks. Perhaps, like me, she's weighing the significance of his prediction. "I have not yet asked about your day," she comments, shifting her attention to me. "Which house was your favorite?"

I decide to turn the question around. "Do you have a favorite?"

She laughs, glancing at Kit again. "My house is my favorite."

"Has Kit neglected my education?" I ask.

"This house dates to the same decade as the Greene-Mildrim House."

"Same architect," her son adds.

Sitting at the round cloth-covered table, I study the room. The toile wallpaper depicts ladies in hoop skirts and big hats under spreading trees. The gentlemen courting them wear tail coats and carry walking sticks. Honey-stained wainscoting lines the walls below the paper. Even though the room is used for family meals, the ceiling has an ornate plaster medallion and elaborate picture molding, from which paintings hang. "It's an amazing house," I say.

"Built by Kit's great-great-great-grandfather. He was a well-known lawyer. I'd show you around, but it really is best to see the rooms in daylight. I'll give you a tour next time you visit."

"I'd love that. Was this the Jewish grandfather?"

"Yes. Kit tells me you are Jewish."

"I am, although growing up in a small New England town and living in another as an adult, I lead an entirely ecumenical existence."

"Where do you worship?" Maddie asks, as if my answer wasn't satisfactory.

"Ashburton has a lovely little temple built at the turn of the last century. I confess, however, that when Diana wasn't interested in being bat mitzvahed, we stopped attending services with any regularity. I've reverted to what I've been since college—a High Holiday Jew. I visit the synagogue on Yom Kippur, mostly."

"My husband, Lee, was never one for organized religion. The boys take after him. I grew up Congregationalist, as did Lee, although his antecedents were mixed. I'd rather my sons attended church more regularly, but I measure their goodness by their characters, which are far more substantial than their commitment to religion."

"I feel the same way about my daughter. Diana isn't the least interested in religion, although she loves Christmas."

"Christmas is irresistible," Maddie says.

"To me, too," I admit.

Kit's mother laughs, a tinkling sound, light and sweet.

"I understand your family is almost as old as ours in the Americas, although we've mixed in some newer blood. Sam's wife, June, has history in early Virginia, but Eleanor's family were newer immigrants—Irish, as I remember—though they were quite enterprising."

"All that family history is neither here nor there, is it?" Kit's says, before I can contradict her about my family tree. His voice is pleasant, but the look he bestows on his mother holds a warning.

Keeping the spotlight on me, Maddie turns in my direction. "You are from Ashburton? That's a pretty town with a famous college, yes?" She lays a beringed hand over Kit's. "Didn't your daddy's cousin's daughter—oh, what is her name? Samantha, that's it—didn't Samantha graduate from Ashburton College?"

"You would know better than I."

"I'll have to ask Mary-Sue. She'll know. And you, Liz, did you attend Ashburton?"

"I went to school in California."

"But grew up in Ashburton?"

"My ex-husband did. Dan has ancestors buried in the historic church's graveyard there, members of the first congregation. A couple of them fought in the Revolution. My side arrived a century and a half later," I say, finally able to correct her ideas about my antecedents. She seems to view Eleanor as peasant stock. If that is the case, I'm no different.

Maddie manages to find a silver lining in the news, "How lovely that your daughter's heritage makes her a member of the DAR! I am also a member, but I've already said as much. It is a nice coincidence, don't you think?" Maddie pronounces as she stands to clear the table.

I glance at Kit before answering. He is frowning at the window.

I say, "May I help?" I begin to rise.

"My son will do the honor."

Retaking my seat, I wait while Kit dutifully clears and heads into the kitchen, his mother following. She returns with a tray supporting a delicate porcelain teapot with matching cups and saucers, and a short stack of delicate dessert plates. He carries a bowl of cookies and another of grapes.

"Those are benne seed cakes," Maddie says.

"Sesame seed cookies," Kit translates. "A tradition around here." He pops one of the tiny cookies into his mouth. I nibble at mine.

Over drinks, we talk mainly about the history of Savannah. I don't see why Kit thinks his mother is such a canny interrogator; so far, I see her as a charming conversationalist and hostess, although there was that dig about Eleanor, which I might not even have noticed if it weren't for Kit's response to it.

"I understand your daughter is around Noah's age?" Maddie says.

I select a cluster of grapes. "Diana is a little younger; a sophomore at the University of Vermont. She plans to continue on for a master's in international conflict resolution."

"Maybe Sam can help her when it's time to find work," Maddie says.

"What a generous idea. It is so helpful to have connections when you're trying to break into a tight field," I say.

"I should have thought of it," Kit says.

"And what about you, Lizbeth? It sounds like your daughter is interested in a life that may include a fair amount of travel. Are you entirely settled in Vermont?"

Is she asking whether I'm willing to relocate to Georgia? I glance at Kit. He is looking at the cookies.

"I did a lot of traveling in my youth, but this winter is the first I've had a chance to explore so far from home since Diana was born." Uneasiness is rising. Kit is too quiet.

She lifts her cup and takes a dainty sip of tea. "I grew up in Charleston. But Lee wanted to live here." The last word comes out *hee-ah*. "It didn't take me long to fall in love with Savannah." She pauses then asks, "Do you think being a Yankee that a move to the South—theoretically, of course—would be as easy for you?"

About to take a sip of tea, I set the cup down. I'm pretty sure Kit's mother wants to know whether I'd move here for her son.

"I suppose that depends."

Maddie lifts a brow. "On what, dear?"

I dart a glance at Kit, not sure what answer he wants to hear. He is wearing that blank expression he puts on when he doesn't want you to know what he is thinking. Right now, his blankness appears to be directed at his mother. I imagine he's feeling railroaded into going down on one knee right here, over the benne seed cakes.

Disturbed by Kit's reaction, no politic response occurs to me. He finally interjects, "It depends on how much she likes the hospitality she experiences in our midst."

Watching him, I wonder if he needs rescuing more than I. The mantel clock on the sideboard reads 9:27. Catching his eye, I tug my ear. "It's getting kind of late."

Taking the cue, Kit pushes his chair away from the table. "I have to swim extra early tomorrow, so I'm afraid I have to hurry us on our away."

At the door, Maddie hugs her son, who dutifully leans down to presses a kiss to her cheek. She hugs me, as well. "Don't be a stranger. You come back to see me on your next visit. We'll do some shopping." She offers a warm smile, and then pokes a finger into her son's ribs. "You visit too, Christopher!"

"Yes, mam." He reaches for the door handle.

CHAPTER 32

NEITHER OF US has much to say as Kit drives down Route 16 toward the interstate. It isn't until we are closing in on I-95 that he squeezes my hand. "You okay?"

"I had a good time. Did you? You were awfully quiet near the end."

Kit snorts. "When two powerfully smart women get going, I can't keep up. I knew my mother would like you. The two of you are very alike."

I snuggle my hand onto his thigh, pleased with the compliment. I too felt we'd hit it off.

The car shudders in the draft of a semi roaring past as we merge onto the highway. A few miles later, he muses, "You are both strong women unafraid of being yourselves. And although I hadn't thought about it before tonight, I'm realizing you're a pretty good inquisitor yourself."

"I hope that's a compliment." I brush my hand up his thigh and over his fly.

"The tease part of you I already knew about." He throws a quick glance at me, staying focused on the road.

"And it's one of your favorite parts."

"Because it usually leads to some of my other favorite parts."

This comment instantly heats those favorite parts, including my brain—and other bits further south. My hand continues to play advance and retreat.

"If you keep that up, there will be retribution."

"Do tell . . ."

But he doesn't. Instead he drops a bomb into my congratulatory reverie about surviving the mother test.

"Mom never liked Eleanor. When Maddie met her for the first time, she did not invite her back, which turned out to be a harbinger of inter-actions to come."

My had stills. I pull it into my own lap.

Kit doesn't seem to notice, as he elaborates, "Mom thought Eleanor wanted to separate me from the family. She always said we lived too much in each other's pockets."

"Did you?" I ask. I might as well find out, since he seems to want to talk about it.

"I suppose we did, although it wasn't Eleanor's doing. It's just that falling in love with her coincided with my first attempts at true indepen-dence. As I have already confessed, I loved her a little past distraction. Until Eleanor, my mother was never possessive." He pauses then adds, "Most kids rebel in high school, but somehow I missed that memo. If I hadn't, Mother might have seen the situation with my wife differently."

I don't comment, lest I stop his flow. Kit shrugs. "I don't know why I didn't rebel. Maybe I was too busy swimming and making perfect grades. Or maybe there wasn't anything to rebel against. I had plenty of freedom."

He sighs. "Anyway, after I met Eleanor during my sophomore year at Dartmouth, I didn't go home for summer breaks. The first year, I worked on Cape Cod and shared a beach house with friends from school. Eleanor was one of them. The rest of my school breaks were spent at her family's summer house in Maine with the same group of friends. We all worked at tourist traps in Bar Harbor."

Kit grimaces. "After we married, I was the one who refused family invitations. I'd drag my feet about visiting. Too many times, my par-ents ended up inviting themselves to visit us, or begging that we come down to Willing for family reunions. This was before we moved down here after El got sick."

His attention fixed on the highway, he adds, "Looking back on the early years of our marriage, I know my behavior was immature. Worse, I left it to my wife to be the buffer between my parents and me. She eventually rebelled and I had to do my own dirty work, but by then she was sick, so it looked like I had simply wrestled the reins from her because we needed my parents' support."

"Your mother knows this?"

"She thinks I'm indulging in revisionist history, polishing Eleanor's halo. She refuses to believe her sweet son would have distanced himself from his parents on his own. Maybe if I'd been more than just mischievous as a kid, if I had indulged in outright rebellion before college— Mom would have been willing to accept me as the villain of the story."

"And maybe if you hadn't been who you are, Eleanor wouldn't have fallen in love with you and stayed in love with you, whatever your faults were at the time."

His brow furrows as if this is a point he hasn't considered, but he doesn't say anything more as we cover the next dozen or so miles between Savannah and home.

We are turning off the highway at Darien when I say, "It must be hard to carry that regret." I'm feeling that a piece of the puzzle has been left out, while a few others have fallen into place.

He nods but his silence continues. When Kit's emotions overwhelm him, his defense is to climb inside his shell, where he seems to be hiding out at the moment. He had been his usual charming, accessible self right up until his mother started to compare her daughters-in-law. But when Maddie began her genteel inquisition about how I would fit into the daughter-in-law mix, he started burrowing. The sexy banter at the beginning of our ride had an automatic-pilot sort of flow, now that I think about it.

Wanting to shift the focus away from the painful conflict between his mother and his wife, I say, "It's amazing how we can have grown children ourselves, yet these wounds from our primary relationships remain unresolved. A few years ago, my father was visiting and promised to do a small thing for me—to take my car in for inspection. At the time I was swamped with deadlines and the car was almost out of inspection. I could have used the help. He forgot. I wouldn't talk to him for an entire month afterward—an outsized reaction to his crime.

He'd done similar things many times before, enough times that I'd learned not to rely on him. I'd also spent enough years in therapy to feel confident I'd put those issues aside. But all it took was for Dad to forget another promise and I reverted to my enraged teenage self, no matter that my age at the time was thirty-six.

"And Mom? She's harder on me than she is on my brother, probably because I did the most rebelling. Our relationship is still difficult enough that we do best confining our time together to forty-eight hours or less. So much for the adult I thought I'd become." I let out an exasperated breath. "The incident with my dad forced me to accept my hardwiring isn't so easy to disconnect."

When Kit doesn't comment on my soliloquy, I ask, "Are iffy relationships with parents a deal breaker for you?" I'm trying to lighten us up, because I'm not comfortable with this conversation, or where Kit seems to be going with it.

"At least I won't be making that mistake twice," Kit says, ignoring my bid for reassurance and still inside his own head. Instinct tells me, he's heading in a direction I fear. "My mother thinks you're great. She told me so when we were in the kitchen."

So that's why he had to help clear the table. "I liked her, too," I say, gazing out the window. My stomach begins to churn. Does Kit see me as competition for his dead wife?

Visiting his mother was a bad idea after all. My stomach may be burning but the rest of me is suddenly chilled. I reach for the heating controls and turn the fan up. Arielle may be correct in observing that I look for trouble where there isn't any, but sometimes it is exactly where I expect it to be.

We drive the rest of the way home in silence.

❋

As we pull through Willing's gates, Kit suggests we sleep at his place and he'll bring Obie over. Chella took care of Obs while we were away.

After unlocking the door, however, he steers us through the mudroom by the faint light falling from the upstairs sconces he left on earlier. I'm a little confused about why he's still here instead of going off to fetch Obie.

Nevertheless, his closeness is reassuring, after how unsettling our conversation was on the way home.

He pulls me closer as we reach the hall. "God," he murmurs into my hair. His hands lift to my breasts. "I love how soft you are."

"And I love how hard you are." I push into the firm musculature of body. He rubs his erection into the crease of my ass, his arms tightening, and walks us down the dimly illuminated hall. We step onto the thick oriental runner in front of the picture gallery. His arms relax. I begin to twist, needing to see his expression, to know we're okay.

But suddenly his foot is tangled with mine and I'm falling. I reach for the banister to save myself, heart pounding. Did Kit trip me on purpose? As my hand glances over the railing, Kit's arms tighten around my waist, controlling my fall. He guides me gently down to the carpet. I land forward on my hands. The texture of the rug is rough under my palms.

"First nose biting, now tripping. You are full of surprises," I say as Kit follows me down.

He insinuates his legs between mine. "You have no idea," he growls as he pushes my skirt up and shapes his hands around my ass before coming down over me. He is tall enough for his body to completely cover mine.

Even through his clothes, he is so warm he feels feverish. He bites the side of my neck. I arch to give him better access. He licks away the sting, pressing tighter. I turn my head, trying to see him.

His lips meet mine. I moan into his mouth. He does an exemplary job of kissing me senseless. At the same time, balancing on one hand, he unbuckles and pulls off his belt.

The bestiality of this position is often more arousing in my head than in real time because so many men don't know how to add the external stimulation many women, including me, need in order to orgasm. The position was one of Darius's particular favorites, and because he was good at it, I enjoyed it, too.

Go ahead and argue, but being fucked this way is not about sen-suality or connection. When a man wants to take you from behind, he isn't thinking about love; he's turned on by the fantasy of domination—another Darius specialty—along with the visuals.

It isn't as if I don't enjoy the visuals myself, but what I enjoy most, past my own orgasm, is being able to watch Kit abandon himself to his own pleasure, which is impossible to witness in this position. I shift sideways to solve the problem, but Kit lays a restraining hand on my neck. "No, dahlin'," he whispers into my ear. "Don't move."

Although I've met this Kit many times, the one who enjoys com-manding the action, there's a harshness to his tone I haven't heard before. For a second, I feel a little uneasy, yet I'm aroused enough to let the uneasiness go. Signaling my compliance, I push into him.

He pulls my top up. Cool air hits my bare skin. I feel him fiddling with the hooks of my bra, shoving the shirt higher. The bra releases. Kit rolls my nipples between his fingers, hard enough to hurt.

"Kit," I gasp.

"Don't move." His hands leave off teasing my breasts. I hear his zipper open. Seconds later, cool air hits the skin of my ass as he pulls my panties down. He palms one knee to pull the slip of silk passing for underwear over it and off. Having solved the problem of egress, he chooses not to be fastidious, leaving the panties caught on my other ankle. He also ignores my stockings and boots. Although my heels are low, they are curvy and graceful. The stockings and garter belt are a major turn-on, if past experience is a guide. His hands roam, pinching my nipples, skimming my belly, shaping my ass, until at last, his fingers slide into the lush darkness between my legs.

I moan and push into his hand.

He removes his fingers. This time I moan with disappointment. "Patience," he says, and I feel the tip of his cock make the slightest entrance before he pulls out to rub himself into the slippery heat he's created. I arch to pull him inside me. He refuses to be caught.

His fingers replace his cock. "Kit," I breathe, tilting into his touch. He massages my clit, penetrating me with his thumb. My body tightens. I begin to pant. *He* strokes into me on a powerful lunge. I fall to my elbows, my cheek coming to rest on the carpet.

Ever the master of variety, Kit changes his rhythm, moving slower. Supporting his weight on one hand, he inches the other down my belly until the tips of his fingers rest on my clit. He hilts himself and rocks, hitting the two sweet spots, one with his cock, one with his fingers. A wash of heat rolls over me. I groan and clench around him.

He whispers into my ear, "I'm going to lift you." I have no idea what he is talking about, but he raises my upper body off the floor, so that I am sitting on his thighs. "Hold onto the stair rail," he says, and drives himself into me.

"Ah," I breathe. With his arms crossing under my breasts, he pinches my nipples. I let my head fall back against his shoulder. He whispers, "Touch yourself for me, dahlin'," and twists to kiss me.

There are some lovely aspects to masturbating in company—a turn-on for both parties, as well as efficient, because I am an expert at delivering my own pleasure. In seconds, I'm close. *"Oh God. Kit—"*

My spine bows. He bites the tender skin at the nape of my neck, a gesture so carnally possessive that the orgasm it spawns is almost painful. I cry out, pushing into his chest. His arms tighten around me and he roars, the sound harsh and lovely and profoundly gratifying as we come in unison.

Collapsing onto the rug, we separate. Neither of us seems able to gather the energy to rise.

He's the one who finally manages it first. I miss his warmth as he picks himself off the floor, pulls his pants up and organizes the rest of his clothing before heading out to fetch Obie.

I roll to the side. Grandfather Jarrett stares thoughtfully down at me. I turn away and sit up. Sliding the dangling underwear off, I gingerly wipe up before standing and climbing the stairs.

I'm almost asleep when man and dog return. Kit strokes a hand down my body. I'm warm under the covers and his touch is sensual and lovely. I purr, "I love you."

"Thank you," Kit says and kisses my forehead, holding me close.

After his breathing indicates he's asleep, I gnaw on his "thank you," feeling foolish for making such a novice mistake. I should not have spoken the dreaded "L" word, and definitely not after something went off-kilter during the visit with Kit's mother. It takes a long time for me to fall asleep, because of that stupid "I love you." From here on I'll be anticipating when the next shoe is going to drop, because I'm pretty sure the first one is already on the floor, positioned for one of us to trip over it.

CHAPTER 33

I WAKE IN the morning to find I've slept through Kit's good-bye kiss. After I shower, I return to his brother's house, walking Obie on the way.

There are shots from last week to edit and color-correct. I'm engrossed in the work when, at a little after one, Kit calls to say he isn't feeling well.

He tells me it's probably best if he stays away. I suggest that if he has picked up a bug, odds are I've already been exposed to it, too. I offer to make chicken soup. He refuses the soup and my company.

I don't hear from him for another twenty-four hours, even though I text the next morning to ask how he is. Late in the afternoon, he calls with the same message. When he arrives home, I watch him beeline to his door without glancing in my direction.

Those midnight worries of mine about that potentially ill-timed "*I love you*" seem less paranoid by the minute.

Some men hole up like bears in winter when they're ill. But I don't think Kit is ill. I think he needs some rope. I worry that I was right all along and our visit to his mother tightened an invisible noose around his neck he hadn't noticed until then.

The conversation during our return from Savannah takes on added significance. My guess is that I'm in competition with Eleanor after all.

Talking about these worries will make them real, rather than a paranoid overreaction, so I don't call Arielle.

To while away the time, because I'm too riled up to concentrate on work and don't feel one iota of creative urgency, I take Obie for extra walks hoping to burn off some of the unbearable tension I'm feeling. It doesn't work. The other panacea, watching inane television I won't remember later, also fails to distract me. I manage to hold myself together until day three, when Kit doesn't bother to call. His e-mail arrives at noon, his thoughts organized in bullet points.

Liz—
• Still under the weather.
• Need to talk.
• See you tonight.
• Don't plan on dinner.

It's a good thing that I'm supposed to be at Pamela's in an hour. I can't imagine how I would spend the time until Kit arrives home except hanging from my fingernails.

❋

Pamela loved the photographs and ordered the triptych Kit and I imagined: the chapel interior, the exterior, and the view out the open front doors. We decided on five-foot by four-foot prints. I'll have Rick, who does my printing, produce them.

I told her I wanted to discount the price because I photographed the chapel without permission. She wouldn't hear of it and insisted on "the going rate." Since I don't have a going rate for the landscape work I have so rarely sold up to this point, I suggested a price based on Rick's advice.

Pamela's response was, "I'm discovering you, dear. In a couple of years, your prices will be three or four times what I'm going to pay, so I'm giving you more than you're asking and getting a bargain at that."

"You have no idea what your vote of confidence means to me," I said, tearing up. She surprised me by opening her arms.

Driving the causeway home with my pocketbook considerably fatter than it was on the way over, I realized if I want to rent a house somewhere warm next winter, I can. The elation I've been feeling about my work, as well as the lovely number inked on Pamela's check is, however, tempered by what is or isn't going to be said when Kit shows up later.

Arriving at Willing, I take Obie out to the river. Seating myself in one of the Adirondack chairs Kit and I set out a couple weeks ago, I hear my stomach rumble. I managed to down some coffee this morning, but have had no appetite for food and still don't.

Kit's car is in the drive when Obie and I return a little after 4:00. Maybe he really is sick, but I can't wait another minute to see him. My dog and I change course and steer toward his house.

I knock. When Kit spies me though the glass door partition, he pauses for a second before stepping down from the hall into the mud-room. Catching sight of his pal, Obie whines, his tail swishing. Kit opens the door and bends to pet Obs. He says, "I'll be over in a minute, okay?"

His eyes are red rimmed. His color isn't good. The hollows under his cheekbones seem more pronounced than when I saw him last. He looks sick and I feel ashamed of myself for doubting him.

"Liz," he says, straightening. "I'm glad to see you."

"I'm glad to see you too," which is true, although I also want to say, *What the hell is going on with you?*

But I can't form words with my insides twisted into a knot of long-ing and concern and apprehension. I nod and turn away.

Not long after I've given Obie his treat and settled myself—if my restless shifting around on the sofa can be called settled—Kit knocks and lets himself in. At least that much is normal.

What isn't normal is the way he folds himself wearily into his chair without making either of us a drink. Nor does he offer his usual hello kiss. I chalk up the lack to not wanting to infect me with whatever he's got. My head says wrong, he has bad news. I tell my head to shut up.

"You look like I should have made that soup, after all," I say, know-ing I didn't make him soup or challenge him these last few days because I was too chicken to face whatever was going on. So much for mon-ster-slaying. I'm surprised the sock monkey isn't sitting in the chair opposite Kit leering at me. "Do you want a drink?" I ask.

Kit rubs the back of his neck and shakes his head, regarding me bleakly. "I'm sorry I've gone missing. I owe you an apology." He tries to smile but can't quite make it work. He grimaces instead.

"Okay," I say, my voice rising on the *ay*, turning it into a question.

Kit sighs and looks away.

The voice in my head—the schoolgirl, not the Victorian—climbs an octave, shrilly predicting doom.

"Here's the thing," he says.

I tell myself to remain calm, with the opposite result.

Bright spots of color appear high on Kit's cheeks. Hesitating a beat too long, he rubs his nape a second time, and in a rush, declares, "I'm in love with you." His eyes hold a defiant gleam.

Whom is he defying? Certainly not me. Maybe himself. Or his mother. Or, more likely, Eleanor's ghost.

Kit's avowal is my wish come true, although it's hard to feel anything but dismay at his lack of enthusiasm for what he's confessed. I smile and attempt to look encouraging. "I love you, too," I say.

"Good. That's good. And reassuring after I disappeared the way I did."

"You don't sound like it's good. Do you usually get sick when you decide you're in love?" I ask, my propensity to make light when my own emotions overwhelm me having been activated. There's more going on here than Kit working up the nerve to express those magic words. And, if he doesn't explain himself soon, my nervous system is going to blast me into orbit.

"Since I've only experienced it once before—" He doesn't finish his thought. "Liz, I think I need a little space to get used to the feeling." His forehead creases. "That's what I've been doing these last few days, trying . . ."

I wait for more. It doesn't come. "I'm guessing trying hasn't worked so well," I say.

"I need some time to myself. Some time alone." He sighs again and puts his head in his hands.

I don't know what this means. The only happy news is I don't start shaking.

"I hoped I'd have this resolved in a couple of days, but it isn't happening and I couldn't continue to leave you hanging."

"Thank you," I manage. I appreciate his wanting to spare me anxiety even if his message isn't adding up the way he seems to think it should.

"I need you to define 'some time to yourself.'"

When he doesn't immediately respond, I suggest, "Do you need a few days? A week? Six months? Forever?" The last is another joke, or so I hope.

"Not forever," Kit says seriously.

"So a little short of forever?" I frown, a red haze exploding inside my head. I feel like my brain is on fire. This is exactly what I feared. "God, I've been stupid," I say and like Kit, put my head in my hands.

"How does what I said make you stupid?" Kit sounds genuinely perplexed.

I let my hands drop. "For not being more skeptical when you swore you knew your own mind."

"Of course I know my own mind! I absolutely know I want to be with you."

"But doesn't needing space amount to not wanting to be with me?" I clutch a pillow to my chest as if it will hold me together and draw a shaky breath. Maybe I'm overreacting. But why should being in love mean Kit needs to stay away from me?

"My feelings haven't changed." He looks down at his hands. "I just can't cope with them right now."

He deserves credit for his self-awareness, but I'm having trouble delivering any. My stomach cramps. I recognize how tsunami-big it is for him to love me, but it doesn't make his needs less painful to accept. I toss the pillow aside and bend over my knees.

"Oh God, Lizzie. Please, don't be hurt. This is temporary." He rises and starts toward me.

If he touches me, I don't know whether I'll fall apart or hit him. Since neither result is going to be helpful, I hold out my palm to keep him away.

He stops, looks down at his feet, rubs the back of his neck, blows out a breath. Finally he returns to his chair.

I recognize the way I'm reacting is as much about past experience as present, but my big new rule about staying in the here and now is impossible to execute at the moment. I take a deep breath, trying to figure out how to change his mind, but right or wrong, bitterness and chagrin are my overriding emotions.

"When a man tells the woman he purports to love that he needs a break, she thinks . . ." I stop to correct myself. "*I think* I know where this is leading. *The* 'some time' you say you need is going to become more and more time, until—*surprise!*—there's no time left."

"That isn't what I'm saying." Kit sounds—I'm not sure. Frustrated? Angry?

"We've known each other barely three months. Our expectations— my expectations—were mistaken," I say. "Let's be honest."

"I've meant every word I've said to you!"

I sigh and try again. "Look. We've both experienced heartache. If you've decided you don't want to open yourself up to the possibility of that kind of hurt again, I'm the last person who would argue with you. But *you* need to understand that when I said I couldn't go through anything like what happened with Roland again and asked you to be certain about what you were promising, that was my line in the sand."

"Nothing has changed!"

"Everything has changed! You swore your feelings were true. But now you say you love me but you can't be with me *for a while.* You also swear we have a future together, except you don't know when that future might recommence. Come on, Kit, you're a man of logic, you can't deny there are some major holes in your equation."

"You're making too much of this. How many times do I need to say I'm not Roland? I just think we should see less of each other while I figure myself out."

I surmise that he spent the last couple of days wrestling with his possessive blond ghost. For eight years he invested in the idea that Eleanor was his only enduring love. Now, he can't figure out how to integrate me into his love story, and he feels like a traitor to Eleanor for trying. Loving me might have been a struggle, one he could have overcome, but the fact his mother likes me when she didn't like Eleanor has probably made his betrayal of his poor wife seem even worse. More worse, apparently, than he can bear.

I stand. Obie scrambles to his feet, glancing back and forth between me and Kit. I put my hand on his back. "Can't you see why I'm having a déjà vu moment?"

"Of course I can, but this isn't about the past, it's about us."

"Okay. Well. I *know* what I want. I want you. And because I love you, I can't live across the drive for the next couple of weeks and watch you wrestle with whether loving me is something you can do."

He doesn't dispute my version of what he's going though. I clench a fist against my lips, feeling sick, worried that Eleanor's ghost will take full possession of Kit after I leave Georgia.

Unable to look at him, I stare out the windows at the meadow turning gold in the late-afternoon light. I suspect this is my last Willing sunset. With a shaky hand, I brush away the tears beginning to drip down my cheeks.

Pushing out of his chair, Kit says, "I didn't mean for this to happen, Lizzie. I promise it isn't forever, only for a little while. I swear it! Honestly, I understand this is upsetting, but our future isn't changing—not if you don't want it to. I expect you to use those gift cards this summer. We're going to be fine."

I shake my head. "I can't put together your confidence about the future with what you've said you need today." I walk to the foyer. Obie trots after me.

When Kit catches up, he hesitates, and then steps close, lifting his hand to brush at a tear sliding down my cheek. When I don't pull away, he touches his lips to mine.

"Oh, Kit," I whisper. He wraps his arms around me. I allow myself to lean into his warmth. Even with him holding me, I feel helpless and alone.

Obie forces himself between us. Kit bends to pat him. "It's going to be okay, Obs. I'll see ya soon, buddy." This bit of optimism is sweet, although I won't count on it and think my dog is bound to have his hopes dashed as well. Kit straightens and holds my gaze, but he's hiding behind that unreadable expression I've seen before—he's gone inside himself.

"We both carry some baggage we need to dispose of, dahlin'. That's what I'm trying to do. I hope this doesn't sound wrong, but maybe you need to look to your own."

"Where do you recommend I start? At least I know my heart can expand to contain as much love as I'm offered. Why do you think yours can't do the same?"

This may be a little too much transparency, but it might also be something he needs to consider.

It takes a few seconds for him to decide what I'm talking about and then his expression hardens. "You think this is about my wife?" he says incredulously.

Isn't it? But even in my current state, I know better than to say so. Instead, I tell him what is also true. "This isn't about me or Eleanor. It's about you." I thump his chest with the palm of my hand. "Do you remember the morning you bought those gift cards? I pointed to my baggage and asked you to respect it. I know I have issues about trust. But my issues don't change that you promised you knew what you wanted."

"I'm not leaving you."

Aren't you? I reach up and run a hand through his lovely wavy hair. "I'm sorry, Kit," I say gruffly. "I'll get over this eventually. And, yes, I'm willing to give you the time you need. I just—"

Kit cups my cheek.

I wrap my hand around his wrist. "I'm sorry." I whisper. "*I need* to go home."

Releasing my hold on his arm, I step away and push the screen door open. If only he'd say, "This is wrong. Let's go to bed and erase the last three days."

He walks out the door. But as it snaps closed, he pivots. My heart soars, the foolish organ. I hold my breath, hoping—

Pressing the palm of his hand to the screen between us, Kit says "I'm not Roland. Believe in me, Liz." He sounds as weary as I feel heartsick.

"I want to," I say hoarsely. "You have no idea how much."

Oh God, this hurts! I press my hand over his. For one long second I hold it there, the screen separating me from his warmth.

His hand drops. That's when I close the door.

CHAPTER 34

NINETEEN HOURS and thirty-one minutes after exiting Willing's gate, the morning after Kit's three-day hiatus, I turn into my driveway. I didn't break the trip with an overnight stop. I needed the comfort of home.

He called the next day to assure himself I arrived safely. The conversation was stilted, neither of us knowing how to make the situation better.

In the month since, I've received a couple of Kit's lawyerly bulleted e-mails, every one of them about the weather. Apparently coastal Georgia is experiencing a heat wave. Kit says the waxy magnolias will bloom in the next couple of weeks. This fact adds to my melancholy. Had everything gone as Kit promised when he bought the flight gift cards, I would have been there to see the magnolias flower.

Kit's bullet points frustrate me. The fact that he signs his e-mails "love you" confuses me. How can you claim to love someone and not yearn to be with them? Or want to hear their voice?

Calling to ask how this is all working out for him isn't within my skill set. I tell myself I'm better off perfecting my version of the woman of valor archetype, giving Kit the space he needs to figure out how to love me, no matter how excruciating I find the wait. Unfortunately, my current head space is more Cowardly Lion than Wonder Woman.

Maybe the coward syndrome—big on avoidance, low on confrontation—is contagious, because Kit hasn't called again. E-mail is his communication medium of choice. I'm going along with it, though I indulge in complete sentences and paragraphs. I also eschew bullet points, though I stick with his safe subjects, sending along progress reports about the slow beginning of our Vermont spring. I don't report on my inner workings because they haven't changed.

I'm using a fair amount of energy to squelch the conviction that he's Roland all over again. I'm trying to have faith in Kit and patience with his process—a different sort of patience than the kind he used to tease me about. How long will it take him to figure out we deserve our chance at happiness together? I worry I can't go the distance. It is torture, not knowing what he's thinking.

A month into this vigil, the big newsflash—absent one from Kit—is that in spite of the dashed dreams weighing me down, I've been able to enjoy the present.

At a reunion dinner with my necklace-making friend Evie and her husband, Dov, his droll sense of humor had me wiping tears of mirth from my eyes. I spent a fun day of shopping therapy with Sheri last week. And Arielle and I have shared many evenings curled in my wing chairs with wine or tea and something sweet. She has caught me up on local gossip, Miu-Miu's antics, and her attempts to tame a feral cat that recently showed up in her backyard. Some sort of reserve holds me back from talking much about Kit with her or with anyone else. Maybe because the situation is so unresolved. Or maybe I don't want to talk about him the same way I didn't want to celebrate my revived creativity, afraid I would jinx it. Arielle has heard enough about him anyway. She spent hours talking me down as I drove home from Georgia.

I haven't seen the Larkins yet, although I did call Mel last week. She told me C. is loving New York and has plans to work there this summer. He will be in Vermont for just a week between the end of school and starting his job. It would be lovely to see him, but I can't imagine he'll have time for a visit. I wonder what is playing at the movies.

As for Darius, I assume he's home from his travels. I should stop in at the shop, although I'm reluctant to see him. No matter his denials, I think he hoped Kit and I would get together. I'm not ready to face his critique of what I did wrong—the Darius version of tough love.

Next weekend, Diana is coming home to visit before she takes up residence with friends in Burlington for the summer. It's hard to believe we're already in the first week of May. She's bringing Marc with her. They've been together for over six months, which makes the timing perfect for such a visit, unlike mine with Kit's mother.

Sitting at the table, working on my second cup of coffee, I consider the day ahead. There are abundant household chores and wedding work. I need to do the first edit of last weekend's shoot, the booking I would have traveled home for if Kit hadn't—

Oy. There's no point in going there. Pushing my half-finished toast away, I try to ignore the way my heart wobbles and the sinking feeling that clogs my throat every time I think of him.

If there's anything good about falling in love so precipitously and losing it as fast, it isn't the pounds I'm shedding, it is the weirdly kick-ass version of the blues I'm experiencing. There is a Gloria Gaynor "I Will Survive" militancy about my days. Also, another new rule—or maybe it's more of a mantra, one that sounds cheesy, but it is the most important of the new Rules to date. I repeat it to myself now, as I check my e-mail and see there is nothing from Kit: There is someone out there for me. I will find love again.

If Kit and I don't work out, I fully expect my heart to break, but this time, I am confident it will mend. Recovery won't be easy or fun, but I won't be shutting myself away for another five years afterward. If I'm lucky to have love walk into my life one more time, I'll be ready. Since the last set of Rules were predicated upon *not* surviving Roland, Arielle and I agree this new attitude shows major progress.

Turning my attention to the weather report, I note rain in the prediction. New England weather notoriously resists behaving as predicted, and thus far this morning has delivered exactly what an early May day should be. The temperature is mild, the humidity is light, and while there are clouds scuttling across the sky periodically throwing the world into shadow, sunlight is beaming through the windows.

I decide the photo editing can wait until later this afternoon. The house cleaning can wait longer than that. Putting my empty coffee cup in the sink, I fill a travel mug, grab the Nikon, tripod, and, of course, Obie, and head out to explore.

Forty-five minutes later, I'm standing at the crest of a hill high above Ashburton. The panoramic landscape below me is impressionistic, as if Mother Nature has taken up pointillism, dotting the patchwork fields in vibrant greens and browns, the woodlands in acid shades of yellow and vermillion. The mountains—the Taconics to the west, and Greens to the east—haven't yet been painted. They retain their blue winter tint, the deep red of tree buds barely coloring their lower slopes as spring color begins to creep out of the valleys toward the summits. Zipping my jacket against a brisk breeze, I watch shadows climb and shift over the eastern mountains as the cloud banks ride the wind toward New Hampshire.

There are a couple of pleasing images on the camera card already, proving that my creative resurrection in Georgia was no fluke. The morning's take includes a shot of a solitary apple tree—a vision of white-petaled fertility crowning a fallow field and defying the brooding gray clouds massing behind it. The other image I like is of a group of spindly saplings with lacy new green leaves clustered in front of budding red maples. At the edge of the field behind the trees, a copse of birch forms a black-and-white boundary.

At present, I'm waiting for the "fingers of God," as Pamela Tisdale described the streaks of light inside the chapel, to slant out of the sky and into the valley. A new gust of wind shakes buds from the trees behind me, sprinkling tiny maple flowers over my shoulders. I'm reminded of the yellow jessamine dropping from the trees at Willing.

This thought is followed by a twinge of yearning. At the same moment, sunlight pours into the valley. I check the light meter, make a quick adjustment, and click the shutter. In mere months, my camera has gone from being my greatest frustration to my best therapy. Perhaps that is what Georgia was meant to be—the beginning of my creative renewal, not the beginning of a perfect love. No matter that my heart aches, a revitalized creative life might be good enough, even if my heart greedily demands more.

※

"Mom." Diana narrows her eyes. "I know something isn't right. And please"—my daughter waves her potato peeler at me—"don't make me use this handy tool to pry whatever it is out of you."

We are in the kitchen, preparing dinner. Marc is out for a run with Obie. Arielle will be over shortly.

It is hard to know if my daughter would be sympathetic about Kit should I be interested in discussing him, which I'm not—particularly since he's still sending those bulleted e-mails and I'm beginning to wonder how much distance there is between valor and despair.

I slice into an onion.

Being her usual relentless self, Diana says, "It's that guy Kit, isn't it? Do I need to go down to Georgia to mess him up?" There's a menacing gleam in her eye. She brandishes the peeler a second time. Diana reserves the job of being hard on me for herself and is fierce about defending her turf.

The corners of my mouth twitch as I imagine Kit discovering Diana on his doorstep wielding a potato peeler. "If I'm depressed about him, it's my own fault," I say, since, knowing Diana, she isn't likely to let the subject drop until she has her answers.

"Meaning?"

"He changed his mind. Not a big deal. We had a winter fling that ran its course." This isn't the whole truth, but my nose is probably not going to grow long over it.

"Really? It's over but for some reason you haven't moved on." She narrows her eyes. "This is progress."

"How, exactly?" I ask.

"He dumped you, which I assume is the case because you're never sad when you dump *them*. And you have feelings about what happened. That's progress, in my book."

"Maybe some feelings are involved," I grumble.

She stares at me. I suspect she's trying to estimate how many feelings are defined by *some*.

Putting down the knife, I say, "He's renewed an invitation for me to visit this summer. Specifically at the end of June, when I'm delivering those prints to the Tisdales." Needing to put this in context, more for myself than for Diana, I add, "He's not much of a correspondent, so I can't figure out how much significance to give the invite."

Diana tilts her head inquisitively, this time waiting for me to define how *not much of a correspondent* fits into the spectrum of communication with an ex-lover who asks you to visit.

I sigh, unwilling to share this level of detail with my daughter.

Reading my sigh correctly, she says, "You're thinking of going? Why? He dumped you."

If your worldview is as black and white as Diana's tends to be, wanting to visit Kit makes no sense. I see her all-or-nothing approach as the result of her youth, as well as her status as an October baby. Diana has probably placed what I've said on her Libra scale and decided Kit is weighing me down.

In contrast to her sharp-edged reasoning, mine is a hundred murky shades of gray. I'm considering Kit's offer because I find hope in his wanting me to visit, even if his miserly communication style is not as encouraging.

While I decide how to answer, the door opens. Arielle walks in.

"I didn't hear your car," I say, reaching to take the basket she's carrying.

"Pretty day, so I walked." She peeks around me. "Girl," she says affectionately to Diana.

My daughter grins. "Glass of wine?" Diana asks her honorary auntie, stepping around me to give Arielle a hug.

"I'll help myself. You keep doing what you're doing." She looks around. "No Obie?"

"Out with Marc."

"That explains the lack of greeting." Arielle pulls two quarts of hand-packed ice cream out of an insulated bag in her basket and puts them in the freezer before taking a wineglass from the cupboard.

"So are you going or not?" Diana asks, as if our conversation hadn't been interrupted. Since my best friend already knows more of the story than I've shared with Diana, I don't have to explain what we're talking about. Arranging onion slices over a bowl of salad greens, I answer, "He should come to me if he's motivated to restart the relationship."

"Excellent thought, Mom."

I reach for the potatoes she prepped and toss them into the pot of cold water in the sink. "You might as well peel those last two." I point at the nearly empty bag. "I'll make hash with any leftovers."

"Mom," Diana says impatiently. "Are you going or not?"

"Okay, okay," I mutter. "Since the invite was part of our original plan, I might as well go."

"Why aren't you making him come to you?"

Because he can't commit himself that far. But what I say is, "*I'm delivering those prints to his friends, so it makes more sense for me to go there.*"

My daughter does this thing with her face, something between a frown and a sneer, as she quarters the last two potatoes. I know the expression well. It means, *Do you really expect me to believe this crap?*

She turns from the sink and says, "On the bright side, he doesn't seem to be another of your harem men even if he's making you sad." She gives me a piercing look.

"I'm with her," Arielle says.

"Harem men are useful. They're helpful, generous in bed, and have never broken my heart."

"Plus they don't hang around long term. Don't forget that little detail," my daughter says.

"Hand me the salad servers, will you?" I ask Arielle.

Sipping her chardonnay, my friend studies me with too much focus. Finally, just as I'm beginning to squirm, she turns to find the servers.

Diana puts an arm around my shoulders and leans in to kiss my cheek. "I'm proud of you, Mama. You gave love a try, didn't you? Admit it." She gives me a squeeze. "Too bad if this asshole doesn't recognize how special you are." She releases me to throw the last two potatoes in the pot and carry the pot to the stove. "I wish you didn't need to go down there to prove his assholeness to yourself, but if that's what it takes, that's what it takes." She returns to my side. "But, can we agree? No more harem men? There's a better man out there than this Kit person, a guy who actually deserves your wonderful self."

My daughter's vote of confidence, along with the pain associated with this loving business, tears me up. I sniff, rubbing at my eyes. "Those onions were strong," I choke out.

Since I don't want to cry about Kit, at least not until he makes the decision to completely break my heart, assuming that I allow him to do it, I've refocused the need for a good cry on other sad situations. The horror of world events as reported by the nightly news is an excellent source of cry-worthy horrors.

A commotion at the door brings Marc and Obie bouncing into the room. Marc is tall and slim, built like the runner he is. His entrance is fortuitously timed, a redirection that saves me from further contemplation of the painful men I have known.

Obie strains to be released from the lead. Once freed, he offers Arielle his usual enthusiastic greeting before trotting to his water dish to slurp with equal enthusiasm.

I watch him for a few seconds. "Can you pick the dish up, Marc? Too much food or water before or after exercise isn't good for deep-chested dogs like Obs. I'll put water down in a few minutes, once he's less revved up."

"Oberon, treat!" Diana says. He trots to her. When she doesn't immediately hand over the goods, he sits at her feet. "Good dog." She puts the small biscuit in his mouth. Two chews and it's gone.

"Anything else I can do for you, Ma?" She ruffles Obie's head.

"Let's see . . . the salad is ready to go, chicken's in the oven, potatoes on the stove, and Arielle bought dessert. I think we're covered. Dinner in half an hour."

"Gotcha. Marc needs his shower but that should work." The two of them walk toward the living room discussing what's playing at the local cinema. They are arguing about which movie to see, their heads close, her blond against his deep brunette. The sight makes me happy. The ever-present tears well again. "What do you think of him?" I sniff.

Arielle was invited to dinner specifically to inspect Marc, a detail I doubt my daughter has shared with her boyfriend.

Instead of answering the question, Arielle says, "You seem better."

I laugh. Arielle has the patience of a saint, which she's needed of late. I'm fairly sure she's been waiting for me to draw her into a dissection of my relationship with Kit. My usual style is to saw apart a failed relationship until it isn't just dead, but dismembered into itsy-bitsy pieces. She had to have been sick of my infinite-loop tape after Dan, and then Roland, the last time I let my heart destroy my ability to make intelligent conversation. I don't want to start in about Kit because I might never stop.

Obie leans into Arielle's legs. She strokes his head. He rolls his eyes to hers adoringly.

"I'm pretty sure he's after more biscuits," I say, "but I could be tarring him with my own Machiavellian brush." I hand her a dog treat.

"I like the dynamic between Diana and her boy." She offers the cookie to Obie. "Did you see how he didn't let her push him around about which movie to see?"

"He's a subtle negotiator. Part of his technique is to ignore her tone. And he's great about teasing her when she gets strident. But I haven't observed him forcing her into doing what he wants, either. That boy is a master of compromise. I love the way he kids her until she laughs and her irritation melts away. It's amazing. I can't say teasing Diana works well for me, but then, I'm her mother."

"And he's cute," Arielle says with a twinkle. "That dark hair and those bright blue eyes are a spectacular combination—speaking purely from an artistic perspective, of course."

"Of course. I share your artistic eye." We grin at each other. "Not that my daughter let herself fall for his looks. Marc worked hard to woo her, and had the smarts to see through the tough persona she hides behind."

"I'm delighted for them both." Arielle gives Obie's head another pat then nails me with her gaze. "So about your Southern friend . . . any news on that front other than what you shared with Diana?"

"Nope." I gaze out the window. The maple in the yard is almost fully leafed out, dappling the grass with speckled shadows nothing like the linear patterns thrown by Willing's Spanish-moss-draped oaks.

My throat fills with longing. I say gruffly, "There is one thing. I finally couldn't stand it anymore and called him last Thursday. He seemed happy enough to hear my news, but when I asked how *he* was doing, the conversation died an instant death. We used to be so easy together, but now there's a huge chasm. I hope it will disappear once I'm down there."

The ice in the whiskey and water I made for myself when I began preparing dinner has melted. I take a sip anyway. Drinking whiskey without Kit is bittersweet. I'm doing it, though, as if Jack Daniel's is the talisman that will draw us closer. That's my big fear. With me so far away, he'll find it easier to revert to business as usual.

Arielle shakes her head.

"E-mail is better. He's right about that. Even if his bullet points never total more than a hundred words. Most of the time, far less."

"You're sure he isn't just a terrible correspondent?"

Ignoring her attempt to comfort me, I wail, "Those stupid e-mails as personal as a grocery list. You would think an articulate lawyer could do better. And the dastardly man always closes with, 'Love you.'"

"Maybe that's the only factor of significance. Maybe he does love you even if he isn't a great communicator," Arielle suggests. "I believe many men get tongue-tied when they feel emotional or are emotionally confused."

"You have a point. Kit retreats inside himself when something intense is going on. I saw it a couple of times, although he definitely held up his end in our last conversation at Willing. He's managing to surmount his feelings and express himself. I suppose that's why I still have hope."

For a second, Arielle and I look at each other. We heave simultaneous sighs. My sigh is mostly frustration. Hers is likely more philosophical.

"Are all men this difficult, or only the ones I fall for?" I ask rhetorically. "You would have thought that after all these years, I'd make better choices. Why can't I fall for someone a little less complicated?"

Wisely, Arielle ignores the question. "So when exactly is this trip, and do you need help with Obie while you're away?"

CHAPTER 35

"THEY'RE GORGEOUS, RICK."

I survey the prints spread out on the shop's long worktable and beam at the owner of my favorite photo lab. "As always, you are a magician!"

The Photographer's Lens in Albany, New York, is one of the few professional labs left in the region, and there's a reason why they continue to prosper. Rick Douglas is brilliant at what he does, although to hold the bottom line, he and his team produce everything from inexpensive digitally printed business cards to family calendars to the big, pricey art prints on the worktable in front of us.

On a computer monitor, images look two-dimensional, but the technology delivering them is three-dimensional. There are wires, a logic board, and chips, not to mention the thickness of the display's glass screen and whatever else is in there to produce what we see. Plus, the source of illumination is from back to front, as the innards of the machine translate digital impulses onto the translucent monitor screen. In contrast, a paper print exists purely in opaque, two-dimensional space with light shining onto it, not surfacing from within it.

Translating an image from a computer monitor to paper is like taking a spherical object and flattening it pancake thin without a noticeable difference. There is alchemy involved and Rick is my master magician.

"I'm relieved you're happy. They were a challenge—a fun challenge." He glances with pride at the thirteen prints in front of him including the supersized images for the Tisdales.

To keep my promise to Pamela, I wiped the metadata from the shots of the chapel before transferring them to Rick, and made him swear he will delete the file on his end after I call to let him know I've backed up the electronic file he gives me this afternoon.

Also arrayed in front of us are smaller-format prints, though none less than eighteen by twenty-four inches, all taken in Georgia. There is Kit's pink-barked clearing—dawn was indeed the perfect time to photograph it, the shot of the cloudy sky and blurred grasses, a couple of images I took at the nature preserve, the marsh on the southern approach to Darien, and what have to be my favorites, the shot of the mist rising from Willing's meadow and the abandoned house under the blooming wisteria vines. I took that one the week before I left.

Minus the chapel shots, the others are slated for display at Sal's Place. I contacted Sally right after Diana and Marc visited and asked if she had room in her schedule for me. The show is going up next week and will hang for a month. I'm thrilled, even if the gallery is only a local restaurant. After such a long hiatus, however, it's the start that counts.

"This is gorgeous work," Rick says, as the chime signaling door-open sounds. He gestures for me to wait while he shoots around the workroom partition to take care of business.

"Arliss!" I hear him exclaim. "What a nice surprise."

"You know I like to visit my favorite printer when I'm at the house," a cultured voice trills.

"You've stopped by at the right moment. Some fantastic work is in on the table. Come see."

Rick and his friend round the corner. The woman at his side is petite and city-thin, older than me and very chic. She is wearing skinny black pants and a narrow white linen blouse with an asymmetrical neckline. I judge it to be Japanese couture. Her eyes are rimmed with dark blue liner, but what is most attention-grabbing and also iconic—because I've seen plenty of photographs of her in the *New York Times* style section and in the pages of *art magazines*—is her hair. It is dark with a natural white streak at the temple. For as long as I can remember seeing pictures of this woman, her hair has been bobbed, but also styled as if a gust of wind kicked it high on her head.

A protégé of Andy Warhol and friend of Robert Mapplethorpe, she is the owner of one of the most prestigious photo galleries in New York

City. I knew Rick had opened his shop here after years of working in Manhattan, but I had no idea he had worked with Arliss Kline.

"Let me introduce you to Lizbeth Silver, Arliss. She's the most talented landscape photographer in the area. Liz, Arliss Kline; Arliss, Liz."

Arliss offers a limp hand. She is, however, interested in the prints and glides over to the table.

I motion to Rick. Understanding what I'm signaling, he moves to the far end of the table to cover the pink chapel print with one of the others. There's a whole lot of quiet as Arliss studies the prints, moving slowly from one to the next with no discernible expression on her face.

It's unnerving to watch her judge my work.

Finally, she looks up. "Rick is right. You have a distinctive viewpoint. Why haven't I heard of you?"

"Uh, because—"

Rick jumps in. "Because I've been remiss in not bringing her to your attention." He smiles at me.

Arliss produces a card from a small bean-shaped handbag. "Do you have representation?"

"Not at the moment."

"Now you do."

My brows shoot up. She is so sure of me and of her power, but she has a right to be as the owner of one of the most important galleries in the photography world. I'm speechless at this amazing good fortune. My reaction must be written on my face because Arliss laughs, making her seem almost approachable.

"I'll look forward to hearing from you," she says. "Do you have a website?"

"I don't have one for my landscape work."

"Good. I prefer to control how images are released."

Rick gives my arm a squeeze. "Do you have a few minutes?" he asks Arliss.

She nods.

Rick turns to me. "So how do you want the prints for your client mounted?" We've already discussed the mounting and framing of the smaller prints. I'm using museum clips because I like them and they are affordable.

"I'm going to let her decide. That's why I asked for the extra clearance around the edges—in case she wants to stretch the prints on frames."

I've already told him I'm making the delivery. He nods. "We can roll the prints into a drum. I'll lend you one." He points to a group of tube-like containers that sleeve and buckle together. They look like elongated matte-black bongo drums.

"Keep the prints flat until you leave for the airport. The UV coating makes them more flexible, but flat is always better. Unroll them as soon as you reach your destination. It's summer, so the humidity will help flatten the prints if there is any curling. It won't matter once they're mounted, anyway." He strokes his chin for a second. "Can I offer another piece of advice?"

"Go for it."

"Hand-carry the drum onto the plane. You may have to buy a seat for it, though."

"Thanks for the tip." I wonder if it would be unethical to buy a seat for the drum with one of Kit's gift cards since I doubt I'll have much use for them after this visit.

Rick packages the chapel prints, making small talk with Arliss, while keeping her at a distance so she doesn't see the pink chapel we hid from her. When he's finished, he offers to help me to the car.

We head into the June sunshine. I unlatch the back hatch so Rick can slide the drum into the storage compartment. He says, "Remember to lay those out when you get home. And Liz? This work is really, really fine. I see a lot of landscape photography. Your work is special. I'm glad to see you taking it up again."

I give him a hug. "Thank you. It's great to be excited about what I'm doing. It's been too long, you know? And Arliss Kline—*oh my God!*"

He grins. "You're on your way, Liz. I'm already looking forward to printing the very expensive prints you will be selling from here on out!"

❋

"I'll pick you up."

Kit and I are having our third conversation in the three months since I left Georgia.

"I told you, I appreciate the offer but I'm renting a car. The plane lands really late, around midnight, so I'm staying near the airport. I'll drive to the Tisdales' the next morning and meet you there."

This is the second time I've had to say this. There isn't a chance in hell I'm going to allow myself to be stranded at Willing without a car if our visit doesn't go well, even if I've agreed to spend the night there.

He blows out a breath. "Okay. You win. But will you at least meet me for breakfast before driving out to Little Hampton? I can't wait to see you."

This statement sends a tingle through me. I can't wait to see him either, but, after so many e-mails about the weather and inconsequential local news along with conspicuously little information about his inner workings, I don't know what to expect. "I'm going to have a large carrier with me. I can't leave it in the car," I say.

"We can go to Palmer's and sit in the back room. There's space to set the carrier in a corner there."

I hesitate for a second, then give in. "Okay. That should work."

Having made all the arrangements with Pamela about flying down, although I'm using one of Kit's gift cards to do it, I'd e-mailed him my plans. It seemed like a promising development that we're talking after all of those bullet points.

"And after Little Hampton, let's stay on the island. We can stroll around, have lunch, and explore. In all the time you were down here, we never got around to doing much there."

"I'll meet you in the village at 9:00."

"June twenty-fourth. Got it. Do you need directions to Palmer's?"

"I've got Google Maps."

"Sure. Forgot about that."

I can't think of anything else to say. Apparently he can't, either. The pause becomes too long, just like the wall between us. "So, I'll see you at Palmer's," I finally think to say.

"Looking forward to it, Lizzie. See you then."

✳

A technical delay in Baltimore sets me down in Jacksonville at 12:16 a.m. on Wednesday instead of 11:30 p.m., Tuesday, the arrival time on my itinerary. Keyed up by the flight and practically vibrating with anticipation about seeing Kit, the last time I tossed myself to the side of the bed facing the clock, it read a little after 2:00 a.m. Even though I'm groggy, I'm out the door at 7:45. The hotel's complimentary coffee keeps me awake for the hour's drive north.

When I came in last night, I laid the prints flat on the second bed, wishing Obie were lying there instead. Sherry's daughter is staying with him, so he has 24/7 in-home company while I'm away. He is probably missing me way less than I miss him.

At least the separation between me and my dog will be short. I'm shooting another wedding starting on Friday. I also have editing to do on the last one, so I have to head home tomorrow. I'm here mainly to enjoy Pamela's and Marshall's reactions to the prints. And, obviously, to discover what has changed between me and Kit. I'm afraid I already know the answer, so my anxiety is high. By the time I'm on the island cruising Mallery Street for a parking space, I'm vibrating with tension, as if I'd imbibed five cups of coffee rather than one.

The street is lined with restaurants and shops. The vibe is one I associate with upscale vacation destinations. I circle a couple of times before a parking spot opens up near the pier. The day was hot when I started out. A little over an hour later, the heat, compounded by heavy humidity, slaps into me as I open the car door. I've been led to believe it is more temperate on the island than on the mainland, but you can't prove it by me. The prints can't return to air conditioning fast enough. I move briskly up the street.

A block from Palmer's, sweat begins to slide down my back. I raise the flat of my hand to my forehead to flick off the moisture also gathering there. I will not look cool and collected when I greet Kit. *Great.* But then, why should my outside not match my inside?

He is sitting on the bench in front of the restaurant's narrow facade and doesn't look as hot as I feel. Maybe if you live down here you acclimate. And maybe he feels my eyes on him because he looks in my direction. Our eyes lock. His are bright with good cheer. Who knows what he sees in mine. Longing? Anxiety? Hope?

I glance away. I don't like feeling vulnerable any more than I ever have. I've vowed honesty in my dealings with Kit, but I fiddle with the drum, trying not to telegraph the jangled emotions I'm feeling.

After Roland, I promised myself I would never allow a man to make me this unsettled again—a big consideration in creating The Rules. The Rules kept me safe and would have gone on doing so if my impetuously optimistic and ever foolish heart hadn't decided to rebel.

It's no surprise that I'm working on a new set of Rules. I think they are pretty solid and might outlast the old set. Unfortunately, they are much harder to enact. I recite them quickly to keep my mind from twitching itself into idiocy.

1. Be as honest and transparent as possible.
2. Be present—don't get so caught up in my head that I discount what's in front of me.
3. Be brave enough to step into the unknown.
4. I am strong and resilient; I've survived heartbreak before. I will love again.

And, practice makes perfect, I think, darkly. Schooling my face into a pleasantly neutral expression, I lift my eyes from the drum.

Kit is working his way through the throng crowding the sidewalk between us. He's wearing a loosely woven cotton shirt open at the neck, sleeves rolled to his elbows. The shirt is untucked over slim-fitting jeans. They look new, which makes me smile.

Even in casual attire, the man remains his elegant self, upright yet at ease in his tall, supple body. The bright morning sunlight renders his shirt sheer where it isn't touching his skin, silhouetting his perfect torso.

Longing almost flattens me. My smile dissolves. I have to stand in place in order to breathe.

Kit closes in, offering his crinkly-eyed grin, and without waiting for permission pulls me into his arms. His touch is strike two, making it even harder for my lungs to pull oxygen from the air. His clean lemony sent surrounds me. I remember when he teased me about smelling like food. Both happiness and sadness roll over me as I wonder if there is any significance in his continued use of the cologne he bought, as he put it then, "in homage to my 'tastes.'"

It's not easy to stay upright for the bone-melting pleasure of being in Kit's arms. Too soon he steps away and asks, "How was the trip?"

"Easy enough." I dab my forehead with my free hand, checking the other to make sure I've still got a grip on the drum.

"Good. Glad to hear it." Kit tugs the drum away and falls into step beside me. We thread through the crowd in silence for a couple of seconds. I steal a glance at him out of the corner of my eye to find him doing the same with me. His mouth quirks. I return my focus to navigating around tourists, unable to help the smile lighting my face.

When we reach the restaurant, Kit pulls open the door. Once we are inside, he props the drum in front of him and lifts his hand to the small of my back.

The spot under his touch feels like fire. Or ice. Desire, as sharp as electrical current, zaps through my body. What should be a harmless and chivalrous gesture, one I've experienced many times before, suddenly feels as if it will incinerate me if I have to withstand the warmth of his hand invading my senses for another second.

Waiting for the receptionist to notice us, his hand rises to my shoulder and begins to brush gently back and forth, moving incrementally toward my nape. *Oh God.*

He used to do this a lot, this idle touching, as if he needed the connection and also as if he weren't conscious of his need. I stiffen. After months of yearning, suddenly, all I want is to pull away.

The restaurant is crowded and narrow, the entry tiny, and another couple is behind us waiting to be seated. There is nowhere for me to go.

What is wrong with me?

I glance at Kit. He smiles. The touching continues. If he noticed my tension, he is ignoring it. I can't decide whether what he's doing is presumption or play-acting or if he's finally done with all the damn space he needed.

Sympathizing with what he's been through doesn't prevent an overwhelming resentment for the way it has kept us apart—which likely has everything to do with my reaction to his touch.

Thankfully, the waitress arrives to lead us to a table. Kit holds the drum in front of him, as, in single file, we follow her past tables crowding the aisle.

The annex is lighter and brighter than the front room. We are seated at a corner table, which allows for Kit's promised storage spot for the drum.

Every table is occupied. The volume of talk is loud, bouncing off the plasterboard walls and hardwood floor, too loud for more than superficial conversation.

"I bet you've never experienced heat and humidity like this before in your sweet Yankee life," Kit says.

"Don't be so sure. I have relatives in Baltimore."

"Sorry, dahlin', Baltimore is not the real South. Maryland is borderland South."

"Maryland was on the losing side of the War along with the rest of the Confederacy. That makes it the South-South." I offer a smug smile while I unfold my napkin and arrange the utensils it contained on each side of my plate.

He laughs.

It's nice to know we're still masters of light banter.

"So, what are you having?" He picks up his menu. "Everything is good."

I order the shrimp and gravy omelet. Kit chooses the Vermont cheese omelet. "This is the first time I've seen Vermont cheese on a Southern menu," I remark.

"They did it for you."

I shake my head, beginning to melt into his charm. He talks about a case occupying him. I relay my good fortune in meeting Arliss. When I called her a couple of days after receiving her card, she asked for digital images to choose from and sent a contract.

"Want me to look over the contract for you?"

I consider. Elliot has reviewed it, but I'm pleased Kit is taking an interest. "That would be great. I'll forward it to you." I pull out my phone and do it then and there. I hear his phone ping.

"It sounds like you're about to get the kind of attention from the art world you deserve."

"Rick, who introduced me and Arliss, said the same thing!" I beam. "It's so exciting! I've been walking around with a big ol' grin on my face since I met her."

The waitress delivers our omelets and side orders of cheesy grits. Kit looks at his watch, then at me. "If we are going to be at the Tisdales' at 10:30, we'd better eat fast."

※

"These are just spectacular!" Pamela clasps her hands, gazing down at the chapel prints on the long table in Little Hampton's great-room.

"Very fine," Marshall concurs, patting me on the shoulder.

I grin. Kit catches my eye and winks. I wonder if he is remembering, as I am, the perfect day when I took these shots.

"I've thought about your suggestions for framing them," Pamela says. "I like the idea of a frameless mount."

"That's why I had them UV coated. You can clean the prints with a damp cloth. Do you use the frame shop off of Frederica? It has a good reputation, from what I've heard. I'd be happy to discuss the particulars with the shop if you'd like."

"That would be lovely." She smiles. "Oh, I have a terrific idea." She turns to her husband, "Marshall, let's have a party to show off Liz's photographs!"

Addressing me she says, "There are no other pink chapels on the island, but many of our friends have spectacular views as well as lovely gardens. After seeing what you've done for us, I'm sure they'll want you to photograph their properties."

"Thank you, Pamela. That's very generous. And I'd love to celebrate with you, but I'm booked with weddings every weekend into the fall. Could a weekday work for your party? I can probably get away for a midweek overnight."

"Our friends are retired just like we are. A weeknight would be fine. Not that waiting until the weather cools wouldn't be advantageous. That would allow the party to spill out onto the veranda. Will you have a weekend in the fall?" Then she says, "Shoot! I forgot. We're going to California during hurricane season to stay with Tolland. I'll e-mail, all right? We'll come up with a date sometime before the next century."

I laugh. "I'll look forward to hearing from you."

"Maybe the party can wait until you are here next winter. Although I want to hang the photographs as soon as possible."

I do my best to ignore her expectation that I'll be coming to stay again and don't look at Kit. The next twelve hours or so will likely push the decision in one direction or the other. "I will look forward to the gathering, whenever you schedule it."

Pamela nods, and gives me a pointed look. "I can be patient. I hope you feel the same way, dear."

"I do." I also feel like we are having one conversation out loud, another in the silence behind it.

Pamela and Kit's mother are friends. She must know what's going on. Maybe I'm imagining that she's rooting for me and implying patience is the key. If only the key didn't fit such a difficult lock.

"Great," the lock keeper interjects. "I'll look forward to showing Liz off. Do you want us to drop the prints at the frame shop for you?" Kit begins sliding the prints together.

"Thank you, dear. What a nice offer."

We work the prints into the drum. At the door, Pamela busses my cheek. "See you this winter, Liz," she says as she waves us off.

※

"Let's go in here." I point to a window where an impressionistic painting of a marsh sits on an easel. We are walking around Redfern Village, an area of upscale shops. "Is this the same artist who did that landscape in your brother's living room?" I ask.

"Hester Dorn," Kit confirms. "She lives on the island."

Kit holds the door for me. A blast of welcoming cool air washes over us as we enter a gallery space where ten paintings hang on bright white walls.

"These are really fine." I stop to study a landscape of a marsh on an overcast day. "Which do you like best?"

Kit pivots to study the other walls. "This one," he says, walking toward the back of the room where a large square canvas is on display. The painting is of billowing clouds in a pale morning sky, with a narrow band of marsh grass at the bottom, divided by a water channel.

"My favorite, too." The painting reminds me of the composition of my shot of clouds over blurred marsh grass, except my image isn't as sunny. "The artist has captured the coast here so well. There is so much sky, dwarfing the landscape beneath it." The identification tag next to the painting reads, *Morning Clouds*, $3,750.

"Definitely not in my price range," I say wistfully.

"Wouldn't Pamela's check cover it?" Kit asks.

"Earmarked already for other uses. But if Arliss Kline is right and my work sells in New York, I'm putting a Dorn on my splurge list."

"Life can surprise you, can't it? I bet you'll have your splurge sooner than later."

I shrug. "You never know." I wonder which way he feels life is currently trending for him. At the moment, Pamela's pleasure with my photographs and Arliss taking me on has me pretty upbeat—about my career, at least.

Kit cocks his head to study the painting anew. "Maybe I'll buy it. I've always been covetous of Sam's painting."

He catches the gallery assistant's eye. She joins us and the two of them step aside for a hushed conversation. She writes something on her pad. He hands her a business card and his American Express and returns to my side. "Let's see what's in the next room," he suggests.

It's ridiculous to feel blue because Kit can buy himself that sublime painting, while I cannot. At least I've gained the potential to sell my work to people who can afford it, which bodes well for buying art in the future, and, as Kit noted, maybe sooner than later. This thought buoys my equanimity, although being with him, I'm finding calm in short supply.

Later, in a gallery specializing in crafts, I give myself permission to spend a small amount of Tisdale money on myself, Diana, and Arielle. A wide brushed-silver cuff calls my name. It has an irregular-shaped piece of celery-green sea glass in a bezel setting at the center. The piece costs $3,500 less than Kit's painting. For Diana, I choose a pair of chunky dangle earrings made by the same artist. Arielle gets a slim silver chain with a group of small stones and sinuous silver drops dangling from a toggle ring.

Although Kit shakes his head with exasperation, arguing about whose credit card the sales girl will run, he eventually gives up and lets me pay. He doesn't understand that if he buys the bracelet and our weekend ends in disaster, the piece will be weighted with too much significance for me to enjoy wearing it. I like this cuff too much to let that happen, although there is a possibility that if our visit doesn't go well, the bracelet will be tarnished in my eyes, nevertheless.

Kit leaves the store more subdued than when he entered. I offer him a bright smile. He manages a tight lift of his lips. I think he's annoyed that I insisted on paying. After several monosyllabic responses to my conversational overtures, I give up and consider current Rule Number One—honesty. "I hope I haven't offended you," I say.

Kit swivels to face me. "I was going to ask the same."

"Not about the bracelet conversation. As to the rest, I'm not offended. Hurt, bewildered, and angry are the overriding emotions. Oh, and let's not forget frustrated. But this is all old news by now." I shut up, surprised by my outburst. On the other hand, one of us has to toss a ball over the wall separating us, so I might as well start the volley.

Kit opens his mouth to speak then closes it. No doubt it isn't his style to air his private business in the middle of a public thoroughfare. I hold his gaze.

"Okay. I deserved that." He looks away. "You already know how sorry I am about you leaving early." Reaching for my hand, as if physical contact will bridge the gap between us, he twines his fingers with mine. "I'm so glad you're here." His gaze returns. He squeezes my hand.

I squeeze back, pleased that I didn't frost up when he touched me, but then I frown. We've lost so much ground. His statement is significant for what he's left out. He didn't say he's sorry for his communication gaps, or whether he's feeling any different than he did three months ago.

Kit squeezes my hand a second time. I let the subject drop, doing my best to ignore that damn sock monkey. The nasty thing has materialized behind Kit, pretending to vomit. I'm not so oblivious that I don't know that the two of us will eventually have to deal with our situation. I point this out to my monkey-monster. As much as I'd like get the discussion over with, however, I reluctantly agree with Kit about this not being the place to do it.

"Let's head back to the village," he suggests. "We can have lunch at Grogan's or one of the other places with a view of the water, maybe take a walk on the beach since it's low tide."

"Isn't it too hot?" I ask, pulling at my damp T-shirt. "The heat and humidity are going to suffocate me. I need air conditioning."

"There will be a breeze by the water. It's cooler there."

"Relative to what?" I grumble, consulting the weather app on my phone. "It's ninety-two degrees and eighty-five percent humidity, according to this." I hold up the phone so he can see. "What will it be by the water? Eighty-eight degrees with a single percent drop in humidity?"

"So you admit Georgia isn't Maryland-hot but something else altogether?" Kit asks. "Score one for my team?"

"If you admit Baltimore is a Southern city."

"Fine, since it means so much to you. As a gentleman, I give way to the lady."

I snort. Not a ladylike sound but I'm too hot to care.

Kit laughs and loops his arm around my neck, pulling me into his side. We have a lot to talk about, but the easy kidding between us feels like progress.

❋

In the end, we decide we aren't that hungry. Buying ice cream cones, we amble onto the pier. Afterward, we walk along the beach, all the way to the Coast Guard Station, which is a mile or more away. When we return to Mallery Street, we are ready for an early dinner. Kit drives us to Echo, a beachfront restaurant. The view of the shoreline is spectacular.

Great view notwithstanding, I want to be at Willing where we can have a conversation that matters. We've spent the day in a holding pattern, a pleasant enough holding pattern, talking about our children, our work, and world news, but I can't wait for it to be over.

An hour and a half later, I follow Kit's Audi down Route 17 in the rental car. Early dusk has descended, casting the landscape in thin silver light, moss hanging ghostly gray against the dark summer-green of the oaks. I step out of the car and grab my overnight bag from the back seat. Kit takes it from my hand. He pulls out the empty drum, too. "I'm going to ship this to your photo shop, so you don't have to deal with it on the plane. Okay?"

"Thanks!" I say.

He deposits it in his trunk.

Inside the mudroom, the light is defused and soft. No surprise, I begin to shake. Kit meets my eyes. My breath catches. He drops the bag and we step into each other. It doesn't matter what is between us, or isn't; our physical connection compels us together.

Our lips meet. We kiss as if this is the first time and also like we're coming home. My hands are unsteady as I pull at his shirt, needing his skin under my hands. I touch the familiar places, his trim waist, the ridge of muscle banding his spine, the roll of his ribs, his nipples.

Pulling my top off and bra straps down, Kit groans, his mouth never leaving mine as his palms shape my breasts. I unzip his jeans and push them, along with his briefs, to his knees. We moan in unison when I wrap my hand around him. He reaches under my skirt. I'm drenched.

I want to bottle this moment, to savor it and keep it close, my thoughts moving from the present to a future that may be without him. But I pull myself into my body, into the moment. Lifting onto my toes, I rub myself against Kit's erection. He bends, pushing between my legs. Frantic to feel him inside me, I pull my panties to the side.

He thrusts, filling me. His forearms under my thighs, Kit carries me to the bench. I settle on his lap, my arms wrapped around his neck for balance. He kisses me again. I love him so much. So desperately. I feed my desperation into a kiss that goes on and on, while his fingers find my clit. I grind down.

Seconds later, clenching around him, the orgasm begins. It's quick and explosive and takes me apart. Kit throws his head back, groans, his arms wrapping tightly around me as he spends.

I rest my cheek against his chest, placing a kiss over his heart. I don't know whether the intensity of what we just did means anything or nothing.

A minute later, Kit pulls away. He looks . . . he looks sad.

"Was it as good for you as it was for me?" I joke, because I'm suddenly afraid "no" is the answer, and using humor to defend myself is a habit I've yet to break.

Kit smooths my hair. "It was better for me." He raises his brows, daring me to contradict him. When I don't, he looks at where we remain joined. "Things are about to get messy," he says.

And not only down there, I think.

We spend a comical minute inching toward my pocketbook and the tissues inside, with the predictable result that we both need to change our clothes. Kit suggests I go upstairs, he'll bring us nightcaps.

I retire to his bathroom with my overnight bag. The nightgown I change into is a strappy bias-cut shift made of cotton lawn. Transparent enough to tease, it stays on the subtle side of sexy.

Kit is in bed when I return, propped on pillows with the sheet discreetly pulled to his navel. Two glasses of whiskey and water sit on the side table next to the bed. I assume he used the bathroom on the opposite side of the hall because when I bend to kiss him, he tastes of mint as well as whiskey.

Instead of climbing in on the other side of the bed, I sit down beside him, forcing him to scoot over to make room. He lets his long sheet-covered thigh rest against mine.

I sip, allowing myself a few seconds to enjoy the view. I have photographed Kit in bed, though I haven't been able to look at the images since I returned home. Pushing a breath out with an audible hiss, I set my glass on the night table. Usually smooth, the whiskey burns its way down my throat.

"Hey," Kit says. "Earth to Lizzie." He touches the gown where it's ridden up. His fingertips follow the hemline, tracing a diagonal path from knee to inner thigh, his gaze on the skin he reveals.

I cover his hand to keep it from moving higher because as lovely as it would be to make love with him a second time tonight, I need to know a few things first.

"Why am I here, Kit?" I ask.

"To deliver the photographs to Marshall and Pamela." He offers a smart-ass smile.

I push his hand off my thigh.

"Come on, Lizzie." He sighs. "I was teasing. You're here because I missed you and I hope because you missed me."

I like this answer better. He carries my hand, curled in a fist, to his lips and kisses the soft underside at the wrist. When he's finished, he rubs his cheek against the skin he kissed, breathing me in. "I've missed your smell," he murmurs.

I shudder. My fingers uncurl. Kit's tongue flicks, dragging into the center of my palm. Attempting to ignore his seduction, I say, "I think we should talk."

"Oh, we're are talking, we're just not using a whole lot of words."

"Are men deliberately obtuse or is it a natural phenomenon?" I murmur, loud enough for him to hear. I pull away and prop elbows on knees, dropping my cheek into my hand.

"Isn't being together enough for now?"

Weighing my vow to stay in the present against this concept, I straighten. With my initial hunger for him appeased, no, it isn't enough. "I need to know what you want, Kit. What you want. Not just right now, but tomorrow and maybe even several tomorrows after that."

"*Right now*," he says tightly, "I want to sleep with you."

"Sleeping with me isn't what this is about and you know it."

His hand slides through his hair. I give him time, but he doesn't offer a countering argument.

"How about I'll tell you what I want? I want what we had last spring, before you changed your mind."

"Stay with me tonight. We can talk in the morning." Cupping my neck, Kit pulls me closer. Our lips meet, and then our tongues. He hugs me tight. He wants me, and I love him, so when he tilts us into the sheets, I go. I want to forget about trust and distrust, about tomorrow rather than simply right now.

I close my eyes, concentrating on the feel of him under my hands, on the whiskey taste of his kiss, but my mind refuses to disengage. Hiding my face in the curve of his neck, I breathe in. Kit smells delicious, like lemony cologne and arousal and himself. I want to be drugged by his kisses and shattered by his touch. *I want to stop thinking.* And, I want to take him into my body and glory in his cry when he comes.

Yet, I remain separate and sentient and alone. Rolling onto my back with a shuddering breath, I turn my gaze to meet his questioning look.

"I need to know what is going on with you. I need to know if anything has changed," I state.

"I love you," Kit answers, but he looks away. "Lizzie," he says to the ceiling, "I just want us to enjoy tonight. We'll talk in the morning." He lays his hand over mine. Only a few inches of mattress separate us, but I might as well be in Vermont for the emotional distance I need to travel to reach him.

"Why can't you talk to me? The conversation we had before I left might not have been a happy one, but at least we were communicating."

He sighs. A couple of seconds pass in silence. Finally he says, "Because I don't know myself anymore." He looks at me. "Do you remember when we were sitting on the chapel steps and I said I didn't know how to let myself love again?"

"But you managed it didn't you? What happened between us wasn't all my imagination!"

"You know it wasn't." He blows out a breath and knots his fists against his forehead. "I guess the lights came on, then went out again. I can't figure out why, and the switch to turn them on for good is eluding me."

I squeeze my eyes shut against my worst fear. Once I've mastered myself, I say, "I want you to be happy, Kit. I hoped you could be happy with me." Rising on my arms, I lean over and kiss him on the lips.

He wraps his arms around me. "I love you, Lizzie, but I'm locked up, or locked out, or—*God!*—I just don't know!" He releases me, sits up, and drops his head into his hands.

Scooting over to sit next to him, I rest my palm on his back. "Do you think this is what Eleanor would have wanted for you?" I ask. "Do you think she wouldn't want you to love someone new, the way you loved her? To not always be alone?" These thoughts, held inside me since I left here in April, have finally forced their way out.

Kit stiffens. Then he stands. He shoves his arms into the sleeves of his robe, and stalks out. A few seconds later, I hear the outside door bang shut.

I don't go after him. I remind myself that Kit shuts down when his emotions are raw. The clock ticks. A few minutes later I hear him come inside, but he stays downstairs. Should I go to him? Or remain where he's left me?

My heart pounds. *I wasn't unkind or disrespectful.* I consider my judgmental tendencies and whether I've been doing some extreme judging here. I don't think so. I am frustrated beyond bearing by his inability to understand the structural composition of the wall between us. That frustration pushed me to say what I felt.

I truly believe Eleanor wouldn't want Kit to worship at her shrine for the rest of his life to the exclusion of a fulfilling relationship. Eleanor would understand that falling in love with another woman honors the love Kit felt for her.

I don't know how to make him understand he can love her and me, and only gain by the experience. Plumping my pillow, I toss myself onto it.

Making her first appearance in months, the Victorian joins Eleanor's ghost inside my head. It's a strange pairing. The Victorian notes that I haven't been in charity with Darius since he tried to make me face truths I didn't want to acknowledge, so why am I surprised Kit feels the same way about what I'm trying to force on him?

I admit she's right, calculating that the odds of Kit returning to bed are slim. Pulling the covers over my shoulders, I curl onto my side. An hour later, giving up on sleep, I hear the clock chime midnight. The tomorrow I can't accept—a tomorrow without Kit—has arrived.

CHAPTER 36

WHEN I WALK into the kitchen, the microwave's clock reads 6:30. I need to be out of here at 7:30 at the very latest to drive to Jacksonville for my 9:55 flight. Kit is wrapped in his robe, standing by the windows, coffee cup in hand. His eyes are as red rimmed and shadowed as mine. With a grim nod in his direction, I pour coffee into the mug he's left out for me and add milk.

From the look of the bare kitchen counters, his interest in food is on par with my own. We sip our coffee in silence. A few excruciatingly awkward minutes go by. Kit puts his empty mug in the dishwasher and offers to put my overnight bag in the car, the first words either of us has managed since our fight last night.

When he returns, he stands in the doorway rubbing the back of his neck.

"I hope you don't play poker," I say, "because that neck thing telegraphs how you feel about the cards in your hand."

"I don't gamble," he says without humor.

I set my mug on the counter.

Kit pushes away from the door. He shakes his head. "I'm sorry. I don't mean to be sharp." He comes to stand at my side, resting his butt against the counter, an improvement in togetherness, if staring at the same four feet of floor counts as togetherness.

"Liz, I need to apologize for last night. Walking out on you wasn't my finest moment." He knocks his shoulder gently into mine.

"I'm sorry for what I said, too." Not so much for the truth of my words, but for how upsetting they were to him.

"No. I needed to hear it." He frowns. "And, I need to tell you something you aren't going to like, so I'd be grateful if you would hold your fire and hear me out."

At this point I don't think there is any news worse than what I already know, although his admission sparks a twinge of hope. I nod that yes, I'm listening.

He steps in front of me and regards me gravely. "After you left in April, I was confused about how I felt. I was stalled and trying to figure out why. I'd been alone for years and managed it fine until you came along. And when you left, I just—" He reaches out to caress my cheek, but rethinks the idea and lets his hand drop. "The truth is, Lizzie, I found it easier to go back to the way things were before."

Maybe, because it isn't a surprise, even if it is as I feared, I don't cry or shake or fall on the floor. I think for a few seconds, and Kit gives me the space to do it.

"Then why keep e-mailing?" I sigh. "Why extend the invitation to visit?"

"The e-mails? I don't know." He shakes his head. "I guess I couldn't quite say good-bye." His hand rises, but once again, he hesitates midgesture, then drops both hands into his robe pockets.

"After Pamela mentioned she was trying to convince you to deliver the prints rather than mail them, I couldn't stop thinking about you. I needed to know if seeing you would change my feelings."

"I guess it didn't," I say quietly, and because I can't help myself, I reach out to lay my palm over his heart.

He covers my hand with his own. "No, Liz, this is my long-winded way of telling you it absolutely mattered. It's just—" He shakes his head.

"The thing is, and I'm sure you know this from your own losses, trying to survive without Eleanor was—" He swallows. "I don't have words to describe what it was like to lose the person who was my center. I was lost for a long time. It took years to regain any equilibrium. Eventually I managed by following a pretty rigid script. But when I fell in love with you, I tossed the script out the window. Last night, I finally realized that for the last eight years, all these years Eleanor's been gone, I haven't been as content as I believed, although I also didn't feel a lot of pain."

"What I did with my Rules," I say.

"Pardon?"

"I had rules, you had a script." I wrinkle my brow, considering. "When I met you, I was in the same place you seem to be in now. I was ready for a change, but not sure how to get there."

He nods. "But you figured it out. I see the problem, but don't know how to fix it." This time, he cannot resist touching me. His fingers skim my hairline, knocking a few strands back into place. "What I do know is that I have been fooling myself for the past three months. The minute I saw you on Mallery Street, I knew I couldn't let you walk out of my life a second time."

"Why didn't you tell me this last night?"

"Admitting what I've been going through seemed like a guaranteed way to lose you. But, this morning I figured I'd probably lost you already, so I might as well tell the truth."

"Thank you." My voice cracks.

"Lizzie, am I asking too much for you to be patient a while longer?" His voice is gruff with suppressed feeling.

My eyes squeeze shut and suddenly I'm fighting tears. "I want to be patient," I choke, "but I'm not very good at so much waiting, although the fact that you've finally shared what you've been going through gives me hope." I offer a tremulous smile, and curl my fist into the terry of his robe. "Is there anything I can do to help speed you a long? Because I'm a fan of speed."

Kit's eye's light. "I love it when you're funny about difficult things. And if you have any tips for finding that switch, I'd appreciate them."

"I'm being serious."

"Oh, I get that, too." He sets his hands on my shoulders and leans in to kiss my forehead.

"I wish I did know how to help. For me, it just happened when I met you." This is a loaded statement, because obviously meeting me wasn't open sesame for him.

But he only says, "You can help by not giving up on me, Liz. I'm not whole, as I'm sure you're aware. I don't know if I'll ever be, but I owe it to us to find out if I can get closer to that line."

As Kit plants a sweet kiss on my lips that promises to be more, his pocket vibrates.

"Damn." He reaches between us for his phone. "I set the alarm as the five minutes-and-counting bell. You need to leave if you don't want to rush for your flight."

"We're not done with this conversation!"

"Then miss your plane."

"I wish I could, but I can't blow off my clients." I step out of his arms. "I love you, Kit, but it's time for me to go."

"Give me more time, Liz?"

I rub my eyes. "This may sound demanding, but I need deeds to go along with your words."

"I'm calling the therapist I saw after Eleanor died. I'm doing it today."

My eyes widen. "That's big. Good for you. It's probably time." This remark may be a little too honest and sound condescending, but screw it, that's how I feel.

Instead of being insulted, Kit relaxes his shoulders and quirks his mouth. "Spoken like the honest, brave, spunky, Jewish, Yankee woman I love." He swoops in to lift me off my feet.

"Mr. Couper, I warn you," I say when he puts me down, "there is a lot of ornery woman in that description."

"Trust me, Ms. Silver, I'm committed to making this work."

I nod, but my skepticism doesn't stand down. I've waited three months for him while he was working himself out of love with me, and now I'm supposed to wait who knows how much longer.

He kisses the tip of my nose.

"The ball is in your court, mister," I tell him and pull his head down for a quick and final kiss.

"In our court," he corrects, as I move away.

"You need to come to Vermont." I pick up my handbag from the counter.

His mouth twists. "Since I hadn't planned on it—"

My expression must telegraph my feelings.

"Look, I messed up." He lifts his hands. "So, among the other major things I need to do is clear a few days from my schedule so I can come up during the week when you aren't shooting."

"Come for my birthday. It's six weeks away. I'm planning a party on August 17. That's a Sunday; the only one I have free until late September. Be my best birthday present ever."

"I'd like to be there."

"Then do it."

Kit gives me a sharp look, obviously hearing the doubt in my tone.

If he is truly committing himself to a relationship with me, he needs to show up. I think he knows it, too.

I yawn; sleep deprivation, adrenaline, and a pileup of mixed emotions are flattening my get-up-and-go. I slide limply into the car.

"Are you okay to drive?" Kit asks.

"I'm pretty sure this morning has me jangled enough to keep me awake to the airport, if not all the way home."

"I'd be happy to take you. I can get the rental back later."

"You're sweet, but I'm fine. I'll sleep on the plane."

He bends into the car and kisses me on the cheek. Shutting the door he says, "I'll see you soon, dahlin'. Count on it."

CHAPTER 37

"WHAT DO YOU THINK of the invitation?" I ask Arielle. I've opened a draft of the birthday party invite I plan to send this afternoon. It's a close-up of a sweating whiskey on the rocks, a picture I snapped quickly yesterday for this purpose. I've already told my friends to hold the date, so the e-mail will be mostly a reminder. I scroll to the message.

FROM: LSilverphotography@gmail.com
TO: <Distribution>
SUBJECT: Birthday on repeat

Although I've tried to prevent it, my birthday rolls around each and every year, although the celebrations are less frequent. This year the two collide.

Please join me Sunday afternoon at 2:00 p.m., August 17, to celebrate the forty-seventh time this date has come and gone during my existence down here on planet Earth. Celebrate the auspicious day with me and my many summer-born friends, making this a five-star celebration. Karl, Janey, Amy, and Geoff, expect your own candles, although I'll leave it up to you to divulge your years on the planet.

Owing to my winter sojourn, the theme is Southern, as is the liquor. I'm stockin' plenty of bourbon and whiskey, y'all. Barbecued chicken, ribs, corn and black-eyed-pea salad, tomatoes, and biscuits round out the menu. Peach shortcake (more biscuits) with a whole lot o' whipped cream for dessert.

No presents. Your presence is the present.
RSVP please. We need to know how many platters to fill.
See y'all here—
XOXO Liz

"I like it. I'm glad you're having the party. I was afraid you would mope the summer away," Arielle says.

"I save my moping for bedtime."

She pats my shoulder. "A little moping is healthy."

Since my return two weeks ago, Kit's e-mails have doubled in frequency. They are chattier, too. In his last message, he broke the bank with seven bullet points. One of his points was three sentences long! While he hasn't called, the subject matter of his missives continues to center around the weather, but he's also mentioned some day-to-day activities, although not what he's thinking or feeling. For Kit, I suspect, this is a giant leap forward. To me, it seems more like a baby toddle forward. The one personal thing he's shared is that he called the therapist the day I left and has seen him twice already. To me, that's a way bigger deal than e-mail frequency or content.

"I did think about canceling the party, but I figure acting *as-if* might be the best therapy." I swivel to face Arielle.

"Good thinking. And I'm here to help. Speaking of which—I talked with Diana and we have the prep covered. She said Marc will also arrive a day early to help."

"She mentioned that. Thank you for taking charge. I planned the weekend to be free, but I couldn't resist taking on a last-minute anniversary party since it only involves Saturday afternoon."

"For once, you won't be throwing your own party. Diana and I think that's a good thing."

I shrug. "I don't have any complaints about how full my shooting schedule is this summer, but it's left little room for party planning or leisure."

"Or moping," Arielle says. "Don't forget to emphasize the positive."

"There's always a yin to go with the yang, right?"

An e-mail alert pings. Kit's name shows up on the notifications panel. My stomach flips. "Speak of the devil," I say.

"The object of mopedom," Arielle comments, which makes me laugh.

"Want to place bets on how many bullet points in this one?" I ask.

"I'm more interested in meeting him."

My stomach flips again. "He said he'd make that happen for my birthday."

I shift to face the computer and click on Kit's e-mail.

No mention of his visit. He's forwarded an article that mentions Vermont and the Sea Islands of Georgia.

"It's early days yet," I sigh, "but since he's decided he wants to pursue a relationship . . . I don't know. Instead of feeling more optimistic, I'm feeling more detached."

"That's weird."

"I guess. As much as he says he is ready to try, there were those months of not trying. Plus, you know me, patience is more your virtue than mine. I want to be with him. All it takes is the sound of an e-mail ping and hope spikes—Pavlov's dogs have nothing on me. But he lives there. I live here. I'm ready, while he is not. I believe both of us wish it were otherwise, but it is what it is." I cross my arms.

"Huh. Remember my idea about him being the practice guy? I'll be sorry if it turns out to be true." She lets the thought hang.

"All I know is the suspense is killing me, and it's only been two weeks since I saw him."

Arielle points to the e-mail. "Click on the link."

The *Washington Post* article is about wedding destinations.

"Interesting," she says. "Seems like he's not shy about the subject of marriage."

"Did you spend the morning gardening? You must be sun-addled if you think Kit sent this for any reason other than the coincidence that it mentions Vermont, specifically Lake Champlain, Stowe, and the Manchester area, as well as the Golden Isles."

I close his e-mail and hit Send on the birthday invite.

✳

Two weeks after the invitation went out, all the RSVPs have arrived except Kit's. Tim, my videographer, and his wife, Vanessa, will be at the

Cape that weekend. Sherri has another party but hopes to drop in late-ish with her kids. Ryan and Harold, my musician friends, will be touring in Europe. Mel wrote to say she and Ham will be there, although the boys are all busy, including C., who won't be home to visit for another couple of weeks. I'll be feeding nineteen, if Kit shows as promised. That he might not sits like a lead ball in my stomach.

Call me as Victorian as my mother, but when an invitation asks for a response, the inviter should not be forced to track her invitee down. In a less-courtesy-driven modern world than my mother's, *Répondez s'il vous plaît* no longer means say yes or no. Saying nothing is also an option whereupon the invited hedge their bets until the last possible moment, when it doesn't mean no. The party is barely two weeks away. The day before yesterday, I gave in and e-mailed Kit about his itinerary. His nonresponse has me riled, as well fearful that he is backpedaling again.

Opening yet another image from the Thompson-Ivvy wedding I shot last weekend, I begin correcting the usual flaws. When an e-mail alert pings, my eyes immediately shift to the message panel.

Maybe I'm not as detached as I suggested to Arielle. The message isn't from Kit. My stomach returns to its normal position.

A musical phrase, the one for the *Jaws* shark's approach, sounds from my phone. I assigned the ringtone to Arliss. It seemed appropriate. There is just something about her no-nonsense, no-humor approach that triggers humor in me. Everyone else in my phone directory gets the old-fashioned dial phone ringtone, even Kit. Especially Kit.

He returned Arliss's contract a couple of days after I arrived home, saying it seemed fine, although he added some language defining media rights. Meanwhile, Arliss chose four images from the assortment I sent her for consideration: the house with the wisteria, the blurred grass above the overcast sky, a shot I took on a solo trip to Sapelo Island with moss swaying from oak branches above palmettos, and the glowing ball of mist rising out of the meadow at Willing.

I pick up the phone and say hello.

"Please hold for Arliss Kline," the male voice on the other end intones. I find this so silly, but Arliss is a busy woman. Having her assistant dial her calls and forcing the rest of us to wait while she comes on line emphasizes just how busy *and* important she is.

"Lizbeth," she says. "How are you?"

"Fine. And you?" I've learned not to elaborate with her.

"Business is excellent."

It didn't take long to figure out that if business is good, Arliss is good, body and soul—although I'm not sure she has a soul, and she's reduced her body to its most compact form possible.

Courtesies observed, she says, "Some of that good business belongs to you. I've already sold two of your prints. Congratulations."

"That's fantastic! I never thought they'd go so fast."

"Your images are singular and fill a niche. They are beautiful and also a little bit Southern gothic without being altogether sinister. Beauty always sells." She sounds as if she wished it didn't. "So," she says more brightly, "I'll need more from you. Also, I'd like to see the wisteria house in black and white. Do you have a different angle on it?"

"As it happens, I have it without the vines blooming. I'll get the file to Rick to print. You should have it by middle of next week."

"Good. Your check will go out shortly."

"Can I ask the amount?"

"Minus commission, $3,073. And Lizbeth? I assume you have been working in Vermont. I'd like to see those images, as well." She doesn't wait for me to affirm her assumption before disconnecting. I wonder if she treats her famous photographers in the same no-nonsense, no-charm way. Not that it matters, really. She is honorable and very good at what she does, and I am grateful beyond words for what she's doing for me. The prestige of being represented by Arliss is huge. Some of the value of art is based on prestige, as well as fashion. I couldn't command prices like these without her representation.

After I put the phone down, I sit for a moment absorbing my good fortune, not only the money, but also that people find my images gripping enough to pay substantial sums for them. I grin, and then, like Obie when he's given a big peanut butter biscuit, I jump up and dance around my office. Obs scrambles to his feet, trying to figure out what's going on.

"This time, Doggerel, life isn't just okay; it's better, better, better than okay!" I dance into the kitchen to give him a treat. Why should I be the only one having fun? When I return to the office, I plop into my chair and spin. My glee not yet exhausted, I pick up the phone and dial Arielle, who says she's coming over with a bottle of champagne as soon as she's finished unmolding the bowls she made this afternoon.

Next, I call Diana, who screams her excitement into my ear. I even call my mother, who manages to congratulate me without comparing my accomplishment to Henry's accumulated accolades. When she says good-bye, I make one last call . . . to Kit.

"Couper Clairborne," Kit's assistant answers.

"Is Mr. Couper in? Tell him Lizbeth Silver is on the line."

A second later Kit picks up. "Lizzie!"

The sound of his voice clogs my throat.

"Liz?" Kit says again. "Is everything all right?"

"Arliss sold two of my Georgia photographs," I blurt.

"That's wonderful!"

"It's almost hard for me to believe that a year ago I didn't have a creative spark left in my head and didn't know where I'd find one. Yet here I am, selling my very fine work"—I laugh at my bravado—"at the most important photo gallery in New York! Cause for celebration, don't you think? We'll have a special, private celebration when you arrive. When are you flying in?" I'm so giddy, I've forgotten he hasn't confirmed he's coming.

There is a second of silence. "I've been meaning to call you."

"And?" I prompt, hoping this isn't what I think it is.

"I'm sorrier than I can say, Liz, but I can't make the party. I have to testify in a land dispute and the hearing is early that following Monday morning. I can't change the court schedule."

Buoyed by today's good fortune, I don't immediately despair. I say, "They couldn't take your deposition?"

"I did attempt to get out of it." Again, a small hesitation before he says, "Then, Levi decided to drive down for the weekend with his recently acquired girlfriend, whom I haven't met. I'm really sorry, Liz. I'm working on coming to Vermont in early September."

Something inside me snaps. I swear I hear it go. But I am preternaturally calm as I ask, "When did you know all this?"

He sighs. "Why is that important?"

"Never mind," I say. "What is important is that another of your promises wasn't a promise after all."

"I said I'd try," he says defensively.

"You said 'Okay.' And then you said, 'I'll see you soon, dahlin'. Count on it.' Your exact words. I took that as a promise."

"I tried, Liz. And I'm working on early September."

"I don't think you're ever coming."

"Lizzie, come on. I'll be there, only not for your birthday. We'll have a special celebration all our own."

I think about this and decide that sure, we could, but I'm at my limit.

"You know what? For all that your e-mails are more frequent and a little more chatty, we haven't had a meaningful conversation since I delivered the Tisdales' prints almost two months ago. There was a big gap before that, too, as I'm sure you remember." I stand and pace through the dining room. "I know I shouldn't be so upset, but when I left the island the first time, you said you knew your own mind, *after* telling me you needed a little space to assimilate your feelings. Then you decided it was easier not to bother. I'll grant that you said you were calling a therapist and did, a step I laud, but you also implied you would visit *for my birthday*."

"We'll talk about this when I get there."

"Will you have anything different to say? Has anything changed?" My hand covers my mouth. Having paced myself into the living room,

I plop down on the couch, trying to calm my thoughts. Apparently nothing has changed because Kit is silent. I let out a shaky breath.

"I hope seeing a therapist is helpful to you. But I—" I break off again. "I think it's my turn for a time-out. I can't keep hoping, Kit. I just can't."

"Dahlin', I'm coming. I promise. We'll talk. It's only going to be an extra couple of weeks."

"Please, Kit. No more promises. We're out of sync with each other. We need to accept that I'm ready for more than you can handle right now. We need to stop doing this dance." My voice breaks. "I know I should keep hoping. I should believe in you. But, the same way you can't seem to figure out how to let yourself love me heart and soul, I can't endure waiting for it to happen."

"Lizzie," Kit says. "Stop this."

"We're in a holding pattern and it needs to change. So, I'm changing it. Don't come here—not ever—unless you've found the right switch. Until that happens, I'd rather we aren't in touch." My voice is so rough it's little more than a whisper as I say, "I love you, Kit, but I can't do this anymore. I know it's not fair, but it's how I feel."

Is this the stupidest thing I've ever done or the smartest? I don't know. I only know that as full of renewed creative purpose as I've become, I'm empty of hope that Kit will find his way out of the dark, as valiantly as he may be trying. Even if he were to show up, if he hasn't decided he can love me without Eleanor's ghost getting in his way, there's no point.

"Liz!" Kit says sharply.

I choke out, "Godspeed, Kit." Before I can change my mind, I disconnect, and then I put my head in my hands and sob.

❈

When I'm completely wrung out, I text Arielle that I'm not feeling well and let's celebrate tomorrow. We will be having a wake when she shows up, but I can't deal with communicating that to her right now.

Upstairs, in the drawer of my bedside table, there's a lone Xanax I've been hoarding for the right catastrophe. I drag myself up to get it, padding over the rugs I laid in April after returning from Georgia. It took me a while to appreciate their loveliness unencumbered by the feelings evoked when Darius gifted them to me.

I fetch the Xanax and return downstairs. As I pass through the living and dining rooms a second time, I think about the rugs; their beauty is eternal, even if the person who gifted them to me was not as constant.

At my desk, I swallow the pill, staring at the jade plant and its seductive friend. Both seem to be thriving. I have no idea why. At the moment, the orchid and its obviousness offends me. I share my water with both plants anyway. Darius's rugs have sparked an idea. So has the orchid, which lives contentedly with or without my love or censure.

I type "Hester Dorn paintings" into the Google search window and hit Go. I'm thrilled to discover a website and scroll through the paintings available for sale, with prices upon request. I choose two, both with low slivers of landscape and a lot of sky. I'll make my final choice after I hear from the artist. Opening a contact link, I type my request.

When Kit bought his painting in June, I made a promise to myself that if circumstances allowed, I too would buy a Dorn.

I'm having another good year in the wedding business. The check from Arliss should arrive this week. I banked most of the Tisdales' payment. I'm optimistic about my financial well-being, even if I can't be optimistic about Kit. I swear to myself that I won't cry every time I look at the painting I'm about to purchase even if it reminds me of my former lover.

Arielle is right. I'm more resilient than I used to be. Yet, I wonder, if I am as strong as she thinks, why can't I wait a little longer for him? I guess because Kit has had five months to show up and couldn't manage it. And, he made promises he didn't keep. Not one, but three. People who don't keep their word are a sore point with me. Does that make me wrong? *No,* the Victorian whispers proudly, *it makes you like me.*

"I don't think so," I tell her. "It makes me like me, for good or bad, probably a little of each. And I *really* need someone to keep faith with me right now."

And, since no one else is volunteering, it looks like the only person willing to do the job is me.

Maybe this is the lesson Zeus had in mind, and not the one about being careful about dissing May-December relationships. I'd thought I was taking charge of my own happiness during the years between Roland and Kit, enjoying men without the pain love has the potential to deliver. What I didn't understand was that I left a level of joy—the level I apparently need—out of the equation.

Maybe the lesson is to keep the promises I make to myself and to believe in love—only not in love with Kit. If so, it is a hard and painful lesson.

CHAPTER 37

A BRIGHT BLUE 4 X 4 is parked in front of my house a month later when Obie and I return from our walk. I recognize the vehicle. It belongs to the Larkins.

I've been in an antisocial mood since I told Kit not to contact me. He didn't quite uphold the letter of the law when he sent me a huge arrangement of dahlias and delphiniums and fancy chrysanthemums for my birthday, which made me hope he would ignore the rest of what I'd said and show up.

He didn't. And if he was going to show up two weeks later, he hasn't. He's either as stuck as ever and honoring what I asked of him, or he's lost patience with me, the same way I've lost patience with him.

The point of letting Kit go was to stop living in limbo and move on. Instead, not only do I long for him, I've compounded the longing with the fear that if there had been a chance for us, I've destroyed it. Knowing I have probably hurt him is like . . . is there a reverse metaphor for icing on a cake? Sludge under mud?

The flowers made me wonder if all hope was not lost. The bouquet arrived without a message other than "To: Liz" and "From: Kit." I've heard nothing since. Maybe I should have done more than send him two words of my own upon receipt, one bullet point: Thank you.

I don't know. I will probably never know.

Obie and I turn up the walk, my resistance to visitors softening when I see C. unfold himself from a wicker porch chair. He meets us midway between the house and the sidewalk.

"Hey, Liz," he says and smiles.

I haven't had a glimpse of him since last summer. My dark mood lifts a little. "Hey, yourself."

He bends to greet Obie, who has muscled past me to lean into his friend. C. scrubs Obs behind the ears, adding a couple of thumps to his ribs for good measure. If the dog were a cat, he'd purr. Instead, he grins at me as C. scratches up and down his spine. In homage, Obie sweeps his tongue across our long-lost visitor's cheek.

Wiping at his face, C. straightens. He looks meaningfully into my eyes. "I've missed you a lot, Liz. It's been too long."

I cannot begin to guess whether this opening gambit is truth or smarm, since he's always been charming in his goofy, overconsidered way. It's been more than a year since our adventure together, however, so I question how much I know about the current iteration of this young man, as well as how much he has or hasn't missed me.

"It's lovely to see you, too, C."

He nods, a forward ducking of his head.

Bringing a hand up to shield my eyes from the sun's glare, I look him over. His hair has grown out, falling to mid-shoulder in golden waves. I've always loved C. in long hair. I decide his jaw is more chiseled, on the way to losing its boyish softness. There is an increased breadth to his shoulders, as well. They strain the fabric of his white T-shirt.

His manufactured ease is the same, yet I sense a low hum of energy I don't remember.

Whatever the differences, including internal changes not manifest to an exterior inspection, the cumulative effect is that C. is less boyishly beautiful than before. He's beginning to look like a man—a very fetching man, who is no less desirable than his former iteration.

My old attraction to him slides between my legs.

It seems indecent to desire another man so soon after saying goodbye to Kit, a thought that dulls my interest in C. under the ache of loss.

I say, "When I saw your mom and dad at the party, they mentioned you'd be up." I'm curious about how C.'s life has progressed past the big-picture outline supplied by his mother.

"I drove up yesterday. Sorry I missed the party. I would have liked to have been there." He smiles and shrugs, shy with me in a way he wasn't the last time we were together. The inability to draw easy conversation out of him is another change. My assessment alters: His essential breezy C.-ness seems diminished, as does his knowing intellectual sparkle.

Perhaps all I'm sensing is a new maturity weighing him down, but I feel the need to investigate. "So, you're home for a visit before school starts."

"We're slow at the gallery. Our customers are just returning from their summer places, so David, DLG's owner, gave me time off. I don't have to be at school yet. Incoming freshmen are on campus now, but the rest of us don't return for another week."

"It's nice that you're getting a little extra time to relax before school ramps up." I wonder if he's having girl trouble. I bet the current version of the man I took to bed has only to stand in one spot for a couple of minutes before women begin to line up, although there remains enough of the geeky-boy about him to make friendships more likely among his brainiac brethren than the more typical bar-and-bed-hopping kids in his age bracket.

Obie, sitting politely at C.'s feet, has been tilting his head at me or C., depending on who has the conversational volley. He stands and shakes himself. I let his lead play out. He trots the rest of the way up the walk, throwing a glance over his shoulder—standard poodle body language for *Are you coming or what?*

Taking Obie's cue, I ask, "Do you have time to come in?"

C. nods. The look I see in his eyes confirms my intuition that his visit is about more than nostalgic small talk and the beverage of his choice.

In the living room, he pauses to notice the Dorn I've hung over the sofa in a defiant attempt at desensitization therapy. Like the bracelet, the painting is all I'll ever have, even at a distance, of Kit. No surprise, he didn't need to purchase the bracelet for me to consider tucking it into the back of the drawer with the gifts from Roland, a too-vivid reminder of a dream unrealized.

I am, nevertheless, determined to ignore the bracelet's connotations and wear it, just as I finally gave Roland's gifts to a friend who is an eBay queen. We're going to split the profits.

Kit was absolutely right: He is not Roland. And, as it turns out, I am not the woman I was five years ago when Roland left me. I learned from Darius that feelings should be allowed to fade, while good artwork remains forever potent. Someday, my lovely Dorn will spark positive memories of my career-changing trip to Georgia. Unfortunately, right now, "someday" is far in the distance.

"I don't remember this canvas. It's good," C. says with new gallery-assistant authority.

"Yes," I sigh, glancing at the painting, "it is." I'd bought the one with the sunnier sky, for obvious reasons.

"There's a story," C. comments, turning to meet my eyes. Something in the tone of my response must have alerted him that all is not right.

"Isn't there always a story?" I say, remembering Kit and his offer of a story the night after I arrived in Georgia. *Oh God.*

"And?" C. says.

"How about we talk about it later?" I suggest, moving ahead of him through the dining room and into the kitchen. "I need to give Obie his treat." The implication is that we will discuss the painting after I deal with my dog. What I really hope is that C. will forget about it entirely.

He leans into the counter watching me, looking not exactly tense, but not exactly relaxed either.

"What do you want to drink?" I glance at the clock. "As usual, this is a Scotch-free zone but I have iced tea. And wine. Or I could make gin and tonics."

"Whiskey?" C. suggests. Rocking on his heels, hands in his jeans pockets he adds, "Whiskey is my new drink."

My face must not look right because he quickly interjects, "A gin and tonic would be great."

"I'm sorry. I'm out of whiskey." I try to correct what my expression betrayed.

I'm lying about the whiskey. But the Jack Daniel's, the house brand at C.'s and at Willing, is tucked away on a back shelf in the pantry. I can no longer bear continuity in my cocktails, and C.'s request reminds me too much of what I've lost.

An object or gesture—a thick-bottomed tumbler, the turn of a stranger's wrist, the scent of lemons, or the way shadows streak across grass—can plunge me into memory and grief.

A bottle of Jack Daniel's has become a reliable trigger; hence it's banishment. I'm not sure why my bracelet and the Dorn, though both are triggers, haven't proven as potent. Maybe because the bracelet was my own purchase and never worn in Kit's company. And, although his brother has a Dorn in his living room, the one Kit bought was incidental to our courtship. It hadn't been delivered before I left. The Jack Daniel's, on the other hand, was different—we flirted and fell in love over our almost nightly whiskey. Since neither of us has an alcohol problem, it is mildly amusing that so much alcohol sloshed around our relationship. Sadly, at the moment, I'm too lost to fully appreciate that humor, nor am I willing to pull the Jack off the shelf for C.

Every great loss is its own dark labyrinth. I know this now. I also know that struggling against the journey, against the twists and turns and dead ends, will only make the trip take longer to navigate.

Diana has suggested, and I want to believe, there is a man out there who deserves my love, as I will deserve his. Yet, I remain stymied by a tiny drop of hope. Stuck inside my labyrinth, facing a dead end, I yearn for a love, Kit's love, that although brief, was wonderful and amazing and just—

Inside my head, I recite my new number two rule: *Be present.* "You've got it," I say to C. "Gin and tonics, coming up."

He pushes away from the counter. "Limes in the fridge?"

"Bottom left-hand drawer. Here's a knife." I pull a paring knife from the wooden holder on the counter and set it on the cutting board.

When the drinks are made, I ask, "What are we toasting?"

He thinks for a moment. "Old friends and lovers."

I detect a note of bitterness in his tone and frown. Whatever is going on with him—because I'm pretty sure something is—I hope it's not about me. Did I hurt C. in a way I didn't foresee?

He grimaces, which isn't reassuring, and then taps my glass with his and takes a generous swallow.

"Shall we sit in the living room?" I pivot to head in that direction.

His hand closes around my wrist. "Liz? I—"

Surprised by his touch and the urgent way he's said my name, I don't pull away.

"I might as well say it," he mumbles, and then, in a rush asks, "Can we go upstairs?"

The gods have obviously decided to play another joke on me. In consolation for Kit's loss, they are offering up a potent young man—this particular young man—as their antidote to heartache.

The Yiddish word for what Zeus and his children are up to is *chutzpa*, audacity almost comic in its insensitivity. Until I'd slept with C., I hadn't been subtle about my contempt for men whose worldview includes cavorting with inappropriately young women as a go-to cure for what ails their egos. I would laugh, except C. might misinterpret my glee, which isn't about him but about imagining my deity-frenemies lounging on their gilded clouds, laughing their heads off as they present their comely temptation. For the second time.

I remind C. of our pact. "We agreed to once."

"I need twice." There is defiance in the eyes meeting mine.

Good for him. What he's doing takes courage. Or desperation.

The idea that C. might be feeling desperation or something like it—I don't think he's propositioning me for the thrill of it—keeps me from giving him an outright no. When I don't immediately reply, however, he releases my arm.

I sort through my feelings. How could I not find C. desirable? He's lovely. And, on the heels of losing Kit, to have this beautiful young man desire me is balm to my ego. Okay, score one for the gods.

Rubbing my forehead, I contemplate why going to bed with C. this afternoon should be any more harmful to either of us than it was the first time.

Something is wrong and I feel a responsibility for getting to the bottom of it. C. is tamped down, his exuberant intellect hardly in evidence. If he thinks sex with me is going to help, how can I argue he's wrong?

Yet the thought of going to bed with him causes another fathomless pit to open inside me. Sleeping with anyone other than Kit feels like cheating. Or moving on. I'm not sure which concept is more disturbing.

"Maybe I'd better go." C. sets his glass on the counter.

"Wait." I step into him, lifting my palms to his chest, the heat of his body penetrating his T-shirt into my hands. C. is muscular but so different from Kit. He feels foreign and not what I know. For a moment I'm repulsed by the idea of being intimate with a male body other than the one I yearn for. A new wave of sadness washes over me, but I master it to meet C.'s gaze.

"What's going on, C.? Why have you suddenly decided we need to sleep together?" I step away.

He shakes his head and expels a breath. I suspect he may be more confused by his inability to express himself than I'm surprised by his proposal. He gathers his hair high at the back of his head and holds it there. His eyes close for a second and then blink open. "We'll talk about it later," he says.

I used almost exactly the same words when I put him off about the Dorn. But more than that, I realize with a start—we have both echoed Kit's response that last night at Willing.

Would Kit have found the truths he discovered in the wee hours of that morning if we had slept together? I'll never know.

C. lets go of his hair. There is so much tension in his gesture, and yet as I watch the golden strands glinting in the light from the windows, I'm smitten by the flex of muscle in his arms and shoulders. I'd like to photograph him naked. Although I can't imagine his parents' reaction, I'm sure C. would love posing. A dark twist of arousal sparks and flares, a clench and release that leaves me unsettled. Even so, for good or ill, I am not going to deny myself the chance to live inside desire instead of grief, no matter that the pleasure will be fleeting.

This realization leads to another—I should have given Kit credit for trying to communicate his needs that night, whether it was comfort or oblivion he was seeking.

"Okay," I tell C., "but we will discuss why afterward. Agreed?"

C. nods. "Yeah, okay. After." He pushes out a harsh breath.

I want to warn him to be careful about what he wishes for. The gods can be deliberately obtuse about the specifics of fulfillment. You may think your wish was clearly defined, yet somehow the results will not be as predicted. Payment will also be demanded, although the exact form can remain a mystery for years—or be specified the minute your wish is granted. I wonder if C.'s request is my payback for taking him to bed in the first place. Just as I wonder what he will pay for this.

Heading for the stairs, I say, "Come on, then," and beckon him to join me.

He shakes himself loose from where he's been planted, likely stuck inside his own internal dialogue, the one *I will* be hearing later. Ambling to where I'm waiting at the foot of the stairs, he looks me over before taking another step closer. Then he slides an arm around my waist, pulling me into his chest. His kiss is sweetly tentative. When I respond, he hums low in his throat and, emboldened, pins me to the wall.

✳

An hour later, we are sweaty, relaxed, and adrift on a sea of orgasm-induced endorphins. C.'s head is thrown back, his neck arched, displaying the slight rise of his Adam's apple. One shapely arm lays against his forehead; the other is wrapped loosely around my shoulders. As ever, his body is a delight. I run a hand slowly down the concavity below his ribs, over his belly, and then retrace the path in reverse.

Our breathing and the whir of the ceiling fan, a birthday present to myself, are the only sounds in the gathering dusk. Shadows blur the room's outlines. I'm blurry, too. C. has filed down my sharp edges. I'm hoping I've done the same for him.

I turn my head toward the windows. The afternoon shadows have lengthened. One branch of the maple has turned orange overnight. In the woods the oaks are shedding their acorns, a nuisance underfoot for Obie and me on our walks. Yet, on such a fecund late-summer afternoon, it is hard to accept that autumn is almost upon us, winter soon to blow in behind it.

I would love to head South again and miss the worst of the cold, but Georgia would be torture without Kit. Maybe I should consider South Carolina or Arizona. Sedona is supposed to be lovely. I curl into myself, the bliss of the last few minutes dissolving. As lovely as C. is, he is not the man I love.

Staying present is my goal, but beyond my abilities at the moment. Most other moments, too.

I press my palm over C.'s heart, hoping to distract myself from thoughts of Kit by its steady beat. C.'s lips curl into a smile. I trace my fingertips over his collarbone, into the light furring of hair at the center of his chest, hair that wasn't in evidence the last time we shared my bed.

Dipping a fingertip into C.'s belly button, I circle once, then twice, drawing a fingernail across his pelvis, enjoying the twitch of his stomach as I inadvertently tickle him. Unable to resist, I kiss his softening cock where it lays sweetly spent among his bronze curls. I have tender feelings for a man's penis in the aftermath of good sex, especially when it performs so satisfactorily. C.'s lashes flutter at my homage. "Ummmmm," he says and his cock twitches.

If I stop touching him, I might think, so I don't. Rising to my knees to straddle my young lover, I press my palms flat against his concave belly. He contracts his muscles at my touch. I trail my hands up his chest, to his jaw, and lay them against his flushed cheeks. His eyes remain closed. I lean in to study his features. Not a single crease mars his forehead, the skin around his eyes, or corners of his mouth. How long will it be before the inevitable frown lines appear? I would rather he never experience my own soul-deep knowledge of loss.

Having taken copious instruction from literature and film, I'm sure C. believes he's quite the expert on the human condition. Inevitably, however, he will discover how little he actually knows. His intellectual citadel *will* be stormed by disappointment, which is when the real learning begins.

As I study him, thought creases his brow. His mouth hardens into a tight line. He is not as relaxed as his posture would indicate.

I tap the arm resting over his forehead. "We've had our fun, sweetie. Time to talk."

"Let's have more fun." In a flash C. rolls and lands me on my back, positioning himself between my legs.

"If you tell me what I want to know, we'll have more fun *later*," I promise. Pushing at his shoulders, I attempt to shove him off.

Refusing to go, he grinds me into the mattress, angling his mouth over mine. "I want more fun now," he whispers.

"We had a deal," I remind him, turning my head to the side. "First fun, then talk." I shove at his shoulders again. "Apparently you didn't read the fine print where it stipulates one round of fun." I sigh, remembering the amusing contractual language of Kit's negotiations. It seems I'm engaged in a threesome, although there are only two of us in bed.

Thankfully, C. gives in with a good-natured peck to my cheek. He flops to his side, shooting his shoulders into a pile of pillows.

I throw on my shirt and face him, curling one leg beneath me. To ensure I don't get distracted, I pull the sheet over C.'s lap. "Not that what we've been doing hasn't been delightful," I comment, "but I sense a greater purpose to your visit than a mere afternoon's delight."

His mouth twists and, just like that, his mood shifts, although he remains mum. I wait him out. Finally he says, "That time with you—" He shakes his head, his brow furrowed. "It was . . . mind-blowing." His chin lifts. He meets my gaze as if he expects me to challenge his truth.

I'm flattered and also a little alarmed by this confession. "It was lovely," I confirm, stroking his sheet-covered thigh and hoping I'm not disavowing his experience.

I've been told by a couple of men whose honesty I trust that their earliest sexual encounters were a little too memorable and difficult to equal. One believes he's spent most of his adulthood trying to duplicate the intensity of that youthful coupling. He's been married three times, and all of his marriages ended by affairs. The idea that I could do that kind of damage to C. is upsetting.

"Maybe it was only a pleasant fuck to you," he says tightly. "I tried to see it that way, but then it got more complicated. That's why I needed to be with you again. I had to know if what I felt was about you or not."

I don't ask what he's decided, my new transparency rule be damned. "I'm guessing this is about a particular complication," I say, praying the complication isn't me, because it is beginning to sound that way.

"It's about James." He sees the look on my face and snorts. "James is a girl."

"Well, you can see where I'd be confused." I laugh, delighted that neither I nor a team switch is C.'s complication. I want all of the sweet pretty men on my side of the aisle, as politically incorrect as the sentiment may be.

"I like exotic women," he says, looking me over assessingly. "James is exotic-looking, though she doesn't look anything like you."

"I'm flattered that you think I'm exotic. What is exotic about James? The name sounds so White Anglo-Saxon Protestant."

"Her hair is darker than yours, but wavier. And long." He draws his fingers down his stomach, indicating how long. "Her eyes are almond shaped like yours, but brown." He offers up a smile that seems part pride and part derision, a contemptuous curl at the corner of his mouth.

I ponder that curl but say only, "How did you and James meet?"

"At a bar. I was out with some of the guys after class. James and a couple of her friends came over to our table. I ended up at her place." His mouth twists again.

Moving way too fast, from my perspective. Not that I say so. Most of us move too fast at his age, making trouble for ourselves in the process. "And?"

"She's a little older than me." I hear a challenge in his tone. At first, I have no idea why. Then, I get it.

"Do you think you have a thing for older women?"

"I might." His eyes dare me to deny this assertion.

Instead, I ask, "How much older is James?"

"Six years."

I weigh the pros and cons of having created a fetish in him for older women. Not that a six-year age difference constitutes a fetish, at least not yet. There is also the strong possibility that his preference developed before he climbed into bed with me.

Rather than explain the age thing, C. says, "James is a painter. Creative, like you." He touches my knee. "You know my family. We're all science geeks, except for Dad, who is geeky too, except he's geeky about history. I figure that's why artists attract me; they're the opposite of what I know."

I decide to be amused that he thinks he already has a type—older artistic women. But maybe he does. He leans in to kiss me. It's a good kiss, sensual and distracting.

"You're sure you don't want to . . ." he breathes against my lips, insinuating his hand inside my open shirt and rubbing his thumb over one nipple.

I push his hand away and insert a couple of buttons into their respective holes. "Oh, I'm tempted. So when you finish your story . . ."

C. retreats, shoving himself into his pillows. He stares at the foot of the bed and says, "James isn't afraid of butting into other people's business. Like, if we were waiting in line to see a movie, she'd start talking with the couple behind us and in short order they would end up our best friends for the evening. She's charming and beautiful and people wanted her along for the ride. With me trailing," he adds ruefully.

"As if you're not beautiful and charming in your own right," I comment.

He ignores this reality check. "The constant connecting ended us up in interesting places. One night, she struck up a conversation with the couple at an adjacent table in a tapas bar. The next thing I know, we're at a jaw-dropping after-hours flamenco show."

"She sounds exhilarating."

He nods. "That was James's public side. Her other side . . ." He mutters something I don't catch, looks at his hands, and says, "I needed a change of scenery. I couldn't stay at the gallery after what happened." He fists his hair and tugs it up.

What the hell did she do? It seemed obvious from the moment he started talking that a breakup would end the story.

I should say something sympathetic, but you never know, not everyone wants sympathy. Even if C. does, getting the right balance could be tricky. If I'm too effusive, he may decide I think he's weak; what seems like kindness to me could look like pity to him. Yet, if I downplay my reaction, he could feel I'm insensitive to his pain.

I decide to go with the basics. "I'm sorry, C." I lean my head into his shoulder for a second. When he doesn't recoil, I kiss his bicep.

"I thought I loved her." He shakes his head, studying the end of the bed. "But she was . . . and she . . ." He clears his throat and says in a rush, "She was fucking me and someone else at the same time. I don't know if he was the only one, either."

"Oh, honey—"

He squeezes his eyes closed. "His name was—is—Ste*phan*." He mimics a French accent, pronouncing the name Ste-FON. There is an abundance of disdain in his tone, as well as a whole lot of hurt.

Making a pretense of readjusting the pillows behind his shoulders, he pulls the sheet up to his waist before adding, "I couldn't figure out what she was doing with me, if you want to know the truth."

I frown. "You're kidding, right? You're brilliant and funny and ethical and kind. You play the piano like a dream. And let's not forget the fencing or the skiing. Plus, you aren't exactly hard to look at. What more could she want?"

"She could want danger and adventure," C. counters. "And someone more sophisticated than me." Obviously he's given this way too much thought, or, more likely, his former girlfriend provided a list. "With money," he adds, "and the ability to further her career."

"Did she say that?" I ask, appalled. "Is this Stephan person dangerously sophisticated and dripping in money?"

C. throws off the sheet and projects himself across the room. When he reaches the windows he pivots, paces to the door on the opposite wall, and agitatedly reverses direction.

Although he is magnificent in his naked glory, my focus is on the frown lines bracketing his mouth—those hard, pained creases I hoped never to see. Suddenly he stops and, crossing his arms, knocks his head into the wall behind him with a hard whack. Rocking, heel to toe, the way he did in the kitchen, he seems to be trying to transition into neutral without visible success, his feelings so chaotic and unresolved that he can't find a way to calm himself.

"She told me I was provincial and old-fashioned and judgmental," he says, his focus on the floor.

I would laugh at the absurdity of these accusations if they weren't clearly causing him pain. "You believed her?" I ask, unable to contain my outrage at what this girl has done to him. "C., look at me," I command. After a second, he shifts his eyes to mine.

"You are not any of those things."

Unable to hold my gaze, he glances toward the window. "Maybe I am," he replies with a shrug, as if, really, who cares? As if he doesn't give a damn.

"Did you hear what I said? You are not provincial or unsophisticated." I try offering examples to help convince him. "You are widely traveled on several continents. That makes you worldly and independent. And, who else has read *Moby Dick* and *Ulysses* before they were sixteen *and* enjoyed them? You've seen more movies than I have, which is saying something, and many of them were foreign. Let's also note that on the Spanish and French films I need the subtitles but you don't. Plus, even though I said this before and it seems shallow to repeat it, you have an athletic and very beautiful body."

This last statement draws a smile from him, but it fades too quickly, prompting me to continue my list of virtues. "Do I have to point out that you attend a highly competitive and intellectually challenging university? Your mother tells me you are on the dean's list. Also, you don't merely play the piano well, you do it with the kind of skill and artistry too often lacking in professionals." I take a breath. "Do I need to keep going?"

He shakes his head as if I'm talking nonsense.

"For goodness' sake, C., *do not* believe a word that awful girl said." I study him for a moment then ask, "What aren't you telling me?"

He doesn't answer. He climbs onto the bed, crawling from the foot to where I'm sitting against the headboard, close enough to rest his forehead against mine.

I stroke hair away from his face. C. shudders. Leaning away, he sits on his calves and scrubs his hands over his eyes.

I wait, suspecting we are both suffering from the same disease, unable to stop loving someone too damaged to love us back.

"She was like an addiction," he says, his hands falling to his thighs. "Just being near her was an adrenaline rush. Like getting high."

Exactly how high has he been getting?

"Don't look at me like that every time I mention drugs! Honestly, Liz, I'm sure you smoked a little marijuana in your salad days. For all I know, you still do."

"Sorry," I say sheepishly.

"She made me feel really alive, hyperaware when she was around."

I nod, thinking Kit made me feel the same way.

Looking toward the window, C. says under his breath, "The sex was fucking *hot*." His mouth thins to a grimace.

"Hot sex is good." I smile and lean up to kiss his cheek, resting a hand over his, where it's clenched on his leg. "I don't want this to come out wrong, because you know I adore you and find you exceedingly hot, but I'm curious what you think attracted James to you. If you are as devoid of interest as she claimed, why did she pick you in the first place?" I'm hoping the question will help C. see how ridiculous it is to believe her criticisms.

He snorts. "I worked in a gallery, remember? An important gallery. She wanted in."

"She befriended you to get shown?" I ask incredulously.

"Liz, she wasn't *befriending* me, she was fucking me over for what she thought she could get from the connection, although I didn't see that until the end, which proves James was right about me being too stupid to live."

"Would the connection be this Stephan person?"

"I finally figured out James doesn't talk to people because she is interested in them, she talks to people because they might know someone or something that will take her places she can't go on her own, like all those openings and shows and parties we never would have attended otherwise."

"Lovely. So she got a show at the gallery with your help?" I insinuate my fingers into his fist.

"She got the show by fucking Stephan. That was the 'leg up' I gave her." Pulling his hand from mine, he crosses his arms and adds, "James liked to meet at the gallery when we were going out after work. I was oblivious to what she was up to. Maybe I am provincial. I was blind, that's for sure."

"Listen"—I rub my hand down his arm—"believing the best in people isn't a crime, nor is it provincial."

He rolls his eyes. "Sure. And sometimes it pays to open your eyes and see what's going on in front of you. If I had, I might have enjoyed a hookup with her and that would have been the end of it."

"Not in your nature, I don't think. You aren't a love 'em and leave 'em kind of guy."

"Whatever." He sounds irritated, maybe with me for my unwillingness to confirm the way James has convinced him to see himself.

"Do you want to tell me about Stephan?" I ask softly.

"Not really." Then he contradicts himself. "Ste*phan* is one of those people who is totally sure of himself and totally sure he's right about everything else. His father is the Duguay half of DLG, Duguay-Lang Galleries. Stephan is heir to the Paris branch. He's on this side of the Atlantic, staying with David Lang to learn the New York art scene. I'll tell you, even without James and Stephan, I'm done with the mannered, snotty, my-shit-doesn't-stink pretentiousness of the New York art scene. Anyway—"

His mouth snaps shut. A few seconds tick by and then he grunts and forces the rest of his story out. "Stephan Duguay was curating a show featuring emerging artists. James heard about it from me and asked if I would talk her up. She's talented, no matter what else she is. By then, Stephan already knew her as my girlfriend. He told me she was charming." His tone turns bitter. "The two of them must have had a great time charming the pants off each other. Literally."

"She got a painting into this show," I surmise.

"Two. I was excited for her, flattered to have my opinion of her talent confirmed by someone who mattered in the art world." He takes a deep breath and then adds, "The show gave her a reason to visit DLG that didn't have anything to do with me. She and Stephan would disappear into the back while I was busy out front. I figured they were talking about the show." He shudders, as if he can't believe his own naïveté.

"When did you figure it out?"

"James sold both paintings at the opening."

This statement isn't an answer although I assume it relates. "Was she thrilled?" I think about how I responded to Arliss's call about my first sale.

"Halfway to the moon. But weirdly jittery, too. Later I decided she'd taken something. At the time, I thought it was because her parents showed up. I hadn't met them before. James acted as if they weren't there.

"Her parents were more blue collar than blue blood. Nice normal folks. That surprised me, since James had such an entitled attitude. Her parents assumed we would go for a celebratory dinner together after the opening. James declined. Her mom and dad came all the way from southern New Jersey to be there for her.

"I was over art-world parties by then, but James wasn't done being the bright young thing. She wanted to continue basking in her spotlight. And I get it. Who would blame her? But more important was her need to continue trawling for influence, so we went to the after-party at the Langs. Once we arrived at their Park Avenue apartment, I hardly saw her. At a little after midnight, I was ready to get out of there, so I began looking for James, but I got waylaid by David. He wanted to talk about a catalog I was editing. The print deadline was coming up. I was standing with him, off to the side of the living room, when I finally saw her.

"David's co-op is one of those grand old prewar apartments—a half floor of a really huge building. The bedrooms were off a long hall at the back of the living room. I watched James and Stephan come out of what must have been his room, since he was staying with the Langs. I looked at her, she looked at me, and I knew she was daring me to make something of it."

"What did you do?"

"I managed to keep myself together until I could finish the conversation with David and get her out of there. Then I accused her of cheating on me with Stephan."

"Oh boy," I exhale.

"At first she denied it."

"The girl had *chutzpa*," I say.

C.'s jaw clenches. "Why did she bother leaving the party with me?" He answers the question himself. "Maybe she was afraid I was *provincial* enough to cause a scene and didn't want it to happen in front of her new entourage." He pauses, breathes out sharply and asks, "Remember when you made me take a shower that first time?"

I nod, not sure where he's going with this.

"The smell of sex is unmistakable, isn't it?" He leans into me. As I imagine he did when he got that horrible girl outside, he inhales through his nose, sniffing the curve of my jaw, the corner of my mouth, and behind my ear, sending a shiver down my back before he pulls away. I sense the violence of his feelings in the rigid way he's holding his body. In my mind, I see C. with a wild, disheveled girl, pressing her into the wall of the building they've just exited.

"And then?" I ask.

"What do you think? I had my answer." His jaw clenches. "I wanted to hit her. In that moment it was all I wanted. But I don't hit women." He looks into my eyes and smiles bleakly. "Reassuring, isn't it? The only good to come out of that night was learning I'll never hit a woman, though I couldn't be near James a minute longer. I started walking."

"That wasn't the end of it?" I guess.

His shoulders twitch. He throws his head back and growls, "No, it fucking wasn't the end of it. James had to have her say. She may not have wanted a scene at the Langs', but she didn't mind having one in the street. She followed me spewing all kinds of toxic accusations, most of which you've already heard. She told me I was a stupid provincial hick-boy from Vermont. She said I bored her with my clueless old-fashioned ideas. Even the sex bored her. She said she'd stuck around because she knew I was her best chance for a show at an important gallery, the kind of show that would launch her in the art world. She said she was finally on the map and that Stephan was into her. In her immortal words, I could go fuck myself because I wasn't going to ever fuck her again."

"Oh, sweetie," I murmur.

"Her delivery made it worse. She didn't shout; she just said what she wanted to say in this cold, even voice. Her tone made it more true, you know?"

"Not true," I say, putting my arms around him. He doesn't pull away but he doesn't relax into me either. His long hair falls forward, a curtain between us, hiding his expression.

"Don't believe her, love." I push his hair away, tilting his face up until his gaze meets mine. I know he fears everything James told him is true. He is here for me to do exactly what I'm attempting: to convince him otherwise. I kiss his cheek, surprised when he captures my mouth in a demanding kiss. He topples me onto my back. It takes a second for me to catch up.

Straddling my legs, he traps me between his thighs. When I don't resist, he insinuates his knees between mine. I set my hands on his shoulders. He captures my wrists with one hand and lifts my arms over my head. Bracing himself on his other arm, he bends to kiss me. I taste his desperation.

I rub myself against him, knowing I can trust C. not to hurt me, no matter the turbulence he's acting out. If this is what he needs, I'm happy to give it to him. His full weight lands on me as he breaks the kiss. He bites my neck. I arch, tugging my wrists free from his grasp to pat the night table, feeling for a condom. But C. doesn't wait. He slides into me on a swift, breath-hitching thrust. I stiffen. Not because I'm in pain, but because God only knows about this girl he was dating and the numerous partners she undoubtedly had before C. and while she was with him as well. He should be using protection. As I begin to protest, he turns his mouth to my ear and says gruffly, "I swear, Liz, I always used a condom with her. And when I found out about Stephan I got tested. I'm clean."

I nod, closing my eyes. The damage, if there is any, has already been done. Not that I don't trust C. I trust him in a way I wouldn't trust another twenty-four-year-old. Or most other men, for that matter, which the ignorant James could never understand.

C. works himself into a pounding rhythm. I suspect he needs to prove he's the dangerous alpha male James wanted him to be. We both make little grunting noises as his powerful thrusts drive me up the bed.

Suddenly, hilted inside me, he stops moving. Both of us are panting. I raise my pelvis, lock my legs around him, and squeeze my inner muscles around his lovely cock, letting him know I have no objection to what he's been doing. His eyes open. I watch his focus shift from wherever he's been to include me. He lowers his head, resting his cheek against mine, and begins moving more slowly, savoring the pleasure of his unsheathed cock embraced by the liquid heat of my body.

It is inexplicable to me that the mean girl he involved himself with—I recognize the type—could suggest C. is boring. More likely James had that perfectly honed, nasty-girl intuition about where the chinks in C.'s armor lay and stuck her knife where she knew she could do the most damage. Or maybe she was too young to understand that a man who relishes the pleasure he gives his partner is never boring. With the kind of nonexistent self-esteem she was probably trying to hide from herself as well as from everyone else, I'm betting gentleness and sensitivity were not what she thought she deserved.

Was I as foolish as this girl when I was her age? Sadly, the answer is probably yes, although I wasn't mean, only ignorant of what really matters.

Regrettably, C. has undergone his first bruising lesson in who not to love. At least when I fell for Kit I didn't fall for a jerk, although there were far too many of those in my youth.

To be fair, men do not hold a monopoly on boorishness. James is living proof of that. I'm hoping it only takes one of her stripe for C. to learn his lesson. I don't want him doing what I did and spend the next twenty years choosing nasty partners before deciding there has to be a better alternative. At least, even if I'll never be with Kit, I know what I want. My next man will be one who touches me tenderly, who tells a funny story when I'm cross. He will be constant and ethical and not a cheater like Dan. Most important of all, he will know his own mind, unlike Kit and Roland. If he comes wrapped in a comely package—viva la bonus. I'll swoon for him either way.

Hear me, ye gods on high? I know what I'm looking for. Now you know it, too. And it isn't the least bit funny that if C. were older, he'd be my perfect match.

Having returned to himself, C. is making love with the sensuality that comes so naturally to him. He murmurs, "Are you okay?"

"More than okay," I answer, happy to have C. in my bed, although I'm heartbroken for both of us, and for Kit, too.

His mouth moves to mine as he slides his hand into the space between our bodies. I moan as he strokes with his thumb, his touch light, matching the gentleness of his cock's glide.

I was right about C. being a quick study. And I am touched that he sought me out, that he feels safe about unburdening himself. Dare I label what I'm feeling as love? Not the kind I have for Kit, but love nonetheless.

My hands glide over his shoulders and down his back, delving into the deep furrows along his spine, over smooth skin and taut muscle. I shape my palms over the globes of his ass, fingers finding an indentation, a handhold. I lift into his stroke.

We slide and spark, desire spiraling into the air like smoke, enveloping us in its sensual mist. I sigh into C.'s mouth. He kisses me, no longer urgent, but unhurried and sweet.

The sun is descending, dipping behind the mountaintops, shadows lengthening. Inside the soft twilight, our focus is encompassing yet trained narrowly upon the graceful glide of in and out, of touch and caress, of care and caring.

I've taken men to bed for nothing more than self-gratification or to release tension after a frustration-filled day. I've had sex that made me laugh and wild rides that left me spinning, unable to find my balance afterward. A few times—fleetingly, at the beginning with Dan, later with Roland, and for those brief incandescent weeks with Kit—sex was more than physical; it was intertwined with love and joy and possibility. In those moments, with those men, I was as elemental as the earth, so high on good fortune and gratitude that I glittered like the stars.

C. and I are engaged in something else entirely. This is sex as an elegy, a tone poem Ravel or Debussy might have composed as a requiem for heartbreak. I wish it were in my power to erase his unhappiness as well as my own. I don't understand, and probably never will, how Kit could have found it so difficult to choose joy.

C. buries his face in the curve of my neck. "Liz," he murmurs, perhaps sensing I have drifted away from him once more.

"Here," I whisper, nipping his ear.

He shivers. I shiver, too, returning to the present, returning to my body. I breathe him in, angling my mouth over his. We kiss and separate and kiss again as his thrusts become more insistent. I clench around him, tilting to take him deeper.

Exigency claims us. We are hunger and need and the potency of pleasure. Time suspends itself until, inevitably, orgasm blows us apart. I want to believe that as we fracture, our grief fractures with us. For a moment, the merest second, we are nothing and everything.

CHAPTER 39

IT TAKES SOME minutes to re-form from the bits and pieces we have so therapeutically disassembled.

"God," C. groans, opening one blue eye.

"Or man," I say, "who would be you." I tickle his side. He wriggles away from my fingers. "I hope we've put paid to any doubts about your masterful bedroom skills."

He grins. Pushing up on his arms, he disengages, provoking a small mew of displeasure from me. He flips onto his stomach and props up on his forearms. "That was really, really—" He doesn't finish the thought, leaning in to kiss my breast.

"It certainly was." I close my eyes and stretch, savoring the lightness I feel. Testing what will happen if I think of Kit, I find I'm sad but not desolate. Perhaps C. has begun the process of emptying the storm of grief I've been lost inside since I decided I couldn't wait any longer for Kit to choose me.

Another peaceful minute goes by before C. says, "I forgot to tell you the best part about James. Her dirty little secret."

I turn to catch his glance. "Is this something I should know?"

"Oh yeah." He walks two fingers up my stomach and then skips to my chin. "The name on her birth certificate is Jeanette. Turns out James Marigold Archer was, and for all I know legally remains, Jeanette Marie Cardinelli."

"Oh, that's lovely," I say. "Where do you suppose she got the Archer part?"

"I only discovered her name change when her parents talked about her at the opening. After what went down, I never got to ask. Maybe she named herself after Isabelle Archer from *The Age of Innocence*, although I doubt James was ever innocent."

"Ha! In any case, it's a wonderful, silly secret."

"Isn't it?" C. laughs.

I suspect I'm witnessing his first foray at putting the awful James behind him.

When he stops chuckling he says, "Can I ask you a name-related question?"

"What?" I shift toward him.

"Why do you always call me C.? How come you never call me Ford anymore? Unlike Jeanette Marie, I'm down with the name my parents gave me. What's the deal?"

"Well, it's because . . ." This is a tough one. I sigh. "It's because I met you when you were a child. And then you grew up. By the time you were sixteen, you were so—" I hesitate.

"I was so . . . ?"

"Oh God," I groan. I can't believe I'm admitting this. "You were so gorgeous. Sexy—even if you were keeping your light under a bushel." I stare up at the ceiling. "It's definitely not okay for a woman more than twenty years older to notice such a thing unless it's in an admiring, motherly kind of way. I was noticing you in an *I'd-like-to-have-my-wicked-way-with-you* way. A person could go to jail."

"Not for sinning in her mind," he says, grinning and referencing Jimmy Carter's famous comment. He adds a Groucho Marx twitch to his brows, provoking a smile from me. His knowledge of popular culture more distant than the last few years and the way he mashes it all up is utterly delightful. I believe it's another characteristic that makes him unique among his peers.

"You thought I was hot? Lizbeth, how naughty." He grins again, then sobers. "No kidding?"

"As if I would kid about such a thing. Tell me you never noticed," I plead.

He shakes his head.

"Well, that's a relief. I thought you might have, since you didn't seem surprised when we ended up here the first time." I pat the bed.

"Thankfully, your mother doesn't seem to have noticed, either. Or Diana." I pause, because this is a thought I've worked hard to lock away, yet here it is in all its excruciatingly awkward glory—leering at me and way too close for comfort. I groan again and ask, "By the way—does your mother know you're here?"

"Sure. But she thinks we're friends in an Auntie Mame and her nephew kind of way," C. says blithely. "But what about you? Didn't you know I had a crush on you? When you took me to bed, it was a wet dream come true. And Liz, I'm not saying this in a metaphorical way. Finding out you thought I was hot?" He wiggles delightedly. "Kinky."

Rubbing his thumb over my nipple, he asks archly, "Did you masturbate while you fantasized about me?" He sticks out his tongue and rolls it over his upper lip. "How fast did it go?"

I swat his hand away. "That isn't funny."

"No," he says. "It isn't funny. It's fucking hot. I bet you didn't know I noticed you way before I was sixteen. Ten, more like."

I raise a skeptical eyebrow.

"You know I've always been precocious." He brings his index finger together with his thumb and pinches the nipple he's been playing with.

"C.," I hiss.

He leaves off to wipe the pad of his thumb over my bottom lip. I bite him. He laughs and pulls his thumb away, flopping onto his back. "I still don't get what our mutual attraction has to do with my name." He rubs his thumb where I nipped it.

"I needed to disassociate you from the boy I'd known. It wasn't comfortable having sexual thoughts about a kid I'd watched reading his first volume of Harry Potter as a six-year-old. When we began seeing foreign films together, some of the subject matter didn't help either, which, you might have noticed, was when I started calling you C."

"We did see some sexy stuff," he says, twisting onto his side to face me.

"Not on purpose. God, that last one was a doozy." I shift to meet his glance, remembering the emotional violence of that movie. "Calling you C. put a little metaphysical distance between the child named Crawford and the man you were becoming."

He regards me for a second, still grinning. "Who you lusted after. Deviant decadent Lizbeth." His eyes sparkle. "You don't suppose I got my taste for kinky women like James from you?" He's obviously delighted by what I've revealed.

"Don't join me and James together in the same sentence! And sweetie, ten-year-olds who beg their parents for a pet boa constrictor come by their kinks naturally."

He laughs. "I grew out of my snake phase pretty quickly, though. Obviously, I'm more consistent in my women, though I do need to figure out how to attract a *nice* kinky woman."

"Amen to that," I say, happy he's figured this out for himself.

"I hope the next time you and I are around my parents and you call me C., I don't blush or something. That's going to have all sorts of erotic overtones now that I know why you use it."

"Don't you dare."

"Is this a potential bargaining chip?"

"For what?"

His grin gets wider but he doesn't elaborate. "I think I could eat a house," he says instead. "Are you hungry? We must have used hundreds of calories in the last couple of hours. Want to get some dinner?"

"I have a couple of steaks in the fridge. How about we grill them? I also have heirloom tomatoes and lettuce from the farmers market."

"You grill, I'll make the salad."

"Are you trying to pervert gender stereotypes? Wouldn't you rather *man* the grill?"

"I'm not as useful with forks and spatulas as I am with knives and swords," he says, dipping his head to nip at my breast.

"Touché." I laugh. Swinging to my feet, I give one of his handsome buttocks an affectionate slap.

With another grin, he rolls to the edge of the mattress. "I'll shower, shall I? I smell a little too delicious." He raises one eyebrow suggestively.

"Wouldn't want Mommy to know what we've been up to."

"Ick. TMI. I do have some residual guilt about us. You aren't making me feel any better."

"Not to worry. I can make you feel better any time you want to give me the opportunity."

I shake my head. "Only if you knock that off—"

"C." He winks knowingly.

I look toward the heavens for patience.

"Meet you downstairs in five." He lets out a delighted bark of laughter, opens the bedroom door, and heads for the bathroom.

"I like puppies," I say to Obie, who is happy to be allowed into the room. "Honestly, I do." And I'm happy that particular puppy is feeling so much better.

✳

During dinner, I pepper C. with questions about his family and school experience, staying away from our entanglements. He gives me the lowdown on Harry and Drew. Mel and Ham talked about his siblings last week, but a brother's perspective is often different from a parent's. The tension C. arrived with is hardly evident this evening. It's wonderful how a couple of good orgasms can make the world a better place. Although, eventually, I'll need to express a few more opinions about his experience with that dastardly ex-girlfriend.

The double dose of endorphins didn't hurt me either. I'm more relaxed than I've been for months. After C. leaves, I'll probably tumble back into my pit, but for the present, I'm feeling damn good.

By the time we finish dessert and clear the table, C. and I have satisfactorily covered our family news as well as dissected the current cultural zeitgeist via film and art. C. can make connections between past and present in such interesting ways. There has to be a girl out there who will appreciate him, and not only for his looks. This thought brings me full circle to the dreadful James. To help C. learn how to avoid the Jameses of this world, I will be offering a few helpful tips.

Deciding those tips will go down easier with an aperitif, I suggest cognac in the living room. I developed a taste for the pear-infused version under Darius's tutelage. Shallowly filling two small, etched, crystal goblets, I hand them to C. He gathers the glasses in one hand and grabs the cognac bottle with the other. I pull a box of dark chocolate truffles out of the refrigerator. I'm friendly with most of the other vendors—florists, wedding planners, musicians, and caterers—who regularly service the events I shoot. Those connections net me bounty like these fancy champagne truffles with the bride's and groom's initials in tiny pink icing letters calligraphed across the tops, which they did not go home with the bride's family because the initials blurred into little pink puddles during the reception.

In the living room, I glance at the Dorn as I move toward the sofa. A twinge of sadness returns, although I don't become unhinged. C. joins me, flopping into a loose-limbed sprawl, his head cushioned on a pillow braced against the armrest. He salutes the painting with his glass before saluting me. "I want to know why you were scowling at that lovely canvas." He sips his drink and reaches for a truffle.

My eyes widen. I had no idea I was doing that. "Eventually," I stall. "Right now, I'd rather talk about James."

"Haven't we covered the topic ad nauseam?" C.'s vocabulary has returned to his usual intellectual high ground. Another good sign.

"You did. I did not."

He downs a generous swallow of his aperitif. "Fire away. The sooner you talk, the sooner you stop talking," he says, pushing his knee against my thigh.

I ignore the knee and the snarky comment. "Do you remember saying you need to figure out how to pick a *nice* girl?'"

"A nice kinky girl. Don't forget that all important characteristic. But I was kidding, Liz."

"On fact, sweetie."

He raises his eyebrows. "Do you have a Nice Kinky Girls for Dummies handbook you want to share with me?"

I smile and lean in to kiss his cheek. He pulls me against his chest, scooting over so I can stretch out next to him.

"Nope. But I do have a white paper on the subject in my head." I tap my temple with the foot of my glass for emphasis.

"Somehow I knew you would," he says with a sigh.

"I promise to keep this short. Okay. First point: Don't confuse bitchiness with strength."

His mouth thins. "Got it. Next."

"Be wary of girls who want to pick you up in bars. It isn't as if every girl who approaches a guy in a bar is going to be a James, but there are better ways to meet women."

"Liz, bars are for pickups. It's been going on since bars were invented. And I liked that James came over to break the ice. Girls do it all the time. And guys like them to do it. I like them to do it."

"You like intellectual challenges as well as physical ones. The chemical mix gets your blood flowing. So a woman who challenges you is going to turn you on. It's the challenge-to-nasty-girl ratio you need to get better at assessing."

C. groans. "I like strong women. I like you, don't I? Though it's true James had a darkly mean side, whereas you have a darkly sexy side."

"Thank you." I bite into a truffle and hold the rest out to him. He takes it with his teeth. "I'm a little worried you aren't as over your boa constrictor phase as you think."

"Low blow." He laughs.

"Moving on . . . don't think you can change anyone. You can change people's little habits but you can't change their hard wiring."

"Doesn't everyone hope the bad stuff can be changed, that a person can transform?"

"Nope." I shift to sit up. "Look, I appreciate that you want to believe people can be motivated by your love. But in my experience, it is rare for anyone to transform themselves because they love you enough to do it. There are always exceptions, but hanging around waiting for one generally isn't cost effective." As I say this, I think about Kit again, about whether I should have waited longer. I still don't know. I needed him to transform, then and there, but he didn't or couldn't share that imperative with me.

C. shifts his shoulders, not willing to argue. "What else?" He drains his glass.

"If you find yourself in a bad relationship, consider therapy for yourself or go with your partner if she is willing. If your lover won't go with you, therapy on your own can still offer insights into your relationship's dynamics and help you decide whether you can stay." I think about Kit again, wondering if his therapy is helping him. Then I think, whatever he's getting out of it, a relationship with me probably won't be part of the outcome. "Bottom line?" I say. "Relationships are full of compromise, and if your partner can't make any, it's probably a relationship you should reassess."

C. leans up on an elbow and reaches around me to pour another cognac. "No second chances? Isn't that a little harsh?" he says as he resettles.

"Therapy is the second and third chance."

If I'm being fair, I didn't give Kit's therapy time to have an effect. But then, he made three important promises and broke them all. How many is it okay to break? Three seems like enough. In baseball, it isn't strike four and you're out. A lot of mythical tradition rides on the number three: three chances to answer the Sphinx's riddle, three spinners of fate, three magic wishes, to name but a few examples.

"Anything else?" C. asks, twirling his glass.

From his tone, I can tell he's done with the advice, but I keep going anyway, because I wish someone had said these things to me when it could have made a difference.

"How about, a really strong woman can meet you halfway without compromise pushing her buttons?"

"I'm done." C. twists and climbs over me to stand.

I'm pretty sure he didn't just reference the absence of alcohol in his glass. Reaching for the cognac bottle, he pours a larger draft than before.

"Go easy on that stuff, will you? You aren't driving down the block to get home. It's miles through the woods."

"Liz, I am six feet tall and weigh enough that a couple of glasses of wine and a little cognac are not going to wipe me out. I can handle a seven-mile drive."

"I stand corrected. But humor me anyway?"

He gives me a cognac high-sign, takes a sip, and sets the glass aside.

I sit up and pat the cushion next to me. "See? This is what happens with strong women," I say. "They tell you what they think. But when you don't agree, they don't punish you."

"James would have said, 'Drink up baby, you're not keeping up,' but if she did make that same suggestion, I probably wouldn't have pushed back." He sits on the far end of the couch.

"Because she might have erupted and the emotional fallout would have been too intense?"

"A creepily accurate observation."

He downs his cognac in two gulps, saluting me with the empty glass. I shake my head.

"It wasn't fun," he says.

"What? My lecture?" I lean in to take the glass from his hand and set it on the table. "I'm sorry. I felt compelled."

"That wasn't great, although I probably needed to hear it," he admits. "What I meant was being with James wasn't fun. It was exhilarating and addicting, but by the time we broke up it hadn't been fun for a while." Agitated, C. springs to his feet again. "Shit," he says, swaying a little.

I don't say *I told you so* but I'll make sure he doesn't go anywhere for a while.

"The good news is that most bad experiences teach profound lessons even if the lesson is only that you don't want to repeat your mistake. You're a smart guy. I have total faith that you won't date another James. I do have one more suggestion though."

C.'s brow creases. Plopping back onto the sofa, he leans his head against the back.

"How about getting to know a woman for more than a few hours before falling into bed with her?"

"Is this another archaic dating rule?"

"A timeless dating rule," I correct.

C. slumps sideways until his head is in my lap.

Combing my fingers through his hair, I say, "I'm really sorry if my lecture laid you low."

"The culprit was the cognac, not you." With a sheepish grin, he closes his eyes.

Stroking hair away from his forehead, I consider C.'s experience with James and hope some of what I said will stay with him. A couple of minutes into my mull, I notice he is asleep. He continues to snooze as I remove myself from the sofa and stuff a throw pillow under his cheek. I consider waking him for the drive home but decide that six feet tall or not, he drank too much. I may not have quite enough compunctions about sleeping with men half my age, but I do retain a mother's instincts. Heading into the kitchen, I call Mel.

CHAPTER 40

"Lizbeth here," I say when Mel picks up.

"Oh, hi," she responds. Then, with a note of tension in her voice she asks, "Is Ford with you? Is he okay?"

"He is here and he's fine. He's also asleep on my couch."

"That's a relief. Ham and I were beginning to worry over his whereabouts. He said he was thinking about visiting you. But that was this afternoon."

I wince. If she knew what went on this afternoon, she wouldn't be as happy about his visit.

"He hasn't been himself since he got home," she confides. "Has he said anything to you about what's bothering him? He won't talk to us."

I glance through the doorway at the young man on the couch. "It's his story to tell, not that you should worry. He's experiencing the growing pains that happen to us all."

"His grades are great. And David—Ham's friend who owns the gallery?—says Ford was a terrific help this summer."

I'm guessing Mel is probing for intel in her gentle way. I don't bite. "As far as I know, that's all true."

"So is it that girl he was seeing? We haven't met her yet."

"Diana has been with a boy for the last year and I only met Marc at the beginning of the summer," I respond. "Honestly, Mel, Ford is fine. You'll see. He's just really tired from school and a busy summer."

My statements are true although I'm leaving a lot out. "That's why he passed out on my couch." I wince at having told her where he's sleeping twice. I sound suspicious to my own ears. Then again, what parent is going to suspect her twenty-four-year-old son is sleeping with his forty-seven-year-old movie pal?

"I'm afraid once Ford's down, he's down for the count. He probably won't wake until morning," Mel informs me.

"No problem. I'll throw a blanket over him and ply him with caffeine before he drives home."

"Thanks, Liz. We appreciate you letting him crash."

"Anytime," I say with another wince. I know I'm not technically doing anything wrong by sleeping with C., but *technically* isn't the same as *ethically*.

Mel and I exchange a few more pleasantries and hang up.

I tidy the kitchen, take Obie for his last out, and throw the promised blanket over C. Grabbing a pad and marker, I write a note to tell him his parents know where he is and don't expect him home tonight. It's too complicated to explain how that went down, especially in inch-high Sharpie letters, so I save the details for later and prop the pad against a pile of books on the coffee table where he'll see it. I also leave the lamp on the side table switched on, so he doesn't wake in the night and wonder where he is.

Because it's only 9:30, after I take Obs out, I brush my teeth, take a shower, and decide to read for a while. Two-and-a-half hours later, I'm still bright eyed. Maybe it was the wine, or maybe too much physical and emotional stimulation. Unlike C., I'm wired.

I turn the light off anyway, hoping sleep will come. While I wait, I can't help contrasting C.'s experience with my own, coming back to the question of whether letting him into my bed is an admission that I've given up on Kit.

Five months was a long time to be strung along. Yet I continue to wonder if I was too precipitous in letting Kit go. The wondering is making me crazy. I need to accept that I'll never reach a definitive conclusion and let the question go.

I'm drifting off when a soft growl from Obie jolts me awake. I listen for a moment.

"That's C. climbing the stairs," I reassure him. Obs drops to the floor. He approaches the door, his tail down.

C.'s footsteps reach the second floor hall. Obie's tail begins a slow swish. A couple of seconds later, C. appears, pausing in the doorway. "Is this okay?" he asks, stepping into the room.

The old C. would have said, "Might I join you?" hiding behind an arch delivery. The new and improved C. has the courage to be direct.

When I nod yes, he strips, dropping his clothes on the floor in typical guy fashion. He climbs into bed. Obie shakes himself out and retires to his dog bed near the windows.

I scoot to the far side of the mattress and face away from C., not wanting him to get any ideas about doing more than sleeping now that I'm finally tired. He seems to understand and spoons himself around me, anchoring us together with an arm hugging my waist.

It's lovely to have a man at my back, if only for the night. I relax— which is when C. says into my ear, "Liz, why does the painting make you sad?"

I sigh and roll onto my back, one hand pressed over my heart, which is suddenly pounding. C. lifts himself over me, examining my face in the darkness. He gives me a sleepy smile. "Come on. Your turn to spill the state secrets."

"The painting was a consolation gift to myself after I fell in love in Georgia this winter and it didn't work out. The last time I gave myself a consolation present, it was Obie."

"You have great taste in consolation gifts. I do, too. You are mine." C. grins. I smile back. Then he sobers. "Too bad about the guy."

"Yeah," I say. "It is too bad when a man convinces you that he loves you, and then can't make up his mind about the significance of his feelings."

To be fair, I admit to C. that I sympathize with Kit's issues, up to a point. "But, my understanding doesn't change that he hasn't yet dealt with why it is so hard for him to find space in his heart for his wife's ghost and for me." Having said this much, I lay out the rest of the story, including the details of how Kit convinced me to take a chance on love, along with the wretched, wonderful, and wrenching rest of it, culminating in my purchase of the painting. I leave out the morose, champagne-infused evening with Arielle the night after I hung up on Kit.

"I'm sorry, Liz," C. says. "You deserve better."

Not that it's hard to undo me these days, but the genuine sorrow in C.'s voice works like a telephoto lens, zooming in on the events of the last nine months with too much focus. The feelings I've been working so hard to push away smash into me. My eyes tear. Biting my lip to keep from crying, I attempt to force my emotions back into storage. My role tonight is the sanguine older woman and full-out sobbing doesn't fit the picture. Yet, it is also true that I have to stop stuffing grief into boxes, and then shoving those boxes into dark corners. All of my dark corners are full up. It is time to clean them out.

Being C., he has noticed my mood shift. He murmurs, "It's sad, Liz. You're sad. I'm sad, too. Go ahead and cry." He wriggles his arm under my shoulders to hug me close.

His empathy unlocks the floodgates. I turn into his chest. He doesn't say a word, he just holds on, forcing me to revise my opinion about all men running in the opposite direction when confronted by a crying woman.

"I will not waste tears on a hopeless man," I choke out.

C. laughs, a reaction I don't understand until he says, "I wish I had your attitude about James." Apparently he's done some crying of his own. I pull him tighter.

When the tear well runs dry, I roll back to my side of the bed. C. shifts to rest his cheek between my nightshirt-covered breasts. I rest a hand on his head. We lie together, thinking our own thoughts, until he lifts up to kiss me lightly on the lips. I reach for a tissue.

He says, "I've been thinking. This guy Kit doesn't sound like a bad person, you know? I also think you've been assuming he's capable of analyzing his feelings. But, from what you've said, he's proved over and over that isn't true, over and over."

In response to my silence he adds, "Why do you think I finally got past my reserve about what kind of reception you'd give me if I asked you to go to bed a second time? It wasn't bravado. I respected our agreement. But I needed help with a mess of feelings I couldn't sort out. I was pretty desperate by this afternoon, so I braved the chance of rejection in hope that you might change your mind."

He squeezes my hand. "Don't be mad at me for expressing this opinion, but I think you were wrong to cut Kit off when he couldn't come to your party. He had a legitimate reason, and it seemed like he was committed to visiting you, only a little later than your deadline. And when you were so disappointed, I'm betting he understood that he'd tried your patience to the breaking point when you visited him in June. Although I agree that he should have visited long before now, I'm also betting that if he is sorry about what he did and didn't do, even if he knows what he wants now, he isn't as sure of what his reception will be as you might think."

"How do you figure that?"

"The reason I like girls picking me up in bars is because I'm risk adverse. Maybe he is, too." He lays a hand on my shoulder.

I rock forward and hug my knees, twisting my head to meet his gaze. "I'm not adding this up." I sigh, straightening. "Let's suppose you're right. Where does that leave me, guru-man?" I contemplate C. Somehow, since he arrived, our interactions have offered new insights into what went on with Kit that I haven't seen on my own.

He grins. "Give your friend some encouragement now that you've cut him off at the knees. Even if he was going to work on his issues, I doubt he was motivated to do it after you told him to go to hell. Guys are as sensitive as women, maybe more so." He narrows his eyes. "I see the skeptical expression on your face. But in my opinion, you have wounded him deeply."

"Hey, I didn't cut him off at the knees or tell him to go to hell. I just told him he needed to figure himself out."

"Right." C. pauses a beat. "It's a wonder the man can still walk."

I don't argue because my thoughts veer in a new direction. "That would be admitting . . . That I still want him."

"Lizbeth, correct me if I have this wrong, but isn't that why we're having this conversation? You told him you want him. Unfortunately, you were running him down at the time, so he may have only heard the running-down part. Take a risk, strong women that thou art"—he throws his arm around my shoulder—"offer him a ray of hope. Trust me, he needs encouragement, especially because, after that birthday fiasco, he may be as hurt by you as you are by him. From his point of view, he was planning to come, although just a little later than expected. He was doing what he said he'd do. You broke up with him over a two-week delay. I get it, you were tired of waiting, but, I'm sure to him, what you did felt crazy punitive."

"Huh . . ." I consider C.'s take on the situation. "This is giving me a headache." I press a thumb into one temple. "Why start hoping again? It's too late." But my stupid heart fills at the possibility that Kit and I could find a way back to each other. I'm reluctant, however, to admit it to my bed partner.

"It's not too late," C. says. "And come on, Liz, you want this kind of trouble. I guess it's a good thing a whole lot of other women do, too, or our species would have died out eons ago."

I laugh. Laughing feels good.

"I'm serious, Lizbeth."

"I'm aware, *Crawford*."

He opens his eyes wide, looking skeptical. "Have some compassion for the guy. And don't wait too long to make your move."

"Okay, okay."

Wisely, he drops the subject. I lie down and punch my pillow into sleeping shape. C. presses close.

"So how did you get so smart all of a sudden?" I squeeze the hand he's dropped over my waist.

"You think I'm smart about this stuff? Excellent." He blows into my ear, making me squeak. I shift onto my back to have a better view of where the next attack will come from, because I don't doubt there will be one.

"I may not know much about women *yet*," he says, "but I've been a guy for a good twenty-four-odd years"—he pauses to move his hand to my breast—"so I do know something about how the male mind works."

"Wise at such a tender age. You've always been an impressive specimen," I tease, as he squeezes the flesh under his hand. "I'm not kidding," I say, a little breathily. "I *am* impressed."

"Of course you are," he responds with his old self-possession. "You don't believe you are attracted only to my body, do you?"

I laugh. "Absolutely not."

"Just as I thought. But maybe we should pretend that's why you adore me, if only for the next half hour or so." He moves his hand into the curls at the apex of my thighs and strokes a fingertip lower. "Let's pretend you can't get enough of my glorious body."

I laugh. "I don't have to pretend." I turn into him, my arms encircling his neck.

Liking my answer, he bends to touch his lips to mine. "Then let's be glorious together," he says and kisses me.

We do just that. No pretending required.

CHAPTER 41

When I break rules, even self-imposed ones, my tendency isn't to rein in and stop the runaway wagon. *No.* I let it careen down the road, thrilled to be aboard. So, when C. suggests he return Sunday afternoon—I'm shooting a wedding starting with the rehearsal Friday night and won't be available again until then—I don't hesitate to say okay. By mutual agreement he returns every afternoon. C. spends another night, as well. Our excuse is that he consumed too much caffeine and had a bad night before and exhaustion has suddenly hit him hard. He's the one who calls home with this news—pretend news to protect the innocent and us, too.

The following Saturday I have work, so it's time to say good-bye. C. must return to school for his sophomore year the same day, leaving town before the shoot is over.

Rolling to the side of the bed, he sits up, knotting his hands at his nape, letting them rise into his hair as he stretches. I watch his broad shoulders flex, all sorts of muscles rippling in his arms and back. It's a pretty sight.

We dress in silence. My guess is that C. hasn't got a handle on the exact etiquette for our situation any more than I do. He isn't one of my inappropriate men, at least not in the usual sense, since our connection is more intimate. He's a true friend, but up until this week, in a much more casual way. Now, he's a friend with benefits, as much as I hate that term. It sounds so easy, when what we've shared has been deeply intense.

C. and I have spent the past week comforting each other, our therapeutic method including talk, wine for me, and whiskey for C. after I "found" the Jack Daniel's. A lot of time in bed figured into the repair work as well. Long pleasurable hours dosing each other in endorphins.

I'm grieving and C. is grieving and we have found solace in each other's arms. It turns out the gods are not wrong. Having a lovely young man—this particular young man— desire me has been balm for my broken heart. I believe I've been the same balm for his.

C. doesn't shower. He says he plans to stop at the state park on the way home for a swim.

As we descend the stairs from the second floor to the first, each step puts distance between us. By the time we reach the front door we are separate, as we will be from here on. We've shared a unique interlude and it's time to move on.

I don't hug him. I place a hand on his blue T-shirt, over his heart. "Don't be the stranger you've been for the last year and a half," I admonish. "I expect to see you with the rest of your family at the Thanksgiving leftovers party."

"Count on it," C. says, and, unlike with Kit, I believe I can. He covers my hand with his own and leans in to kiss me lightly on the lips. Then he gives Obie one last full-body scratch. When he's done, he steps onto the porch.

Perhaps I should close the door before he is completely gone, my usual farewell strategy with departing lovers. Yet because C. has never been one of their ilk, I stand in the open doorway, holding Obie by his collar as I watch C. progress across the porch with that wonderful bounce off the pads of his feet I've noticed only in young men. At the stairs, he turns, searches my face, and returns.

"Liz," he says sternly, placing his hands on my shoulders. He gives me a little shake. "You *will* make contact with your Southern friend."

He's been at me about Kit every single day. Sometimes two or three times a day. I nod.

"That wasn't a yes," he says.

"I promise to think about it." And I do think about it. Every day. What I think about mostly is how devastated I'll be if Kit doesn't respond, should I try to contact him.

C. rolls his eyes, unable to believe my stubbornness. "Just do it," he says, sounding exasperated. "I don't want to leave here concerned about you."

"My knight in shining armor," I tease, trying to deflect him with humor. I really need to decide if this humor thing is a habit I should change.

"I'm wise to your tricks. Don't try to make me laugh. Just do it."

"C., I said I'll think about it. That's the best I can do."

He grunts and rolls his eyes one more time before turning away. "I have your e-mail address," he warns over his shoulder.

"Love you." I'm being ironic, although I do love him.

He gives me the finger, but with a wide grin, and jumps clear of the porch. Of the many lovely images of C. I hold in my head—and there are some mighty fetching ones—this is the one I know I'll always see first: golden hair streaming, body poised in midair.

Landing on the walkway as softly as a cat or a ballet dancer, and as light on his feet as the fencer he is, he offers a last jaunty wave, and sprints the rest of the way to his car.

✴

I am a bad Jew—or so my mother says. I eat shellfish regularly and show up at synagogue rarely. It is true that I give the organized trappings of my religion a wide berth. If this is a sin, I'm in good company. Like me, the majority of American Jews live a secular life. What is hard for outsiders to see is that Judaism is the ballast that keeps many of us afloat, the philosophical underpinnings that define who we are and a source of joy and sustenance. It is also the scale upon which we value and weigh the difficult choices life foists on us.

Entering the sanctuary for Yom Kippur, one of the two holidays I'm guaranteed to show up for services, I notice Evie, my friend and designer of the favorite Bakelite necklace, hailing me from a pew halfway down the aisle.

Evie's blond curly hair tumbles past her shoulders in contrast to her husband Dov's hair, which is long too, but coal black and tied away from his face with a narrow strip of white fabric. He usually uses a leather twist, but on the Day of Atonement, tradition dictates we leave leather goods at home.

In the ancient world, leather was a status symbol. On this holiday, we are meant to be humble before God, hence the prohibition against leather.

"*Shanah tovah*," I say, seating myself next to my friend. I've wished her good year in Hebrew, which is a traditional greeting during the holidays. Dov leans past Evie. "*Shanah tovah*, Liz. Good to see you."

I thank him. We exchange a few more words of welcome. He returns to his siddur—Hebrew for prayer book. Dov grew up in a Hasidic household. Though he attends our Reconstructionist temple, he holds more tightly to tradition than I do, wearing white for the purity of the day, including white canvas sneakers. Being Dov, the sneakers are Converse high-tops.

During the High Holidays, as on the Sabbath, we are meant to leave our daily concerns behind, no going to work or driving, which is why I walked to services on this gorgeous late-September morning.

Other prohibitions include no turning on lights or performing any household task, including cooking. Bathing, eating, drinking, and sex don't make the cut, either. Turning on lights used to require a candle and flint, more work than flipping a switch. Although we no longer beat rugs, or stir our clothing in large pots to launder them, also involving fire—the prohibitions remain, because they are about more than physical labor. Not doing work means not having the distractions of daily tasks to take our thoughts away from more lofty matters.

Fasting and abstaining from bathing are meant to remind us that too many people in the world do not have their elemental needs met. Going without is a call to compassion and to charity and activism on the behalf of those less fortunate. I'm not sure why there is a prohibition against sex, although being distracted by pleasure is the opposite of introspection. I should ask the rabbi to clarify that one for me.

While sex hasn't been on my radar since C. left, I am, as my grandmother used to say, "*So hungry my belly button is hitting my backbone.*"

Her exact words in American-Yiddish vernacular were "My *pupik* is clopping," which is how I'm feeling after not eating or drinking since an early dinner last night. Nine hours to go and counting.

Evie asks, "Will you break fast with us?"

Did I forget to reply? I've been a little distracted. "I have two freshly-baked challahs in my kitchen to contribute."

"Great. And how could I say no to your challah? Dov says mine doesn't taste like a Jewish girl made it."

Evie converted when she married Dov. She elbows her husband. He leans in our direction. "I am glad you made two because I'm reserving one for my exclusive consumption." Hugging his wife, he adds, "I like to tease Evie. She knows I love her baking."

Pointing at something in the prayer book, Evie listens as Dov says something into her ear. I look around the small shul, smiling and exchanging waves with other congregants.

The Yiddish word for genuine is *haimish*, a good descriptor of our temple. Built at the beginning of the twentieth century, the Ashburton synagogue is a humble building that mixes Yankee austerity, Arts and Crafts architecture, and decorative flourishes that look as if they were inspired by Scheherazade.

The building accommodates no more than a hundred and fifty people. Its human scale and integrity remind me of the pink chapel. Both the pink chapel and the shul promote thinking, which is what I'm here to do.

I don't come to services to recite prayers. Unlike Dov, who is studying his prayer book with intensity, mine is closed. The praying I do on Yom Kippur is from my soul, not by the book.

The Bible says God created us in his own image. If that is true, then logically, as our pater, God shares our sins. For me, that goes a long way toward explaining why God is always so irritated with us, as the prayers continually point out. What parent enjoys seeing his children repeat his own mistakes?

Most of us, however, understand that when you say no to a toddler, the first thing the child will do is test your mettle. Adam and Eve may have had adult bodies, but they were totally ignorant about the true consequences of eating that apple. The way I see it, God should have begun with several other less-dire lessons, so that by the time he got to the apple, Adam and Eve were clued in to the kind of retribution in store when God said "don't."

In my opinion, God needs to take more responsibility for his less-than-successful parenting.

His parenting skills are also why the siddur's seven-hundred-plus pages of "I am lowly and unworthy" don't work for me. The promise of retribution has never been a great way to control human behavior. Follow the news if you need examples. I don't understand why God doesn't put more emphasis on practical steps toward transformation, including immediate rewards for good deeds. But then, I'm not privy to God's big-picture plans, which is probably why I'm missing the genius of his game.

After years of reading the prayer book and leaving shul so depressed I would have thrown myself upon the nearest burning bush if one had presented itself, I forgo most of the prayers to concentrate on my specific spiritual issues, allowing my mind to wander in its own wilderness until a solution presents itself. Surprisingly often, one does.

Rosh Hashanah, the birthday of creation, focuses on thankfulness, but grief and forgiveness rule Yom Kippur. Today is for acknowledging the mistakes we have made that hurt us, as well as those around us. We are meant to mourn our imperfections and those we share collectively with our species. And, as the year passes into memory, we remember what and whom we have loved and lost.

This may seem majorly depressing, but there is an upside. If we do what we can to make amends, if we are genuinely sorry for our trespasses, whether deliberate or not, God is amenable to giving us some slack, although he/she likes it best if we atone to those we have wronged, preferably face to face. The ten days between Rosh Hashanah and Yom Kippur are specifically set aside for this task.

I believe atonement motivated Roland to apologize to me when we met at that wedding a year and a half ago. It is hard to believe how quickly time has passed from that February afternoon to the present, and also how rarely I think of him anymore. In hindsight, accosting me at that wedding was good for both of us, though I didn't think so at the time. Being able to express my feelings to Roland contributed to finally separating myself from the trauma of our parting.

If we are heartfelt in our sorrow, God wipes our slates clean and grants us another year to do better. That's his special deal of the day.

But if we aren't heartfelt, it's like taunting God to go ahead and do his worst. A superstitious bunch—not only Jews, but human beings of every stripe—most of us prefer not to throw dice against those consequences. The idea of trudging through the year without this reckoning, carrying the weight of so many transgressions, seems like an exhausting prospect when you are used to the gift of yearly absolution.

I don't know if the Bible is literally true or a compilation of stories meant to impart ancient and still universal truths. Whatever it is, a proscribed day to appreciate the world and, close on, another for absolution and renewal is a great mitzvah—an immense blessing. This sums up why I'm sitting here contemplating the trajectory of my life over the previous twelve months.

The good news: I haven't indulged in any terrible crimes against humanity, animals, or the environment. I haven't cheated on a spouse, traded junk bonds, or kicked my dog. I'm a good friend to those I love. I recycle, give to a charity that helps women who are mistreated, and to the ASPCA. I buy Obie his favorite peanut butter treats, and I participate in Green Up Day.

But on the flip side of the coin, I've been snippy with Diana when understanding was called for. I forgot to call my brother Henry on his birthday. I have shortened Obie's walks when I'm busy with deadlines, and for the last few months, I've been more than a teensy bit self-involved and impatient. Nor do I communicate with my mother as often as I should.

The rabbi interrupts the contemplation of my shortcomings by calling out the page number of the blessing that begins the service. I shift in my seat. The bench, though well cushioned, is not meant to be comfortable. I flip to the blessing and view it without reading, asking for forgiveness of my trespasses against Diana, Henry, and Obie. I decide I have some making up to do where Arielle is concerned as well. She deserves more and continued thanks for trying to cheer me up about Kit. Maybe it is time for a Miu-Miu portrait. As for him—I am still trying to figure that one out.

On Rosh Hashanah, I thanked God for the people I love, including Mr. Couper. As Darius pointed out, you can never be too grateful for the gifts life offers.

But no surprise, being thankful is easier than forgiving.

This year, like all the rest, I can't forgive my mother her continued judgment of me. I do love her and know she loves me. Luckily, so far, God has been willing to let me and Mom inch our way toward each other. Hopefully, he's still okay with the slow pace of our progress.

Also on my conscience: a couple of clients obnoxious enough to provoke less than stellar behavior on my part. In my favor, I completed the work to my usual standards despite the Bridezilla behavior of the brides and their mothers.

So much for the easy stuff. There are some harder bits. Chief among them is that I have been remiss about not visiting Darius, because going to see him means telling him about where his insights have led. He sent two postcards in March that I didn't receive until I returned home. Fate hasn't pushed us together, so I swear that I will stop at his shop in the next few days. I promised to show him my new work. It is time to fulfill that promise.

C. was on my sins list last year, but no longer. Sometimes I view C. as the catalyst that forced the rest, leading to what Darius taught me and to the new direction my career is taking. He was the beginning of many lessons, some deeply painful, some lovely. Looking back, I see how my dissatisfaction with work and The Rules kicked into overdrive about the time C. and I saw that odd French movie. I hope our time together propels C. toward happiness. In my mind's eye, I see him leaping off my front porch. He e-mailed yesterday, saying he isn't letting women pick him up in bars while he tests out what he refers to as my "Archaic Dating Rules for Dummies." His news included a piano audition he's taking next week for a big band forming on campus. I send up a prayer that he wins the gig. Being in a band could expose him to fresh venues and people and, perhaps, the right girl.

C. remains adamant that I contact Kit. In his e-mail he asked whether I'd done it yet. I don't know why I'm so resistant.

When I imagine Kit these days, I picture him in that Tom Ford suit, a friend with benefits on his arm. It's a reliable way to torture myself. I want to be the only woman on his arm—forever—which is a truth I force myself to accept as the trending reality.

Rabbi Simcha instructs the congregation to rise for the opening of the ark and the reading of the Amidah. We stand, as one. The Amidah is a complicated prayer beginning with a recitation of our ancestors— Abraham, Isaac, Jacob, Sarah, Rebecca, Rachel, and Leah—before turning to the subjects of understanding and return, repentance, forgiveness, and healing. The last stanzas are entreaties to God for more years to enjoy life and serve "the eternal one."

Once the opening section of the prayer is said in unison, we read the rest silently at our own speed. The room is quiet enough to hear the rustle of each thin page as individual congregants turn them.

The Amidah is the only prayer that feeds my soul. Yet, as I begin the reading, entreating God for forgiveness and for the personal guarantee of another year to improve myself, as well as to give back to the world, my thoughts return to Kit.

I ask God if he/she can explain why a relationship so ephemeral, a relationship tallied in months rather than years, should be so difficult to let go. Admittedly, I didn't do any better with Roland, although we knew each other far longer than I've known Kit.

How do I let go?

God doesn't answer. Or maybe the answer is in the Amidah's appeal for forgiveness and healing. *Heal me, then,* I silently entreat. My tone, though unverbalized, makes what I'm asking more of a dare.

Again, I receive no answer.

I imagine loosening the bonds of indecision and yearning that bind me. I imagine that being released I would float through the glowing light of the stained-glass Star of David window over the ark and out into the sky like a character from a Chagall painting.

The sun slides behind clouds. The window darkens. I sigh, returning to the liturgy of the Amidah. I ask myself why I'm so stubborn. Why can't I make the decision to contact Kit or to let him go?

The congregation reads in unison. I join my voice to theirs:

Hear our voice, Lord our God; merciful Father, have compassion upon us and accept our prayers in mercy and favor, for You are God who hears prayers and supplications; do not turn us away empty-handed from You, our King, for You hear the prayer of everyone. Blessed are You, Lord, who hears prayer. Show us mercy . . .

If God is willing to offer me so many second and third chances, having kept his side of the bargain for lo these many years, especially during the last five years when he might have turned away in disgust while I busily deceived myself about my own happiness, then . . . then my worst sin isn't my stubbornness to forgive.

My worst sin is my belief that paring away emotions I deemed undesirable—paring away love—could lead to happiness. It seems incredible that I didn't see the fatal flaw therein. By protecting myself from heartache and exiling pain, I also exiled too much joy.

Oh, I have lived a full, emotion-fueled life with my daughter and friends and family, and I have an intensely intimate relationship with the world. The images I capture with my camera are proof of that. It turns out, however, that I need more.

God! I hope you are listening because I'm about to admit that Darius was right about everything. I crave the joy and challenge of an intimate partnership. The pleasure my affairs offer is no longer enough. It has never been enough.

Since I talk to Yahweh and to Zeus, I might as well add a little Chinese philosophy to my melting pot. For thousands of years, humans have understood that a life without balance, without the yin and yang of joy and despair, cannot be wholly complete or completely happy.

I have to grab the pew in front of me as a new truth smacks into me. No wonder I've spent most of the past few of years stumbling around in the dark. My life was out of balance. If I find no other truth today, at least I've found the key to that mystery!

A chill runs up my spine as sunlight spills through the windows, so bright I have to squint to see into it. If I believed in signs and portents—which occasionally I do—I've just received an answer from on high.

Rabbi Simcha asks us to read aloud and in unison the urgent words of the last section of the Amidah, exhorting us to make our choices, to forgive and to repent. God will be closing his gates at sundown. Within the framework of this healing ritual, if we don't come inside now, if I don't come inside now, I will be locked away from life's full embrace for another year.

Five years is definitely enough. It is time to open my own gates. It is time to unlock the door to my heart, and to welcome whatever is on the other side, which nevertheless has as much chance of being sorrow as love.

I realize that I'm not supposed to stop loving Kit. I'm supposed to accept my feelings without trying to hide from them. They will change or not. They will be fulfilled or not. Whether what life delivers proves delightful or depressing, the point isn't to deny the feelings that rise in response, but to travel through those feelings with a modicum of forgiveness and grace.

Before Kit entered my life, I believed the fortress around my heart was unassailable. I believed that if my heart broke one more time, I wouldn't survive. But the opposite has occurred. Although Kit and I are no longer together, my heart is more whole than in a very long time. The new me, forged as a result, is stronger as well as wiser than the woman Dan and Roland rejected.

It is possible love may never walk through the door again, but as I lift my eyes to the sun, I thank God—all of my gods and goddesses—for the infinite second chances they offer.

C. is right. It is time for a last attempt to breach the walls around Kit's heart. He may not have been able to give me what I needed when I needed it, but I didn't do any better by him. He needed time and I refused it.

No matter the outcome, I will find a way to hold out my hand. If Kit doesn't take it, I will survive. I have learned to grieve and forgive. I have learned how to begin again.

CHAPTER 42

"DARIUS?" I CALL, entering the shop with my laptop under my arm. Looking around, I see his inventory no longer includes the Biedermeier pieces or the wonderful yellow-striped Empire sofa I admired last fall. The chiffonier is the only piece I remember. There are new acquisitions to enjoy: a long cherry sideboard, Deco in style, eight beautiful mixed-wood chairs from the 1930s, and a high Victorian dresser with a polished stone top that looks as if it lived a past life in a great house's kitchen.

I pick a red maple leaf that blew in with me off the parquet as the sharp clip of hard-soled shoes moves in my direction.

"Leezbeth!" Darius exclaims as he comes into sight from the other side of the hall. "How delightful, *chérie*!" He sandwiches my hand between his own. "I have been hoping you would stop by."

We buss cheeks. "I was hoping the same of you," I tell him. Getting myself here proved far easier than figuring out how to approach Kit, but I'm working on that, too.

Darius laughs, not the least offended by the pushback. "I assume we have both been very busy," he says. Extracting his ever-present pocket watch from his vest, he flips it open. "Close enough to the end of business hours to offer a drink. Shall we?" He motions toward the stairs.

In his great-room, we carry our French chardonnay to the sitting area.

"I brought my computer to show you images from Georgia as promised."

"I saw some of them at Sal's. The photographs are very fine."

I set the laptop on the bench as I settle on the couch. "Thank you." I grin. "In fact, I'm not sure I can thank you enough for encouraging the trip to Georgia. I loved it there and found fantastic subjects for my camera." I reach across the table to him. He leans forward to squeeze my hand.

"You know, I bought one of your pieces."

"Sal didn't tell me!"

"It was last night." He walks to the back wall and turns a frame resting on the floor to display the image of mist hovering over Willing's meadow. "I like your title."

"*Hope Rising.*" I was both apprehensive and hopeful that morning. Swallowing my feelings I tell Darius about Arliss and Contact 32.

"Congratulations, Leezbeth. I am so delighted."

"And you? How was Europe? I appreciated the postcards you sent but you didn't offer details."

"*Très bon.* I delight in the bosom of my family. As for the treasures I returned with, I am sorry you did not visit sooner. The shop's poverty of inventory"—he waves a hand—"indicates it is time to depart, as much as the calendar says the same."

As usual, his narrative is the bare bones.

"Can you believe it is just short of a year since I've seen you?" I say.

He nods. "Life moves too quickly." His twinkling eyes meet mine. "What of you? The South is almost another country, *oui*? I can tell from your pictures your time there was productive. And Christopher? He was a good host?"

"Has he reported in?"

Darius gives me one of his dead-eyed looks and says, "He told me he loved having you with him."

"And I loved being with him." It takes effort to continue meeting Darius's gaze.

His eyes hold mine as he sips his drink, but he doesn't press for more information, which makes me want to share it—likely his plan from the start.

"Do you remember the night when we fought about love?" I ask.

"I remember a dialogue."

"An intense dialogue. We held very different views about relationships. Since my return from Georgia, I've wanted to tell you that you were right more than I was."

Darius's expression says, *Well, of course.*

"Kit and I—" I put my glass on the bench between us and rub my eyes. "I thought it might be—"

"I admit, *petit colombe*, I thought you would be good for each other," he interrupts, a kindness because it is still hard to say aloud that I thought we were in love.

"As prescient as you were, in the end we didn't want the same thing," I say instead.

"It is regrettable about his wife." Darius tsks. "Such a tragedy can create a wound that never truly heals. Although I had hoped—"

"Me too," I interject this time, seeing no point in rehashing what happened.

He leans over and touches my knee with his fingertips. "You are sure Christopher does not want what you want?"

Before I can ask if he possesses information I don't have, a petite woman, perhaps a little younger than Darius, walks into the room carrying a string bag filled with groceries.

"Gertrude," he says, getting up to relieve her of the bag. A smile lights his face. Darius pronounces her name the French way; Jerrr-trued.

I stand to greet her.

"This is Leezbeth Silver. Remember at Sal's? It was her photograph I purchased." He walks to the kitchen island. I follow. He pours another glass of wine.

"*Oui*," she says. "Of course. It eez a pleasure to meet you. Your work is lovely." Her accent is strong. She is also *très* chic, with expertly colored blond hair worn in a loose knot at the back of her head. Something about the elegant cut of her knee-length skirt and tailored blouse, as well as the way she wears the antique moonstone necklace roping her throat with several strands of pearls, seems quintessentially Parisian.

"I'm delighted to meet you," I reply. Gertrude is an interesting twist to Darius's story. "How lovely that you could visit."

"I think so, too." She smiles at Darius, taking the glass he offers. "I am learning the town. I hope to know all of its streets by the time we return to Paris this winter."

We walk to the seating area and share the couch.

Darius takes his usual chair. "And then we will come home to Ashburton, if she does not grow tired of me." He leans into his wing chair. Ever Mr. Mystery, he adds, "Gertrude and I have known each other a very long time. I am hoping she knows my faults well enough not to find them terribly disturbing."

"Since university," Gertrude says.

I glance back and forth between them, wondering about their history. The way they are looking at each other makes me think Darius has found a reason to let his own wounds heal. Perhaps this is another one of my delusions, but over the last couple of months I have come to believe there is some choice involved in whether one heals or not. Past the worst grief, a time exists when we must decide whether to live looking only over our shoulders or to face forward and try new paths. It isn't that we shouldn't remember and honor the distance we have traveled, but if we are always facing backward and yearning for what we've lost, we squander the future and the happiness available to us in the present.

Gertrude lifts her glass to drink. A vintage, basket-cut diamond flashes, catching the light. It exactly where you'd expect to see one on a woman who is half of an engaged couple.

I glance at Darius. He meets my eyes and twinkles. I suffer a tiny twinge although I know Darius and I were not right for each other. A voice in my head, the forward-leaning voice, notes that if Darius can fall in love, my own situation may not be as hopeless as I believe.

❉

"The only problem," I tell Arielle, "is figuring out the best form of contact."

"What about you keep it simple and call?"

"Too easy to misinterpret pauses. And excruciating if he doesn't want to hear from me."

We are drinking tea and eating my blondies. With the wedding season winding down, I've finally had time to bake. I brought a tin to Georgie at the nursing home this afternoon, then dropped by to deliver the rest to Arielle. She invited me for an early dinner.

After dabbing a napkin to her lips, she says, "Men are like aliens who walk among us. I have no idea what the protocol is for telling a man you're sorry, though I assume it is the same as when you tell anyone you are sorry. You apologize. You ask forgiveness. Remember how you used to say to Diana when she was little, 'Use your words'? I assume that's a good route to go. Seems like it might be water under the bridge, but you know what they say: 'If you don't ask, the answer is always no.'"

"Nora Roberts, the great sage of our times."

"Is it my fault she got that right—although I think I've read that quote in other places. But as I said, don't ask me. Do what feels right to you."

"I've gotten as far as deciding to send a photograph, only I can't figure out which one." I take another sip of tea. "Hey, did you get a request from Francesca? She wanted a couple of images for a show she's opening for the holiday season. The theme is 'other places.' She said she was contacting you, as well."

"I meant to tell you. I'm making a punch bowl. It's going to be my take on a Greek chalice complete with bacchanalian figures dancing around the center. I've never done anything with human figures before. I'm looking forward to the challenge."

"That's great," I say. "I had to check my contract with Arliss. Apparently I can work with galleries out of the country, but in country she has to be notified."

Diana, Marc, and Arielle accompanied me to New York last weekend for a group show opening at Contact 32. I sold another image that night and the show was covered in The New York Times. The black-and-white version of the wisteria covered house got a mention. Needless to say, I'm thrilled.

My iPhone rings in my purse. I fish for the phone making menacing shark music. "I'm going to be impolite and pick this up," I tell my friend.

She nods and reaches for a second blondie.

After the usual "Hold for Arliss Kline," only a few seconds go by before she comes on line. "I have good news."

I put her on speakerphone, so Arielle can hear the good news with me.

"We just sold *The Trees Whisper*. And I've got someone interested in *Needwood Church at Twilight*. I'm going to ask Rick to print another set of the images we've sold, but larger scale this time. And I'm upping your prices."

"Great!"

I turn to Arielle after Arliss hangs up. "Did you hear that? Oh my God!"

My friend says, "We need to celebrate. I've got my ever-present bottle of champagne in the fridge. It's been waiting for fun, rather than tragedy. Shall we?"

"Absolutely!"

CHAPTER 43

DATE: October 25
FROM: LSilverphotography@gmail.com
TO: edschriver@goldendov.com; TDonaldson@gmail.com;
darius@barbariantiques.com
SUBJECT: Thanksgiving Leftovers Party

Diana and I hope the annual leftovers party is on your calendar.
The party starts at 5:00 p.m., the Saturday after Thanksgiving.

As always, bring leftovers repurposed or straight up and let
us know by end of day Friday whether you are bringing a before,
during, or after, so we can fill in the food triangle as needed.
Looking forward to seeing you—

Liz & Diana

Realizing I already have an address group from my birthday, I delete the addresses I just added to the "To" field, select the summer distribution list, and hit Send.

With this small task accomplished, I return to work and pull the new shots Arliss and I selected, as well as two for Francesca.

Today is also the day I've set aside to finally choose an image for Kit. I've decided that pictures speak louder than words. I plan to send along a few words as well, but I'm relying on the shot I pick to convey my message.

Having narrowed the choice to two contenders, I contemplate the photograph of the glowing mist rising off the meadow that Darius bought, and Kit's pink trees. I decide to go with the meadow, probably because the title, *Hope Rising*, sums up my feelings about this endeavor.

As I move the image into the Dropbox for Rick to pick up and wait for it to load, I click into the folder where I've tucked all the snapshots of Kit, and scroll through the thumbnails. I must make a sound of distress because Obie, settled at my feet, rises. He pushes his head under my hand. I inhale, forcing myself to breathe deeply. Patting Obs to reassure him I'm okay, I scroll through the photographs of the man I love.

Not all attractive people are photogenic, but Kit is. I hesitate over a shot of him lying on his stomach, hair tousled, his head nestled in the cross of his arms, a smile on his lips and a mischievous glint in his warm brown eyes. Kit was never afraid to show himself to the camera just as, for a brief time, he showed himself to me.

I draw a shaky breath and scroll faster. The shots I want are among the last. My hand stills as the images I took the night of the gala come into view. Clicking through the six shots from that evening, I choose the last one. Kit's mouth is tipped up on one side in his signature grin, his hand over his heart, the full wattage of his Kit-ness on display.

I convert it to black-and-white, sizing it to fit one of Kit's 5 x 7 frames. After I add the shot to the Dropbox folder for Rick, I order a frame online. In the shipping form, I type in The Photographer's Lens address.

Whether Kit adds the framed shot to his hall gallery or not isn't within my control. What matters is for him to see how lit he was for me. For us. I don't think I'm imagining that he was as lit up as he was in his wedding pictures. Along with my note, I'm hoping the image will allow him to acknowledge the joyous future he seems intent on throwing away.

Composing a message to include in the shipping box with Kit's gifts is more difficult than choosing the images. I spend an hour typing and erasing. Finally, I give up on a message of wit or great insight. On a plain blank card I write, "I hold the memory of the joy you shared with me close. I'm sorry for my part in what happened between us. Love to you always. Liz"

✳

Two days after FedEx sends the confirmation that Kit received the package, his e-mail arrives.

- Package received.
- I realize I'm breaking the rules, but I want you to know how much I appreciate your gifts.

There is no greeting or salutation bracketing his two concise bullet points. Also, no "love you."

I pour myself a glass of wine, saluting the man's uncanny ability to keep me tethered and yet in limbo. The wine doesn't do much to dull my disappointment. I conclude that neither photograph offered Kit the epiphany the decision to send them was for me.

For as much as I had riding on his reaction, I don't implode. Maybe I'm finally getting over him. Or maybe, like any overtaxed muscle, my heart is too exhausted to feel much of anything.

The person I share the news with is C., who has been keeping me apprised of his own adventures, including a girl named Mina, the lead singer for the band for which he is now the pianist. C. says they play Dixieland and Bluegrass with a modern twist. He promised to send me a YouTube link as soon as their first video is finished. To my missive about Kit's reaction, he responded:

Hang in there. This is good. I can see you rolling your eyes from here BUT give him time. He has some reconfiguring to do now that you've made your move. See you at Thanksgiving. Okay if I bring Mina?

Ciao—
"C."

AFTER

"DO WE HAVE enough pie?"

I glance at the four pies lined up on the sideboard, two apple, two pumpkin. "Probably not," I tell Diana, "but Arielle is bringing an apple cake, and Evie mentioned a pecan pie or pumpkin mousse."

"I forgot about those. Mar-kie?" Diana sings. "Can you get the chocolate down from the top shelf where we stashed it to keep Obie from trying to kill himself again?"

Marc and Diana drove into town late yesterday afternoon after spending Thanksgiving with his parents. It was Diana's first visit with Marc's family, a sign that all is well with my daughter and her mate, because that's who Marc seems to be. Right from the start, he's been relaxing into his role. It was Diana who was less sure about committing herself. I'm delighted she seems to have moved past her doubts, which were related to past experience, not to Marc. Having the wisdom to know what parts of the past should be allowed to color the present is difficult to decipher—I should know.

The outside door is shoved open. Cold air rushes into the kitchen along with my best friend. I take the apple cake from her and set it on the counter. Obie offers his usual effusive greeting, which becomes more effusive when Arielle pulls a dog treat out of her pocket. It must be peanut butter because he heads for the living room to savor it in private.

"Snow coming." Arielle shivers as she takes her coat off and hangs it on the portable rack I've erected next to the door.

I look out the window at the heavy gray sky. "The weather had better hold off until the guests have come and gone." Most Vermonters can drive in all weather conditions, but we are smart enough to stay inside during a storm unless it is absolutely necessary to go out.

Arielle turns to me. "Is there something I can do?"

I point at the oversize cutting board on the dining room table where the orchid, blooming profusely, holds pride of place. The plant and I have made peace with each other. I've even come to appreciate its straightforward come-on. Knowing what it needs, it presents those needs without apology, along with admirable artifice.

"Can you open the figs and cut apart the grapes?" I put the kitchen shears in her hand. "The cheeses in the fridge go with the fruit."

Arielle gives me a Girl Scout salute.

The doorbell chimes. I send Diana to answer it. She returns with Jill and Alex. Alex carries a huge turkey pie.

"This is for the drinks table." Jill holds up a bottle of Prosecco.

I direct her to the cloth-covered folding table in the living room where I've arranged various types of glassware, liquor, and a wide tin bucket filled with ice and stocked with white wine, beer, and soda.

The rest of the guests arrive in a flurry soon after. Diana and I take turns manning the door. Evie and Dov show up with sweet potato pasties and the promised pecan pie. In the kitchen, warming trays I've collected over the years fill with other contributions: turkey chili, squash soup, and a casserole made from layered leftovers—potatoes, peas, stuffing, and gravy-soaked sliced turkey. Side dishes, including relishes and breads, gradually crowd the kitchen counters.

The Larkins arrive last. Mel steps inside, carrying a large bowl of roasted vegetables. She busses my cheek and hands the bowl to me. Ham gives my shoulder a squeeze. Harry sidles in after his father. Drew isn't here. He chose to attend a gaming convention in Burlington. C. brings up the rear, a beautiful mixed-race young woman at his side.

"C.—" I start and then correct myself. "Ford! Come in, come in."

He laughs, gives me a knowing wink, and motions the young woman in ahead of him.

"Mina?" I ask.

She nods hello. C.'s new girlfriend has coffee-colored skin and eyes more gold than brown. Her hair is arranged in tiny braids. Each tawny strand capped with an assortment of colorful beads and tiny bells, pulled away from her elegant bones into a loose ponytail clasped high on her head. A drape-necked top falls off one of her slim shoulders. Below her Band-Aid skirt, her legs are encased in striped leggings. Wearing platform heels, she's only a couple of inches shorter than C.

"Ford has likely explained I'm his honorary Auntie Mame," I say to her.

C.'s mouth quivers with suppressed amusement.

"He told me you're one of his 'other mothers,'" Mina answers.

I can't help glancing at C. He shrugs. Then, apparently unable to contain his mirth, he whoops.

Mel gives me a significant look. "He's been in high spirits all weekend. It's nice to see him so cheerful." Her glance holds mine as we remember how unhappy he was the last time he was home. "Mina is from Belize," she adds.

"It's so nice of you to invite me to your party," Mina says.

"It is so nice of you to join us," I answer sincerely. "I would take your coats so you can pour yourselves drinks, but my hands are full."

"I'll deal with those." Ham gathers the coats.

"Thanks, Ham."

Mina rubs her arms as if she's cold.

"Can I get you a sweater?" I ask.

"Here." C. peels his off, exposing a T-shirt that reads, "There's no place like 127.0.0.1." I have no idea what it means. He hands the sweater to her.

"Thanks, babe. I wish I could get used to the cold."

"Liz doesn't like the cold either. She went all the way to Georgia to escape it last winter." He looks at me and says, "Are you going back?"

"It doesn't look like it," I answer, understanding the question he's really asking.

"Too bad not to be somewhere warm in winter. I should have considered the weather before I decided on Barnard, but New York does have its compensations." Mina grins at C.

He grins back and rubs his hands together. "Let's see what there is to drink."

Before we separate so they can peel off toward the drinks table, C. offers my shoulder a commiserating pat. "I'm disappointed," he says. "I was hoping you'd have better news."

"Me too." I had so hoped. I ask C. to pour a glass of the Prosecco for me. Turning to his girlfriend, I say, "Mina, I hope we'll get another chance to chat once the food is situated."

"Can I help?"

"My daughter and I have it covered, but thank you. I need you to save your energy for eating a lot of what we put on the table!"

I leave them to their drinks and round up Diana and Arielle. Diana gathers Marc into our serving group. We remove the appetizer detritus to the kitchen and begin transferring main and side dishes to the table. Counting heads, I tally all twenty-three guests who accepted the invitation.

Once my helpers and I put the food out with dinner plates and utensils, I tap the side of my glass. It takes a minute for conversation to die down. Diana stands next to me. I put my arm around her waist.

Scanning the smiling faces of my friends, I allow myself a few seconds to feel fortunate there are so many lovely people in my life. Like Arielle, many of them have been friends of mine for decades.

C. leans into the archway between the dining and living rooms with his arm around Mina's shoulders. Our eyes meet. He raises his glass.

If I hadn't slept with him—my sweet catalyst—would I be represented by a major New York gallery today? Taking him to bed was an impetuous decision that led down a winding road to some pretty amazing places. And, he's been a help not once but twice, the second time when we consoled each other for our losses.

Though contacting Kit didn't work out the way I'd hoped, C. was right about my need to do it. Whatever mistakes I made with Kit, I have a modicum of peace I wouldn't have if I hadn't attempted to make amends. That Kit didn't change his mind, or couldn't, doesn't negate the worthiness of taking the chance on love.

Discovering it is possible to open my heart without losing it utterly, along with the exciting recognition and remuneration from the landscape work I love best, connect back to that February evening with C. His new confidence and happiness, the interesting Mina at his side, is, I believe, confirmation that I have been as much a positive catalyst for him as he was for me.

"A micro minute before we all dig in," I shout to the group assembled around the table. "Let me start by saying thank you all for attending the thirteenth annual Thanksgiving leftovers party!"

Mel yells, "A lucky and auspicious number!"

The rest of the group laughs.

"The jury is out on that one. But—what's without doubt is how lucky I am to have such wonderful friends in my life."

"Back at you" and "Here! Here!" rise from the crowd.

"Eat, drink, and be merry!" I proclaim. *"L'chayim! Salud! Bon appétit!"*

"L'chayim! Salud! Bon appétit!" echoes around.

Arielle and Marc pull lids and foil off pots and casseroles. I gesture to everyone to take a plate and start eating.

Diana turns to me and says, "Mom, you seem to have returned to your old self. I'm glad."

"It's possible the woman before you is not her old self, but a new and improved self." I give her waist a squeeze. "I meant what I said—I'm so lucky." My voice fills with emotion. "I may not have a *beshert*"—I pause, letting my feelings settle so I can continue past the tightening in my throat—"but I do have friends and family who love me as much as I love them. And you, my darling daughter, are the icing on my cake."

As heartbreaking as it was to love Kit and not have him love me the same way, I survived his loss, and though my heart remains bruised, it is in one piece. Maybe Arielle was right and Kit was for practice, because if the door to love were to open again, I won't hesitate to step through it. Love is worth the risk.

"I have a wonderful life," I tell Diana.

She doesn't roll her eyes. "I'm glad you feel that way. I know I give you a hard time, but for the record, you're an amazing woman and I'm lucky you're my mom."

"Awwww, honey—"

"Don't let that go to your head," she snaps but leans in to kiss my cheek.

I laugh and gather her in for a hug.

"Okay, sentimental journey over." She pulls away. "Let's get the apple pies into the oven."

"Yes, ma'am." We each pick up a pie from the sideboard and carry it into the kitchen. Once the pies are warming, I suggest to Diana that she get herself some dinner.

"I did too much munching. But you should have something." Opening the refrigerator, she begins sliding cartons and containers around, making room for more leftovers.

"Uh-oh," she says, still bent into the refrigerator. "There's no heavy cream." I hear a note of exasperation in her tone. She means, "You forgot to get the cream."

"We can manage without. There's vanilla ice cream in the freezer."

"You can manage, not me. Pecan pie has to have whipped cream. I'm willing to slum it and buy the stuff in a can, but there will be whipped cream on my pie!" She grabs her coat and handbag.

"Really, Diana—"

In the light from the street lamp outside the window, I see a few fine snowflakes have begun to swirl. While I'm studying the weather, Diana disappears into the dining room, returning with Marc in tow. His plate is full. From his body language he appears about as inclined to venture into the cold for whipped cream as I am. After a bit of back and forth, he gives my daughter a broad smile and follows her to the coat rack, wolfing his food. I don't know what she said to get him into the car with her, but I see regret in his eyes as he sets his plate aside.

"You're a good man," I tell him.

"I'm a crazy man."

I laugh. "I'll keep that warm for you." Cutting off a piece of foil, I wave them out the door.

After I've covered Marc's plate and set it on a warming tray, I select a few bites and wander into the living room. Alex pats a spot on a bench I've set in front of the bookcases.

"This is a great crowd. A foodie crowd," he comments. "I love your parties both for the food and because your friends are so interesting. You know people from all over the place, and most of us don't see each other except for your birthday or Thanksgiving leftovers."

"I used to worry about being the only common denominator, but the mix seems to work."

"It definitely does."

I finish my food and excuse myself, heading toward the kitchen to make tea and check on the coffee pots. As I move through, I scan the crowd to make sure everyone has what they need. I see Harry pass Obie a piece of turkey from a platter and stuff a piece into his own mouth. As I stare at C.'s brother feeding contraband to my dog, my empty plate gets tugged from my hand. I follow the plate to see C. adding it to a stack on his arm. He moves toward the kitchen. I follow.

"Drop those in the sink, please."

He does as asked and then turns to face me. "It didn't work, huh?"

"I guess not."

"Damn. I was sure I had that right."

Rather than discuss Kit, I say, "So, Mina? Good going. She definitely seems strong and nice."

"And she's twenty-seven." A cheek-splitting grin overspreads C.'s face.

Laughing, I shoo him over so I can get to the sink to put water up for tea. I glance at the clock on the stove. Diana and Marc left twenty minutes ago. They only went to the corner store. What is taking so long? Maybe the store didn't have any cream and she had to go somewhere else?

C. and I begin clearing the food from the table. Mina and Arielle join in. As soon as Diana and Marc return, we'll serve dessert.

When the dishes are rinsed and in the dishwasher, I ask for the pies and other desserts to be taken to the table, while my alarmist tendencies kick in and I begin worrying about Diana in earnest.

I'm pulling out dessert bowls and setting up pitchers of cream and sugar when the doorbell chimes. "Odd," I say. Everyone I expected is here. Could Darius and Gertrude have come home early from his annual Thanksgiving trip to New York and decided to join us?

C. says, "I'll get it. You're busy."

"You can't manage the cream and sugar?" I tease, pulling the milk jug out of the fridge.

"Not that kind of cream." He winks and turns to weave his way through the crowded dining room.

Cocky bastard. I grin.

The pitchers and sugar bowls are arranged on a tray when C. returns. He puts his hand on my shoulder. "Liz?" His tone is grave. "You're needed at the door."

There is something in his expression that pulls my heart into my throat.

"Oh God, has something happened to Diana and Marc?"

"Oh—! No." C. rubs a palm down my arm. "Nothing like that. As far as I know, they're fine. But you need to come."

His assurances don't make me feel better. I consider the safety of my loved ones. If something had happened to my mother, who is with my brother and his family for the holiday, I would have received a call. Dad is in Florida for the winter, so if he were in trouble, there would be a different call, but not the police at my door. Are we making too much noise? Is that the problem? Has someone parked where they shouldn't?

C. tugs me through the living room, then retreats toward the kitchen.

Taking a deep breath, I swing the front door open, expecting to find a policeman on the other side. Instead, standing under the porch light, I see a man with salt-and-pepper hair, his broad back covered by a heavy navy overcoat, snowflakes glinting on his shoulders. He turns to face me. There are dozens of dusky pink roses in his arms.

The jolt is so strong, I have to steady myself in the doorframe.

We look at each other for what feels like a minute, but is probably only seconds. As usual, I have no idea what Kit sees in my expression. I see he is tired. And thinner. But his eyes are bright, his cheeks red from the cold.

"I'm here," he says.

"Yes . . . yes, you are." I can't get past the fact that he's standing on my porch.

When I don't say anything more or step aside for him to enter, he says, "You invited me."

"I did?" I try to think past the fog in my brain. Then the answer comes: I used the e-mail list for my birthday party, and he was on it. I hadn't noticed because I hit Send without reviewing the list.

His brow knits. "Maybe I should have called, but you were pretty specific about the rules of engagement."

I rub my eyes, just to make sure I'm not imagining him.

"I took too long," he says when I still can't get a coherent sentence out of my mouth. He takes a step toward me.

"Maybe a little long," I say, both dumbfounded and delighted, "but not too long."

"Good. So you wouldn't object to inviting me in? It's kind of cold out here for a Southerner."

"What? Oh. Yes. Right." God, I'm bowled over. Knocked on my ass, more like. I step aside.

Kit enters the house, which is when Obie, his sensitive ears alerted to his favorite's presence, skids into the room barking ecstatically.

"Obs!" Kit grins. He holds the loose bunch of roses out of the way just in time, as Obie leaps, almost knocking me over. His front paws land on Kit's chest.

"Obie," Kit says again. "Buddy—" He tries to pat him, but Obie is too excited, his joyous energy impossible for his body to contain. He pivots and gallops up the stairs. Short ecstatic yips echo as he runs from room to room over our heads.

"Are you okay?" Kit asks, probably because of the stunned expression I can't seem to wipe off my face. He holds the roses out to me.

Before I can decide whether I'm okay or not, Diana, who I'm relieved to see has arrived home safely, and alerted by the dog, hurries into the room. She holds a can of whipped cream in each hand. Behind her, silhouetted in the living room archway, Marc, Mina, and C. have congregated.

Diana glances at me for a second, reads my face, and turns her attention to our new guest. Her eyes widen. Though she's never met him, she instantly understands who he is.

Handing the whipped cream to Marc, my daughter looks Kit over. "Hi," she says. "I'm Diana." She holds out her hand.

Kit gives her one of his crinkly smiles. "A pleasure to meet you." They shake.

"Let me put those flowers in water," she offers, taking charge. Noting the living room has emptied, she suggests, "Why don't you and Mom sit in here. I'll get you some pie."

Why she thinks I need pie, I have no idea. Then I realize she's trying to give us some privacy. She reaches for the flowers I haven't taken from Kit. At the same moment, Obie careens down the stairs with something in his mouth. He knocks into Diana as the flowers are moving from hand to hand.

I will probably see this moment in my mind's eye for the rest of my life. Roses fly into the air, tumbling in a blur of pink and green, raining down on the bookcase and into the bookcase, falling over the dog and all over the floor. One lands on my shoulder, the stem catching in my hair.

Undaunted, Obie drops a stolen dinner roll at Kit's feet and looks up at him with a big doggie grin. His dust-mop tail swishes wildly. Kit takes in the flowers strewn at his feet. He glances at the roll, and then at me. Reaching out, he plucks the rose from my hair and offers it with a flourish.

And just like that, the two of us are laughing. Doubled over, can't stop, full-out hysterical.

At some point, Diana manages to turn C., Mina, and Marc around and herd them into the dining room, taking Obie with her. I watch, my stomach aching with the laughter I can't stop, as she rounds up our guests for dessert. A couple of curious glances get thrown in my direction but everyone stays in the dining room.

Kit stops laughing first. I'm not laughing any longer, either. I'm sobbing. All the feelings I've been struggling with have exploded out of the boxes where I've stashed them. I have imagined Kit at my door a hundred times. In my fantasies I'm in control; I'm cool and so collected. But here he is, and I can't collect a thing—not the roses, not my emotions, not the reality of his presence.

Wrapping an arm around me, he pulls me through the front door onto the porch where I can cry without an audience. He wraps his arms around me. I let him.

"You told me not to show up unless I knew what I wanted," he says into my hair.

I can't respond for trying to catch my breath. I start to shiver as much from the temperature as the adrenaline rush. Kit unbuttons his coat and wraps it around us. His warmth enfolds me with the scent of lemons.

"I know what I want. I want you," he says softly, resting his hand over mine where it lies against his shirtfront, where it feels right. When I don't resist, he brings my hand to his mouth and kisses the palm.

"Lizzie?" Kit says. "I'm sorry it's taken me so long to sort myself out. I was a little stupid."

I have finally calmed enough to produce a few words. "It's a failing of your sex," I sniff.

"I feel better knowing that. It's good not to carry a burden of such magnitude alone."

My mouth curls into a smile as I lean into his body. He kisses my forehead. We stand for a minute breathing each other in.

"Damn, this is better," Kit finally says.

"Better than what?" I ask. "Better than being alone? Better than being in Georgia?"

"Better you have expressed an opinion. You not having an opinion, dahlin'? I can't describe how truly disturbing the last few minutes have been for me."

"I'm pretty sure I've got a few more. Give me a little time."

"All the time you want." He pulls a handkerchief out of his pocket and dabs at my eyes. I snatch it and blow my nose. One of his expressive eyebrows rises, but he doesn't comment. Instead he says, "While I wait for you to come up with the rest of those opinions, I'm thinking some of that pie would be nice. It's been a long trip."

It sure as hell has, I think, but I say only, "Sure. Why not."

He takes my hand, the one not holding the handkerchief, and twines his fingers with mine.

Life can face you one way for a really long time and then, in a flash, spin you in a wholly different direction. What you know to be solid and sure can explode in an instant and you are forced to rebuild reality from the ground up. The process can be a halting, death-defying act. It can also be unalloyed joy, the kind that lifts you off your feet and carries you away. I know I'll ruminate more about this later, but for now all I'm capable of is basking in this utterly perfect moment.

Kit steers me toward the door and pushes it open. Warmth, light, and the murmur of good cheer spill out to greet us. I give his hand a squeeze. He squeezes back. We step forward together—over the threshold and into the wonder of whatever comes next.

ACKNOWLEDGMENTS

THE GREEN MOUNTAIN GODDESSES, Carolyn Haley and Cynthia Locklin, are beloved friends and authors who gave unstintingly of their creativity and honesty to shape this novel. Their acute reading skills and encouragement were priceless gifts, as were our writing retreats fueled by good food, fabulous cocktails, and glorious Vermont sunsets.

An extra special shout out to Carolyn for teaching me so much about writing, including how to stand up for what I believe is right, instead of being whipped around by the winds of uncertainty every time one of my beta readers offered an opinion. Those beta reader opinions were also invaluable gifts, whether they all made it into the story or not.

Thank you as well to Jill Shultz, whose developmental edit resulted in much hair-tearing *and* a better, stronger story.

A final thank-you to the smart, savvy team at Smith Publicity who understood my goals and helped me push *Willing* into the world for you to read.

LESLIE NOYES a graphic designer and writer living in Southern Vermont. Her writing is inspired by her adventures in love. When she isn't designing magazines—or playing competitive croquet—she is texting with her daughter, sending overlong e-mails to friends, or plotting her next novel while also fighting a never-ending battle against the clutter that tries to colonize her desk.

Visit her at LeslieNoyesAuthor.com, where you can learn more about the places and issues that inspired Willing, listen to a Spotify playlist themed for the novel, and read Leslie's musings about the minutiae that capture her attention.

Follow her on Facebook and Instagram at LeslieNoyesAuthor.

Made in the USA
Las Vegas, NV
17 May 2021